REACTIVE

THE ELITE TRIALS

REACTIVE

BECKY MOYNIHAN

BROKEN
BOOKS

Published by Broken Books
www.beckymoynihan.com

ISBN-13: 978-1-7327330-0-8
ISBN-10: 1-7327330-0-7

Cover design by Becky Moynihan
Cover model by Neostock
www.neo-stock.com
Edited by Jesikah Sundin
www.jesikahsundin.com

To my daughter,
You are strong and brave and beautiful.
Even when you're afraid.

THE BEASTS

Ninety seconds and counting.

Water sought entrance into my mouth and nose. Long, undulating strands of hair blocked my vision. The pressure in my throat was unbearable. I couldn't think, only feel. Just how I liked it. Ninety-five seconds. Ninety-nine. One hundred. My body bucked and writhed, the gnawing hole in my chest too great.

I shot to the surface. Air hit my face and I inhaled a mouthful. More, more, until the ache in my starved lungs eased.

"Yes!" I sputtered on a wet cough and smacked the lake's surface. I had just beaten my best time.

Holding my breath under water was a game of mine. Maybe a foolhardy one, but it was all I had.

Under the water, I felt most at peace. All the noise and colors and cares of the world slipped away as fluid silence filled my being. And, in those moments of silence, I could more easily remember her face. Graceful lines, vibrant hazel eyes, sweeping dark locks. Her memory was now an impression than an actual image. Too much time had passed by since I'd last seen her.

Soon, the weather would be too cold for my early morning swims in the lagoon—truthfully, it already was. But a moment of peace was worth the chill in my bones.

I rubbed my eyes and frowned as the sun peeked through the trees. I wouldn't have time for breakfast. Again. After wading to shore and unsticking a wet shirt that was determined to showcase my assets, I grabbed my boots and made a dash for the training barracks. I kept my eyes downcast for as long as I could, but the pull was too strong. My gaze flicked up past the tree line to the pale, castle-like structure sitting atop the waking horizon.

My upper lip curled and I focused on my bare feet. From the multitude of windows, eyes were always watching. The attention warmed my chilled flesh—but not in a good way. And *he* could be watching. I broke into a sprint.

Today was the same as any day. Outdoor training. Seven days a week—even during hail-studded downpours, skin-blistering heat, and frostbite-inducing winters. At the end of each day, I collapsed into bed only to do the routine again the next. But there was one minuscule difference about today, a milestone that no one here knew about.

My birthday.

I'd been alive now for eighteen years, but I'd survived the past eleven of those years in this prison they called a city. At its heart, the city was black because of the people in power. But, to the naked eye, it was a beautiful jail cell—miles and miles of thick pine and oak, rolling emerald hills, and lush grass. The great outer wall wasn't even visible, its eastern gate a good three-mile walk from here, the city's center. Despite the surrounding nature, a faint static hummed through the air and never stopped. Perhaps the sound was just a figment of my imagination, but the buzzing undercurrent taunted me. A reminder that I was nothing more than a trapped creature who was subject to the whims of her master.

While the other trainees finished their breakfast, I jogged up the stairs to my room on the second floor, dripping a trail of water on the dull concrete. With a click, I locked myself inside the only place I felt relatively safe, then towel-dried my hair and set to work peeling off my wet shirt. A throb of pain punched my shoulder; I hissed, glancing at the dark purple bruise. *Push past the pain*, I berated myself and rolled my shoulder back. *You are not weak.*

The memory of yesterday's spill on the track sent a shiver down my spine. That obstacle shouldn't have bested me. I should have seen the simple hurdle.

My charger had suffered the most from our fall, sustaining a bloodied right foreleg. Her vet had prescribed a few days of rest before allowing her to work again. So today marked another new milestone. For the very first time, I would be riding a charger other than Freedom. Officially, my charger's name was Cleopatra, but the name held no meaning. A wild light glinted in my beast's eyes, one that refused to dim. She yearned for freedom—like me.

Soon, I hoped to give her that very freedom. A fool's dream, most likely, but one I desperately clung to.

Every day I whispered of freedom in her twitching ears when no one else was around—a reminder to us both of why we trained so hard. Why we risked our lives. Why each challenge and hardship was worth the fight. Being free was more important than anything to us, but the only way out of this city was through the Trials. The problem was, no one had ever won all three Trials and earned Title of Choice, which also meant no one had ever exited the wall's reinforced steel gates.

Not that the people wanted to leave. The outside was dangerous, an unknown to most of the ignorant residents. They feared what lay beyond the wall and clung to the protection Tatum City offered. The Trials were created to form order and hierarchy, two things I'd been told were paramount to the success of a community. Those who dared contend in all three Trials only desired status and every-thing that came with a superior title.

But I didn't.

Day in and day out I trained, my sole focus on beating my time, my aim, my endurance. I had to win. Not for a secure position in the city. No. I had to see her face again, before the impression became a wavering mirage. I had to find her. And I only had one chance at making that happen. If I lost in the Trials this year, that was it. No do-overs.

I donned my protective training gear: a long-sleeved gray shirt tucked into leather pants, a thick leather vest snug across my chest, and knee-high boots. I stuffed my riding gloves into the waistband of my pants like I always did, not planning on wearing them. They were an unwanted bar-rier between me and the reins that controlled a ferocious animal. Besides their bite—which could sever a limb—the wiry coat and serrated mane and tail were a charger's natu-ral weapons. The tail alone acted as a whip, easily slicing through unprotected skin. That's why the riders wore raw-hide leathers. I had more calluses and scars on my palms than I could count from Freedom's sharp mane, but the pain was worth it.

Control was everything. Without it, I never would have lasted this long.

Lastly, I grabbed the whip. The leather felt cold and cruel against my roughened fingers. I stifled a shudder. For a split second, my grip tightened and I imagined throwing the thing as hard as I could, watching with satisfaction as it sailed out of sight. But I couldn't. Rules were not to be broken. I clipped the whip to my belt.

Another rule—mandated five years ago—was a ban on using helmets. Helmets were for the weak, my trainers said. Proving one's mettle was more important than safety. I snorted, thinking of all the head injuries I'd seen since then. The gory image of one man's head, exploding like an overripe melon dropped onto concrete, would forever haunt me. Humans were no match against a vicious kick from an agitated charger.

Before leaving the room, I peeked at myself in the small, broken mirror above my dresser. I looked like *her*. At least, I liked to think I did. Same hazel green eyes. My hair hung in long damp strands, almost black now. But once dry, slashes of brick red would chase the darkness away, especially when sunlight struck it just right. Sighing, I quickly tied the mass into a messy knot. A lock tenaciously fell over my left eye, a byproduct of my stubborn cowlick. I forced the strand behind my ear.

"Who's tough?" I poked a finger at my cracked reflection. "That's right. You are." My fake bravado was more than obvious. I scrunched up my nose and wrenched the bedroom door open. As soon as I stepped into the hall, I was swept into a sea of other trainees. Someone bumped into my sore shoulder and I clenched my teeth.

"Watch it, tier five," a short, dark-haired girl snapped. "Just because you have your own room doesn't mean you

5

can take up extra space in the hallway." She pushed past me when I didn't bother responding. These people were not my friends—they were competition.

I'd discovered that fact in a most horrific way during my first year as a trainee. I'd asked a girl if she wanted to be my friend and received a bloodied nose for it. Soon after, a rumor spread that I was sniffing out trainee weaknesses and should be avoided at all costs. After several threats and bouts of hazing, I had learned my lesson: keep my mouth shut. Better to blend in than create enemies.

We clamored down concrete stairs and burst into sunshine. I slowed, soaking in the warmth, but an elbow dug into my back.

"What are you doing? Keep moving," a guttural voice said.

Before I could react, a young man with black hair stalked past, obsidian-edged blue eyes practically shooting venom my way. I quickly broke the stare but glanced at him again when something on his neck snagged my attention. It was a black tattoo, bold and striking. I squinted for a better view, but his long legs carried him away to his designated training field.

I arrived at the stables a few minutes later and took a moment to breathe in the aroma of hay and horses. Well, not horses in the usual sense of the word. What little I knew of our land's history suggested that the beasts in this stable did not exist one hundred years ago.

But that was before the Silent War—a war of such epic devastation, the world was forever changed. The end didn't arrive in clashing colors, fire and chaos, screams and bombs. No, the end stole over the land like a masked thief, invisible, untraceable. Silent as death. The who and why of the attack was still, to this day, a mystery. But the deaths had been global. The world's population count was now back up into the millions, most people living in small rural communities since the old cities were overrun by wild beasts and clans. I had no clue if there were other cities like the one I was now trapped in.

Whatever had been done a century ago altered the entire ecosystem, choking off at least ninety percent of all life. Yet, a few living organisms had survived and gradually adapted to a harsher habitat. Some of the animals became smarter, stronger. Some didn't change at all.

And others morphed into monsters. The new normal.

Not all the predators were evil, though. Chargers were just extremely large carnivorous horses.

As I entered the two-story stone building, I whistled and several curious equines leaned out of their stalls to watch me as I strolled by. A small smile bled onto my face at their response. I didn't mind being noticed by these creatures. I was friends with them in a way I never could be with the humans in this place.

I scooped out a slab of bloody meat from a bucket that was pegged to a support beam, then continued on my way. One of the chargers lunged for the meat and I danced to the side and out of biting range. "Tut-tut. This isn't for you, jug head," I chastised the impatient miscreant. Nearing the last of the stalls, I laid eyes on my favorite charger.

She nickered at me, her harder-than-brick jaw rippling. I could barely see her pupils, her irises a glowing yellow in the morning light, like a lion's.

Despite her mutated appearance, my charger was sweet.

I had been there as she entered the world, as she blinked at me with large, intelligent eyes and bobbed her head, like she was saying hello. Like she knew what I wanted most, communicating how she wanted it, too. Without hesitation, I petitioned to be her rider. I had been too young for the Trials at the time, but my guardians—my adopted parents—bound us together in a contract anyway. And now, no one could ride her but me.

We shared a special bond. An unbreakable one.

"Hey, Freedom," I crooned as I approached her on silent feet. She grunted as I offered her the meat, her large teeth flashing as she snatched the juicy morsel from my palm.

"I'm sorry about yesterday, girl. The fall was my fault," I said, carefully stroking her prickly chestnut coat. She eyed me sideways, looking far too accusatory for my liking. I sighed. "If anything had happened to you, I—"

But I didn't finish the thought. If anything happened to her, it would break me. My throat tightened. These feelings I had for her, they were dangerous. If anyone discovered how strongly I cared for this beast, they would use those emotions against me in the Trials. People controlled through weakness. I had to be more careful.

I only knew of one soul in this entire messed-up prison who wouldn't—

"Thinking about me?"

Startled by the voice in my ear, I spun, almost punching the person behind me. My fist stopped just shy of his nose. Freedom shook her head, agitated at the interruption. "Asher Donovan! One of these days you'll learn. I almost rearranged your face!"

The stable hand grinned, unfazed as I smoothed a hand

down Freedom's nose. "Sorry, Lune. But was I right? Your cheeks are as red as your hair."

I snorted. "My cheeks are *always* red. Thinking about food makes them turn red."

His dimples puckered. As fast as they appeared, they winked out. "That was quite the spill you two took yesterday. Do me a favor, will you? Don't get yourself killed out there."

I waved his concern away as usual. "I'm fine. We're both fine, actually. Minor scrapes and bruises. Comes with the Rasa Rowe contract."

"Oh, that reminds me, I'm here for a reason—not just to chat your ear off." He chuckled. "Your father—" He choked on the word when he saw the look I gave him. Asher knew better than to call my guardian that. "Sorry. I meant to say 'Renold.'" When I nodded, he continued. "Renold asked me to introduce you to your temporary charger. Come on, he's this way."

Dread weighted my ankles as I followed him down the aisle. I'd never ridden, let alone socialized, with another charger before. Some of them were unattached to a rider, contract-free for one reason or another. Usually either too young or too wild. Anyone brave—or stupid enough—could ride them. But without a mutual respect between beast and rider . . . things could get ugly fast.

"I know what you're thinking, Lune." Asher glanced at me. "Stalin is a handful . . . but so are you. Your temperaments are similar." A dimple slowly indented his cheek. I whacked the back of his head.

Laughing, he casually bumped my uninjured shoulder with his. "Okay, I deserved that." He stopped in front of a stall and ran a hand through his ash-blond locks, making the strands stick straight up. Why was it that boys looked cute with messy hair, whereas I looked like an electrocuted squirrel? "Here he is." He ticked his head toward the stall, then crossed both arms over his chest.

I stepped up to the window and peered inside. Immediately, a dark blur rushed me and, on instinct, I leapt back out of biting range, crashing into Asher in the process. Arms wrapped around my middle, preventing a tumble to the cement floor.

"Whoa! He doesn't like people much. Sorry about that," Asher said.

"Hm. Maybe we are alike after all," I muttered, shaking off my nerves and Asher's touch at the same time.

"Here, let me help." Asher went over to a meat bucket and returned with a sizable chunk, placing it in my palm. "I'm just going to put my hand underneath yours when you offer him the meat. He trusts me, so it should work."

"Okay," was my only reply. *You can do this*, I told myself. *It's not a monster. Just a horse with a craving for blood. No big deal.* I felt Asher slide behind me and my back stiffened. Now *this* was a big deal. He had given me the courtesy of a warning, but it wasn't enough.

I focused on my breathing as the warmth of his body pressed close, suffocating me. I bit my lip, forcing myself not to react. *It's just Asher. He's harmless as a snail.* His hand underneath mine was almost my undoing, but I held it together, my breaths shallow. His touch right now was only for Stalin to smell a familiar scent. To further distract myself, I asked, "So are we still a go for tonight?"

Asher's leg moved, nudging mine, and I took a step

forward, then another. Stalin squealed, his teeth almost peeling off a layer of skin as he snatched the offering from my palm. "That wasn't too bad," Asher said, as if giant canines scraping your skin was an everyday occurrence. Probably was in his line of work. "And yes, we're good to go for tonight."

I stepped to the side, needing space. I didn't do well with people at my back. Even him. "Yeah, I think Stalin and I are best friends already." I rolled my eyes. Asher just stared at me. "Uh, you want me to get him out or . . . ?"

"Oh! No, I'll do it," he said, stirring into motion. "You might want to stand back in case he, um, doesn't behave . . ."

"Right." I gave them both a wide berth. "Wouldn't want him to trample me before I can even get a foot in the stirrup. How embarrassing."

Asher didn't respond. Sometimes I got the impression he didn't understand my sarcasm.

I followed them out of the stable, getting my first good look at the terrifyingly magnificent creature I would soon ride. He was built like a Clydesdale, but I knew he had the speed of a Thoroughbred. Not a single speck of white marred his body, his hair jet black, darker than a moonless night. I slowly approached his left side, making sure he could see and hear me. "You are a beautiful animal, Stalin. I'm surprised no one has claimed you."

He watched me with a keen yellow eye as I slowly placed my hand on his coarse coat. I fought for calm. More than anything, animals could smell fear. If I wanted to ride this beast, I couldn't reveal the turmoil raging inside of me. Stalin swiveled his gigantic head and Asher slackened the reins, allowing the beast access to me. As his nostrils flared, I softly blew on his nose, introducing him to my scent. He snorted and swung his head around, relaxing.

I passed the test. I breathed a sigh of relief. At least he wouldn't eat me. Not right now, anyway.

Before Stalin had time to think, I launched onto his back, exerting more effort than usual to mount the huge beast. "All right, Asher, I got this. Hand me the reins. And what's the code word for tonight?"

With a salute, he placed the reins in my hands. "How about 'gloves.' You really should wear your gloves this one time. I've heard he pulls at the bit like a—"

I never heard him finish the sentence. Like a punch in the gut, a terrible feeling twisted my insides. I hadn't felt the warning in a while and the sensation startled me. All I knew was that something bad would happen if I didn't react swiftly. "Ash! Get back!"

He backpedaled and, in the next instant, Stalin exploded into action. All four hooves left the ground as he jumped and bucked, trying his best to dismount me. Letting out a bellow that had the hair raising on my neck, he charged forward.

He was out of control. *We* were out of control.

As we careened down the dirt road, my legs gripped his massive sides, the only thing keeping me upright. If I fell . . . No. I wouldn't fall. My hands tightened on the reins, the tough leather scraping my palms, and I pulled, forcing Stalin into a turn. He plunged through thigh-high grass, having no choice but to obey my command as I kept the reins taut, arm muscles burning with the effort.

Control. It would be mine, not his.

Every time we made a full loop, I tightened the reins more, spinning us in ever-shrinking circles until the landscape blurred and lurched around me. If we didn't stop soon, I would be sick.

His abrupt jerk to a stop sent my legs flying backward and my stomach smacking into his neck. Well, then. Maybe he could read thoughts. I blew out a breath. Far too late, I realized his ploy. A spike of fear finally leaked through my defenses when his head whipped back so fast that I barely had time to shift my own to the side. His sharp mane lashed my neck a second before his jack-hammer head rammed into my cheekbone.

The impact struck me deaf and blind.

I felt rather than heard a groan leave my mouth as pain roared in my cheek, throbbing like a second heartbeat. "Ouch," I managed to utter, my face numb and on fire all at once. "You asked for it, you stubborn lummox." Unclipping my whip, I hesitated a moment, poised to inflict pain but hating the very thought of it. I ground my teeth together and brought the whip down on his rear. "Haw!" I shouted, digging my heels into his ribs. With a surprised shriek, Stalin whirled and broke into a reckless gallop.

But this time *I* was in control.

His hooves tore up the road, clods of dirt spraying in his wake. The wind whipped my hair free of its bindings and dark red locks streamed behind me. I threw my head back and whooped to the sky.

I embraced the danger, I craved the adrenaline, I needed the speed.

And, for a moment of suspended time, I pretended that I was flying.

Even more, I pretended that I was free.

THE SUPREME ELITE

This had been a test. I was sure of it. And the request reeked of Renold. He must have hand-picked this half-wild beast just to see how I would cope. Well, I had won and that's all that mattered.

As the stables came into view, so did Ash's familiar tall, lean figure. I gave my friend a cocky salute and plastered on a confident smile. The smile slipped a second later. It hurt my still-burning cheek too much.

"Are you okay?" he yelled as he jogged toward us.

"Yeah, I'm fine. And thanks for the tip. He really does pull at the bit something fierce." I grinned, but it probably looked more like a grimace. My poor aching face.

I slowed Stalin to a walk as Asher closed the distance between us. He offered me a hand, always the gentleman, but he knew better. I slid down on my own.

Abruptly, he lifted a hand toward my cheek. I flinched. Whatever he saw stopped him in his tracks and his hand lowered, slowly curling into a fist. "Blasted beast. I hope you gave him a solid whipping for doing that to your face."

My eyes widened. *Did my gentle, animal-loving stable boy really just say that?* "I did, actually. Ripped him a good one. But this was to be expected, you know that. He was just testing me."

He blew out a breath as he raked a hand through his hair, shoulders loosening a notch. "I know, I know. Sorry. I worry is all. Um, so a message came for you while you were out taming this stupid beast." I felt my body relax as he attempted to lighten the mood. There's the Asher I knew. "Your fath—I mean, Renold cancelled the rest of your morning training. You're to attend lunch at noon in the banquet hall."

Time stopped.

It had been almost two months since my last visit to the one hundred and seventy-five thousand square foot house—if one could call it that. The four-story, pale stone creation with jade turrets slicing at the sky wasn't exactly homey. It was intimidating. Or maybe it was just the people living inside that made the house appear so.

Why was I being summoned now? There were no important social functions scheduled this month, so I must have done something to displease Renold. I locked my jaw and inhaled through my nose, then exhaled slowly. Asher didn't need to see my growing anxiety. He couldn't help me, and I didn't want him to. Not with this.

I cleared my throat. "Right. Guess I'd better go then. I've only got two hours to make myself look and smell presentable. An impossible task, but I'll try my hardest. Wouldn't want a delicate elite to faint at my mere presence."

A laugh burst from him and he nudged my uninjured shoulder on his way over to collect Stalin's reins. "Just a bit of friendly advice? You might want to keep that sassy mouth shut during lunch."

"Hey!" I aimed my palm for the side of his head, but he caught my wrist mid-swing. "Your reflexes are improving, stable boy. Must be all that dung-slinging you've been doing."

His hand on my wrist pulled me closer. "Or maybe I've been secretly watching your training sessions."

My humor vanished, replaced by a sick sensation souring my stomach. "Ash . . . please don't sign a contract. I know things are hard, but . . ." I wanted to throw up as I envisioned him pitted against a segment of blood-thirsty contenders. "The Trials are brutal. People die in them every year, even with years and years of training under their belts. You wouldn't make it. A part of you has to be cruel and you don't have a mean bone in your body."

"You don't either, Lune, no matter what you might think of yourself. I can see the real you."

My heart skipped a beat. What could he see? I was too afraid to ask.

"What do you call a house full of holier-than-thou snobs?"

No one answered my question, of course.

I was keeping myself preoccupied with stupid jokes as I walked along the opulent house's outer length. I was certain eyes followed my path, so I whispered the answer. "An Elitist Clubhouse."

I snickered. *Good one.* I mentally gave myself a pat on the back.

Truthfully, the bright sandstone structure wasn't unpleasant to look at. The stone-carved leaves and filigree shapes, edging the windows and roofs, were intricately designed. My gaze lifted higher until I had to shield my eyes from the sun's glare. The gargoyles and grotesques that watched me from atop the parapets I could do without. They gave me the creeps.

As I climbed the stairs to the main entrance, I passed between two gigantic lion statues. They had loyally guarded this house for over two hundred years. Surviving the progression of time, their stone bodies were surprisingly intact. A few scars, but that was to be expected. I could respect that. I patted one on the chest. "How are you today, Lennie? It's been awhile. I promise I haven't been avoiding you. It's the location . . . not you. Say hello to Benny for me. I gotta run!"

My eyes landed on the arched double doors, made of glass and iron, and I squared my shoulders. Time to face the *real* Trials. I pulled on the ancient butler doorbell, cringing at the shrill dinging sound. Nothing good lived inside this house. As a whole, the walled city was a mix of old world and new, pockets of untouched history next to random high tech. But inside the grand house, a bygone era had been reborn, and the current inhabitants lived a lifestyle very different from the rest of the city.

How or why it was this way, I couldn't fathom. But it all seemed to stem from the chaotic whims of Renold Tatum.

One of the doors groaned inward, revealing a thin, sober-faced, middle-aged man. Hooded gray eyes looked down a prominent nose and settled on me. "Your name and business, miss?"

"The Queen of the Underworld here to collect the souls owed me."

His nose twitched. "I'm afraid we weren't expecting you.

18

Do make an appointment next time." Before he could shut the door in my face, I stopped the heavy wood with my boot.

"Don't be cheeky, Dobson. You know I could do this all day." I invoked a superior tone. "My father summoned me to lunch."

"Of course, Miss Tatum, this way," he droned. As he turned, I made a face at his back. No matter how many times I heard it, I loathed being associated with that surname.

Through another pair of heavy doors we went, into the grand entrance hall. Light marble floors gleamed, disappearing into several open-arched doorways. The most astonishing feature of this place was the ceilings. Each room had a different pattern, from mahogany wood beams to billowing print fabric. Often, I'd catch myself staring upward, despite the crick forming in my neck.

I glimpsed a sea of green to the right, but now wasn't the time to enjoy the exotic plant life. The butler steered me left, pausing at the foot of a magnificent stone staircase that spiraled upward and out of sight.

"You know where to go from here?"

I rolled my eyes in reply, making my way up. "Feel free to come search for me if I don't make it back down in the next year."

"Remember, lunch is served promptly at noon. Don't be late." I bit back a groan at his parting words. I'd gotten into trouble more than once for being late to a social function. Mealtimes were political events. That's why I hated them and why I dreaded the summons I had received today. Something was going to happen and I wasn't going to like the outcome.

I trailed a hand along the wrought-iron railing, the wooden top smooth under my fingers. Probably the heaviest black chandelier ever crafted hung from the ceiling several floors above, dropping down the center of the winding staircase in tiers laden with electric candles. But it was the windows that lit my ascent. Dozens and dozens of them adorned the half-circle wall. I took a moment to thank my lucky stars that I wasn't a maid. Cleaning those windows would be a pain in the butt.

I stopped at the third floor. Everyone with the last name of Tatum haunted these halls and I didn't want to be seen by them quite yet. I was a mess. The judgmental stares would be harsher than usual if they caught sight of me now.

Tugging off my filthy boots, I slipped past the living hall on silent feet. I could see my bedroom door straight ahead—I just had to get there. The doors leading up to it were shut but I still held my breath as I passed them. Did doors have ears? They could probably hear my rapid heartbeat.

Finally making it to my room, I loosed a breath. Piece of cake.

As I touched the handle, the door flew open, a figure framing the doorway.

"Lune, Lune, as pale as the moon," a high-pitched voice singsonged. "You look awful. Did your charger finally grow a backbone and trample you to the ground? Or was it that delicious trainer of yours?"

Oh, how I wanted to run and hide right now. The petulant, condescending voice belonged to my guardian's biological daughter, Rose Tatum. Pretty and covered in wicked thorns, she was. She teased, taunted, and tortured me the three years I had lived in this house. Moving into the barracks at the age of ten had been a mercy.

She tossed her heavy mane of platinum curls when I didn't respond to her barbs, sliding out of the doorway and into my personal space. She knew how much I despised that. "I heard you would be joining us today and father *finally* gave me permission to switch rooms with you. What a tease he is, denying me for so long. It's not fair that this larger room goes mostly unused while you roll around the countryside, not appreciating it. So, it's mine now. But don't fret—you can earn the room back *if* you win your Trials." She smirked, confident that I wouldn't win, then winked a doe brown eye at me.

Life was a game to her, and she usually won. She had Renold wrapped around her conniving little finger. It was no use fighting, but my hackles rose—she had taken something else from me. Soon, I would have nothing left.

I slouched against the wall, feigning boredom. "Suit yourself. It makes sense, really. I mean, you have more stuff than me. All that makeup, jewelry, clothes . . . You take up a lot of unnecessary space, Rose."

She must not have appreciated my humor because in the next moment her eyes glittered, and she swung at my face. I easily caught her fist and twisted her arm behind her back. She gasped in shock, but I couldn't stop myself from gritting out, "Try that again and I'll give you a black eye. Then it'll be *you* who looks awful."

She struggled and I let her go. "You'll regret this! I'll make sure you're punished." Her glare was murderous. Before all my years spent training for the Trials, I might have peed my pants at her words. Now I just felt detached from the drama. Her methods of abuse were nothing compared to what I'd experienced under my trainer's care. Especially my latest one.

But there was Renold, and I felt a moment of regret for my hasty reaction. I shivered. Would she tell him about what I had just said and done? Maybe I should have kept my mouth shut as Asher had suggested.

Rose paused in my bedroom doorway. "Now that you *touched* me, I'll need to change and freshen up before lunch. Do the city a favor and take a bath or something. Anything. You reek of dung." She slammed the door behind her.

I sniffed myself in mock concern. "Uh-oh, you're right, I do smell. I'll make sure to scrub off the stench of spoiled brat until my skin turns red."

Too bad she didn't hear that last line. It was a really good one.

I opened the door to her old room and sighed at the disarray. Rose had been busy. The few belongings I kept here were scattered across the rug. I groaned when I spotted my fancy dresses balled into a pile. They would need ironing now. Such a waste of time.

With a sigh, I picked them up and hung the blue dresses of varying hues in the room's armoire. I hadn't always hated blue, but being forced to show my support and loyalty for the Tatum family by wearing their color made me cringe every time I saw a shade of it.

Now I just needed a bath. Admittedly, I was looking forward to the luxury. The barracks had running water, but it wasn't heated, not like here in the big house. Only the elites had access to it and, since I was being forced to dine here, I might as well take advantage of the amenities.

After slipping out of the room, I scurried down the hall

and locked myself into a bathroom. Layer by layer, my training gear plopped to the white-tiled floor and I kicked them into a corner. The knob on the claw-foot tub creaked as I twisted it and out spewed gloriously hot water. As the tub filled, I secured my hair in a knot, glancing at my reflection in the silver oval mirror.

I prodded my purpling cheekbone and grimaced. Several thin red lines ran along my neck where Stalin's mane had struck. *Ugh. No wonder Rose said I looked awful.*

I stuck my finger in the bath water and turned off the flow. *Hot!* Slowly, I slid beneath the surface. My skin started to bake. *Perfect.* The aches and pains in my muscles eased, replaced with a feeling of languid weightlessness.

As I floated in blissful silence, my pesky thoughts stirred to life. I grasped the leather cord around my neck, and for the thousandth time inspected the bear tooth looped through it. Water droplets plinked softly as I rubbed the smooth surface; terrible memories shot to the forefront of my mind. No matter how hard I tried, I would never be free of that painful day.

The day that changed my life forever.

If I could revisit time and say one thing to my younger self, I would say, "Don't trust little boys with honey-gold eyes." No matter *how* innocent he might have looked. He had given the necklace to me that day—exactly eleven years ago. It was the worst memory of my life running into him. Literally.

And yet I never took the stupid necklace off, even though it represented everything I loathed.

Maybe because it reminded me of everything I had lost. That I had lost *her*. And I never wanted to forget.

Eyes the color of warmed gold.

A teasing lopsided grin.

I dropped the tooth.

No.

I would not think about *him*.

My head plunged beneath the water's surface, drowning my thoughts.

I rubbed at a long indent on the skirt of my royal blue dress. "Stupid wrinkle," I muttered. The wispy fabric was stubborn, not wanting to hide imperfections. I almost liked the dress because of the flaw. The only problem was the open back, which meant I had to wear my hair down to cover my exposed skin. Why had I gotten my hair wet? I hadn't intended to, but thoughts of that *boy,* his memory an ever-present thorn in my side, had affected my ability to rationalize.

"Stupid boy."

I knew what I needed to do, but first, I needed to hide the darkening bruise on my cheek. My makeup kit was nowhere to be found, so I crouched in a very unladylike fashion and poked my head under the bed. Sure enough, the kit was there. Grumbling, I crawled underneath and snagged it. After several attempts, I managed to conceal most of the bruise, fading the purple to a dull pink.

It now looked like my right cheek was forever blushing.

Shoes in hand, I exited the room and snuck to the staff's stairwell, then tiptoed to the fourth floor. The less power-ful elites lived up here, so I was extra careful not to be seen.

They were always scheming, always clamoring to climb the social ladder. If the observatory wasn't on the top floor, I would never step foot in these halls.

This time of day, the observatory was empty, making it all too easy for me to hurry up the spiral staircase propped in the far-left corner. A catwalk led to a set of French doors which I opened. Immediately, a gust of fresh air hit my face, fluttering my damp hair.

But this wasn't my destination.

Stepping outside, I climbed a set of iron stairs which dumped me onto a narrow balcony. A waist-high stone parapet was the only obstacle between me and a staggering fall to the ground far below. I pressed my legs against it and leaned my upper body over the edge, deeply inhaling the spicy scent of autumn leaves. My body tingled as if charged with electricity and my laughter danced on the breeze as I threw my arms wide, wishing I could fly.

No one came up here but me. I was glad my childhood sanctuary remained a secret, but the elites didn't know what they were missing. The view was breathtaking. Trees as far as the eye could see dotted the horizon, a speckled mass of yellows, greens, oranges, and reds. And rising above the vibrant colors was a wall of mountains. I focused on the tallest peak, knowing it must be tremendous in size; yet, the mountain looked so small from here. Unattainable. Untouchable.

Blue.

My lips pursed.

Even the mountain's grandeur was tainted by Tatum family blue.

A faint whisper of voices reached my ears and I looked

down. Far below, I could see the top of a dark brown head of hair being ushered inside the main entrance. I leaned farther over the edge, my almost dry hair framing my face as I strained for a better view of the unfamiliar person. And then the head tipped back, revealing a young man.

My breath caught as our gazes met.

Even from this distance, I could see his eyes.

They were gold.

I must have seen wrong.

The sun must have infused his irises with its amber rays.

Yes. That was it.

The velvet heels pinching my feet punctured the silence with their clacking beat, carrying me across the entrance hall and past the circular room brimming with greenery. All was quiet. Too quiet.

I was late.

My heart flapped against my sternum like a trapped bird, becoming more frantic with each step toward the tall stone archway looming closer and closer.

Be brave.

Dobson stood just inside the arch, ready to announce me to the room's occupants.

Be strong.

The stoic butler's voice rang loud and clear. "Miss Lune Tatum."

I felt the color drain from my face. Saliva rushed into my mouth and I swallowed, the sound loud in the deafening silence.

Show no fear. Fear is weakness. I am not weak.

My spine snapped straight, chin raised high. My face cleared of emotion, transformed into an unbreakable mask—one carved from years of pretending. Of preservation.

I stepped into the room.

Despite its sheer size and soaring barrel-vaulted ceiling, colorful tapestries, and triple fireplace, the banquet hall held no appeal for me. The occupants soured the surroundings. In the middle of the room sat a never-ending mahogany table laden with power-hungry elites. At least four dozen pairs of eyes turned as one, carefully watching me enter.

But only one set of eyes pierced through mine. They stripped away my mask and grabbed ahold of my soul, squeezing it slowly. My steps faltered as a shard of panic stabbed my heart. A single look from *him* and once again I was pinned under the overbearing control of my guardian, Renold Tatum—the Supreme Elite of Tatum City. All my training felt insignificant, pitiful, as he studied me with those all-knowing eyes. Eyes of blue ice. They could capture and freeze their prey if they so desired.

In his presence, I was reduced to a helpless child.

My wooden legs propelled me toward him while my mind screamed at me to run. But I couldn't act on my impulses. The consequences would be too great. On his left sat an empty, high-backed chair—the seat of honor. I quickly scanned the table, noting the chairs were filled to capacity.

Dread ate at my gut.

I was meant to sit in that prestigious spot. I'd never felt so low. A game was being played at my expense and I didn't know the rules.

I came to a halt behind the blue velvet upholstered chair, afraid to touch it. Afraid it would burn me. Before the chair could devour me whole, my guardian's deep and cultured voice, smooth as molasses, cut the tension. "Lune, I have someone to introduce to you. He's from the Recruiter Clan. Meet Mr. Brendan Bearon."

Renold motioned next to me and my gaze left his as chair legs scraped against the wood floor. A man rose, unfolding his long limbs. He was incredibly tall. Maybe six-foot-three? My head probably didn't even reach his shoulders. Curious, I looked into his face, an obligatory smile on my lips.

My smile froze, then disappeared. The whole room vanished when I saw his eyes.

There was no mistaking them this time.

Only one person had gold eyes like that—eyes I would never forget.

The boy from my past had found me.

My vision blurred as I was wrenched back in time to the worst day of my life.

REUNITED

I should have listened. I should have waited.

But I'd been too caught up in the moment. I just wanted to feel the sweet embrace of water on my skin. So, when my mother had paused to gather nuts for the evening's community dinner, I had balked. Had pleaded for permission to run on ahead. Alone.

She sighed. One beat of silence, two. Then, "Go ahead." She had given in so easily, something I wasn't used to. But it *was* my seventh birthday, after all.

I squealed and grinned so wide, my cheeks throbbed.

"Hold up, LuLu, you know the drill. What are the rules that keep you safe?"

I stumbled over the list in a rush, excitement tangling the words in my mouth. "Always stay on familiar trails, steer clear of strange noises, never speak to outsiders—they are not to be trusted."

She waited a beat. "And?"

"And if anyone approaches, run."

Her approving smile was all I needed to see. I took off like a rabbit, my skinny legs flying down the trail as fast as they could go. The trail ended at the tree line and I skipped to a halt, gazing at the other-worldly reflections sparkling on the lake's surface. The sight always took my breath away.

It looked like one of the fairytale scenes Mum had described during community story time.

I searched the nearby trees and found a branch the size of my arm. With much grunting, I severed it from the tree's trunk. The adults wouldn't let me have my own weapon yet, but I could carry a stick. I raced full-tilt for the lake, brandishing the stick like a sword.

I would slay the water dragon with it.

Water sprayed high as I jumped into its depths, legs pumping. And then I was diving deep, fingers brushing the lake's clay bottom. I wished I could be a mermaid, like in the stories. They didn't have to worry about the land beasts. But my lungs demanded air, so I kicked off the silty floor, rocketing to the surface.

The sun's glare blinded me, and I scrunched my eyes shut as I popped my head above the water. I kept my lids closed as I floated on my back, enjoying the sun's warmth on my face. It wasn't long before I heard a sound like fire popping. *Crack!* I jerked my body upright and blinked water from my vision as I searched the shoreline.

Nothing.

The noise must have come from the forest. Was something—or someone—watching me?

"Mum?"

No reply.

What should I do?

Another rustle broke the silence, and this time I recognized the telltale sound of twigs snapping underfoot.

What are the rules that keep you safe? The words rolled around in my head until a single thought finally broke through.

Run.

Frantically, I splashed to shore, my water-logged clothes making me clumsy. I slipped and fell in the grass. Picking myself up, I barreled toward the woods, only to smack into something barring my way. The solid object tipped over backward, latching onto me. A surprised squeak left my mouth as I tumbled to the ground once again.

I flailed and twisted free. Rolling to my feet, I spared a glance at the object that had tripped me and almost loosed a blood-curdling scream. Instead, I blurted, "Holy stars!"

A boy blinked up at me, dazed. I didn't recognize him. His dark brown hair hung past his ears in a shaggy mop, partially covering his eyes. I watched him warily as he stood and inspected the scrape on his elbow. I noticed with a small amount of satisfaction that I was at least an inch taller than him.

"Who—who are you?" *I'm talking to a stranger. I'm going to be in so much trouble!*

The boy peered up at me shyly. "I'm Bren." Glancing over my shoulder, he shivered. "Who are you?" he asked, his voice a notch braver.

I shook my head, flinging water droplets every whichway. "Nah-uh, I can't tell you. I'm not supposed to tell strangers my name."

"Oh." He rubbed at his arms. He looked nervous again. Now *I* was starting to feel nervous.

Ever so carefully, I backed up a step toward the woods. I bet I could run faster than him.

I heard his sharp intake of breath. "Don't go! M-my sister, she got stuck in a tree a-and I can't get her down. You're taller than me so-so maybe you could help me reach her?"

"What about your parents? Can't they get her down?" I was still slowly backing up. My fingers tightened on my stick weapon and I raised it an inch. I'd use it if I had to.

His eyes flicked to the stick, then he sniffed, and sniffed again. Was he crying? "They won't be back until after dark. By that time, maybe a bear will have eaten her or something."

That did it. I loosened my grip on the stick. There was no way I was going to let a wild beast find and eat her. "Where is she?"

He breathed a sigh of relief. "Come on, I'll show you." His hand reached for mine, linking our fingers together before I could protest. He started guiding me into the woods, away from the trail I knew. Away from my mother.

Mum!

I craned my neck around, searching for her. I was going to be in so much trouble. The boy tugged on my hand and I turned my head. He was staring at me, and with his free hand, brushed the hair out of his eyes. Wow. I'd never seen a person with eyes the color of gold before. Suddenly, those hypnotizing eyes warmed to a honey hue and a lopsided grin tipped his lips. "My sister needs you. Follow me?"

His words gave me courage. And purpose. Someone needed my help.

My smile was tentative, but brave. "Okay."

The little boy led me deep into the woods to a group of rough-looking men, no sister in sight.

"What did you bring us, little man? A wee strumpet?" A man covered in dark tattoos chortled. "What is she, then?"

Bren was shaking head to toe. "I-I don't—I don't know. The feeling is strong, though. I—I did what you asked.

Please . . . please let my—"

Crack!

His head flew back as the man boxed his ear with a meaty palm. "No one likes a beggar, boy."

That was the first time I felt it. My gut churned violently, warning me of danger before my mind could react. But the warning came too late. Large, callused hands smothered my screams, tied my hands and feet, and carried me far, far away from my community. From my home. That first night—the first I'd ever spent without my mother—I huddled in a ball on the forest floor, scared and shivering from the cold.

Silently, the boy slipped a leather cord around my neck, a large tooth dangling from the end. "I'm sorry," he whispered. "My—my father made this for me. It's all I have." The men broke into raucous laughter as they ate and drank around their meager campfire. With a gasp, Bren crawled away before they took notice.

The next morning, the group split in two—the boy responsible for my kidnapping went west, and I was taken north. Eventually, the men brought me to Tatum City and shoved me into the hands of the Tatums. Running away wasn't an option. The wall around the city was charged with so much electricity that one touch could stop a heart from beating.

My pleas fell on deaf ears, my cries ignored.

I never understood why the Tatums took me in. All I knew was that they were never letting me go.

And my life as their prisoner daughter had begun.

———○———

"Lune, where are your manners?" Renold's lightly accented tone of warning jolted me into the present.

I sucked in a breath, almost choking on it. The memory had been visceral, leaving a bitter taste in my mouth, and making me feel seven years old all over again.

Squeezing my eyes shut, I wiped away the sting of that horrendous day and exhaled silently. I had a part to play. This would have to be my greatest performance yet if I was going to make it through lunch unscathed. Lashes fluttering, I looked up at Bren, a little boy no longer. All the soft edges that I remembered were now hard, stubble dusted a square jaw, and his floppy hair was now styled.

But his eyes were the same.

Then he smiled at me.

Oh.

The crooked grin. That was the same, too. It appeared genuine when I knew it was an act. Like mine was.

I smiled so big, my injured cheek throbbed. "Forgive me, Mr. Bearon. I was struck by your eyes. They are a very unique color." I stuck out my hand and he didn't hesitate, firmly clasping it in his. As we shook hands, I couldn't help but notice how ghostly pale my skin seemed compared to his dark tan. And his hands were huge. No matter. My grip tightened, and I watched with satisfaction as his eyebrows lifted in surprise.

That's right, pretty boy. I've grown a backbone.

His grin broadened. "That's all right. I get that a lot." His voice sure wasn't how I remembered it. And not only because of the deep, rolling timber. There wasn't a note of shyness. Now it was more . . . self-assured. No, I was going with deeply-laced ego.

34

Renold cleared his throat and I took that as my cue to sit. I saw Bren reach for my chair, so I grabbed it, pulling and twisting in a swift move of independence. He took his seat next to me, glancing at my profile, but I ignored him and waited for Renold to drop the other shoe. I knew there had to be another.

My guardian leaned to the side, whispering to Blanca, his petite and always quiet wife who was seated next to him. He meant to keep me waiting. As the staff slipped into the room, arms laden with large silver platters, I studied his body language, desperately wishing I could read minds. Dressed in his usual formal attire, sapphire rings flashing on long, elegant fingers, he looked perfectly at ease. In his late fifties, Renold had the grace of a king. Everything about him spoke of effortless, aristocratic class.

Appearance was the great deceiver.

I knew what that placid face could do to self-esteem. I knew what those elegant hands could do to a body and spirit.

I was staring so hard at his hands, I didn't catch the first few words he threw my way. ". . . very important purpose. Mr. Bearon came highly recommended for the Trials and so he will become the newest citizen of Tatum City. But he wishes to contend in the Trials *this* year, not leaving much time for training. I need someone who will train him one-on-one for the next few months, so he will be ready. And it can't be just anyone. He needs the best training possible, and what person better for the job than my own daughter?"

No. Please, no.

Blood rushed to my head, knocking against my skull. Tremors worked their way into my hands. I stuffed them under the table out of sight.

I knew I shouldn't question him, knew it with every survival instinct I possessed. Yet my mouth opened and words came spilling out. "But, sir, I'm not qualified. I'm not a trainer." I hated how weak my voice sounded.

He smiled indulgently, but I saw the dangerous glint in his eye. "You are now. I'm temporarily promoting you."

This had to be a sick joke. It had to! The Trials were my one chance at freedom, and now I was being forced to train the boy who had taken away my freedom in the first place? A boy that I was starting to think didn't even remember me.

The room was so quiet I could hear my faltering heartbeats. I knew every little movement, every expression, every word I uttered would be scrutinized by all. The pressure was unbearable. I didn't know how much longer I could keep my mask in place. I felt it slipping, cracking, revealing the raging inferno inside.

My reply came out stiff, but at least it was free of emotion. "Thank you, sir. It would be an honor to train Mr. Bearon."

His face brightened in false appreciation, the intensity rivaling his white-blond hair. "Good. I knew I could count on you. Your new duties begin in two hours." After my affirming nod, he dropped the third shoe. "Oh, and one more thing. I have a personal matter to discuss with you after lunch. You know where to meet me."

My gaze whipped to Rose, sitting across from me. Her malicious smirk confirmed my fears: she had told Renold about our earlier altercation. For the next hour, I avoided conversation by staring holes into my plate, listlessly pushing my food around. But I didn't eat. My stomach would revolt against being filled anyway. Thoughts of what awaited me consumed every molecule of my being.

GAME ON

I'd endured worse over the years, but today had felt different.

Although my wounds were shallow compared to previous ones, the look in Renold's eyes as he had approached me in the cellar promised more than just pain—he wanted something from me. No, he *needed* something from me.

When I had placed my hands against the chilled wall of our secret meeting place, Renold swept my hair over a shoulder, exposing bare skin.

"You know I do this because you broke the rules, right? The rules cannot be broken. Ever."

"Yes, sir," I had said, breath hitching. No matter how many times this happened, the moment before the first strike was always the worst. I wanted the punishment to start so that it could be over. But he took perverse pleasure in prolonging my torture. I heard his calm breathing as he slowly rolled up his sleeves. Heard the slither and creak of the two-foot-long leather whip being picked up, the same kind used on the chargers. I waited, an unstoppable quiver shaking my bones.

A pause. "It's about control, you know. Control your impulses, your wayward reactions. You are never to threaten a Tatum family member. Until you learn that . . ."

The whip's high whine alerted my senses a second before the pain hit.

The sharp sting was manageable at first, but quickly morphed into a pulsing slap of heat. He struck again, stealing breath from my lungs and steel from my limbs. I almost crashed to the floor, knees knocking together as I fought to remain upright.

You cannot break me, I chanted. The same chant I repeated during every punishment.

"Beg," Renold ordered coolly, composed as ever. I was glad I couldn't see his serene face as he beat me. "Beg me to stop. Beg for mercy, you disloyal child."

He knew I wouldn't. I never did. And I knew it drove him mad. The beating increased in pace, leaving me gasping and nauseous, my back a never-ending blaze of agony.

Push past the pain. You are not weak!

My nails dug into the unforgiving cement wall, gouging, scraping—a distraction from what lay behind me. For a blessed second, at least.

With one final heave, the whip sliced through skin, then fell away. I bit my lip so hard, blood pooled on my tongue. I almost gagged on the coppery tang. My tormenter withdrew into a corner, locked the whip into a small wooden box and shrugged into his suit coat. The blanket he draped over my shoulders could almost be mistaken as a loving gesture, so gentle was his touch. He reminded me to take the back stairs, then slipped out of the room like a phantom.

I waited for the retreat of his footsteps. Then waited another minute, just to be certain I was alone.

Deafening silence.

I finally gave in to my weakness and slid to the crimson-speckled floor, curling into a tight ball.

My tears mingled with my blood.

As I exited the house two hours later—now late for my new duties—I didn't stop to soak up the sun's warmth. My training gear kept rubbing against raw skin and fresh bandages—it was all I could do not to hunch over. My boots were heavy as I trudged down the house's front steps. I began the trek to the stables in search of my . . . student. Bren was to meet me out front. Where was he? We had a long journey ahead of us.

"Hey." A hand touched my shoulder from behind. My reaction was pure instinct. I grabbed the wrist and yanked it forward, crouching as a body slammed into my back. For a second, the heavy weight pressing on my tender skin left me paralyzed, unable to draw air. Then a cry of rage ripped from my lungs as I heaved the attacker over my shoulder. The body flipped and smacked the ground with a jarring thud.

Someone groaned loudly.

After several moments of catching my breath, I looked down and immediately wished I hadn't.

Bren blinked up at me.

I was in so much trouble.

"Sorry about that," I wheezed, then cleared my throat. "Not fond of people sneaking up on me." I offered my hand, not because I cared that he was hurt. If I didn't play nice with Renold's new pet, he might snitch on me.

He waved my hand away, stumbling a bit as he rose to his feet. Huffing out a laugh, he replied, "I'll remember that next time. Nice hip toss, by the way. You know judo?"

Wait, what? He was impressed with the toss? And he

wasn't mad at me? My eyes narrowed on his face.

"Yeah, I know judo. Do you?" I continued walking toward the stables—maybe a touch slower than before now that my back was cursing me for my antics—and he kept pace. Quite easily, in fact. His legs were ridiculously long.

"A little," he replied. "Self-taught, mostly. Life on the outside—Uh, let's just say self-defense is a must."

I laughed mockingly, a surge of heat licking my neck. "I bet. Save anyone from danger with those fancy skills?"

He looked at me like I had zapped him with a taser. I barely held in a derisive snort. What a pretender. The innocent act didn't fool me.

I gestured at the stables and spoke again before he could spin a tall tale. "This is the Equestrian Center. Inside are seventy-five highly-trained chargers." As we entered, Bren whistled appreciatively. Several chargers poked their heads into the aisle in response. His eyes widened in wonder.

"You've ridden a charger before, right?" I asked. If not . . .

"No. Always wanted to though. I hear they're wicked fast." He stepped forward and reached toward one.

I grabbed his wrist, stopping him just in time. "Don't. Unless you feel like losing a hand." The beast yawned and flashed its enormous teeth.

Turning, I raised an eyebrow that said, *See what I mean?*

Bren cleared his throat nervously. He should be nervous. *Very* nervous. "Thanks. Seems I have a lot to learn about this city."

You have no idea, pretty boy. You're as good as dead. I kept my thoughts quiet by sheer force of will. This arrangement was growing worse and worse. Why had Bren been recommended for the Trials? He was a complete idiot. Renold's newest game was beyond twisted.

We moved to Stalin's enclosure and I paused, studying Bren's reaction. He had a look of awe on his face when he saw the black giant. My eyes rounded as Stalin craned his neck and sniffed at the newcomer, seeming for all the world like a docile creature. I blinked—hard. But the beast continued to sniff without baring his teeth. Was I hallucinating? I hadn't eaten yet today after all . . .

"Do you think he'd let me pet him?" Bren asked, a little boy's hopeful face peering down at me. I did a double-take. Why did he have to be an animal person? Did villains pet animals?

Apparently, they did.

"Um, maybe. But offer him some meat first. There's a bucket over there." I pointed, hiding a smirk when Bren mouthed the word *meat* as he went to grab the food of carnivores. Was he expecting the beast to eat an apple?

When he hesitated in his approach, I rolled my eyes, annoyed that I had to help him. Maybe I should just let his hand get bitten off. Then I wouldn't have to train him.

Pushing the morbid thought aside, I went to place my hand beneath his like Asher had done for me, but I couldn't make my arm move. Ugh! *I can do this. He's just an overgrown boy,* I scolded myself. But I couldn't stop myself from adding: *A lying, betraying giant of a boy.*

After a couple of false starts, my hand finally slid under his. He glanced at me in surprise, but I ignored the look, as well as the way my palm lit with warmth. Like holding a sunbaked rock. "Here. He's somewhat accepting of my scent, so this should help with the introduction phase.

42

Just . . . no sudden moves, okay?"

I was still wary of Stalin. He probably wouldn't mind sampling a piece of me. I fought the urge to pull away from the foreign sensation of touching this boy-turned-man. Instead, I nudged us closer to the hulking beast. Stalin seized the meat from Bren's palm, making disgusting smacking noises as he chewed.

"Lune?"

Startled by the unexpected voice behind me, my hand jerked upward, whacking Stalin's nose. Immediately the animal bellowed and lunged for the offending object. A scream lodged in my throat. *I'm going to lose my hand!*

One second, big scary teeth were closing in on my fingers and the next I was spinning out of control, my body wrenched away from danger. I gasped, disorientated as the world tilted sideways and, yet, I somehow remained on my feet.

"You all right?" The deep voice vibrated through my palms and I looked down, confused. What the—*How come my hands are on a chest?* A hard, muscular—

I leapt backward, only to plow into another body. My back flared with pain and I swallowed another gasp. Fingers grasped my arms, steadying me. "Whoa, whoa! You okay? I'm sorry, I shouldn't have snuck up on you." I recognized Asher's panicked tenor and stopped myself from elbowing him in the gut.

I eased out of his grip, inspecting my hand. Five intact fingers wiggled at me. "Thank the stars," I breathed. Louder, I said, "It's fine, Ash, no worries. I should have been paying attention." I really should have. My new student was already turning into an unwelcome distraction.

"Who's he?" Asher ticked his head toward Bren.

"Mr. Bearon is, uh . . . He . . ." I stammered to a halt. Heat fanned my neck, cheeks, and temples. The temptation to snarl "Meet my kidnapper" was overwhelming.

"You can just call me Bren," he said, completely at ease with the awkwardness that was me. He raised a hand for Asher to shake. "Miss Tatum has agreed to train me."

"Asher Donovan," the stable boy replied, and they shook hands. And then Bren's words finally sunk in. "Wait, *train* you?"

"Yes. I've been told she's the best. And I entered the city just this morning, so that would explain why you haven't seen me around."

Asher's eyes bugged out at that, and he looked to me for answers, but I wasn't going to give him any. He was acting too friendly with us and that had gotten him into trouble more than once. He was too nice for his own good. I had to end this conversation. Now. Before Bren reported him for socializing above his station. "Don't you have things to do, stable boy? Because if you don't, I could always have a word with your boss . . ."

Shock registered on his face, quickly replaced with hurt. I felt the weight of it, like a boulder sitting on my chest. I had to look away before I took the words back, making matters worse. I heard a mumbled, "Yes, ma'am." Then he shuffled down the aisle and out of sight.

My stomach cramped painfully, and I bit back a grimace. I *never* spoke to him that way. I might have just lost the only human friend I had.

Bren was watching me—I could feel his heavy stare. I met his eyes, expecting to see approval, but what I saw sent my pulse tripping. Disappointment. Shame rushed through my veins, heating everywhere it touched, but I clenched my jaw, turning the emotion into anger. *He* was disappointed in *me?* He had no right. No right at all. Not after what he had done to me.

I tore my gaze from his and inhaled a cooling breath. "So, we have a slight problem. You've never ridden a charger, and riding is the only way we could possibly visit all three Trial sites before nightfall. Maybe they have a couple of old bicycles around here . . ."

"I'm fine with riding double. That is . . . if you are?"

Was that a challenge? Because that certainly sounded—

My eyes flicked to his again. They were suppressing . . . laughter?

Yep. Definitely a challenge.

I envisioned him sliding off Stalin's rump and breaking a leg, too injured to train for the Trials. A tiny smirk formed on my lips.

This could work.

"Sure. We'll take Stalin."

My grin stretched, and I didn't even care if I looked downright evil.

Ten minutes later, I was definitely not smiling.

Bren had vaulted onto Stalin's back without the aid of a mounting block or stirrup, now settling himself directly behind me.

"I thought you said you've never ridden a charger," I all but snapped. I rotated in the saddle, so I could see him better, and clenched my teeth as the movement agitated my wounds. He was such a liar.

He wouldn't meet my eyes. "Uh, perks of being six-foot-four?"

Holy stars, he really is a giant.

"Is that seriously your explanation?" No way was I falling for that lame comment.

He laughed, sounding uncomfortable, making *me* uncomfortable. Suddenly, the space between us felt thinner than paper. His chest was almost touching my back and hot revulsion surged up my throat. What was I doing? I couldn't do this—not with anyone. But especially not with him!

I was about to swing my leg over the saddle and call this whole thing off when he finally replied, "Okay, so I may have ridden a horse or two in the past. Not a charger, but a regular horse, yes."

"You've got to be kidding me," I spoke without thought, irritation heavy in my tone. I flicked my finger back and forth in the minuscule gap separating our bodies. "Was this your idea of making me uncomfortable? Because I don't appreciate it."

In a rush, he said, "No, no, I didn't mean to deceive you or anything. I've never ridden a charger before and just thought I'd learn best this way." He scratched the back of his neck, looking apologetic. I almost believed him. Then, "So I make you uncomfortable?"

With an irritated sigh, I faced forward. He was *not* going to get to me. I'd endure this painful trip even if it killed me. "Make sure you hold onto something, Mr. Bearon. Stalin's gait isn't exactly smooth, especially his takeoff."

I bit my cheek to rein in sinister laughter.

This should be entertaining.

Very entertaining.

"Yeah, I'll . . . maybe I can just . . ." His uncertainty eased my phobia at being so close to him. Maybe I could deal with this, after all.

Before he could secure a handhold, my heels kicked Stalin's sides, jolting us into motion. But my plan backfired terribly. Bren didn't fall—didn't even flinch. No, he wrapped his arms around me and held on tight. I could feel the length of his body brush against mine, scratching against my new wounds. A cry almost slipped past my tight-lipped grimace.

The pain sent a fresh wave of fury through my blood and I urged Stalin faster, leaning as far away from the man behind me as I could.

Maybe this trip wouldn't kill me but resisting the urge to kill *him* was going to be harder than I thought.

Tatum City was sprawling, yet rural. More a forest dotted with small villages, patches of farmland, and an over-sized house than an actual concrete-and-brick-infested, overpopulated city. The three Trial sites and their correlating training fields were spread out, separated by miles and miles of hills and trees, and I preferred it that way. Easier to avoid certain people I didn't like, namely the elites and my peers.

After several minutes of steady cantering, we arrived at the Rasa Rowe Trial site where silver high-rise stands encompassed an oblong track. Bren slid to the ground and offered me a hand, looking up expectantly. I glanced at the offer of help, then very deliberately dismissed it, jumping down on my own. Wrong move. Jolts of pain ran up and down my back, stealing my breath.

"You all right?"

With a shallow inhale, I straightened, and ignored the question. "How did you enjoy your first ride on a charger, Mr. Bearon?" I slowly looped Stalin's reins over the track's outer fence.

He didn't reply right away and my jaw clenched. Finally, he said, "It was . . . fast. But I'll admit, I was a bit distracted by all the red hair in my face. Spent most of the time dislodging it from my mouth." His eyes laughed at me. "And please call me Bren. 'Mr. Bearon' makes me feel like an old, stuffy geezer."

My mouth opened so wide, an army of flies could have flown in. I choked, breaking into a fit of coughs. *Geezer? What does that even mean?* Giving my head a shake, I secured my wayward locks into a messy knot at the base of my skull. There. Problem solved. The thought of my hair brushing against his mouth . . .

I grimaced. "So, this is the Rasa Rowe Trial site. It looks like a harmless racing track, but the inner walls and the ground hide obstacles meant to create a challenge." Not to mention the objects thrown by the audience. They loved being able to participate in this Trial.

"What kind of obstacles?"

"The better question would be, 'What obstacles *aren't* there?'"

Bren released a low whistle. "And you've practiced with these mysterious obstructions?"

The question rankled my nerves. "Of course. I've been running the training track since I was ten years old."

"Well, color me impressed."

Wait, what? Was that a compliment? Or was he just

teasing me? I squirmed. Either way, his words made me feel odd. I didn't like it.

"I don't know what contracts you've signed, but the Rasa Rowe Trial is the one that requires you to have a charger. Only trainees with an elite patron can afford one of these beasts. Do you have a patron?"

At that, his eyes probed mine. For some reason, he hesitated, like maybe he thought I wouldn't approve of the answer. My lips tightened, unease twisting my gut as my mind connected the dots before he could confirm it.

Finally, he said, "Yes. Your father."

My blood chilled. I knew Renold funded other trainees, but something felt different about his relationship with Bren. It was more than a calculated investment in a promising Trial's contender. I needed to figure out their connection. My freedom counted on it.

Bren cleared his throat, the noise almost nervous. "I suppose you should know I've signed contracts with all three Trials."

Everything in me froze.

Then heated words, hot enough to match my internal rage, exploded from my mouth. "*What?* Are you crazy? That's suicide! You don't even know how to ride a charger, you stupid fool! It takes *years* of intense training to contend in a Trial without dying. Do you even know what the other two Trials are? They're more dangerous than this one, I can tell you that!" I briefly came up for air, then dove in again. "Have you even had training or have you just been skulking around in the woods for the past decade?"

My throat burned as I took great gulps of air, trying to calm myself. Bren stared at me, still as stone. Did I scare some sense into him? Then he burst out laughing, the sound rich and full. Argh! I was going to punch him in the face. With my fist!

"First off—" He paused to wipe at his eyes. *The nerve of this guy!* "I'm flattered that you care so much. I was beginning to worry. Second, I know the odds are against me, but I've actually had some training. I haven't been—what did you call it?—*skulking* in the woods for the last decade. Why would you think I'd be doing that anyway?"

Uh oh.

And just like that, the heat in my veins extinguished.

I'd suspected he didn't remember me and now I was fairly certain of it. But there was no way I was going to walk down memory lane with him right now. That confrontation would come when I was good and ready. If I ever was.

Instead, I shrugged off-handedly. "Renold said you were from the Recruiter Clan. I assumed you all skulked, doing whatever you pleased, kind of like pirates. Pillaging, plundering, that sort of thing." *Kidnapping,* I ached to add.

"Pirates? That's an interesting description. But no, I didn't do whatever I pleased. Far from it. Sometimes you don't have a choice in what you do." I watched curiously as his hands clenched and unclenched, the knuckles bleeding white.

I pushed off the fence and untied Stalin's reins. "You always have a choice." But did I really believe that? To myself, I muttered, "You just have to be willing to fight for it."

I fidgeted with the reins, nerves twisting my stomach into tense knots when it finally dawned on me that we were completely alone at an empty track. Brendan-the-boy was a kidnapper, but who was Brendan-the-man? Would he . . .

try anything? My grip tightened. Let him try. He'd regret it after losing an important body part or two.

Bren broke the silence. "It's quiet out here. It almost feels like we're on the outside."

"No. It's not the same. Not even close."

"Have you always lived in Tatum City?"

I should have kept my big mouth shut. Should I lie?

"No," was all I said. Let him wonder. That's all he was going to get.

Before I could mount, Bren was already astride Stalin, waiting for me. I gaped. "He let you mount him? And he didn't go tearing off into the woods with you clinging to him like an unlucky flea?"

Bren snickered. "Maybe I'm a *lucky* flea." He offered me a hand up.

"So not fair." I glared at Stalin and dismissed Bren's hand. "Hold still," I ordered them both. Taking a running leap, I planted my hands onto Stalin's hip bone and swung a leg over his back. My fresh bandages tugged at raw, sensitive skin and I gasped. Then lost my balance. I started slipping but Bren twisted in the saddle, wrapping an arm around my lower back, the only spot not injured.

My face burned. I was used to feeling heat in my face, but now I was feeling heat creep up my side where his arm held me up. And it wasn't the usual painful kind. *Traitor,* I internally fumed at my body. I righted myself and mumbled a quick, "Thanks." I doubted he could hear it.

"No problem," he said. Guess he could hear my pathetic gratitude after all. My embarrassment knew no end. "Where to next?"

I pointed over his shoulder. "Take this road due west. Are

you sure you can handle this big beast?"

"Oh, I think I can manage him. Just like riding a horse, right?" I wanted to smack him for his arrogance. He looked back and caught me mid eye-roll. His face lit up with mischief. "Better hold onto something, little bird."

My mouth opened, a retort heavy on my tongue at his audacity. *Bird?* But the words never came, my objection pushed aside as Stalin shot forward on Bren's command. My fingers dug into the sides of his jacket and I leaned in close, not used to riding without my feet in stirrups.

Bren's laughter floated on the wind as we raced down the dusty road.

I knew in that moment my life would be changing yet again because of this insufferable boy. He knew how to play my games. Maybe even better than me.

My lips curled. *Game on, pretty boy. Game on.*

5

FEARS & WEAKNESSES

He was a natural, I admitted to myself begrudgingly.

Bren handled Stalin as if they'd been riding together for years. It would make my job easier, as his trainer. But, as my competition, he might prove a challenge. Fifteen minutes later, we reached the French Broad River. Cutting through the heart of the city, the wide river had survived the test of time and kept us alive. Without this resource, Tatum City would cease to exist.

The bubbling noise, as water eddied up and over flat rocks, calmed my mind. I closed my eyes, letting the sound sweep me away. A memory floated behind my closed lids— the first time Bren and I had met as children. The picture was serene and peaceful, surrounded by water, until . . .

Exhaling through my nose, I opened my eyes, dispelling the vision. I wouldn't let Bren ruin water for me. Water had been my last moment of peace as a free human being and it would remain a source of comfort to me as a prisoner. Not pain. I wouldn't let it become that.

It was then I noticed we had stopped at the bank's edge. "There's a bridge farther upstream," I offered, "but that will take us out of our way. We can cross here. The water is fairly shallow this time of year."

I tightened my knees against Stalin's sides in anticipation

of the slight drop into the river, but nothing happened. I chewed on my lip and felt my brows lowering in confusion. I couldn't see Bren's face. Was he sightseeing? We didn't have time for that.

Impatience had me asking, "What are you doing?"

He cleared his throat nervously. I didn't like him sounding nervous. It made *me* nervous. "Uh, how about we take the bridge?"

"What? No, we don't have time to waste. We have maybe two hours of sunlight left and still have a lot of ground to cover before I'm done showing you the last of the Trials. Come on, I'm pretty sure Stalin's crossed the river before."

His voice rose a notch or two. "You're *pretty* sure? What are you not telling me?"

I shrugged, then realized he couldn't see me. "I've never ridden him before today."

He laughed, but it was strained. "Of course you haven't. This place is crazy." I listened to air expand and contract his chest, like the task was an effort. "I don't think this is a good idea, Lune. Let's take the bridge."

He turned Stalin's head, nudging him upstream, and that's when I lost my patience. I reached around him and snagged the reins, ordering Stalin into the water. My heels into his sides sealed the deal. In we plunged, the freezing river soaking our shoes and pants within seconds.

Bren hissed a stream of words I couldn't decipher, tightening his hands on the reins. They squeezed until Stalin had no choice but to back up. "Stop!" I yelled while wrestling for control of the beast. The conflicting actions confused the poor animal and he lost his footing. His rump disappeared beneath the water as he sat like a dog.

I had an irrational thought that I was going to get my hair wet again, and then I was sliding backward, unable to stop gravity's pull. Before I could think better of it, I grabbed onto Bren's jacket, but that only made him come along for the ride.

One second we were high-and-dry, the next low and utterly soaked. A zip of shock lit my body as I fully submerged into the chilly water. The fall sent river water rushing up my nose and, when I rose to the surface, I coughed and sputtered. The hacking burned my throat and I groaned. And then I was choking on laughter. I laughed until my side and back ached.

An invisible knot in my chest loosened. When was the last time I had laughed like this? It felt . . . good. Really good.

I remembered Bren, feeling a tiny bit guilty for pulling him in with me, but it was soon replaced with satisfaction. He deserved this little piece of revenge. Maybe this would be the first of many. I wanted to bask in his reaction, so I sought him out. My laughter died. He stood in the waist-high water, rigid as stone. His expression was blank. Did he get hurt?

"Bren? Are you okay?" I waved my hand in front of his face, but he gave no indication that he could see me.

Moving nearer, I touched his shoulder. He exploded into motion. Catching my wrist, he barreled into my stomach and flipped my body up and over his. I landed on my back with a splash, water cushioning the impact, and yet my aching wounds screamed their protest. Shocked, I let myself sink to the river bed.

Still holding my wrist, Bren pulled me out of the water

and I coughed anew. I didn't feel like laughing this time. As I bent over, my stomach cramping from the blow it had received, I felt a hand rest on my sore back. I inhaled sharply, not quite hiding a flinch. "You all right?" he asked. How many times was he going to ask me that? I jerked away from his touch and the intrusive weight lifted.

Ignoring his question, I instead blurted, "What the crap was *that?*" I carefully straightened, trying not to wince from the pain.

"Sorry. Natural reaction." His face was a mix of distraction and annoyance. He avoided my incredulous gaze, raking wet hair off his brow. Without another word, he peeled off his sopping jacket while wading to the far bank.

Watching him was like seeing myself in a mirror. Action and reaction. Survival instincts kicking in when fear rendered the mind useless.

And then I knew.

"You're afraid of water." It wasn't a question. I gaped in disbelief. The thing that gave me peace caused him *fear?*

After pulling himself onto dry land, he turned and stared me down.

I held up my hands, palms facing outward. "Hey, we all have weaknesses. Some are just better at hiding them than others." Water, though? Of all things. I kept a tight leash on the grin that wanted loose. I could use this to my advantage.

I joined him on dry land, my boots making squishy noises as I led Stalin to a tree. After looping the reins around a branch, I sat on a nearby rock and untied my boots. A few grunts and tugs later, I managed to wrestle the clingy leather into submission. Tipping them, I watched a steady stream of river gush out. Ugh. Nothing was worse than wet leather. At least my bandages were waterproof and hidden beneath my vest.

All was quiet, and I felt a moment of panic. Now that I knew Bren's secret, was he thinking of a way to stage an accidental death? Maybe drown me? My hand crept to a hidden pocket in my pants as I glanced up at him. He hadn't moved. He stood by the river bank, watching every little thing I did. The hairs on my neck rose.

He looked away and exhaled, releasing the tension in his shoulders. My fingers slid into the pocket and felt for the small knife I carried with me always, for moments such as these. If it came down to me or him, it would be me. Suddenly, his legs ate up the distance between us and my muscles coiled, prepared to strike. My fingertips brushed cold steel.

And then he knelt in the grass before me so we were eye level.

I froze.

His next move surprised me the most. Calmly, he said, "Fear is not weakness. It reminds us that we are human— with limitations. We are not gods. But, instead of hiding our fear, what if we faced it? For in facing what makes us afraid, we become stronger."

My fingers slackened, as did my jaw.

Bren gently placed two fingers beneath my chin and nudged my mouth closed. I was in too much shock to stop him. He looked amused. "I take it no one has told you that before?"

A strange noise came from my throat before I could choke it back. I swallowed, looking at the hands clenched in my lap. "No. No one has." I couldn't bear his attention a second longer. Jumping to my feet, I wiggled my half-numb toes, then quickly sat down again and picked up a boot. "Uh, let me put these on and we'll head out." He gave me space and a quiet sigh fled my lips.

As we mounted up, I couldn't help but mull over the strange words he had spoken with such conviction.

Every step we took toward the Arcus Point Trial site heightened my senses. And my nerves.

No one ventured this side of the river, except for the handlers. It was isolated from the rest of the city and eerily quiet. Even the forest animals steered clear of the area. And for good reason.

Demons lived here.

I squirmed in the saddle until Stalin picked up on my unease. He pranced and bobbed his head, nickering. The sound set me on edge and all I could think about was standing on my own two feet. I slid to the ground, a carpet of pine needles silencing my fall. Bren reined Stalin to a halt and joined me.

I tugged my five-inch blade from its hidden pocket, relief hitting me as I held its reassuring weight. It might not puncture a thick hide, but it would penetrate an eye just fine. Bren was staring at the knife, then at me, then the knife, his eyebrows lost in the hair that had fallen over his forehead.

"What?" I arched a brow in return. "You can never be too careful. This place is isolated from the populace for a reason."

His eyebrows completely disappeared at that.

After tying Stalin to a tree, we left the road and took off on foot. The forest swallowed us whole. It was wild and untended out here, but the trees provided sanctuary if the need arose. I would climb one if I had to. My goal was to remain invisible. For the next several minutes, we walked in silence, avoiding dead leaves and twigs.

No undue noise.

Thank the stars, Bren knew how to be stealthy. But that posed a new problem: he was good on his feet, not just in the saddle. Maybe he wouldn't be hard to train, but he would be hard to *beat* when the time came.

Abruptly, the trees ended and we stood facing a twenty-four-foot-high metal monstrosity. Thick supports burrowed deep into the earth, giving the fence ultimate strength and durability. It wasn't live now, I knew that much, which gave me no comfort. Electrified or not, the last place I wanted to be was locked inside that cage.

"So, what's with this city's cages and walls?" Bren asked.

He didn't know? "To protect the people from mutated beasts and any other outside threats." I slid a glance his way, wondering what his reaction would be to Renold's explanation.

He chuckled. "Or maybe they're to keep the citizens *in?*"

My jaw dropped and I quickly snapped it shut. This was not a conversation I should be having with *him* of all people. I steered the topic to safer ground. "The Arcus Point Trial cage surrounds four square miles of rough terrain—much larger than the training cage. During the Trials, this fence is live to keep the beasts from climbing out, as I mentioned. Both cages house a variety of obstacles, like old buildings and cars, plus many trees. These obstacles can be helpful . . . but not always. They can just as easily play a part in your death."

Bren watched me curiously, but I didn't elaborate. Past Trials gone wrong were not something I liked to discuss.

"Where do they keep the animals?" he asked.

I pointed north. "In a concrete bunker on the far side of the cage. They have handlers on site at all times, feeding them, keeping them contained." Not a job that I would want. On occasion, a mutated beast would get out of hand or even escape. They had no qualms about biting the hand that fed them, or eating said hand.

"Can we see them?"

"No," I said quickly. Too quickly. *Breathe in, breathe out.* More calmly, I explained. "No, we can't. It's against the rules. That's why this Trial is the hardest. No contender is to know or prepare for the breed of beast they will fight in their Trial. But contenders don't fight in the cage alone. In each Trial segment, five contenders and ten beasts face each other in the cage. The contender who kills the most beasts wins the Trial." As I stepped into the safety of the trees once again, I muttered, "If they don't die first."

"And how do you kill the beasts?"

"Bow and arrows."

Bren snorted. "Bow and—"

An animal scream, its eerie wail growing louder and louder, frightened a bird directly above my head. The bird's reaction triggered mine and I whirled into a fighting stance, my knife at the ready. Blood pounded a frantic beat in my ears as I searched for the danger. My throat tightened. Darkness edged my peripheral.

I can't hear. I can't see. I can't breathe!

When something brushed against my hand, threatening to steal my knife, I lost it.

I grabbed onto flesh and bone, twisting my body underneath. But before I could pop the limb out of socket, an arm snaked around my waist, tightly pressing my back against a hard wall. No. A body. The friction rubbed against my wounds and I bit back a cry.

I went limp. My dead weight dropped like a stone, but so did the living thing behind me. We twisted as we fell, my captor cushioning the impact. The grip around my waist loosened as we crashed to the ground in a tangle of limbs.

Now was my chance.

My sharp elbow struck what felt like solid cement and a jolt of pain zipped up my arm. But it had the desired effect. I was now free of captivity. Rising to a crouch, I lunged on top of my attacker and slipped my knife beneath their chin.

And I hesitated, my instincts sputtering. Could I kill? *Should* I kill? My moment of indecision cost me everything, and yet . . . it saved me.

I was flipped onto my back, wrists pinned in vice-like grips as a heavy weight pressed me down into the ground. Trapped. Helpless.

Panic and pain took hold. A scream burst from my mouth before I could stop it.

"Lune!" a voice bellowed. "Would you snap out of it? I'm not going to hurt you!"

My screams faded as I concentrated on that voice. I blinked until the fog receded, revealing honey-gold eyes. The sight sucked the fight out of me, then a second later, reignited it.

Bren.

He was on top of me. Holding me prisoner.

I growled, "Get off!" and struggled against his grip. It was like being pinned down by a steel plank. A fresh wave of panic flooded my veins—even when he released me, rolling to the side.

As I tried to stand, hot pain shot through my body. My muscles shook and black smudged the edges of my vision. No, no, not now! I blinked the darkness away. After a few attempts, I clamored to my feet, then slowly backed away. Tremors gathered in my fingers and stole up my arms. Glancing down, I saw my knife still clenched in my fist. I almost dropped it. Almost. But self-preservation, the one thing that had kept me alive all these years, had me hastily slipping the weapon into my pants pocket.

I continued backing away. Swirls of shame and fury inflamed my face. What had I done? I had almost *killed* someone. My brain skipped over the thought, not wanting to process it. Bren had ruined my life, but still . . .

Space. I needed it. A lot of it. Pivoting, I plunged through the woods.

"Lune!"

No, no, no! I had to get away. He was unraveling me all too quickly, peeking at the darkest parts—the parts I so carefully kept hidden. Their exposure left me weak, vulnerable. I hated it. I hated *him!*

He was going to destroy everything—everything I had worked so hard to achieve. My fears were his gain. He would train with me, use me, then exploit my weaknesses, stealing my freedom once again. Wasn't it enough that he had stolen my past?

Terrible pressure built inside my throat until breathing

was impossible. I slammed into a tree and dug my nails into the bark to steady my shaking body. Rage choked me. I fought the knot in my throat and let loose an unearthly howl. Cocking my arm back, I rammed a fist into the tree.

The pain was instant, sharp and biting. More pain. More wounds to heal. More scars for my body. But the rage was still there.

I hit the tree again and my knuckles split open from the abrasive impact. Whirling, I slammed a boot into the trunk. The satisfying sound of cracking wood gave my adrenaline a boost. I went for another pass, whipping my leg around, but something grabbed ahold of my calf, immediately releasing me so that I stumbled to the side.

I crouched and brought my fists up, prepared to defend myself. And then I recognized *him.* "Why did you stop me?" I spat.

Bren spread his arms wide, like an invitation. "Hit me instead."

I looked away, clenching my aching jaw.

"I know you want to. I saw it in your eyes."

I remained silent, furious with myself for being so transparent.

"Am I right?" he prodded. Again.

He was going to get his wish if he kept verbally poking me. But with a great amount of effort, I gathered my raw emotions, concealing them once again. He wouldn't so easily tear down my barriers next time. *Oh stars*, I prayed there wouldn't be a next time. The stress of keeping everything locked inside would kill me.

I needed distance. From him. From everything. Without replying, I marched to where we had left Stalin and untied his reins. I halted, my head falling back in frustration. I couldn't get away from Bren. I was *stuck* with him. Even now. He stood right behind me, his large body casting mine in shadow.

Words begged to be said. Words that would create a river between us, one he couldn't cross. They crashed against my brain until I was forced to expel them. I spun and stood toe-to-toe with him, glaring up at his grim face.

"Don't," I said curtly. "Don't try to figure me out. Whatever you think you see, you're wrong. You know nothing about me or what I want. I'm your trainer, nothing more. Keep it that way."

"Why?" His confusion permeated the air, so thick I could almost taste it.

But I was used to confusion. If he spent enough time inside these walls, he would get used to it as well. Secrets weren't given away for free. *Not if you want to survive.*

Though stiff, every movement a fresh nightmare of undulating pain, I swung into the saddle before saying, "Come on. Let's go."

THE PEERS

Normally I craved silence, the kind that made me think I was the only being in existence. But, in this moment, the utter lack of noise was torture.

I knew he was there—his legs brushed the backs of my thighs with every shift of the saddle. I felt his fingers tighten where they rested on my sides when we crossed the river, loosening when we hit dry ground. Minutes ticked by, taunting me with their slowness. Would this day never end?

With the sun heavy in the sky and on the verge of plunging below the tree line, we made it to the last Trial site. My shoulders relaxed their pensive hold and so did my tongue.

"You should petition for Stalin as your mount in the Rasa Rowe Trial. He's strong and fast. Stubborn and a bit mouthy, too, but you two have that in common, so . . ."

He chuckled. "I suppose we do. You wouldn't mind?"

"Not at all. I have my own charger, Cleopatra. I'm sure she's jealous that I've spent all my time with another today." Too late, I realized the phrase didn't come out the way I intended. "With another charger, I mean."

"Well, we wouldn't want that now, would we?"

Ugh. He was teasing me. "No, we wouldn't. She might retaliate with her teeth. Who knows what body part she'd target."

He shut up at that. Score one for me.

At the top of a grassy knoll, we paused, taking in the sight of a square gray concrete slab nestled at the bottom of a green valley. If only the earth saw fit to swallow the arena whole. Inside that ugly box was a world of pain and brutality, where only the physically strong—or merciless—survived. Not many women attempted this Trial. Even the very brave knew their limits.

I knew mine, but nothing would keep me from doing what I had to do.

I would win. There was no other alternative.

"This is Faust Night?"

"The one and only." I rested my eyes on the Trial's insignia: crossed swords. It was chiseled onto the concrete wall, duplicated on either side of the front doors.

"Not much to look at. Let's go inside." He was on the ground and bounding down the hill before I could protest.

What did he think this was? A picnic?

With a groan, I followed.

Near the entrance, I tied Stalin to a hitching post, then approached the two guards in blue uniform who barred the doorway. As we neared, their hands crept toward their belts, where I knew they carried electric volt guns. On more than one occasion, I'd seen someone hit by a high-voltage dart—watched as they helplessly writhed on the ground, body madly convulsing. I had no desire to experience that sensation right now.

"Evening," I said, making sure they could see my empty hands.

"State your purpose," the older one on the left commanded and then straightened to his full height when Bren's tall frame filled the space.

"I'm Lune Tatum, in case you haven't seen me around. Newly promoted to training instructor. I have orders from my father—I'm sure you've heard of him—to show this student the Trial sites. He wishes to see the inside."

"Instructor?" The younger one scoffed, looking me up and down. I bristled under his scrutiny. He finally noticed my expression, the one that said, *Let us in or I will knee you in the jewels*. He shared a look with the other guard, who nodded, and they opened the doors.

I breezed inside, head held high. The message was clear: *Your jewels are safe. For now.*

The sound of snickering followed me in and I whirled. Bren tried to wipe the grin from his face without success before saying, "You must have a lot of friends."

Was that sarcasm? Was he using sarcasm on me? "Not really, no. People usually avoid me."

He snorted on more laughter and I rolled my eyes. I could tell this was going to become a habit with him.

I crossed the drab entrance hall and threw open a set of double doors. Stepping over the threshold, a needling chill slid up my spine. The interior was dark except for the middle of the cavernous room, weakly lit from the skylights high above. I touched a metal railing, using it as a guide as I descended the steep staircase. My eyes never left the square patch of light at the bottom, which grew larger and larger with each step.

The trainers called it The Pit. I thought the nickname fit quite well. This place was the armpit of Tatum City.

Sunken deep into the ground, the arena was unadorned and unremarkable—a cement slab surrounded by tall, reinforced glass walls. It was seamless, except for vent holes strategically placed in the floor and on rods hovering above the glassed enclosure.

"What's the glass for?" Bren had followed me to the bottom without trouble. I didn't even see him use the handrail. He touched the thick glass and peered inside the square pit with rapt curiosity.

"To protect the audience." I placed a palm on the cool wall.

"From *what?*"

"Flying debris," I responded cryptically. At his pointed look, I elaborated. "Every year there are four segments for this Trial, since it's the most popular. For each segment, five contenders compete against each other, and the last one not cut by steel wins. But there's a . . . twist, I guess you'd call it. The contenders *also* have to deal with the elements thrown at them."

"You mean, like earth, fire, wind . . . and water?" His throat bobbed, like he was having trouble swallowing.

"Yes, like that." My lips curled reflexively. Was he nervous? He should be.

He didn't respond. He was staring at the pit like it was a torture chamber of death. I guess it kind of was. If he didn't get over his fear of water, it could very well be his near-future grave.

"Bren?"

"Yeah."

"I'll train you." I almost bashed my forehead against the glass, completely shocked I'd said that out loud. But, for some stupid reason, I promised myself that I would. Maybe I felt a small connection with him, knowing he had weaknesses just like me. But I couldn't promise that I wouldn't use his weakness for my gain. Nothing was more important than winning my freedom.

He was quiet for so long, I sought out his reaction, only to find him staring at me quizzically. When his gaze intensified, I struggled with the desire to run away and hit him at the same time. *Why is he looking at me that way?*

"I think," he said, low and soft, "there's a whole lot more to you than fists and sarcasm. And I think I'm going to enjoy getting to know the real you."

My heart blipped to a halt.

Oh crap.

After dropping Stalin off at the stables, we made our way to the trainee barracks—finally. I was almost done with this field trip. My muscles were stiff, hot and aching, exhaustion pulling at me after only a few hours in Bren's presence. Keeping my spine straight was near impossible now.

I didn't understand what had possessed him to say such a thing earlier, about wanting to know the real me. I did know one thing for certain though. He couldn't find out about our childhood connection. Because if he knew, he would have the power to tear down my carefully constructed walls. Tearing them down would expose emotions I had spent eleven years suppressing, and I couldn't be vulnerable like that. Especially not with him. I had to stay focused on training. With the Trials less than three months away, distractions like him would get me killed.

If he tried to unearth any more of my secrets, I would do

whatever it took to keep them hidden—even if I had to fight him. And outside of training, he would find that fighting me was *not* something he wanted to do.

As we neared our living quarters, I ticked off the barracks rules. "All trainees eat and sleep in the barracks while under contract. Except for the elites and house staff, most everyone else lives in the village north of here. Follow the rules and you'll do just fine. Here are the important ones: meals are served three times a day in the mess hall starting at the sunrise bell; head to your designated training field at the second bell; fighting is not allowed outside of the training fields; guests are not allowed inside the barracks; girls' dorms are on the second floor and boys' on the third."

I stopped in front of the ugly building and faced him. "Oh, and relationships are strictly forbidden. Like no, uh, funny business sort of thing. You know what I mean," I finished lamely. So awkward.

Bren's lips quirked, like he thought my embarrassment was cute. I itched to smack his face. "I think I got it. What happens if you do any . . . funny business?"

He thought this was a joke? Fine. "They cut off a finger for each infraction. So, if they catch you touching someone in a manner they deem inappropriate, you lose a finger. Keep doing it, lose all ten fingers. Toes come next." Somehow, I managed a straight face the entire explanation.

He choked on a cough and I decided to help him out, giving his back a mighty thwack. "Breathe," I said, barely restraining a snicker.

"Whoa, whoa, whoa," he said, holding up his hands and avoiding my touch. "Should you be touching me right now?"

A snort left my nose.

Eyes narrowing, Bren dropped his hands. "You were teasing me."

"You're not the only one who knows how to tease, Mr. Bearon. Don't dish it if you can't take it. And touching is unavoidable—we must train, after all. But, if you want to see the inside of those Trials, you'll steer clear of . . ." I raised an eyebrow, daring him to finish.

"Funny business," he dared with a smirk. He was going to be trouble. Giant-sized trouble. The big oaf continued to pursue the subject. "So, what will really happen if you're caught doing funny business?"

Why was he so interested? This was worse than any nightmare.

I puffed out a long-suffering sigh. "When you signed those contracts, you became property of the Trials. As overseer of the Trials, Renold decides on the type of punishment to deliver when a trainee breaks a contract rule. If you're lucky, he'll let Elite Trainer Drake decide. Because, if Renold takes a personal interest in your punishment, chances are your contract will end. No contract means no contending in the Trials. Got it?"

His head bobbed slowly. He wasn't smirking now. Good.

My stomach rumbled like a runaway charger, reminding me that I hadn't eaten all day. "Come on, let's head to the mess hall. I'm starving." I paused with my hand on the door, debating if I should warn him. Why was I helping him so much? No one made life easy for me when I was dropped into this place. When *he* had taken me away from the safety of my mother.

And yet . . .

I cleared my throat, then blurted, "Be careful what you

say around the other trainees. They would rather spite you than befriend you. Not everyone is as *sweet* as I am." I threw him one of my sugary fake smiles, which only made him grin. Ugh. He wasn't supposed to smile at that.

Opening the door, I followed the noise. This was my least favorite part of the day. I could avoid most of my peers during training, breakfast, and even lunch since I oftentimes ate at the village market but, by dinnertime, I was ravenous. Nothing kept me away from the last meal of the day.

The mess hall was packed, the evening meal in full swing. I noticed Bren's gaze went straight to the most predominant feature in the massive room: the rank billboard. Its digital lights flashed dozens of names and ranks from top tier to bottom tier, the majority of the names found in the bottom two tiers. My name blazed bright blue under the tier five rank. I looked away from the stupid shrine and pointed to the far-left corner of the room.

"The beginner trainees—or tier ones—usually sit over there. Groups are formed by skill level, not age. There are five tiers total."

Bren shrugged. "I'll sit with you."

"The tier fives won't like it. Everything is about hierarchy in here. If you sit at their table without earning a spot first, you'll be mocked, ridiculed, teas—"

"I'll be fine, Lune," he laughed. "This isn't my first rodeo."

Rodeo? What's a rodeo?

"Suit yourself," I muttered, grabbing a metal tray next to the cafeteria line. Most of the time I passed through the line unnoticed before sliding into an end seat at my usual corner table. Not many had the nerve to disturb me.

But there was a decided shift tonight. A heavy, curious feeling permeated the air. One I had never felt before—the weight of several dozen eyes boring into my back. I knew it was because of Bren. The city rarely saw outsiders and, even more rarely, witnessed me spend time with anyone but my trainer. Bren didn't seem to notice the attention, too busy creating a mashed potato mountain on his plate. I envied his nonchalance.

Unlike him, I was too preoccupied with the stares to notice what I was putting on my plate. When I spotted a stack of shiny red, I reached for it. As long as I had an apple, I didn't care what else I was eating.

I glanced at Bren's plate again. "Fish and potatoes? That's it? Where's the greens? As your trainer, I'm not impressed with your diet." I was quite pleased with my superior tone. Maybe being a trainer had its perks.

A sound came from deep in Bren's throat.

I blinked up at him. "Did you—did you just *growl* at me?"

He turned, revealing a tiny pile of broccoli sitting on the corner of his plate. "There. Happy?" I nodded sagely, finding delight in ruffling his feathers. He obviously had a vendetta against greens. When his face cleared of annoyance, he drawled, "And I didn't growl at *you*. I'd be too afraid of the consequences. I just growl at anything green."

My brows lowered. "My eyes are kind of green."

"I know." The right corner of his mouth tipped up and he gave me a wink. I almost dropped my tray.

Speechless, I watched him stroll to where the tier fives sat and claim a spot at the head of the table as if he did it every day. He was either incredibly assured or ridiculously stupid. Probably both.

I shuffled after him and took the empty chair on his left. I hated that my back was exposed to the room, especially now that it was freshly injured and vulnerable. Longingly, I stared at my usual antisocial seat at the less crowded corner table. The tier fives near us gawked, clearly confused to see me sitting at their table, and with another person no less.

And then Bren spoke, his voice so loud the entire table fell silent and stared. "Hi, everyone. I'm Bren."

I wanted to wedge my body into one of the cracks in the floor.

"Mind explaining this, Mute?"

That's what I got for being anti-social. My very own nickname.

I looked at the mousy-haired man sitting across from me, giving him my best bored-to-tears face. "One of these days, Lars, my knife might accidentally fly out of my hand and slice off your tongue. It'll be interesting to hear what you have to say then."

Bren guffawed and all eyes returned to him. At least someone appreciated my joke. "I never know when you're joking, Lune. It's hilarious. Hey, everyone, what do you call a man without a tongue?" He shook his head, not expecting an answer, apparently. "Genius."

"You'll have to give Bren some slack here. He doesn't know all the rules yet. In fact, he just arrived from the outside and will begin training tomorrow." And that's all I planned on telling them. I picked up my fork and stabbed a large piece of broccoli, shoving the whole thing in my mouth. I made a show of chewing noisily, sneaking a glance at Bren as I did so. Opening my still-full mouth, I said, "Try some. It's super fresh, crunchy, and oh-so-green."

His lips twitched.

Lars leaned on an elbow, his lithe body inching closer to mine. "You're gonna need to help me out here. Why are *you* hanging out with him? You don't hang out with anyone."

I stopped chewing.

"She's my trainer," Bren oh-so-helpfully supplied.

Several incredulous voices rose at once, asking questions, demanding answers. My sweaty palm tightened its grip on my fork. Hopefully, I wouldn't have to use it for purposes other than stabbing my food. My throat constricted as I breathed in the stench of envy, jealousy, and fear.

Unease slid down my spine.

"Was this your daddy's idea, Princess?"

The noise dimmed as that one question drowned out the others. I could hear my rapid breathing and worked on slowing it. Mention of Renold's preferential treatment never failed to set me on edge. Even as my breathing slowed, my grip on the fork increased until my fist shook under the pressure.

Bren's hand inched toward mine, probably intent on freeing the unfortunate utensil, but I dragged my hands into my lap, out of sight.

"That's none of your concern, Catanna." I leveled a stare at the impertinent girl. Holding eye contact with a she-devil was not an easy task. Her graceful limbs and soft brown skin were deceiving. Even her wide sable eyes, fringed in sooty lashes, suggested innocence. Kindness. But I knew better. She was a snake disguised as an enchantress.

I waited for her venomous teeth to strike.

"Oh, but I think this affects us all, wouldn't you agree,

fives? If she can earn a trainer status *before* winning a Trial, shouldn't the rest of us be able to have titles? She's breaking the order of things." Catanna looked around the table, seeking support. And, as usual, she got it. Several trainees nodded and flicked hostile glances my way. She turned back to me, a dark and victorious gleam shining in those depthless eyes.

I felt caged. Trapped. The walls bent inward, boxing me in. My face numbed and I couldn't speak.

Underneath the table, fingers brushed my knuckles and I jerked, wrenching my hand out of reach. The touch must have come from Bren, that boundary-defying idiot. I had almost stabbed him with my fork.

Exhaling, I raised my voice to the restless crowd. "Once upon a time, a man dared question the Supreme Elite's decision. The next day he disappeared, never heard from again. The end." I focused on each of their stunned faces. "Any questions?"

Silence.

"I didn't think so."

Relief bathed my body when the invasive stares looked everywhere but at me. Just the way I liked it. Chatter ebbed and flowed once again, and I dug my fork into whatever was on my plate. It could have been radishes for all I cared. The meal had lost its taste. If it weren't for the small matter of keeping up my strength, I would be up and out of this room in a flash.

"Sooo, Bren," Lars droned, setting his sights on the fresh meat. "From where on the outside do you hail?"

"Mostly the mountains. Avoiding the beasts of the land." He caught my eye as he bit into a broccoli stem and grimaced. I rolled my eyes. What a big baby.

Lars nodded, as if he understood the plight of the outsiders. "I hear it's bad out there. That food is scarce, people try to rob you blind, safe shelter is hard to find, and that the animals try to eat you in your sleep." He chortled like he found the image funny. "Good thing the Supreme Elite let you in. You must be special or something."

Or just a practiced liar, I wanted to add. I bit the inside of my cheek.

"Guess I'm just lucky," Bren replied. I snorted, earning a scowl from the nosy man across from me.

"Well you're much better off in here. With the right allies, your future could be bright." His greasy stare slid to me. "Choose wisely who you align with."

Bren eyed him up and down. "I'll keep that in mind."

With a parting sneer thrown my way, Lars picked up his tray and left the table. Catanna and several others did the same.

Bren swallowed. "You're right. People really do avoid you."

If he wasn't so right, I would have punched his arm for that comment. My fist itched to make contact anyway, so I sat on it. "They don't know what to make of me because I don't think like they do. And I avoid *them* because I know all too well who they are."

Chew on that, pretty boy.

His movements stilled as he studied my face. "And the plot thickens. Who is Lune Tatum and how does she think?"

At his inquisitive look, my skin buzzed like a live wire. I jumped out of my seat, scrambling to collect my tray without dropping it on the floor and drawing even more attention to myself. I couldn't handle any more probing eyes on me. Before depositing the tray at the washroom window, I grabbed the apple from my plate. No way was it going to waste.

"You all right?"

"Holy stars, stop-sneaking-up-on-me!" I whirled, almost colliding with his chest. How could someone so big be so quiet? It was unnerving.

"I have no idea what you just said but I think I get the gist." Bren grinned, but it fell when he saw my face. I didn't know what he was seeing, but I knew what *I* was seeing. Or thought I saw. Honest-to-goodness concern.

It was all too much. This day had been too much. I could feel myself unraveling, and soon I would lose control. Slowly, I breathed in through my nose, gathered my frayed emotions, and locked them away.

"Let's go. It's been a long day. I'll show you where you'll sleep." I climbed to the third floor, someplace I'd never been before. Males of various age, anywhere from ten to thirty, a few even older than that, roamed the hallway. Some were in a shocking state of undress as they traveled from the public bathroom to their bunks or dorm rooms. A blush crept up my neck.

Awkward.

Stopping at an unclaimed bed, I turned to Bren. "Tiers one through four all bunk out here. Only tier fives have private dorms. Training gear is in the bathroom, and you'll want to wear riding leathers in the morning. Rasa Rowe training is first. Meet me outside the barracks at the second bell . . ." I trailed off, wondering what else I was supposed to say.

And then I knew. A devilish smile took over my lips and I leaned toward him, a boldness creeping over me that I wasn't used to. "Oh, and by the way," I whispered. "I have contracts with all three Trials, too."

His eyes rounded as his jaw dropped. The strange boldness tingling through my limbs allowed me to place a finger beneath his stubbly chin. The blunt hairs shifted, giving way to skin.

"Surprise." I winked at him.

My finger worked on closing his mouth. It shut with a faint click.

THIEF

The crickets were loud tonight, like a discordant stringed orchestra.

I melded with the shadows, thankful that clouds smudged the moon from the sky and obscured my movements. My black pants and hooded shirt further hid my presence as I shifted the precious cargo, careful not to let it bump against my sore back. On nights like this, I found purpose in a world that didn't have one. Even as my heart raced at the thought of being discovered out past curfew with pilfered goods, I beamed. This was my "screw you" to the power-hungry elite class who took and took and never gave.

Tonight, I would contribute to a struggling society. The weight of my treachery dangled over my right shoulder and down my arm instead of my back. The awkward bundle was a reassurance that I would make a difference. Not much of one, but better than standing idle and watching the city's backbone snap. The village people couldn't escape their fate, unlike my possibility. They needed all the help they could get. A madman lorded over them with an iron fist, stealing their toil and labor for himself and his posse, leaving only scraps behind.

But I had access to a solution. And so, I made this trip as

often as I dared, trying to right a small portion of the many wrongs.

Antler Hill Village, the largest and poorest settlement in Tatum City, rose like a phantom in the mist. Most of the population worked and resided here, numbering around six thousand men, women, and children. Asher was born in this village. How he had befriended me, the Supreme Elite's daughter, was beyond my understanding.

It had just . . . happened.

The Trials had brought us together. In fact, the annual Elite Trials were the only reason villagers and elites ever intermingled. It was the great equalizer. Anyone could contend in the Trials, and many did, for the sole purpose of bettering their future. The only way to receive a secure job, or attain more food and accommodations, was through a Trial win. The elites sometimes contended just to improve their ranking; or they became patrons, further solidifying their position—*if* their contenders won.

The worst part was the children. Many, as early as ten years old, were forced by their parents or guardians into contracts. If they were unable to better their family's lives by the contending age of eighteen, it was still one less body for their home to feed and clothe. At least I had willingly signed. So many joined, yet so few returned.

They should be called the Death Trials.

No one currently living in this village had won a Trial. Once you did, you and your family were moved to better accommodations in the smaller Loyalty Village nearby. Renold had named it, of course. Guards, trainers, and doctors, each having won a single Trial, lived there with their families. Some of the advisers did, too, but I was convinced their titles were mainly for appearance. Renold did what he pleased and expected everyone to fall in line—or face the consequences.

He didn't dole out punishment with his own hands. No, that special treatment was reserved for me. And, even then, he always used an object to inflict the pain. It was the guards who kept the villagers working, and the trainers who kept the trainees practicing from dawn until dusk.

Three years ago, a small group of villagers refused to work for a day. The next morning, the leaders of the group disappeared. As for the rest, they were stripped of their jobs and homes. The risk of helping the outcasts was too great; many were imprisoned for stealing or died of starvation.

We were an overworked, mind-numbed society with no way out. Up until now, anyway. I was fighting for myself, but I also wanted to send a message. There *was* another way. A chance to win freedom. To me, the risk was worth taking.

I didn't think I could survive living in this oppressed city for another year, let alone a lifetime.

In Antler Hill, there weren't enough houses for everyone. Many families double-housed, and even more packed themselves into the old white hotel atop the hill overlooking the village. The interior stank of mildewed carpet, but it contained running water, and that was the most important thing.

Even at midnight, the red clay roofs of the village's pale plaster houses shone dully. The buildings reminded me of a fairytale my mum had described once, one where a girl longed for adventure, and wished to escape the small town where nothing new ever happened. So, she did . . . and found herself face to face with a beast.

There were too many parallels between the heroine's story and mine. But the beasts in my story couldn't be tamed, and no enchanted flower could keep them at bay. It was me or them.

I waited behind a tree for the night watchmen to appear. They were lazy, the villagers too exhausted from a long day's work to cause problems. Their sloppiness was my ticket inside. Sure enough, a guard in royal blue sauntered past, his volt gun clinking against his belt. He didn't even look my way. I shook my head. At one point in time, the buffoon had won a Trial segment, probably Faust Night. The Elite Trainer would rip him a new one if he saw how his trainee was making use of his rigorous training regimen.

When I could no longer hear his boots scuffing the dirt-packed road, I slinked up the hill and wove my way between buildings, keeping to the darkest shadows. I brushed up against a small, one-story house, the plaster rough against my fingertips, and pressed my ear to the chipped green paint of the dwelling's only door. All was silent. With one knuckle, I knocked. One. One, two, three. Pause. The shuffling of feet, then . . .

"Code word?"

"Rumpelstiltskin."

A soft groan. "Lune, you do this every time."

I lowered my voice an octave. "How can you be sure that it's me?"

"Because we've been doing this for six years, that's why."

"Then let me in, doofus."

Asher snickered, cracking the door open just enough for me and my bundle to slip inside. When the door clicked shut, I faced him, a shot of nerves zipping through my limbs. I'd rather be chased by a guard than deal with the damage I had done to our friendship, but when he met my eyes and I saw the lingering confusion there, my mouth opened.

"Listen, Ash, about earlier . . ." My chest hurt. I wasn't used to this level of vulnerability. Eleven years of conditioning kept the words trapped inside. They were poison on my tongue.

But I knew that Asher deserved more.

I spit out the foreign string of words, each one burning as it left my mouth. "There's no excuse for how I treated you. I'm . . . I'm sorry."

Naked.

I felt naked.

It was as if he knew how hard it had been to speak that apology into the void. The confusion melted away, replaced with his usual empathy.

"No matter what you do, I will always forgive you." My heart squeezed, and I cherished the words. Yet I was afraid of the power they gave me. "But I couldn't help noticing," he continued, his eyes searching mine, "that you looked scared. Is it . . . is it the new guy? Bren? He didn't hurt you, did he?"

At his stormy expression, I shook my head. "No! No, he didn't hurt me. It's just . . . I didn't know what he would think of you and me—I mean, we're not supposed to be friends, you know that." Ugh, I was so bad at this. "What I'm trying to say is, I didn't want you to get hurt, but I ended up hurting you anyway."

I needed a muzzle.

He smiled, amused. "So, you want to be my friend, but

more like a *secret* friend, right?"

"Yes. No! This is all messed up." I groaned. A tiny cough came from the dark depths of the house and I clamped a hand over my mouth. Asher and I stared at each other in silence, listening to the gentle creaks and sighs of a slumbering household. On silent feet, I crept to his worn dining table and laid my burden on its surface. "There were more leftovers than usual this evening. This should make several meals worth. How is Selah's cough?"

"Not any better, unfortunately. But not any worse." Asher rifled through the bag, pulling out several apples, carrots, and potatoes. His eyes brightened in the dim candlelight and I felt my own well up with tears. Ever since his father passed, the Donovan family struggled to fill their stomachs. Ash's three siblings were too young to acquire jobs, and his mother was often sequestered to her bed, weakened from ailments. They couldn't afford medical treatment, not with Asher's menial job as a stable hand.

"I'm sorry," I whispered. It was all I could think to say.

He glanced at me. "Thank you, Lune. And my family thanks their elusive 'guardian angel' as well."

My throat closed. The more I did this—the more I helped—the harder it would be to leave all the people behind.

"Two villagers went missing today," he continued, even quieter. He knew how dangerous it was talking about the disappearances.

"Did you find out their crimes?" At his head shake, I added, "I'll figure it out. Just . . . keep your head down, okay? You can't be the next to go missing. I wouldn't . . ." I couldn't finish the sentence out loud. I would never forgive myself if he disappeared because of my decision to so blatantly break the rules. This should be my burden, not his. No one needed me. If I vanished, no one would suffer for it.

Before I left this city, I was determined to discover what happened to those who disappeared.

"LuLu, where are you?"

I couldn't see her. She was just out of sight, around the trail's bend. My mouth opened to reassure her, but no sound came. My bare feet left the ground in their attempt to reach her, but I was running in place. Stuck. Trapped. Helpless.

"Lune?" The voice was farther away now, barely a whisper.

"No, don't leave me! Mum!"

I gasped, eyes popping open as I bolted upright.

My pulse evened when I saw the chair still jammed underneath my dorm's doorknob. Thank the stars, I was still in bed. The reoccurring nightmare didn't usually wake me up. No, something else had woken me. Judging by the shadows and silence, it was a good two hours before dawn. Ugh.

Something felt different . . .

I groaned as the reason filtered into my fog-addled brain. Bren.

No, not just Bren. Bren and me.

No!

It was my first day as a trainer. That was it.

Another more sobering thought struck me: I was

probably going to get him killed.

What are you up to now, Renold?

I wasn't trainer material. I couldn't even get the village dogs to sit on command. I hissed as I rolled off the bed, the action pulling at my back's fresh bandages. At least the wounds had stopped bleeding.

The room was especially chilly this morning and I threw on a black sleeveless top and cropped pants as fast as my shaking fingers would allow. What I needed was warmth flowing through my veins and adrenaline pumping strong in my stiff muscles. Maybe then I'd feel brave enough to face my new student.

Flipping my head upside down, I gathered my hair into a high ponytail, all the while watching the bear's tooth dangling in front of my face. At the thought of Bren seeing it, I slipped the tooth underneath my shirt. Before leaving the room, I swiped last night's apple from my bedside table.

I made my way to the gym on the ground floor, the only soul awake at this ridiculously early hour. I flicked on the room's light switch and set my apple down, carefully contorting my body into a stretch as the bare bulbs groggily winked to life. Straightening, I breathed in the stench of stale human sweat, overshadowed by the sweet sound of silence.

Being an early riser had its perks.

My callused hands picked up a steel cable jump rope, the cool, heavy weight promising a rigorous warmup. I stopped counting after fifty cycles, lost to the mindless rhythm of flexing and hopping. My injuries were pushed aside as my body warmed. When sweat trickled down my temples, I tossed the rope aside and lunged into a defensive stance, an imaginary opponent in front of me.

But the face lacked definition.

I closed my eyes, conjuring an image of Lars. Nah, not today. A stronger face appeared, framed by dark brown hair. Gold eyes solidified the apparition until I could easily believe he was there in the room with me. Bren. My lips curved wickedly as I opened my eyes, keeping his likeness clear in my thoughts.

With a quick twist, my fist was in his stomach. I could almost hear the pained grunt as air left his lungs. He came at me but was too slow. My arm blocked his blow. I rained an uppercut into his jaw, knocking his teeth together. As he staggered, I wrenched my leg around and firmly planted a foot into his gut.

And the giant toppled like a felled tree.

I raised my fists as the crowd roared.

"Is that me on the floor?"

A high-pitched squeak ripped from my throat and I jerked around. *Gah, the apparition has come to life!* I looked at the ground behind me, my imaginary foe nowhere to be seen. Closing my eyes, I bit back a groan. That meant . . .

Reluctantly, I looked up at the *real* Bren, his face a mask of amusement. My stomach dropped. Thank the stars, my face was already red from exertion because the flames of embarrassment had taken up residence there. As my lips pursed, I pointed at him. "You didn't see or hear anything. Got it?"

He raised his hands in mock surrender and chuckled softly. "Got it, boss. I must have dreamt it."

"No. You're not allowed to dream up stuff like that, either." His eyebrows rose, and I changed the subject before he could pick apart what I had just said. "Why are you up so early, anyway? Couldn't sleep?" I finally noticed what he was wearing: gray sweatpants and a black shirt that hugged his muscular frame in a distracting way. *Stop looking, stupid!* I refocused on his face.

"I usually start my workout routine before anyone else wakes up. I enjoy the solitude and silence." Great. We had something in common. His eyes slid down my body and a flare of self-consciousness made my arms twitch. "I didn't peg you for a morning person." His mouth stretched into a grin.

"I'm not," I said flatly, giving in to the urge to cross my arms. "Morning people are creepy." I inched my way around him toward the exit.

"I don't mind if you stay. And I won't talk if that helps." His words gave me pause. "Besides, downing a real opponent would be much more satisfying than an imaginary one, don't you think?"

Swiveling, I arched a brow. "Volunteering?"

Bren smiled, his eyes full of mirth. "Definitely."

I cracked my knuckles, then squared off with him. "Okay, I'm game. But this is a lesson between a student and trainer. You can't tell anyone we sparred outside of the training fields." This was dangerous. What we were about to do was technically against the rules.

Bren only flashed his teeth. "Wouldn't dream of it." He crooked a finger in a "come-hither" gesture. "Show me what you got, teacher."

Gladly. A ping of excitement tickled my palms and I forgot about everything else.

I threw a real punch at his stomach. He blocked and

quickly lunged at me. I barely slipped past his counter-punch, but the closer proximity worked to my benefit. In and out I darted, landing a kidney shot before he could grab me.

Bren grunted, and I grinned at the sound. Music to my ears. "You're quick," he puffed.

"I have to be." I aimed a swift kick at his lower stomach. Maybe a little *too* low. With surprising speed, he caught my foot. I jumped, rotating my body up and over until he dropped his hold. Upon landing, my foot lashed out again, this time for a leg sweep.

He easily dodged me, and I rolled a safe distance away, ignoring the sharp pull of my bandages.

"You're not so slow yourself," I grumbled, studying his body language. Would he attack next?

A split second after he faked a low jab, his other fist went for my face. My upper body arched backward. His large knuckles nicked the tip of my chin as his forearm swept past my head. He was wide open. Poor guy, I almost felt sorry for him. Pivoting sideways, I slipped inside his guard again and brought my knee up into his groin. Hard.

Bren exhaled sharply, curling forward.

Game over.

I shook my head and tried not to grin. And failed.

All of a sudden, fingers latched onto my wrist, yanking me off balance. My legs were kicked out from beneath me. And then I was falling.

Ooph!

My butt smacked into the worn floor mat, followed by my spine and skull. Oxygen eluded me as I gaped at the ceiling. Ouch. The hand still holding my wrist pulled me up and then shifted to my shoulder when I swayed.

"Sorry." Bren smirked, not looking sorry in the least. "I couldn't resist. You were all lined up for the perfect leg sweep."

I managed to shuffle backward and dislodge his hand from my shoulder. "So, it's like that, huh?"

"Yes, it's like that."

"Fine. Game on." *Why did I say that out loud? Idiot!*

"Good." He looked far too pleased about this whole thing. "Looking forward to it, *trainer.*"

It was then I noticed he had something in his hand. Something red, shiny, and . . .

"Is that my apple?"

He lifted the object high, which was indeed my beautiful red apple. "Oh, this?" He brought it to his nose and sniffed. *Sniffed!* "Mmm, breakfast is so far away and this smells really good."

In dismay, I watched as a mischievous glint danced in his eyes.

"Don't. You. Dare," I warned, my voice a quiet threat.

Something changed in his expression then. Something . . . intense. "One thing you should know about me, little bird. I. Always. Dare."

And, with that, he took a large bite out of my glorious apple, the sound of teeth sinking into the fleshy fruit a slap to my face. I gasped in horror at the exaggerated wet, smacking noises he made while chewing, looking for all the world like a man who had won a challenge.

I sucker punched him.

Tiny apple chunks sprayed from his mouth as he bent over, coughing on a laugh. I pounced and wrestled the half-eaten fruit from his fingers.

"And you should know something about me," I said, and Bren watched as my teeth ripped into the apple's flesh. I finished my declaration with a wad of fruit in my cheek. "I don't share food."

8

TEACHER & STUDENT

Bren had received training before. Lots of it. And, after only a few days, he and Stalin were the best of friends. I tried not to be bitter as I watched him lean on the training track's fence and scratch the beast's nose with casual ease.

I was bitter.

Besides being a capable rider, he was funny, way too attractive for his own good, and an idiot. He turned heads wherever he went. I hated him for it—all of it. People now noticed me, too. I could no longer stay hidden when a big, giant oaf trailed after me the entire day. My mental walls were the only thing keeping me sane and, even then, Bren seemed to enjoy tapping on them, occasionally prodding and poking.

Somehow, I kept my riotous emotions locked away. Most of the time. But it was getting harder. Especially when he threw me off guard with random nonsense comments.

"You know," he drew out the last word and I braced for impact, "you're not very chipper in the mornings. You should try coffee. It works wonders."

I stifled an eye-roll. The growing habit was starting to wear on my eye sockets. "What's coffee?"

It was as if I had asked what planet we were on. His face morphed into absolute shock.

"You—Wait a minute here. You don't know what *coffee* is?"

I'll admit that his gaping expression almost put a smile on my face, it was *that* comical.

"If you haven't noticed," I said, arching a brow, "I don't exactly leave the city much. Or *at all,* actually. So, whatever this 'coffee' stuff is you have on the outside . . . no, I haven't tried it."

"Hmm," was his reply. And then again. "Hmm. Someday, Lune. Someday I'm gonna find a way to get you coffee. And then you'll see. You'll see how magical mornings can be."

This time I did roll my eyes. "Mornings are only magical in fairytales. Do you have your communicator in?"

Bren stuck a finger in his ear. "Yup. I can hear everything loud and clear, even the grinding sound your teeth make every time I talk."

My eyes narrowed and he grinned.

I instructed the control booth operator to amp up the race track's obstacle settings to difficult, then mounted Freedom. After the horrific spill she and I had taken earlier this week, my confidence had dipped as well. I always got back in the saddle and pushed past the fear but, this time, I had an eagle-eyed student cataloguing my every move. He would learn from my example and, therefore, steal my techniques. Maybe I wouldn't show him *everything* I knew. After all, how would Renold know if I kept some of my training a secret from his prized new citizen?

Bren looked up at me from his position near the gate, and I tapped my earbud. "Watch, listen, and learn, student. Racing is one thing, but overcoming the obstacles is a whole different game. Take notes because you're next." I made the last part sound ominous, then added, "But don't worry. I'll man the controls and put the settings on easy."

"Why does that give me no comfort?" he muttered.

I nudged Freedom through the gate, snickering as we entered the track field. It wasn't my fault that he bit off way more than he could chew. They were called *Trials* for a reason.

"Remember," I said to Bren through the earbud, "the charger takes their cues from the rider. Warn them of upcoming danger before it's too late."

"Roger that."

Roger who? You say the weirdest things, Brendan Bearon.

I signaled the operator, swirling an index finger in the air.

"It's go time. Ready, girl?" Freedom's left ear swiveled in reply. Her muscular body tensed. Ready.

A short buzzer went off.

Freedom leapt into a controlled gallop, fast but not too fast. We both needed our wits about us in this dance with death. My mind cleared away cluttering thoughts and made way for lightning instincts. The dull twinges of pain coming from my back were pushed aside. I saw Freedom's head and the track—all else disappeared.

From the left came a faint tick, tick.

"Gee!" I commanded. The pressure from my knee had Freedom sidling to the right. *Poof!* A burst of air hit us from the vents in the inner wall and we hunkered down, powering through. Any closer to the left and we would have been blown off our feet.

Snap! Without looking, I knew what was coming next.

"High!" I lifted the reins, signaling Freedom. A three-foot-tall hurdle spiked out of the ground. The seasoned charger barely broke stride, neatly tucking her front legs beneath her as she pushed off with massive haunches. My stomach rose and crashed with the jump.

Before I could catch my breath, I heard another noise—this time a sliding whir. "Low!" A thick pole shot across our path, level with my chest.

Freedom ducked beneath the object with ease, but I couldn't lean forward in time. My upper body tilted to the side so that it dangled over empty air. I passed underneath the pole only to see another, this one even lower, coming up fast.

I had to trust that Freedom saw the new obstacle as I focused on righting myself before the inevitable jump . . . or crash. Blindly, I reached forward, tangling my fingers into her serrated mane. I pulled until my arms were able to wrap around her thick neck, chin tucked into my shoulder.

Normally, I loved the feeling of jumping a hurdle, but in the precarious position I was currently in, not so much.

As we returned to earth, I felt the landing in every bone.

And then my boot slipped from the stirrup. I cried out as Freedom's bristly hide dug into my arms; her mane tore at my gloveless palms. With a growl, I heaved my body upright and readjusted my boot. But the action cost me. Sticky warmth coated my hands, making the reins slippery in my grasp. I tightened my grip on the blood-spattered leather.

"Lune!"

The shout in my ear had me looking up. Just in time, too.

"Crap."

Bursts of red-hot flame shot from the ground, several

feet into the air. I squeezed the reins, asking for Freedom's complete attention. Then we danced with fire.

"That was one of the most amazing things I've ever seen."

I spun at the feel of warm air tickling my ear, the action effectively boxing me in—Freedom's wide shoulder at my back and Bren standing way too close in front of me. We had finished the run fully intact, minus a charred hole in my right sleeve. I hadn't even felt the fire licking at the material.

Now I found myself in the dusty track stables, sandwiched between two forces. My brain switched off at the overwhelming proximity, and I stared at him stupidly.

He knew. He very well knew what he was doing and how it affected me.

It was written all over that smug, pompous face.

I slapped a hand to his chest and pushed him back a step. Or rather, he *let* me push him. My palm stuck to his leather vest and when I pulled away, a wet, sucking noise reminded me of my injuries. I winced. "Ugh."

Fingers feathered against the inside of my wrist and I jumped.

"May I?" Bren asked, and my attention shifted from his fingers still touching my skin to his questioning gaze.

I stood, rooted in place, like a cornered animal. I never let anyone tend my injuries, except for the doctors and nurses in the infirmary. I didn't trust anyone else.

But I found myself nodding, warily. Had my brain fallen out onto the track?

"Sit." He pointed at an overturned bucket, and I stiffly

lowered myself onto it.

As with all the training fields, first aid kits were plentiful. He unclipped one from a support beam.

His long legs crouched on either side of mine and I felt boxed in again. He gently flipped my hand palm up. If he wanted to, he could easily snap my arm with that large hand of his. My muscles coiled tight as I watched his brow furrow in concentration. I remembered the knife still hidden in my pants pocket, wondering if I would need to use it.

"What are you doing?" My words were clipped, strained. I clenched my teeth.

He flicked his gaze to mine. "Doing what I do best."

Really? I itched to push him away. "And what's that?"

He raised a bottle of rubbing alcohol over my bloody palm. "Fixing things. Now hold still. This is going to sting a little. Okay, maybe a lot."

"What great bedside manner you have, Dr. Br—" I sucked in a sharp breath at the sensation of a dozen bees stinging my hand. My fingers reflexively curled around the pain and I watched in horror as Bren threaded his fingers through mine.

I stopped moving. Stopped breathing.

And then buzzing warmth soothed the pain away.

"Your doctor orders you to breathe, Lune."

"I *am* breathing," I ground out. "And you're not my doctor. I just find applying bandages with one hand to be quite awkward."

He cracked a smile and I wanted to knock it clean off. "Why don't you wear gloves?"

I snatched my hand back. Was he judging me? Judging my scars? "Control is more important than a few scars."

"Hmm." He stared at the injured hand now cradled in my lap as if hoping it could give him better answers than my mouth. Finally, he said, "I think scars reveal a lot about a person. They show that you've been through tough times but came out stronger than before. They show that you've worked hard, harder than most." He raised his eyes to mine and I was trapped in their snare. "And I think a person should never be ashamed of their scars. Wear them with pride."

He did it again.

Strung together words that felt so utterly wrong in this decrepit city. But he believed them. I could see that in his open expression.

He slowly reached for my hand to finish bandaging it, and I let him.

"Can you hear me, Bren?"

"Aye aye, Captain."

"Where on earth do you come up with these weird sayings?"

Chuckling came from my earbud. "You need to get out more, little bird."

"That's so not funny. And stop calling me that."

"I make no promises."

I groaned. "Focus."

"I'm focused."

"So, I'm going to talk you through each obstacle, okay? No worries, I won't toss any water at you. This time."

"Smart aleck."

"Once again. Weird saying. Go ahead and nudge Stalin into a gallop, nice and steady."

I made sure they weren't going too fast, then let my finger hover over a button on the control panel. To say I was nervous was an understatement. I'd never been allowed inside the booth before, let alone given control over the obstacle course panel. It felt like playing God. Was I a benevolent god or a vengeful god? Possibly both.

"Okay, get ready. I'm deploying a two-foot-hurdle in three, two, one—" I pushed the button. They cleared the hurdle no problem. I grunted. "You're a natural at this." *I hate you.*

"Or maybe I just have an awesome teacher."

I bit my lip. Ugh. He was impossible. "I'm fairly certain a few days in my presence can't account for your skills. I mean, I *am* amazing, but . . ."

His laugh had me smirking, despite myself.

I surveyed the many options before me, glancing at the harder ones maliciously. No, better not to kill the student on his first obstacle course run. "Alright, your next obstacle will be spears randomly jutting out of the ground."

"Say what?" he yelled.

"Calm yourself, little student. Just trust me. I'll tell you where to go. Hopefully," I whispered the last word, but his snort revealed that he heard. My finger hovered over the button. "In three, two, one—" Push. "Go left! Hard right, all the way to the wall! Slight left. Straighten out. And you're through! See? Easy as pie."

Bren whooped in my ear. "Cherry pie is my favorite!"

I shook my head. Adrenaline must make him stupider than usual. "Next is a double jump. Simple wood beams.

The second beam is higher than the first. You ready?"

"Ready, spaghetti!"

My jaw clenched. "Focus, Mr. Bearon, or I'll accidentally switch the controls to difficult." He shut up at that. "Here it comes in three, two, one—"

I pushed and watched as three beams sprung into the air. *Three?* I scrambled at the controls, looking for an undo button. But there wasn't one. "Crap!"

"What?"

"There's a-a-a beam! Another one! A third one! Watch out!"

My inarticulate warning failed to prepare him for the surprise obstacle. It was a low beam, one that needed to be ducked under. Bren didn't duck. It struck him in the chest, swept him right off Stalin's back, and he fell.

I heard a forceful expelling of breath in my earbud, then silence.

"Bren?"

No reply.

I was running before my brain could tell me what to do, hoisting my body up and over the track fence because the gate was too far away.

"Bren!" This time I heard it. A slight quiver in my voice. Panic.

I knew this was a bad idea from the start. I wasn't capable of taking care of anyone else. I had killed my student!

My boots skimmed over the track, barely touching the packed dirt. And still, I wasn't going fast enough. *Please, please, please,* I inwardly chanted, heaving for breath as I finally reached his unmoving form. My knees dug into dirt and rock. I ground to a halt by his side.

"Please don't be dead," I gasped out, straddling his too-still body. I leaned down, my ear pressed to his chest. And quieted my erratic breathing.

There!

Right when I heard the strong heartbeat, he wrapped his arms around my back and flipped me underneath him. I was the one on the ground now, looking up at a grinning Bren.

I went rigid. Deathly still. Finally, my brain caught up, putting together the pieces.

He had played me.

My earlier relief turned to roiling rage and, in a flash, I whipped my head up, aiming my forehead at his vulnerable nose. It met a hard cheekbone instead.

I screamed like a crazed feline. My hips knocked him off balance and I reversed our position. Straddling him once again, I jammed a forearm under his chin, pressing none-too-gently on his windpipe.

The only sound was my hoarse breathing as I sunk daggers into his eyes with my own.

"Don't *ever* do that again! Do you understand me? I thought you were dead!"

The amusement leached from his face.

His arm moved and I tensed, ready for more, but I felt a roughened palm scrape against my cheek. Felt long fingers slide into my hair. I couldn't breathe. Couldn't think what to do. Something in my expression must have changed because his lips formed a crooked smile. "You care."

I pushed off his chest and scrambled away, certain I had just caught fire. I needed space to clear the fog in my head—calm the galloping beneath my sternum.

On autopilot, my body whirled and put much-needed distance between me and him. Then stopped. Marched right back. Jabbed a shaky finger at him. "You! You need to stop. This isn't a joke. This isn't a *game!* People *die* doing this! It's dangerous." My voice was shaking now and I squeezed my eyes shut, fighting for control. When I opened them again, he was standing. Watching carefully.

Embarrassed at my impassioned outburst, I turned away. Fingers trailed lightly over my wrist and I paused but kept my head down. I was mortified. And mad. So, so mad. He was making me lose my mind!

"Lune . . . look at me. Please." It was the last word that did it. No one ever used that word anymore. Not like that. The use of it, directed toward me, was foreign. And nice. It still wasn't easy raising my eyes to his. But, when I did, his emotions were on full display. Raw and real. An aching lump lodged in my throat at the sight of such sadness and remorse. I didn't want to see those emotions directed at me.

Not from him.

It made things . . . confusing.

He spoke again and those emotions became words. "I know this is dangerous. I know it isn't a game. I know the stakes are high, but . . . but when I'm with you, I forget about those things. And all I can see is a girl shouldering the world. And all I want is to put a smile on her face, make her laugh, and assure her that she's not alone. But maybe that's selfish of me. Maybe she has more at stake than I realize. And maybe she wants to be alone."

He sighed and dragged a hand through his hair, dark strands dropping over his forehead. "I'm sorry," he said, barely a whisper.

A deafening silence settled between us. It was silent in my head, too. But the silence was almost peaceful. I could tell, by the tortured expression on his face, that he truly was sorry. I didn't quite know what to do about it. Maybe if I said something, those lines between his eyebrows would erase.

I nodded slowly. "Okay. Just don't give me a heart attack again."

The creases disappeared.

WEAPONS

One week.

I'd managed to avoid the Faust Night training field and Elite Instructor Drake for seven solid days. As a tier five graduate and now a trainer myself, I was given a longer leash, no longer required to report every breath and eye blink. But, Bren needed more than hand-to-hand combat training. It was time to face the cut-throat mob.

"So, what's your favorite weapon?" I asked him as we skirted the training field. Curious stares tracked us, and the invasion agitated my senses. Bren didn't seem to notice their looks, or inspection.

"Guns." No hesitation.

"Like a gun, gun? With bullets?"

The corners of his mouth quirked. "Yeah."

"Well, we don't have any of those in here. They're forbidden. And only guards are allowed the use of volt guns. You'll have to pick another weapon to practice with."

Upon seeing my face, a pair of guards allowed us entrance into the Stahl Hall armory, no questions asked. Apparently, news of my trainer status had made the rounds. I pushed open the intricate, dark wood doors and stepped inside the white glass-domed room. Before the Trials, the long brick-and-glass building used to house exotic flowers, plants, and trees, just for the enjoyment of looking at them. A glorified greenhouse.

"Behold: every man's dream room." I punctuated my announcement with a hand flourish. "Choose a weapon; but while doing so, drooling is discouraged. The tiles can get slippery."

"Too late," Bren murmured, brushing past me, eyes fixated on the walls. He walked in a circle, lips parted.

"Uh, do you need some privacy while you ogle the weapons?"

"Sure," he said, absentmindedly.

"Do you think Lars is cute?"

"Uh-huh."

My head fell back, and I stared through the glass ceiling to the cloudy sky above. Men and weapons. Hopeless.

As I watched his eyes worship each and every steel object, I realized we were going to be here for a while. I slid to the floor and began picking at my cuticles.

Minutes ticked by. Excruciating, snail-paced minutes.

"Soooo, see anything you like?" I droned.

"Yes." When I looked to see where his gaze was, I about leapt out of my skin. He was looking at . . . me.

I didn't know what game he was playing, but he needed to stop. Now. I couldn't focus when he stared at me like—

"The su-yari."

"Huh?" I blinked.

He hoisted a wicked-looking pole from the wall, over seven feet long with sharp blades on each end.

"Your weapon of choice is a . . . a *stick*?" I burst out laughing. I couldn't help it. Eleven years ago, I had almost clocked his skull with a stick. If only I had been smart enough to do so. Oh, the irony.

He stared at me, eyes gradually narrowing as several emotions warred for dominance on his face. Would he laugh with me? Or would he—Oh, he was offended. Good. My shoulders shook harder. He spoke louder than normal, drowning out my laughter. "I'll have you know, this Japanese straight spear was favored by the samurai. Perfect for close combat. It's lighter than a sword, with farther reach, and it has *two* blades. I can fight multiple opponents at once."

Samurai? I had no idea what that was. Yet another conversation that made me feel dumb. And so, I replied, "Overcompensating for something?"

He stilled. Slowly, his lips curled. Then his mouth opened. "You can't judge a man by his—"

"Stop!" I yelled. "Don't finish that sentence. Just don't."

He snickered. My answering glare said, *I'll shove that stick up your*—I cut the thought off. Ugh. His expression smoothed, but a stupid mischievous light still twinkled in his eye.

With casual, precise movements, he twirled the spear in lazy figure-eights. "So, what's *your* favorite weapon?" Although his voice was as relaxed as his actions, I detected a burning curiosity behind the question.

"My fists."

"No, but really. What kind of weapon does the great Lune Tatum like to wield?"

"Sarcasm."

He stopped twirling and gave me a long-suffering look.

"Oh fine," I huffed and picked myself up off the floor. Ever so lightly, I trailed a finger over a row of glistening silver and onyx blades, their sharp beauty mesmerizing, until I paused in front of my twin daggers. They shone a burnished gold in the afternoon light. I hefted them both from the rack, their eleven-inch length perfect for maneuverability. Speed.

They molded to my grip like an intimate embrace.

I whipped around, doing my own version of a figure eight. Blindingly fast. The blades emitted a faint whistle. But I froze mid-swing when I caught sight of Bren's stare.

He glanced away, throat convulsing. A quiet laugh huffed from him and he shook his head. Then he approached me, raising his eyes to mine. The intense look glued my feet to the marble floor.

Stars, what was happening?

He kept coming until my vision was full of him, until I caught a whiff of his unique scent, like pine and leather and sunshine. He was supposed to smell like fire and brimstone, not the smells that I—

Bren plucked the daggers from my limp hands. My swallow was louder than a slap in the too-quiet room. He inspected the detailed hilts while I worked on finding my heart again, which had somehow found its way up my esophagus.

"Beautiful," he murmured.

When I snuck a peek at his face, he was staring at me again. Warmth bloomed in my cheeks, flushing down my body. My chest tightened as I became hyper-aware of his nearness. My instincts screamed danger and I jerked back a step, hating that he was holding *my* weapons.

An intense wave of anger doused the foreign heat in my veins. And the . . . feelings. I shouldn't feel *anything* but rage and bitterness toward the boy who stole my childhood. Who plagued my present and threatened to steal my future.

My competition.

In that moment, I had forgotten.

How had I forgotten something so important?

Maybe I was broken.

Maybe I was just a stupid hormonal girl who had a weakness for giant idiots.

"Bren?"

"Hm?"

"Don't forget that beautiful things can be deadly."

It was telling when an entire building was used solely for weapons instead of daily training sessions. Trainees were forced to practice outside at all times.

Strength.

Speed.

Precision.

The three defining goals of the Trials.

Apparently, these traits could only be achieved outdoors. Surrounding Faust Night's flat training field was a stone wall level with my chest, cracked with age and covered in moss. Over two hundred years old and still standing, its endurance was used as an example on a weekly basis. "The Shrine of Strength," the trainees called it.

Unfortunately, the wall was also used for discipline. At least, that's what the Elite Instructor called his methods of punishment. As Bren and I stepped onto the field, my attention was drawn to the northwest corner that was reserved for these barbaric demonstrations. There, a large crowd circled around something.

Or someone.

I scanned the field and found a cluster of instructors on the far side, casually facing the other way. They knew. They knew what was happening amongst their students yet refused to stop it. Yet again.

In the middle of the circle was a hazing.

My pulse sped up and sent blood rushing to my head as memories of my own hazing darkened my thoughts. Many hazings, actually. If a trainee didn't stand strong against the abuse of their peers and fell under the weight of jeers and physical blows, they lost. And the hazing would continue. Only when they remained upright under the onslaught, un-wavering as the wall at their back, would the hazings stop.

I had endured them for years.

And now someone else was being tortured. I forced air down my tight throat. I shouldn't interfere. I'd kept to myself for so long, avoiding all confrontation. And then, through the writhing mass of bodies, I saw a flash of dark red hair. Like my own. The owner was hunkered down on the ground. Like an animal.

A familiar emotion snapped into place. Rage.

I tried tamping down the feeling. Tried to back away. But Bren was behind me, and he was silently fuming too. I could almost feel the heat pouring off him as his jaw muscles bunched. The fact that this was affecting him, too, stirred something else awake in me. *Don't do it. You'll form enemies. You'll never make it to the Trials.* My head turned away, then whipped toward Bren again.

"Hold these." I shoved my daggers at him, barely waiting

for him to catch them.

I didn't think, didn't let my overactive mind talk me out of what I was about to do. My instincts drove me onward through the grunts and curses, and past the hostile and surprised looks. Despite my reclusiveness, everyone knew me. Knew that I kept to myself and stayed out of trouble. The Supreme Elite's obedient daughter.

Yet here I was, pushing toward the heart of the beast. And to the black ugliness that brewed distrust and detachment in every single trainee.

What was I doing?

You're painting a target on your back.

So be it.

I was sick of it all.

I broke through to the inner circle and there was Lars, the slimy devil, a sniffling human ball at his feet. He circled his prey, taunting, "How do you plan on contending in the Trials someday if you can't even stay on your feet? Give up now. Admit defeat." His boot connected with the child's shin, eliciting a yelp of pain. My vision bled red.

"Lars!" I barked, striding forward.

He slowly raised his glittering eyes to mine, delight shining in their blackened depths.

"Well, well, well," he crooned. "I knew you had a soft side, Mute. Took you long enough to show it. Come to save the day?" He swept his hands out and gestured to the dozens of onlookers surrounding us. "You're highly outnumbered."

I dared a swift look at the faces watching us. Cold. Blank. I was alone in this. *Cowards*, I wanted to hiss at them. Although I didn't doubt that some of them would have Lars's back if he called for aid.

"She has me." Bren's deep baritone rumbled through the silence. For once, I didn't stiffen at the prospect of someone so close behind me.

Lars chortled, wholly unfazed. "She's on the losing side, outsider. Sure that's what you want?" When Bren gave a dismissive shrug, Lars whipped his hand up, jabbing a finger at us both. "Careful," he sneered. "Rumors might start flying about your *friendliness.*"

I ignored the cheap threat, purposely bumping into his shoulder as I made for his latest victim. Quick as a striking serpent, he gripped my wrist, grinding and crushing the bones together until my hand went numb. I choked on the cry of pain searing my throat.

He yanked my body against his and I tasted the sour tang of disgust as his lips caressed my ear. "I did this for you. *All* for you," he whispered.

I was too shocked by the words to react. But Bren shocked me most when he towered over us both—not touching, yet the heat radiating off him fanned my exposed skin. "Let her go. Now."

Lars released me with a savage twist and I grimaced. "She's not as *strong* as she seems. Think hard about who you want to align with, outsider." His lithe frame slithered into the crowd.

My wrist throbbed but I refused to rub at the ache in front of everyone. Instead, I focused on the quivering child at my feet, slowly crouching before her. She was bent in half, knees clasped to her chest, probably wishing she could melt into the ground.

My heart pinched in pity for her. For the loss of precious

innocence.

"Hey," I said, softening my voice like I did with Freedom. "He's gone. You're safe now. Bullies like that should be whipped, don't you agree? I would do the honors in a heart-beat, if I could. Right in front of everyone." I kept my voice light, but I meant every single word. Imagining his howls as I cracked the whip encouraged my lips into a smirk.

Her head lifted a few inches, until I caught a glimpse of large hazel eyes. My breath hitched. *Green* hazel eyes. Like mine. She was about ten years old and strikingly similar to how I probably looked at that age.

So that's why Lars had targeted her. His words made a semblance of sense now. He did this because of me. Because she looked like me. But why? What had I ever done to him? A frown dragged my lips downward. "What's your name?"

She hesitated, uncertainty written on her little face.

I relaxed the tense lines around my eyes and mouth, hoping I appeared friendly.

"Iris."

I almost missed the whispered word. "Iris? That's a beautiful name. I'm Lune." I felt a heavy presence standing behind us and gestured at him. "This is Bren. And don't let his size fool you. His giant ego made him that big."

He laughed and knelt next to me, dwarfing the small girl. Iris's eyes rounded in fear. I couldn't blame her. His size *was* intimidating.

But his voice was soothing, sweet, as he said, "Is this girl bothering you?" He flicked a thumb my direction, flashing a wink at me. My eyes narrowed.

She shook her head rapidly, as if afraid he'd haul me away. He could try . . .

BECKY MOYNIHAN

"Oh good. Deep down . . . deep, deep down, Lune is nice. If you can see past the looks she gives you, like she just finished sucking on a lemon—Ow!" My elbow in his ribs cut him off.

Our antics coaxed a giggle from Iris and, despite the onlookers, I smiled in return. "Come on, Iris, we'll walk you to your trainer, okay?" I held out a hand, waiting for her to decide. I knew this move would draw a line. A line that said, *She's with me now. Mess with her and you mess with me.* But would this doom her to more hazings or save her from them? Only time would tell.

She placed her thin fingers on mine and we rose together, hand-in-hand. The top of her head didn't even reach my shoulders.

The crowd lingered, as if witnessing the most fascinating thing they'd ever seen. Maybe it was. Not often did people help each other in this city, and they certainly had never seen *me* help someone. No one here knew of my nocturnal visits to Antler Hill Village. I stared them down as I raised my voice, saying, "Get back to training!"

Surprisingly, they scattered like ants. A weight eased off my chest and I sighed. Wincing, I carefully rotated my injured wrist now that prying eyes were gone.

I almost loosed an embarrassing squeal when a loud voice spoke beside me. "Miss Tatum, have you been avoiding me?" I faced the Elite Instructor, the thirty-year-old, well-built blond who had whipped me into peak shape for the last two years. Iris's hand was still tucked in mine, and I nudged her behind me, then released her fingers.

Even though I had earned top rank and permission to enter this year's Trials, Drake Stonewood made it his

114

mission to remind me every time we crossed paths that I was still not good enough. To him, his students were a waste of breath until they proved themselves. Of what, I wasn't sure.

He gave Bren a once over, his eyebrows twitching as he evaluated the fresh target. I stifled a chortle when I realized Drake couldn't touch him. He was mine. Mentally cringing at my brain's choice of words, I scolded myself. My student. He was *my student*.

I cleared my throat, but Drake continued talking before I could make up a lame excuse. "So, this is the outsider." His onyx earring winked dully in the waning light as his eyes swung my way once more. He crossed thick arms over his chest. "Did you win a Trial and earn a title while I wasn't looking, *trainer*?" His upper lip rose in a sneer as he derided, "Must be nice to have the Supreme Elite as your father."

No more could I stop my fists from clenching than my teeth from grinding. The daughter treatment. I was sick to death of people thinking Renold gave me special favors. If they only knew the truth of the matter.

And then his lips curved almost gleefully. My stomach bottomed out. I knew that look. I'd rather have him yell at me. "This is perfect, actually. I've been meaning to do a special demonstration and you'll be my assistant." Abruptly, he turned on his heel and barked over his shoulder, "Follow me. And bring your student."

Not good, not good, not good.

I hurried to keep pace, briefly expressing with my eyes for Iris to stay put and Bren to follow. I felt him at my back, a living, breathing shield. Again, his presence wasn't altogether unwanted, and that confused me. My brain was on the fritz these days.

I focused on Drake's wide, boulder-like shoulders plowing through the field's obstacles. Nothing and no one dared stand in his way. We reached the center of the massive field where a lone Smart Bot stood head-and-shoulders above us all, peering down as if it found us lacking. The synthetic legs were bolted to a wide platform—the Platform of Endurance. The trainees called it the Spotlight of Humiliation.

We had all set foot on its lofty perch.

And been knocked down.

Drake hopped onto the platform and wrapped a hand around the robot's neck. "Trainees! Listen up!" his rough voice bellowed. All noise ceased—over two hundred pairs of eyes swiveled to the Elite Instructor. "If you haven't heard, we have a new *trainer*. And not just any trainer. She's still in training while instructing her very own student. They're *both* contracted to contend in the Trials this year! How's that for irony?"

He laughed, and a few trainees hesitantly joined him. Then his eyes locked onto mine and he motioned me forward. A tremor began in my knees and worked its way up my legs, my stomach and chest, and into my arms. My hands formed tight fists around the trembling. I clamped down on the shivers that threatened to clack my teeth together.

My stiff legs carried me up the stairs and onto the platform's thick plywood and rubber surface. The sea of faces staring up at me were ravenous wolves, hungry for my bones. Drake clapped a meaty hand onto my shoulder, jarring me out of my stupor. My spine went ramrod straight and I felt his fingers dig into my flesh, anchoring me in place.

Drake was speaking again and I tuned in. "I believe the Trial's newest trainer doesn't need an introduction, though. After all, this is a small city. Only one Supreme Elite whose daughter left the comforts of Tatum House for the Trials. And contend she will! I gave her the tier five rating. But . . ."

My heart missed a beat. I knew how this would end. He was building me up, high and unscalable as a mountain, so that he could rip me into such minuscule pieces, no one would ever look up to me again. That was his way. No one was higher than him. No one stole his command—especially a trainee. Because he and I both knew that's what I was, no matter what Renold said.

At last, he dropped the ax. "But she still needs to prove herself worthy of a *trainer* status, wouldn't you all agree?" I heard several shouts of affirmation. "We will put her to the test. See if she can learn a new fighting technique. Because she can't teach if she doesn't learn, right?"

The crowd was all-out cheering now, worked into a frothing frenzy. Without looking, I knew their eyes were picking me apart, thirsty for blood. *My* blood. If it wasn't for Drake's fingers painfully wedged against my collarbone, I would have wilted on the spot, making a fool of myself before the real fun even began.

"Lower the Smart Bot," Drake murmured. He must have an earbud communicator in. The floor beneath my boots vibrated as a trapdoor opened, swallowing the robot whole. Solid floor snapped into place, smooth like the rest of the platform.

My stomach twisted into jumbled knots, and a wave of nausea raced up my throat. I swallowed the sea of saliva filling my mouth. I thought he would pit me against the robot. Its motion-detector chip was state-of-the-art. Unbeatable. Most who fought it were sent rolling off the platform in under a minute. I could endure that shame. After all, every trainee did. But no, he had something else in store for me. Something even worse.

My gaze left the rubber floor and fixed on Drake. He was grinning at me—had never stopped. "Up for the challenge?" He knew I wouldn't back down.

"Always," I breathed, rotating my neck and shaking out my hands. Whatever he threw at me, I would be ready.

He raised his voice above the crowd's eager chatter. "Watch closely, students. Up to this point, we've taught you martial arts. But today, you will witness something different. It's fast, efficient—and make no mistake—it's brutal. But when you want your opponent on the ground as quickly as possible, this is the way to do it." My pulse fluttered like a bird's wings when he spread his arms wide and roared, "I introduce you to street fighting!"

I'd never heard of it, and neither had the other trainees, but that didn't stop the hoots and cat-calls, the stomps and whistles.

I was so screwed.

Drake was pacing now, clearly basking in all the attention. "Before I begin the demonstration, here are the rules for this technique." Everyone hushed at that, ready to absorb the lesson. "The rule is this: there are *no rules*! Fight dirty. Hit the soft spots and hit them *hard!*"

Pandemonium broke out. Hundreds of voices rose as one; the terrible sound of approval sunk deep into my bones.

"Let's begin!"

I blinked, wholly unprepared when he came at me like a windstorm. His fist pounded into my exposed ribcage. "Uhh!" Air rushed from my lungs in one giant gust. My spine curled forward to protect my ribs only to be met with a sharp elbow strike. The blow connected between my shoulder blades and I hit the platform with a thwack.

Pain lanced up and down my spine, shooting into my skull in patches of hot, blinding light. But I wasn't broken. Never broken.

I made my move. Twisting my hips, I brought my legs up and jabbed both heels into the soft backs of his knees. He crashed down next to me. I rolled to my feet at the same time he did and we exchanged blows. His fist pummeled my stomach while I punched his throat.

Drake choked, neck tendons bulging as his face turned red, more from fury than lack of oxygen. Oh crap. He swung for my left temple and I ducked, then lashed a leg out. My boot struck his sternum. He staggered. With a bellow, he rushed me. Too sudden. Too unexpected. I went airborne as his body rammed into mine, then crushed me to the platform.

Before I could fight my way free, he flipped me over, my stomach now pressed to the rubber. Then, he grabbed my left arm and wrenched it backward. My shoulder joint screamed in agony.

My vocal chords joined in as I lay face-down, helpless, about to endure my bone being ripped from its socket. *Push past the pain. You are not . . . you are not weak!* Tears leaked from my eyes, blurring my vision, but I managed to lift my head an inch. To do what, I didn't know. Ask for help? There wasn't any. Just a haze of unfriendly faces.

Out of the corner of my eye, I focused on a flurry of movement. Several trainees were struggling, holding someone in place. They were having a rough time of it, too, as legs and arms jerked and thrashed.

Pain consumed me then, a searing wave. I squeezed my eyes shut, desperate for the misery to end. This time when Drake's fist connected with my temple, the blow defused the scorching heat.

Darkness took me.

SAFE

It was the gentle swaying that registered first, the motion smooth, effortless.

My head rocked against something firm, unrelenting. The oddly warm surface thumped rhythmically. Or was that the pounding drums in my skull?

My eyelids wouldn't open. They were so heavy.

The rest of me felt . . . strange. Twin bands wrapped around my back and legs, holding me aloft.

I'd been knocked unconscious before, but this . . . this had never happened. Why did I feel secure?

With a slight shifting of my body, pain returned. Roaring agony, all sharp teeth and jagged edges, stole my breath. A pathetic-sounding whimper came out of me.

"Lune?" The deep voice hummed in my ear that was pressed against . . . a chest? "I've got you. You're safe now. You'll be okay."

Just like that, the questions disappeared. My mind latched onto the one word it needed to hear: *safe*. And, despite my confused state and the fact that my body was forcing me back to sleep, I knew it to be true.

I was safe.

This time when I awoke, my taste buds flared to life first.

Acid coated my tongue. I rolled it around in my mouth, stirring up spit to clear away the nasty flavor. Even that small action caused pain. There was an incessant beat in my temple. More like the pounding of a sledge hammer. I grimaced at the sensation, but that only made it worse.

A groan slid past my clenched teeth.

Something shifted not far from me and I froze, listening. Silence. I pried my lids apart and blinked away the fuzzy haze. Black. All was black. At the realization, it was as if a hand pressed on my sternum with extreme force. Did I lose my eyesight? My eyes moved everywhere at once, looking, searching . . . for anything.

There!

An even darker shape materialized within the blackness and I knew all wasn't lost. Alarm sizzled in my veins as the shape grew larger, heading for my prostrate form. Out of a deeply ingrained instinct, my hand slid under the pillow beneath me and grasped a hidden knife. When the long shadow reached for me, I grabbed hold and yanked it closer, revealing vaguely familiar features. The knife plunged toward the face of—

"Bren!" I gasped. The suspended knife shook in my grip. I released the weapon and Bren. The sound of steel meeting concrete rang through the small room. *My* room. Wait . . . How did I get here?

I was panting now, the movements sharp and painful. My ribs hurt. My brain whirred awake, finally, and I picked through my most recent memories. Drake. The platform. Street fighting. My smackdown.

Gingerly, I probed at the sore spot on my left temple. A

raised lump greeted my fingers. Another groan left me.

Bren responded with soft laughter. "She awakens. I expected disorientation, but a knife? I'll remember that for next time."

I couldn't make out his expression. He didn't *sound* mad. "Why is it so dark?"

"Oh, sorry. I didn't notice." With a faint snick, he turned on the lamp at my bedside table. How had he not noticed?

Weak yellow light bathed one side of his face, leaving the other in mysterious shadow. It was fitting, really. It's how I saw him—a mixture of the two. His irises were a deep amber as they watched me studying him. All of a sudden, I was overcome with nerves. My fingers picked at the scratchy wool blanket wrapped around me. I had so many questions.

"How—" I cleared my parched throat. "How did I get here?"

"I carried you." He sat on the floor beside my bed, forearms resting on knees, like he planned on settling in for a spell. That made me even more nervous than the thought of him carrying me. So, I had heard his heart thumping against my ear then.

I inhaled sharply. "And no one stopped you?" Why wasn't I in the infirmary? And how did he carry me so far? I wasn't exactly skin and bones. My body was encased in lean muscle.

He grunted. "They tried. But a few black eyes later and they let me take you. Drake walked away as soon as you passed out. Didn't even call for a doctor."

My heart was racing now. Not at the mention of Drake's callous treatment—that was normal. But at the hazy memory of a lone figure fighting against the crowd. "I-I saw you. Before . . . before I lost consciousness." Why did I admit that? Stupid. So stupid.

His eyes saddened. "I'm sorry I couldn't save you from that. It was barbaric." His hands curled into tight fists and a flash of anger made his irises glow. "Is that how he usually trains his students?"

I laughed humorlessly. "No. Usually he lets the Smart Bot humiliate us if he's displeased. Which is often. But I . . . I didn't earn my trainer status. He doesn't believe in hand-outs or shortcuts."

"So, he reminded you and everyone else where you be-long?"

"Pretty much."

Abruptly, he rose to his feet and I flinched, then winced at the resulting ache in my head.

"Here, drink this." He placed a clay cup in my hand. I looked up at him in question. He tapped his temple. "For your head. No one would give me pain meds, but this tea will help with the headache."

I was struck speechless. He cared about my headache? How many countless headaches had I endured because no one cared? Because the pain wasn't enough to warrant medication?

My fingers trembled as I lifted the cup to my lips. The dark liquid could be poison for all I knew, but I doubted it. After all, he had carried me for over a mile when he could have just dumped my body into the lagoon. I took a sip. Immediately, my gag reflex kicked in. I almost spewed the contents across the room but managed to down the pungent stuff, not quite masking a grimace as I swallowed.

"Yuck!" I stuck my tongue out and scrubbed at it with a

shirt sleeve. "Wha ith tha?"

The grin he gave me was pure evil. "Willow bark tea. It's a natural pain reliever."

"It's natural all right. Like drinking dirt, natural." I glowered at the cup and made to set it on my nightstand.

"Nah-uh." He grabbed the cup, his fingers curling around mine. I didn't know whether to gape or glare. I glared. His brows quirked. He was obviously hiding his amusement at the situation. "Don't give me that look. Finish the yucky tea, little bird."

"Pushy, bossy doctor," I grumbled, but did as I was told. He looked way too pleased with himself. "Why do you keep calling me that? 'Little bird.'"

He dragged a hand through his hair while looking at the ceiling. My gaze wandered to his throat, at the pronounced tendons. His eyes fixed onto mine and a terrible rush of heat crossed my face. I *really* needed to stop ogling him.

"When I first saw you, you were on the highest balcony of Tatum House, precariously leaning over the edge with your arms spread wide. Like a little bird about to fly. Even now, you seem poised for flight at any given moment." He flashed a quick grin.

I focused on my lap and picked at a slight chip on the cup's rim, embarrassed yet oddly pleased at the comparison.

"You remind me of someone."

My head snapped up so fast spots of bright light interrupted my vision. I hastily blinked them away and pushed aside the new flare of pain. I schooled my features as best I could before replying, "Who?"

He scratched his neck and sighed heavily. "I met her a

long time ago. I had just turned eight and she was maybe a year younger, but taller than me." He smirked at the memory. A swallow got stuck in my ever-tightening throat. "She had long, dark hair that shone a deep red in the sun, like yours. Large, hazel-green eyes, and . . . and these cute little freckles on her nose."

Bren searched my face. Hard. Like he was reading. And then in a soft whisper, said, "It's not possible."

I was still as death. Only muscle memory kept me breathing in that moment. He shook his head and looked at the floor, then started to pace. His nervous energy permeated the room, mingling with mine.

"But the thing is, I couldn't save her either. Like today, when I couldn't save you. And so . . . and so you remind me of her. The girl I failed." He stopped pacing and stood in the middle of my room, shoulders slumped. Heavy shadows masked his features. But I saw, in the glow of his eyes, raw torture. Honest pain. And my throat tightened even more.

Could it be that my kidnapper was haunted by what he had done? Kidnapper. He didn't sound or act like a manipulating liar. Not anymore.

I was so screwed.

Half an hour later, my stomach was eating itself. Getting beaten up must increase metabolism or something.

It was still dinner hour and I had encouraged Bren to head on down. I even told him I wasn't hungry, so he wouldn't feel guilty for leaving me alone. Now I faked sleep, not fooling anyone, least of all my stomach. If I were honest with myself, I was actually hiding. I didn't want to face the trainees who had witnessed my embarrassing takedown.

How would they look at me now?

I tossed my blanket aside and jumped to my feet, instantly regretting the abrupt movement. The room pitched sideways. My hand braced against the cold wall until the dizziness subsided. After a deep inhale, which caused my ribs to ache fiercely, I shuffled to my dresser and wiggled open one of two drawers. Blue greeted me, of course. Cursed blue.

Besides training gear, I kept three outfits at the barracks. I'd never worn them. Fancy clothes weren't needed here—completely impractical. But tonight, I felt like wearing something nice. I laughed at myself. *You'll only draw more unwanted attention!* And yet my fingers reached for the fine fabric and held it up to the lamp's pale light.

The bell-sleeved azure blouse floated over my head as I slipped it on, my ribs protesting each tiny movement. Thin straps kept the off-the-shoulder material from exposing cleavage. I didn't want *that* much attention. Black stretchy pants and knee-high boots completed the ensemble. I dared a peek in my small, cracked mirror and wished I hadn't. If I kept this up, my entire face would be a purple bruise.

I shook my hair free of its tether, letting it hang down my back in soft waves.

Before leaving the room, I gulped down several large breaths. Added steel to my nerves. Tonight, I would make a statement. I might have been beaten but I wasn't beat. Tonight, I'd hold my head high.

You cannot break me.

"Ready or not, here I come." My smile no doubt looked crazy, but it was a smile nonetheless.

A STATEMENT

He wasn't there.

I rescanned the mess hall. It was hard to miss a giant.

Nope. I was alone. Just me and a pack of starving hyenas. Oh, and Iris. She saw me and gave a shy wave. I returned the gesture, then picked up a metal tray and made my way through the cafeteria line. In a different world, I would sit next to her at dinner. But in this world? Too dangerous for her. I didn't look at her again.

My neck tingled, and I knew most of the room's occupants were staring at me. I felt naked under the intense scrutiny but continued dishing food onto my plate, focusing more on the room than on the task before me.

As soon as I turned, I knew someone was coming at me, but it was too late. The collision smashed my full tray of food into my chest. The plate's hard rim dug into my tender ribs and I gasped. I leveled out the tray and peered down at my shirt. It was covered in a food apocalypse. "Awesome," I muttered under my breath.

"Oops. I didn't see you there, Princess." Catanna's deceptively sweet voice rang loud and clear in the ensuing silence. Great, we had an audience. Her hand flew to her mouth. "Oh no! Your beautiful shirt is ruined! But I'm sure Daddy will have a new one made for you, right? After all, he gives you *anything* you want."

I knew to expect the barbs but they still struck home. Tears weren't an option, not in front of a group that was hungry for my demise. So, I did the unthinkable. I broke down laughing. I laughed so hard my head and ribs throbbed in time to the jerky movements. I was a slave to laughter.

Any second now I'd be rolling on the floor.

Catanna snarled, "You don't deserve trainer status, you freak. Just look at you. Pathetic." I saw her hand dip into a pile of what looked like mashed potatoes still clinging to my plate. *Splat!* She plopped the food on top of my head. A large warm dollop landed on my bare shoulder.

My laughter shut off like a switch. I dropped the tray and the crash echoed off the walls.

With bated breath, every soul in the room waited for my reaction. I remembered the promise I had made to myself earlier. How tonight I would make a statement. How I wasn't *beat*.

Okay then.

I'd show them all what I was capable of.

"You know, Catanna," I crooned, inching a hand behind me. "You really need to lighten up a bit. Your complexion is looking a tad mottled." My hand sunk into a platter filled with a soft, gooey substance. Too perfect. I whipped my loaded hand forward and slapped a palm against her chest, then spread the mystery goo around with a flourish.

I stepped back, surveying my handiwork. Her eyes were huge, but her ever-widening mouth was the predominant feature on her shocked face.

"See?" My finger made a circular motion around my own

smug face. "Your skin is turning this weird purplish color. Wow. You might want to get that checked out. Doesn't look healthy."

She shrieked like a banshee and swung a fist, which I quickly smacked aside. "Now, now, Catanna. Don't bring a fist to a food fight. That's against the rules. How about we settle this like ladies, hmm?" My hand went in for seconds and this time shoved the runny goop up her nose.

The room broke out into deafening hoots and hollers, but I was on a roll now. Nothing would stop me from cramming food down that big mouth before this was over.

Long, muscular arms wrapped around me from behind, snapping me out of my food-crazed haze. The pressure was light against my ribs, but the contact still hurt. Without hesitation, I jabbed my booted heel into a kneecap. There was a grunt of pain, but the arms didn't loosen their hold. My head whipped back, seeking a nose, but bounced off a hard jaw instead. Bright shooting stars danced across my vision.

"Lune, stop attacking me!"

I would know that growl anywhere, even hyped up on adrenaline. I sagged in his arms. A tremor of nerves and fatigue shook my body.

"You need to get out of here," Bren practically yelled in my ear, the room still in pandemonium. There might have been a food fight or two taking place as well—it was hard to see anything clearly. I nodded. "Come on," he said, and tugged me backward. I let him, never taking my eyes off a seething Catanna. Her teeth were bared. Her dark eyes promised retribution. A pale glob of goo trickled down her chin.

I smirked.

As soon as we rounded the corner, Bren released me, then promptly latched onto my right bicep. He marched me down the hallway at a fast clip. I practically floated along, feeling unhinged. Invincible.

"You should have seen her *face,* Bren," I all but cackled. "A whole apple could have fit in that big mouth. If you hadn't stopped me, I might have tried it!"

He muttered something under his breath. Before I could try decoding the words, he ripped open a door and shoved me inside a pitch-black room. The door slammed shut, encasing me in complete darkness. A sliver of fear leaked through my adrenaline high. Where was I? Had he decided to get rid of me after all?

With a clink and buzz, a row of flickering light bulbs illuminated my surroundings. I was in the barracks gym.

And I wasn't alone.

Bren prowled toward me, fire in his eyes. "What were you *thinking?*" He kept coming, until his body was inches from mine. I held my ground, but he didn't stop, reaching for my shoulders. Finally, self-preservation kicked in and I backpedaled. He pursued me across the room, never once taking his eyes off mine. They burned me from the inside out, but I wouldn't look away.

Tonight, I was stronger. I was stronger than them all. Including *him.*

My back thumped against the far wall; blue padding cushioned the impact. I had nowhere to go. I should feel panic. Fear. Anger. But I didn't. As he crowded in close and trapped me between his arms, both hands splayed against the mat on either side of my head, I raised my chin and clenched my jaw.

His nostrils flared as he said, "Do you have a *death wish?*"

My hands shook as they formed fists at my sides. "Of course I don't!" I yelled louder than planned. "It's called defending myself. I might not be able to avoid a beating from my trainer, but I'm *done* taking them from my peers."

My whole body vibrated with pent-up aggression. I couldn't get enough air in my lungs. I wasn't beat. I wasn't *beat!* I might have been tricked and mistreated as a child, but I was stronger now. I was done staying silent. The temptation to reveal our past connection, to clear the air once and for all, was a thorn in my tongue. I wanted to rip it out before the wound could fester a moment longer. But I didn't. I bit my tongue.

Stars, why can't I do it?

Bren watched me, utterly still. Holding his expressionless gaze felt like forever. Suddenly, he looked defeated. His eyes slid shut and his head drooped forward, a long sigh puffing from his lips. Hair fell over his forehead, shadowing his face.

But I needed to see. I needed to see what he was thinking. I needed to know if he understood, or if he thought I was insane. Because if it was the latter, I would walk out of here and never speak to him again. Screw the consequences, he could train himself for all I cared. A beating from Renold would be worth it.

And so, I unclenched a fist. And, with trembling fingers, I reached up and touched his hair, slowly sweeping it aside to reveal his face once again. He inhaled sharply. Then his eyes snapped open, so close to mine. I stopped breathing at the sight of those eyes burning hot with emotion. If his were swirling with such intensity, what did mine look like?

I let go of his hair as he captured my fingers with his, keeping our interlocked hands close to his face. Too close. Too close.

Then he pressed his lips to my scarred knuckles.

Warmth pooled on the back of my hand and slid up my arm, traveling all the way to my neck and into my cheeks. And still I held his gaze, never looking away. My frantic rage from earlier was replaced with a bewildering calm. It eased into my veins, leaving me weak and breathless. I slumped against the wall.

Bren's lips curved into a crooked grin. "What's on your hand? It's delicious."

I blinked stupidly, not understanding. "Huh?"

His tongue darted out as he licked his bottom lip. "Hm, I want to say . . . applesauce? You should try it."

My lips parted at the abrupt topic change and his gaze fixed on my mouth. His expression intensified. He almost looked hungry. My spine snapped straight and I slid to the side, disengaging our hands. When several feet of space separated us, I turned around and looked at him. He had tracked me with his eyes, one hand still propped against the wall.

Time to wipe that expression off his face. With a wicked smile, I replied, "As much as I like applesauce, this batch is bad. After all, it was up Catanna's nose."

Pure revulsion was the last thing I saw. And despite my bruised body, I twirled and waltzed out of the gym, head held high.

MONSTERS

"Your turn." I crossed my arms and studied Bren's near-perfect form as he nocked an arrow. Did he have to be good at everything?

He stilled, breathed in, and on the exhale, released the arrow.

It missed the target completely, sailing into the trees beyond.

My jaw unhinged. "Um . . . was that intentional?"

He smirked. "Nope."

He would fail the Arcus Point training at this rate. That little nugget of knowledge sent a bolt of victory sizzling through my insides. I hid a satisfied grin and, a second later, felt guilty for wanting him to fail. I squashed the pesky emotion. *He's competition, stupid!*

"Try again." I placed another arrow in his palm.

He readied his aim and, this time, I stepped in close behind him. "A little higher." My hand raised his left arm an inch. "You can't just aim and shoot—you have to *feel* it. Let your instincts guide you."

There was a hitch in his breathing. His arm tensed where my fingers touched.

"Close your eyes and relax." My voice lowered. His bunched muscles unwound. "Feel the smooth bow in your hand. Feel the tautness of the string. Feel the sturdy arrow between your fingers. They are an extension of your body—your neck, arms, shoulders and spine. Memorize how *this* feels." I paused a beat, then, "Do you feel it?"

"I feel it," Bren rasped.

Something stirred inside me. I took a steadying breath before saying, "Then open your eyes, sight down the arrow, and release."

With a controlled exhale, he fired.

Twang, whir, thud.

A near perfect bullseye.

Crap! I jerked away from him, fists clenching. Why had I helped him so much? He was my competition. My *competition!* I took a step back, needing room to breathe, and collided with a body.

I bounced off, then pitched forward. Bren's back broke my fall. *Why does this sandwich thing keep happening to me?* Normally I would mumble a quick apology and be on my way but, when I turned around, an arctic glare pinned me in place, freezing the words on my tongue.

Ugh. It was the guy with the striking neck tattoo who had elbowed me in the back days ago. I hadn't seen him since.

"You," he sneered. Oh. He remembered me, too. "Do you make a habit of running into people?"

"Technically, *you* ran into *me* that other time . . ." I trailed off as his lip curled, revealing clenched teeth. As he took a threatening step toward me, I fought to stand my ground; my knees locked.

Bren laid a hand on my shoulder. "Who's your friend, Lune?"

I rolled my shoulder to dislodge his hold. "He's not.

We've just run into each other a couple times. Literally. I don't even know his name, so I've decided to call him Tattoo Boy. What do you think? Too obvious?" I tilted my chin until Bren's face came into view.

He grinned. "Nah, I think it's perfect."

The men's gazes clashed, hot and cold, sending a shiver dancing along my spine. Something passed between them, like they were having a telepathic conversation. And then the man with the shocking blue eyes looked away. "The name's Ryker," he growled, pushing past us. "Don't forget it."

As soon as he disappeared, my fists slowly unclenched their death grip.

"Look, you chased off another one," Bren teased, and I felt a tug on the braid running down my back. "We've got to work on your people skills."

If I wasn't stuck training him, I'd have chased *him* off for pulling my hair. Instead, I flipped the braid over my shoulder and out of reach. "Sounds great," I replied, syrupy sweet. "You can teach me as soon as you learn how to avoid my knee in a fight."

He laughed, maybe a tad nervously. "So, now that I hit the target, do I get to practice in the cage?"

I broke eye contact and reached for an arrow, quickly nocking it to my bow. "No. You're not ready." The question had caught me off guard and my fingers trembled. *Show no weakness. Show no weakness.* After a long inhale, the tremors lessened. On the exhale, my hands were steady. I released the arrow.

———◦———

A week later and I was out of excuses.

"I think I'm ready," Bren said.

The late morning sun was especially warm today. I finished tying my hair back, basking in the feel of air hitting my exposed neck. "Ready for what?" I played dumb. I knew what he referred to, what he had been working toward. The final piece of his training.

But, *I* wasn't ready.

"I want to enter the cage. My archery has improved the last few days and I'd like to test it out on something moving." He was leaning against the steel locker that contained the Arcus Point bows, watching as I grabbed ours from their mounting racks. His casual pose was deceiving. I knew he studied my body language, curious how I would respond.

"Sure." I hated that my voice sounded higher than normal.

"Lune."

"What?" I started collecting the supplies we'd need, anything to keep my hands and mind busy.

"Lune, please look at me."

I paused. Sighed. Forced myself to meet his imploring gaze. I was beginning to discover something. Something I was most definitely not comfortable with: he could read me better than I could read him.

His eyes narrowed knowingly. "Are you okay with this?"

My eyebrow arched, daring him to question me again. "Of course. Let's go."

When we arrived, Ryker was preparing to enter the cage. Curious about his skill level, I beckoned for Bren to join me up in the watchtower, but he didn't see the hand gesture. No, he was too busy sidling up to the man with the tattoo.

I sighed and shuffled after him, only to hear him say something that made me want to retch. "Mind if we join you?"

Why did he have to go and ask that? Subconsciously, I rubbed at my wrist.

Bren looked at me. Studied the way I held my wrist. I dropped it. "You game?"

It had been too long. Too long since I'd practiced in the cage. I hadn't been inside for over two months. How I had kept my tier five rank intact with so little practice was beyond me. Surprisingly, Drake turned a blind eye to it, more interested in my archery prowess than actual beast takedown abilities.

I almost told Bren to go right ahead while I observed from the tower, like normal trainers did. But for some stupid reason . . . I didn't. I glanced at Ryker instead, replying, "I'm sure Tattoo Boy doesn't want us interfering with his practice time." The man's eyes narrowed to slits. Guess he didn't like that nickname.

His reply shocked the crap out of me. "Go ahead. I could use the competition. Just stay out of my way."

He faced the cage once again, dismissing us. With a tap, he turned on his earbud and muttered into it. I could see his trainer nod from his place on top of the watchtower, then hold up three fingers toward the control booth operator. Whether he was relaying how many trainees would be inside the cage or how many cyberbeasts, I didn't know.

I didn't have time to ask, either.

The cage door emitted a high-pitched shriek, then slid open on well-oiled rollers. There was no backing out now. My heart rate spiked. On autopilot, I took a step forward, only to be halted by a grip on my elbow. I glanced sharply at

Bren. "What? Having second thoughts?"

He must have detected the thin note of hopefulness in my voice because his eyes softened. Then he lifted a hand and captured a wayward strand of hair, gently tucking it behind my ear. My scalp tingled in the wake of his touch. "You all right?"

"Yeah, fine," I said quickly, pulling away. He didn't say anything else and I didn't look at him again.

As the gate sealed us inside, Ryker took off on silent feet and disappeared from view. I led Bren away from the fence toward the strange urban jungle within. My voice was hushed, barely a whisper. "The fastest way to shut down a cyberbeast is to shoot it in the eye or heart. Whatever you do, don't hesitate. It's programmed to render you unconscious with its electric volt teeth. So, retreat or hide if need be, but don't stand there and let it take you."

"Don't befriend the beasts. Got it," Bren whispered.

The first thing I did was hunt for higher ground. A vantage point. I liked to spot my quarry before it spotted me. An oak tree with low-hanging branches presented itself and I made a beeline for it. I slung my bow across my shoulders and took a running leap at the tree. Boot firmly planted on its trunk, I pushed off and grabbed a sturdy limb, then scrambled up several feet. I peered down at Bren from my perch.

He was looking at me, hands on hips, a spark of impish delight in his eyes. I frowned. What was he doing? Then almost faster than I could blink, he was on the branch next to me. I gaped at him. He winked. What did he—? How did he—?

This is not the time! I silently prepared my bow.

Hunkering down, I waited for the cyberbeasts to find me. They always did, like they could detect my scent. How many had Ryker requested? This was the hardest part—the waiting, the suspense. For machines, they were eerily silent, and not knowing where they were had me on edge. The fact that they were just metal and wires encased in synthetic fur made no difference to me. They were programmed to hunt and attack. So, to me, they were monsters.

Monsters that stalked my dreams. Living nightmares. Goosebumps pricked my flesh.

All my attention diverted to Ryker as he popped back into view. He quietly picked his way through a heap of rubble and sidled up next to a rusted, broken-down car. Surprisingly, all its windows were intact. He gripped the driver's door and pulled. It didn't budge. Pausing to form a stronger grip, he wrenched his hand backward, and the door screeched open.

My heart stopped. The air was eerily silent. Not even the birds chirped. The birds. Warning bells rang in my head.

They were coming.

A faint crunch, like the sound of a dry pinecone being stepped on, came from behind us. My pulse was a drum in my skull as I forced shaky fingers to slowly nock an arrow. I checked Bren's readiness and found an empty branch instead. The sight robbed me of air. I was alone, up a tree, with a predator on my scent. I frantically searched the forest floor for the stalking machine. Nothing.

Where is it?

Pounding, shuffling noises alerted me to the cyberbeast. A black streak raced for my tree hideout and zipped right on by. I couldn't move, could only gape as it went for Ryker instead. He was still beside the car, leaning against the rusted exterior, casually fiddling with an arrow.

He looked . . . bored.

Just as the large panther-like machine opened a maw laced with electricity, Ryker leapt to the side and grabbed the animal's scruff. Using its forward momentum, he shoved the beast inside the car's opening and slammed the door shut. Another dark cyberbeast jumped over the car's roof and crashed into him. They toppled to the ground. In a flash, Ryker planted his boots on the beast's underbelly and flipped the machine over his head. He lunged on top of it and, while the wolfish cyberbeast thrashed side-to-side, maw seeking flesh, he gripped its synthetic ears.

What the man with the tattoo did next was complete madness.

He bit down on an ear and, with a jerk of his head, tore the thing clean off. Dark oil splattered his face. Still holding onto the intact ear, he used his other hand to thrust an arrowhead into the beast's eye socket.

Faint clicking signaled that it was powering down.

He then climbed to his feet and strolled to the car. *Strolled!* I could hear a *thump, thump, thump* as the trapped cyberbeast bashed its body against the windows, attempting to free itself. A window cracked. The door burst open and the beast sprang.

Ryker dove out of the way but, before he could nock an arrow, Bren was there. My breath hitched. He would probably get electrified. Most trainees did their first time in the cage. As the black beast charged toward him, he loosed an arrow, then jumped clear. The cyberbeast crashed to the ground in a pile of twitching fur and metal, an arrow embedded in its eye.

My jaw dropped.

"Lune, watch out!"

But the warning came too late.

A force rammed into me from behind and I fell from the tree. Pain jolted up my legs as I hit the ground hard. I dropped into a roll to lessen the impact just as a large shape soared over my body. I didn't look to see what it was. I ran. I ran like I always did. Because I couldn't help it. My fear was a living, breathing thing, and that thing was now pursuing me.

Oh stars.

Trapped. Always trapped.

A tree root snagged my ankle. This time the fall snatched the air from my lungs. I flipped onto my back and was fumbling for an arrow when the machine materialized. *No. Not that one.* The pale metal saber cat, teeth just as long as the real animal's, prowled toward me. With a grunt, I shot an arrow. It thunked into the cat's tawny chest. The machine kept coming. *No, no, please! Not again!* I lashed a boot out and made contact. As the head twisted sideways, I scrambled to my feet and prepared to run.

It pounced. My spine and skull slapped against a tree trunk as the cat's paws pinned me in place. I struggled and, finally giving in to blind terror, screamed. Screamed as those elongated teeth buzzing with electricity closed in on my neck. No. No.

"No!"

With the teeth only inches away from zapping my skin, I heard a sharp thud. I stared at the gaping mouth. A mouth that wasn't moving. And then the heavy machine tilted sideways and smacked the ground. My eyes settled on its still form.

I heard rustling but didn't dare take my eyes off the cat. I expected it to reanimate any second now—despite the arrow protruding from its synthetic heart.

"Lune." The voice was soft, imploring. I didn't respond. "Lune, it's over."

I blinked. Blinked again. No. It wasn't. It was never over. "Where were you?"

A dark shape grew in my peripheral. "I was watching from the ground. I needed a better vantage point."

I didn't understand. All I knew was that I had been alone. Alone with my nightmare.

"Why are you so afraid of them?"

Just like that, the fog erased. Bren's face sharpened into focus and our eyes connected. His brows were furrowed. Worried.

My lips pursed. There was no point denying it. He now knew my biggest weakness, my greatest fear. He could use it against me in the Trials. But I could use his, too. "Why are you so afraid of water?" I tossed back.

The creases in his skin deepened. He almost looked angry. Good. "I know what you're doing. It doesn't have to be like this."

"Of course it does!" I snapped. "Maybe you're my student, but you're also my competition. Don't for one second forget that. You might know my secret, but I know yours, too." With that, I brushed past him.

"I'm sorry you were afraid," he said, and I paused. "I can help you."

My fingers tightened around my bow. Without turning, I

replied, "No, you can't," and started walking again.

No one can.

13
YOU NEED SOMETHING

Two days later, Bren didn't show up for training.

My first thought was that he must have broken a city rule, then gone missing. I would never see or hear from him again. Renold's latest victim and another casualty of Tatum City.

I should stop jumping to conclusions.

But he wasn't at breakfast hour, the stables, the archery field, or lunch hour. No one else had seen him either. I carried on with my training, body on autopilot, but mentally I was screaming. Was he ill? Injured? Now that he knew my secret fear, had he sought out a more competent trainer? The thought churned my stomach. I should feel relieved to have him out of my hair, but I just felt . . . conflicted.

Why did I care? I didn't have the answer and that troubled me most.

With the absence of Bren came a heightened awareness of my peers. My back was exposed more than ever, no giant shadow to guard it. As I helped Iris with knife throwing, Lars and Catanna openly watched me, whispering to each other. My hands shook with the strain of appearing calm when they ached to hold my twin daggers. Instead, I forced them to gently correct Iris's throwing stance.

Time ticked by, lost in the roiling clouds. With each plink

of freezing rain on my chilled skin, my mood darkened. An unbearable itch wiggled inside of me until my limbs refused to hold still. My movements became jerky, agitated. Iris glanced up at me in confusion.

I tried on a smile of reassurance but failed miserably. The warring emotions simmering in my veins were too intense. All-consuming. "I need to—" Frantically, I searched for something that could help me combat this growing tension. A mechanical dummy stood off in a corner, unused. "Keep practicing, Iris."

Without explaining, I marched toward the dummy and switched it on. A barrel of foam-tipped halberds beckoned to me—mocked me. I yanked one out and sneered at the blunted ends. I couldn't effectively beat on the dummy with padding. I tried anyway, jabbing its side with a solid thwack before it could finish booting up. My feet danced as it swung at me, then I envisioned Bren's face on its blank features.

The face grinned at me.

I bared my teeth at the image and advanced. "So, you think you can just waltz in—" *Whack.* Dodge. "Then disappear on me?" Jab, jab, *thwack.* I grunted as dummy Bren rained a blow into my ribs. "You think I care?" *Smack.* "Because I don't." *Whump.* "I. Don't—" I ducked at the next swing, then landed a hit to its stupid head. "Care!" With a whirl, my boot struck its midsection. Pain jolted up my leg and I welcomed it. No, *needed* it.

In the next moment, that spine-tingling sense of being watched sent me into blind action. I thrust my halberd behind me and struck something solid, the impact jarring my bones. No satisfactory grunt or cry of pain greeted my ears, so I whipped my head around. A hand firmly grasped the pole's padding. My gaze traveled up a well-defined arm, strong neck and jaw, to . . .

Bren dominated my view, his eyes glittering. A forceful sigh fled my nose.

His hair was drenched and now lay flat against his forehead. He looked good wet. For some reason, that realization made me mad.

"It would appear beating me up is a fantasy of yours." An infuriating lopsided smirk followed his statement, then, "I'm flattered."

Impatiently, I pushed soggy hair out of my eyes and, with a jerk, broke his hold on the pole. "Where were you?" I wouldn't be surprised if steam was leaking from my pores. I was relieved to see him, whole and unscathed, and that made me angrier.

The dumb smirk on his face fell. "What's wrong? What happened?"

My arms flew wide. "*This* happened. Training. The Trials. The city. *You.* Did you think I wouldn't—"

Worry. I was going to say worry. But why should I worry about *him?* He was my competition, stars help me!

An irrational desire to hit him pulsed through my veins. I wanted to hit him so badly I burned with the urge. Picking up another halberd, I threw it his way. He caught it with one hand and I growled.

"Fight me." I squared off with him, readying my weapon. "Show me what you got. Show me how *perfect* you are."

He gaped as if I were insane. Or a monster. I wanted to scream at him, "*It's all your fault! I had everything figured out and then you showed up. Just waltzed in here and messed with my head. Again!*" But I wouldn't. And so, I did the next best thing.

I charged him with all my pent-up fury.

Roaring a battle cry, I swung the pole at his head in hopes of removing it from his big, stupid body. He ducked. On the backswing, I aimed for his stomach. He jumped back and out of reach. "Aaahhh! Just—" I swiped at his legs and he leapt. "Hold—" The halberd swooped toward his groin and he caught it. "Still!"

I released the weapon and threw myself at him. My shoulder rammed into his gut as my arms wrapped around his legs. The move must have surprised him because the tall tree-of-a-man tipped over backward and, before I could disengage, took me down with him. He landed on his back with a heavy splat, mud spraying in all directions.

My body collided with his. Air whooshed out of me. The muddied ground would have been a softer landing. In a flash, Bren tossed his weapon aside and flipped me underneath him, pressing my back into the cold sludge. I blinked as rain spat on my face. How did he—? I didn't care. It would not end like this.

I clocked him in the side of the head with my elbow. My hips bucked, sending him rolling off me. I pounced on him once more and tucked my forearm under his chin, applying force. I was seething—air hissed in and out of my teeth. I waited for him to make his next move. I could do this all day.

But when his hand shot up and wrapped around the back of my neck, I never saw it coming. He gave a quick pull. I lost my balance and fell on top of him. With a gasp, I struggled to rise only to have his fingers clench tighter.

Our gazes clashed. How dare he! Then I stilled. My eyes

flicked back and forth over his, stunned at what was written there. The hurt and confusion was a kick to the face.

"Lune." His voice was rough, strangled. "What did I do?"

"You—" My voice cracked. "I—" *You disappeared. I was . . . I was . . .*

But I didn't let the confession take root in my mind. Instead, I stared with increasing mortification. What had I done? And in front of a field of trainees and trainers no less. A wall of shame slammed into me. My bottom lip began to quiver and I bit into it, humiliated. The quivering remained and I bit harder, focusing on the sharp pain. Gentle fingers touched my chin. A thumb slowly rubbed across my trapped lip.

Startled at the unexpected warmth, I released my lip. And wished I hadn't a moment later when Bren's intense gaze zeroed in on my parted mouth. My stomach muscles clenched and spasmed as he shifted beneath me, bringing our heads closer. Panic zipped through my body, spurring me into motion. I yanked my head back and he released his hold.

My boots fought for purchase in the slick mud as I scrambled upright, slipping in my haste to retreat. All decorum vanished when he slowly stood and took a step toward me. I shook my head, hair smacking my face, but he kept coming. Pursued me.

This felt too much like bending the rules. Like testing unbreakable lines.

What are the rules that keep you safe?

Run.

My instincts willed my feet to take flight, and so I did. Regardless of who was watching, I ran across the field, past the outer wall, and down a gravel path. I recklessly raced over uneven terrain, jumping over logs and dodging rain-drenched branches. The grass was slick, but I didn't slow down, not until I reached the marshy bank of a pond. I stripped my boots, then plunged into the murky depths. The temperature slapped my body and a gasp ripped from my lungs.

My flushed skin cooled, but the water couldn't touch the heat still simmering in my veins.

I completely immersed myself in the freezing element, swimming deeper. Soon it was just me, the water, and my endurance. My legs and arms filled with the familiar ache of keeping me aloft, ever churning. I reveled in the consistent strokes, breaths synchronized with the fluid movements.

Water was peace.

It was the only time I could escape the here and now, and the raging thoughts that consumed my being all too often. In the water, thinking was impossible. I basked in the watery grave of silence. Peace . . . I craved *peace*.

And then I clambered onto shore, having reached the other side all too soon. But I wasn't done. Half numb with cold, I trudged up and over a decaying bridge, my toes finding purchase down the loose rock pathway. The air grew heavier with moisture and thunder rumbled in the distance. I breathed in fresh mist and earthy aromas as I finished my descent, turning toward the cascading waterfall.

My final destination.

The water poured over a sheer rock face and pounded onto the smooth flat stones jutting out of the river bed. From there, it navigated the many twists and turns through the forest. I skipped from stone to stone until my back was pressed against the smooth rock behind the waterfall. After a lengthy inhale, my lungs now filled to capacity, I stepped underneath the deluge.

My scalp and shoulders stung; icy needles pelted my skin from above. I squeezed my eyes shut and allowed my head to tip back. And there I froze, my body braced against the water's weight, unwavering. Unbent. The water roared and raged, but I remained unfazed. At peace—*finally*. Time slowed. Every second became a minute.

Under the water I could control my fate.

It pushed me down, but I always ascended. It held me, until I could no longer hold my breath. It stole my hearing, thoughts, and sight . . . and I embraced the simplicity. Water was strong, yet it allowed me to be strong, too.

But then a thought sunk into my mind and my peace shattered into a million jagged pieces. Heat scalded my eyes and I let the tears flow, each one lost in the torrential downpour. A heavy weight constricted my chest, building in volume until the pressure became unbearable. I leaned my head out of the waterfall and drew in air, then expelled it in a tortured scream. The sound bounced off the high rock wall, echoing down the river.

I stood, shaking, my lungs and heart depleted—empty. As the thought sunk deeper, something happened. For the first time ever, the water felt lonely. And for the first time ever, I realized . . .

I didn't want to be alone.

My whole body ached with exhaustion. I had stayed under the water too long, searching for peace—even a thin thread. But it was gone. The dinner hour came and went, and now the moon guided my water-logged boots through the barracks doorway. If anyone was around to witness my half-drowned appearance, I didn't notice.

I was too consumed with my thoughts. Thoughts that plagued my every waking–and sleeping–moment. Thoughts of *him*. My head was so full it was a wonder my neck could carry it.

Halting in front of my dorm room, the first thing I noticed was the faint-yellow light beneath the door. Some-one was in there. Almost too numb to care, I instinctually sought out my hidden dagger, but I wore the wrong training gear. I was weaponless. I softly snorted at my idiocy. I *was* a weapon.

Pushing on the heavy wood, I slid the door open silently. There, sitting on my bed, was Bren. My throat closed. I stepped over the threshold anyway. Our eyes assessed each other. Friend or foe? I wished I knew. He rose, the frame's metal springs creaking. Ever-so-carefully, he crossed the distance separating us, as if approaching a jittery animal.

Maybe he was. I wasn't breathing when he reached around me and nudged the door closed. Silence fell, and I heard drops of water from my hair and clothing plink against cement. He bent his head toward mine and this time, I didn't pull away.

I watched him watching me. What he saw must have been a pathetic sight: a tired, defeated, and lonely girl. My mask was in shambles. But I didn't care anymore.

His lips twitched as he bit the inside of his cheek. I saw

the moment he came to a decision. His face relaxed but his eyes were lined with caution when he finally spoke, voice loud yet painstakingly soft in the quiet space. "You don't have to explain if you're not ready or don't want to. I know you've been through a lot. And that's why I'm here, little bird. I think you desperately need something and I want to be the one to give it to you."

His eyes asked for permission, but for what I didn't know. Was he asking me to trust him? Panic crept up my ever-tightening throat. *I can't. I can't. He shouldn't even be in my room like this. If anyone found out, they would assume that we were . . .* And yet, my feet remained bolted to the floor. My heart fluttered, stomach lurching as I forced myself to swallow and nod. Just once. But that's all it took.

He slowly blew out a breath, then leaned forward and erased the space between us. I'd been near him on many occasions, but this was different. I felt him in every nerve ending as his hand cradled the back of my head and pressed my cheek to his shoulder. His arm wrapped around my lower back and pulled my body to him. And there he held me, his warmth seeping through my frigid skin, kindling my insides to a slow burn.

When was the last time I'd been this close to someone? I couldn't remember. My worry over the rules vanished.

I could feel him breathing in my damp hair. The sensation curled my toes. He rested his chin on the crown of my head, and my brain shut off as my senses sparked to life. All I could do was *feel*. I was swimming in electric fire and I submerged myself in it. My shoulders drooped and a sigh shuddered through my limbs. Bren's arm tightened around me and mine responded in kind, twining behind his broad

153

back without my brain's permission.

But my brain wasn't operating in this moment.

His scent drifted to me and I sought out the source. Before I knew it, my nose was brushing along the bare skin of his neck, deeply inhaling. My head fogged with intoxicating scents of pine, leather, and rich earth. I could stay here forever, my nose buried in his neck.

His soft chuckle startled me out of my stupor, and my eyes flared wide.

"Better?" he asked.

I blinked. "Yeah," I muttered and withdrew.

The moment our bodies separated, a wall of cold replaced the warmth he had infused inside my blood. I crossed my arms over my chest as a shiver shook my shoulders.

"Lune, look at me." My eyes wanted to look anywhere but at him, this new feeling of closeness creating an odd shyness. I would have laughed at the ridiculous notion if it weren't so painfully uncomfortable. When my gaze waveringly met his, Bren continued. "The thing is, I need something too. I need you to stop running away from me."

He held up a hand as I opened my mouth in protest. "I don't care if you have to beat me up when words just aren't good enough. Whatever you need to do to get it out of your system. But"—his fingers trailed down my temple and tucked wayward hair behind my ear—"please don't shut me out. I can't bear it."

I wrenched my gaze away and fixated on my lamp's bare bulb. I couldn't promise that I wouldn't. The instinct was woven into every strand of aware and unaware moment. *Run. Keep your secrets safe. Don't let anyone close. Follow the rules.* Those instincts kept me alive. But when he looked at me like that, and talked to me that way . . . I wavered.

Stars above, I was doomed.

CAUGHT

Splat.

Ugh. Another muddy puddle. I crept into the grass, settling the lumpy bag more comfortably on my shoulder. The
rain had dissipated but the ground was a sludge pit. For the
next few days, cleaning my boots was going to be a pain in
the butt. With the storm came lower temperatures. I shivered in a black sweater while wrestling the hood over my
head.

As I made the unsanctioned trek to the village, my inner
critic listed my many shortcomings: thief, rule-breaker,
failure, weakling. I hadn't been able to collect as many supplies this week. I clenched my teeth. I wouldn't fail Asher. I
wouldn't. The familiar outline of village buildings saved me
from my thoughts and I hunkered down behind my usual
tree, ready to wait out the night watchmen.

Boots clomped along the saturated road, loud and lazy
like always. Just as a guard was about to round the bend,
a figure darted from the shadows and flitted from building
to building. A door rasped open farther down the row of
houses, faint light spilling out from the home. Then the running figure stumbled over an object. Something metal.

The silence exploded into a clanking racket.

The guard whirled, fumbling for his flashlight. "Halt!"

My heart pounded in my chest. I had to do something. If they were caught . . .

"Hey!" I yelled. A volt dart zipped toward me and crackled against the tree's trunk. Crap.

And then a large, callused hand covered my mouth. My scream was muffled as an arm wrapped around my middle and lifted me off my feet. My assailant dragged me backward while I clawed and kicked. But it was as if they knew all my moves. The head-butt was dodged, the kneecaps well out of range, the groin protected. I assumed the person was male judging by the giant hands.

Oh stars, don't let it be Drake.

My attacker pulled me behind another tree and pressed me tightly to his chest.

My back. Someone was touching my back. Air sawed in and out of my nose, but I couldn't get enough. The night wavered.

"Shhh. It's just me." The voice was deep and soft. And Bren. A strange sensation moved in my stomach, like bird's wings. His hand slid away and he slowly released me, only to breathe, "Run."

At the sound of footfalls clambering down the hill, I did. I flew past Bren and made for the nearest copse of trees. Lighter steps dogged mine and I knew they were his, not the pursuing guard's. At least he was chasing us and not the villager who broke curfew. I plunged into the woods and immediately tripped over an exposed tree root. Instead of falling, my body was scooped up and set to rights again.

Bren grabbed my hand and took the lead. I was too shocked to protest as he weaved back and forth, traveling through the dense undergrowth like it wasn't even there.

Like it was broad daylight. *How can he even see?* And then the trees thinned, and the river was before us. I plowed into Bren's back. Huffing and puffing came from the woods behind us. Sporadic beams of light.

"Keep going," I whisper-yelled, and shoved at his shoulders. Nothing. His muscles were wound so tight, he felt like a marble statue. I whipped around him to face his front. "Bren, can you hear me? You must do this. You have to trust me."

He slowly blinked. Good enough. I grabbed his hands and yanked. He jerked forward. One step. Two. I jumped into the river, the icy water rising past my boots, soaking my pants. I kept tugging and Bren sank in beside me. A great shudder racked his frame, vibrating up my arms, but he followed me. I waded to the bridge, our salvation, and ducked beneath its underbelly. There, I let go of him and grasped a support beam. Tucking my legs up, I wrapped them around the beam and hung suspended above the water.

Bren followed suit, clinging to a beam next to mine. I held my breath as clunky footsteps neared the water. They stopped. The guard cursed. Cursed again. Then took off across the bridge. I waited until all I could hear was the gentle rush of the river. My breath whooshed out of me. "Well, that was fun." My eyes met Bren's. He was staring at me, and I couldn't read his expression.

Air hissed through my teeth when I realized I had dropped the bag of food when Bren grabbed me. I quietly lowered myself into the water and made for shore.

"Where are you going?" Bren had found his voice. It sounded rusty.

He followed me out of the river, so I whispered, "I didn't

complete my task. Go back to the barracks, Bren. You can't be out past curfew."

"And you can?"

I didn't answer. I honestly didn't know what my trainer status afforded me. Under the circumstances, probably nothing.

He wrapped a hand around my bicep, bringing us to a halt. "I know what you're doing. I saw you steal the food."

Everything in me stilled. Even my thoughts.

"Why, Lune? Why would you risk doing this? If your father found out—"

I exploded into action, whipping my hidden knife free. The point pricked his jugular. "Are you going to tell him?"

He was calm as he said, "No." The word shifted his neck muscles and my blade drew a drop of his blood. I winced but didn't budge.

"Prove it."

He paused. Then, "I'll share something with you. A secret for a secret."

I eased up on the blade a notch, scrutinizing his eyes. "I'm listening."

He looked upward and blew out a breath, seemingly unfazed that a knife was at his throat. Stupid idiot. "There's only one reason why I was allowed into this city, and that's because I'm different. And so are you."

"What is she, then?" the man had asked the day I'd been kidnapped. My heartbeat picked up pace.

Bren's gaze returned to mine. "In fact, you are far more important than I am. That's why I'll be delivering your stolen goods and completing your *task*."

My grip tightened on the knife as confusion washed over

me. I couldn't help but ask, "Important? Different? How so?"

His expression grew wary before he glanced away. "I can't tell you any more than that."

I narrowed my eyes and waited a beat. When he remained tight-lipped, I dropped the subject. For now. I had a mission to complete. "I didn't steal the food, by the way. It was going to be thrown out. I call that resourceful."

His lips quirked to the side. "Or opportunistic."

With a sigh, I pocketed my knife and traipsed into the woods. "Come on. I want to make sure you do this right. There's no way I'm letting you get caught by the guards." He'd probably tell them I put him up to the task.

"What, no witty comeback?" he asked, following close behind.

"I'm not a night owl. Keep pestering me though. I'll poke your eyes out."

My threat didn't faze him because he began to pester me with more questions. "So, what's the big secret of the Supreme Elite's daughter? Why sneak around at night, and why contend in three dangerous Trials? Don't you already have a secure future?"

I snorted and spun to face him. "How about a compromise?" I said, falsely sweet. "I'll tell you why I signed up for the Trials if you tell me why *you* did. And I can tell if you're lying," I warned, gesturing back and forth between our eyes. "Deal?"

He studied my face for several seconds. His expression gave nothing away as he crooked a finger, asking me to come closer. Oxygen stalled in my lungs as I leaned forward, as his breath fanned across my ear. And then he whispered,

"No deal."

The very next morning, Asher tore my doubts and fears wide open with one simple sentence. "Lune, your father wants to see you and said you'd know where to meet him."

The city's walls crushed my bones to oblivion. Bile raced up my esophagus and my lips pinched tight against the onslaught. I would not be sick. Renold didn't deserve the satisfaction.

"You okay?" Asher brushed a hand along my arm. I gulped down air and relaxed my pensive look before meeting his blue eyes. They brimmed with concern.

"I think I made a mistake last night." I forced down a painful swallow. Bren must have told Renold about my illegal activities. I knew I couldn't trust him. I *knew* it! "But don't worry, Ash. I'll figure it out."

I retreated as he gaped, panic etched clearly across his face. But I had no more words of comfort. They would only be lies.

With one glance, the guard let me into the big house at the staff's east entrance. He knew the drill. I practically tiptoed down the dimly lit stairwell, one flight, then two. Still, my boot's tread echoed off cement and I cringed.

I landed on the sub-basement level, the dark and mysterious belly of the beast. Few ventured down here; and some, like me, had no choice. A bare bulb above my head flickered wanly, casting an eerie shadow replica of myself against the dank stone wall. One foot lifted, then the other, forcing me toward my destination.

Room after discarded room passed by, each containing dusty relics of the past. Unused and wasted instead of put to good use. I silently came to a standstill at the end of the long hall, facing a heavy wooden door. It was closed. But I knew the sole occupant inside was aware of my presence. There was a tension in the air, so thick I wanted to expel it from my lungs. When my vision wavered, I dragged in a breath of the putrid stench and threw my shoulders back.

As my trembling fingers clenched the cold, hard doorknob, I began the silent chant—a habit birthed from ten years of abuse. *You cannot break me. You cannot break me. You cannot break me.*

The door swung inward.

He sat in the center of the room, his formal attire at odds with the simple chair and dingy floor. The room's single bulb shone on his bright hair, bleaching it white. His eyes, however, were sunk in shadow. But I knew they tracked my every flinch and fidget. With practiced movements, I slid into the room and softly shut myself inside.

After a beat, he broke the tension. "Lune, how good of you to come on such short notice. I know you must be busier than ever with your new duties." His solicitous words held false warmth. My spine stiffened. He was pandering, lulling me into a sense of camaraderie. I kept my lips sealed and his ticked up knowingly.

"How is the training going? Is Mr. Bearon making progress?"

"Yes, sir. He is a fast learner, extremely skilled, and has already graduated to a tier five training level in all three Trials."

"Really." His brows arched minutely, giving me a glimpse

of pale blue eyes. They shrewdly studied me. "And what do you think of him personally?"

My heart leapt into my throat. Did he know that Bren had orchestrated my kidnapping all those years ago? But I would never ask. "Uh, I think he's a hard worker, observant, and he abides by the city's rules. He will be a force to reckon with in the Trials and make a good citizen." Stupid idiot. I shouldn't have mentioned the rules. Did he know? Was that why I was here?

He rose, and the room shrunk. I was a little girl, helpless and at his mercy. But he never showed me mercy. Never. I locked every limb in my attempt to stay grounded instead of tearing the door open and running from the room in blind terror. With one step, he was in my personal space. My un-blinking gaze fixed on a speck of dust marring his otherwise pristine suit.

His hands entwined behind his back as he began to circle me. The blood rushing in my ears almost drowned out his next words. "This is good news. But . . . I think you're leaving something out." When he stopped directly behind me, blood leached from my face. In the next instant, my neck spasmed as the sharp bite of a needle penetrated skin, nerves, and muscle. Throat convulsing, I choked on a gasp.

Renold gently laid my braid over a shoulder and contin-ued, seemingly oblivious to my shaking body. "What do I value more than anything?"

"Loyalty." My voice was tight as my body jerked. Another dart of fire ripped through my neck and my spine arched in agony. My mouth opened but no sound came out—yet my insides railed against the mistreatment. This wasn't the first time he'd stuck needles in me, but he was being extra vicious about it this time.

"Correct." He sounded pleased, but then a third needle pierced through tissue and scraped bone. Black spots marred my vision and nausea rolled heavy in my gut. *Push past the pain. You are not weak.* My lips trembled uncontrollably. "The trouble is, I don't know if I can trust you. I don't know if you have the good of your family at the forefront of your mind, and that won't do at all. No, not at all."

I was panting now, fast and shallow, the motions sending white hot agony through my skull and down my spine. Ever so slowly, he applied pressure to the needles still jammed into my neck. Air hissed through my clenched teeth. Then Renold whispered in my ear, "Can I trust you, *daughter?* Can. I. Trust. *You?*"

"Y-y-yes, s-sir," I stuttered through chattering teeth.

"Good." He unceremoniously yanked the objects from my flesh and pocketed them. My whole body slumped a fraction, but I refused to fall at his feet. "I need you, Lune. And now is not the time to go soft on me, not when your Trials are so near. Someday, maybe sooner than you think, you will reap the benefits of your loyalty. Your success in these Trials is paramount. Do not fail me. If you do, our past meetings will seem like child's play."

The threat was delivered with casual flippancy as he faced me yet again. But in his eyes was a deep well of warning and promised pain should I fail. If he only knew what I was planning once I earned Title of Choice.

My head bobbed submissively.

I thought he was finished, but his next words felt like needles sinking into my flesh all over again. "One thing you should know about members of the Recruiter Clan. They are loyal to me and only me. I have a mutually beneficial relationship with them and they believe in my cause. Maybe someday I'll reveal to you what that cause is if you prove yourself loyal to a fault. In the meantime . . ."

He flicked a hand in dismissal. Before I could close the door behind me, I heard him say, "I have eyes and ears everywhere, Lune. You'd do well to remember that."

I couldn't feel my body. Shock had made me blessedly numb. But Renold's words played over and over in my head until I thought my brain would burst. Somehow, I found my way to the stables and into Freedom's stall. She nosed me, searching for meat. I was empty-handed. Still, as if sensing my desperate need for her, she allowed me to wrap weary arms around her neck. I barely felt her prickly hair poke my skin.

A groan fled from the depths of my bruised and cracking heart. Tears poured from my eyes and I let them, my strength depleted. "I need to get out of here, Freedom," I whispered in her ear. "I think I'm finally breaking."

BETRAYED

I think you're leaving something out.

The statement was stuck on repeat in my head. What did Renold know? Was someone watching me, whispering words into his ear? As I approached Bren and Stalin at the Rasa Rowe training track, the questions stirred a growing paranoia inside me. Most everyone would jump at the chance of being the Supreme Elite's eyes and ears. The payoff would be worth any form of betrayal. Desperate people did desperate things.

I was screwed.

I would not live long enough to contend in the Trials, let alone win.

The odds were stacked against me and steadily growing. It was only a matter of time before Renold pulled out his last playing card and turned the tables on me, rendering me useless.

"Where've you been, little bird?" Bren's touch on my elbow jump-started my senses, dispelling the numbness. I whipped around and put space between us. His forehead creased upon seeing my eyes, no doubt puffy and red-rimmed. "What's wrong?"

The idea that had been niggling at me finally burrowed into my brain.

And the realization hurt more than I cared to admit, like someone was squeezing my heart. I almost took off without explanation, too emotional for words, but I needed to know. I needed to hear him say it out loud. My voice crackled with barely restrained fury. "It's you, isn't it? You're spying on me, reporting my activities."

His face turned waxen. "What?"

I scoffed. "You're not a very good liar, Mr. Bearon. I just need to know one thing. Did you speak with Renold yesterday?"

For once, his eyes betrayed him, giving the answer before his mouth could. But I stayed, long enough to hear him say, "Yes."

I hated being right.

The desire to punch him was strong, but the urge to flee was a riptide in my veins. In a flash, I was on Freedom's back and maneuvering around the track's outer edge. Right before I loosened my grip on the reins, Bren shouted my name. It was a plea. I never wanted to hear that voice again. Freedom shot down the road with my heels goading her sides, and I let her go free.

She chose her own path without hesitation, something I would probably never be able to do.

Landmarks blurred as we flew at a reckless clip, but there was no stopping us. Adrenaline spread through my bloodstream, a heady dose of power, and I reveled in it. It made me feel alive in a world that craved my demise. In moments like this, I controlled my fate—not them. If I chose to put myself in danger, it was *my* choice—not theirs.

And so, we charged over the rural landscape dotted with hills and valleys, streams, rocks, and dead leaves. Greens, golds, and fiery reds dipped and swirled around us until, abruptly, a swath of blue cut across our path. We plowed into the river, Freedom's legs leaping over the swells and kicking up chunks of water. The cold couldn't reach me. I was impervious to its bite.

For several minutes, we rode hard, both of us heaving in lungfuls of sharp air. Trickles of thought returned and I batted them away, only for them to nag me in full force.

I have eyes and ears everywhere.

With a pained gasp, I jerked on the reins. Freedom squealed at the unexpected command, flailing her front hooves as her hind legs skid in the loose soil. I was off her back and stumbling toward a scraggly bush before she could come to a complete halt. The nausea was too strong; there was no help for it. My stomach clenched and throat burned as my breakfast gushed from my body. I shook, groaning as cramps and tears had their way with me.

Weak. I was so weak.

I hated it.

That weight sat on my chest again, the one that was becoming all too familiar. I threw my head back and screamed. Screamed and screamed, the noise startling a flock of blackbirds. They flapped into the sky as I expelled my pain. But not just physical pain. Emotional. The hurt and anger from betrayal and threats was more painful than any broken bone or stab wound. The scars, the damage. They were soul deep.

My knees failed me and I crashed to the ground. I welcomed the bark of pain, but the distraction didn't last.

He betrayed me. He betrayed me. He betrayed me.

The truth was a continuous loop inside my head.

Invisible talons clutched my raw throat; I clawed jagged fingernails down the vulnerable skin of my neck. Bren was Renold's eyes and ears. It made perfect sense, really. He was from the Recruiter Clan. They did Renold's bidding. He'd traded his outside job for an inside job. I should have known better.

But I had become weak.

He had fooled me with his warm, honey-gold eyes and innocent smile.

Again.

I was so stupid.

They are loyal to me and only me.

So, I really was alone. He didn't have my back. It was all a ruse to gain my trust and loyalty when he had no plans to give me his in return. I dry-heaved, gut contorting to dislodge any and all contents. But I was empty. Utterly empty.

My stomach was a mess. I skipped lunch.

Despite my newfound determination to cut Brendan Bearon from my life, I couldn't. He was a dogged shadow, practically attached to my hip, and there was nothing I could do about it. But I didn't have to make things easy for him.

When I reached the Faust Night training field, he was throwing knives with Iris. My blood simmered at the sight; my hands formed fists as I strode toward them. Would he use her against me in his desire to get close to Renold? Who knew what tricks he had up his sleeve. But I wouldn't take it lying down, not like I had been for the last couple of weeks.

No. I would fight him every step of the way.

Starting now.

He saw me approaching, a ready smile on his face, but I spoke before he could. "Meet me at the northwest corner of the field with your preferred weapon. We're sparring. Now." I took off without waiting for a reply, and he followed me, ever the shadow. He shortened his strides, remaining a few feet behind me. Every hair on my body stood on end, hyperaware of his presence.

Having him at my back was no longer a comfort. It was torment.

I slammed open the doors to the armory and made a beeline for my daggers. Before I could reach the wall of steel, a dark form blocked my path. I changed course only to be blocked again. My teeth ground together. "Move out of my way, Bren."

"Not until you talk to me." His voice was low and quiet, but his body spoke otherwise. Muscles were tightly coiled, ready for action. Good. I was itching for a fight. My feet pivoted and, when he mirrored the motion, I struck. He jumped aside, barely avoiding a knee to the groin. Next time, his crown jewels wouldn't be so lucky. Their days were numbered.

I resumed my trek toward the weapons wall but only managed a single step before steel bands wrapped around me from behind, pinning my arms to my sides. I roared and pushed off the ground, tucking both knees close to my chest. Under the extra weight, his arms crept higher and higher, until they were within biting range.

And I did just that.

I dropped my chin; my teeth sunk into skin and muscle.

I was out for blood. As the tang of warm copper coated my taste buds, Bren let out a feral growl and hurled me to the floor. With my arms trapped at my sides, I couldn't brace. I detached my teeth from his arm and squeezed my eyes shut. Then my world twisted. Air still whooshed out of my lungs as Bren reversed our positions, taking the brunt of the fall.

In his vulnerable position, I tried to head butt his face but hit rock-solid shoulder instead. I yelled and thrashed for all of two seconds before I was unceremoniously flipped onto my stomach, face smushed against frigid tile. His superior weight pinned me to the floor.

But that didn't stop me from cursing him. A slew of words ejected from my mouth, strung together in nonsensical phrases. I went on and on; the fire in my blood waved and cracked like a whip. And then I stopped. Sealed my lips shut. Focused on my breathing. Great gusts sawed in and out of my flared nostrils.

Bren shifted so his own harsh breaths thundered in my ear. "I swear, if you *ever* bite me again, I will bite you back," he growled.

I was so done with threats. "I demand you get off me. Right. Now."

His answering sigh was heavy; his whole body deflated. Still, I was trapped. "I've decided something, little bird. From now on, when you run away, I'm going to tackle you to the ground and sit on you until you talk to me. Running doesn't solve problems. Stay and face them, no matter how painful."

A shudder racked me. I couldn't face the pain. It would crush me, body and soul. For a full minute, I laid quietly, then whispered, "Let me up."

The brokenness in my voice was unmistakable. He immediately untangled his body from mine. I felt detached from my limbs as I dragged myself upright. My weary eyes took in his taut frame—blood leaked from an oval-shaped bite on his right forearm. He deserved it. That and so much more.

"Lune . . . talk to me."

There was that plea again. Why? What would talking do? He would just use me. Lie to me.

I shook my head and folded my arms across my chest.

He sighed, exasperated. "Are you mad at me?"

My head gave a curt nod before I could stop myself.

"Does it have to do with your father?"

My neck muscles strained against the action, but my head moved up and down again. *Stop answering his questions!* I screamed internally. But it was like a force greater than myself controlled my body now.

"Are you . . . jealous that he spent time with me the other day?"

I almost lost it. My heart-rate spiked and my lips twisted in a sneer as I speared him through the gut with my eyes.

"Okay, okay. You're not jealous. That's good." He heaved a sigh and scrubbed his hands down his face. And then something clicked, like he found the missing puzzle piece. His eyes all but glowed at whatever conclusion he had come to. He spoke in hushed tones, almost too low for me to catch. But I heard every single painful word. "You're afraid. Something happened with your father and it scared the crap out of you. Is that it?"

Carefully, I met his impassioned gaze and shook my head, then retreated a step. Wrong move. His eyes gobbled up my reaction and before I could blink, he strode toward me, saying, "Yes, that's it." I swiftly yanked up a hand and slapped my palm to his chest. He pressed against my fingers but came no closer. His breathing was erratic; I could feel his heart thundering.

I didn't know what to make of his reaction. Was it all an act? I couldn't take any more of this. Trust was impossible with him and I needed to face that fact. Bren was right: the problem wouldn't go away just because I ran from it. It was time for me to acknowledge and accept what stood between us—the thing that would never go away, no matter how much I secretly wished it to.

He and I, we were doomed from the start. Two beings on different sides, fighting for the same thing. And yet, we weren't. What he wanted was different than what I wanted. How could we care for each other if we were fated enemies?

I finally spoke, each word like broken glass in my throat. "Stop. Just stop. I see you clearly now. I know why you're here and what Renold has asked you to do. So, you can stop *pretending*, Bren. Don't act like you care about me when I am nothing more than a means to an end. And I certainly don't care about you."

The anguished look on his face was unbearable. Why wouldn't he stop? Was this some kind of psychological warfare? Because it was working. In a rush, I finished with, "I will continue my duties to you as your trainer, nothing more. Meet me on the field."

I whirled and retrieved my daggers, unable to witness his crestfallen expression a moment longer. He was destroying my mind. A deep growl was the only warning I got before Bren grabbed my shoulders from behind. *No way. I'm not doing this again.* And this time, he made a grave mistake: I had steel in my grasp. But I completely froze when one of his hands brushed my braid aside. Then panicked when he sharply inhaled. "What happened to your neck?"

I jerked away and covered the evidence of abuse. Shame burned my cheeks. He shouldn't have been able to see the marks. Renold had been sloppy. "It's nothing." Even I didn't believe my words.

He squeezed his eyes shut, dug fingers into his hair and pulled. With a groan, he murmured, *"Num acquired me tu es, paulo avis. Non possum resisters dolorem in te videre."* When he finished expelling the strange words, I slowly blinked. Just one more mystery. One more *secret.*

His eyes opened, and the storm within was devastating. He studied me, and I let him. I would not waver. His face fell. "You're not going to let me help you."

It wasn't a question.

As I made my way across the room, his parting words clung to me, like shadows. They were shackles around my feet. "I'm not giving up on you, Lune. You're worth fighting for."

Over the next month, I trained Bren as hard as Drake had trained me. No quarter. No mercy. Sunrise to sunset. He didn't complain, except when I made him train extra hours after dinner. In the dark. In the water.

"Suck it up, pansy. Do you think the Trials discriminate fears? No, they exploit them. Get in the lagoon."

"You're the devil," Bren muttered. But he obeyed,

muscles bunching as he waded toward me.

"Thank you." I dipped into a mock curtsy. "It's what all trainers aspire to be."

He shook his head, jaw muscles flexing. He was angry. My lips curled. Good. An angry Bren was far better than a funny Bren. Or a sad Bren. Our gazes briefly connected, long enough for me to see the half-moon smudges under his eyes and the fine new crease between his brows. I quickly looked away and focused on his hands as they clenched and unclenched.

I bent my knees. Water swished at my thighs as I prepared for our spar. "We're going to keep doing this until you forget you're in water. Until your fear is just a pesky fly in your mind's eye. Until you willingly jump in on your own and start to doggy paddle."

He brought his fists up, his shoulders still too tense. "And what about your fears? Shouldn't we work on decoding them? Because I, for one, am still in the dark."

I bared my teeth as I snarled, "Stop stalling, Mr. Bearon. You know very well that I'm not here to ease your curiosity. Now get over yourself and fight me."

"You know, you're not very fun anymore. You're like a cantankerous old spinster, shriveled and bitter. Like one of those sour green apples." He threw a fist at my jaw and I jerked backward. He really was mad. I leered. Perfect.

"I can be a sour apple if I want. I *like* green apples. All apples." I sprang and his eyes widened as I went for his legs. For some reason this move always worked. My shoulder rammed his stomach; my arms wrapped around his thighs. And he toppled backward with a resounding splash. We submerged in the freezing water but I barely felt it. Rage burned me up from the inside out.

Bren flailed, digging his fingers into my shoulders. He wrenched me off him, then banded his arms behind my back, locking me to his chest. We breached the surface and I gasped. Eyes wild, I glared into his equally tumultuous gaze.

"Let go of me, Bren. This isn't sparring," I growled as I struggled against him. His arms only tightened more.

"What, you don't like this, little bird? Are you perhaps *afraid* of something? You wouldn't want to work on that now, would you? I'm all too willing to help." His warm breath feathered my cheek as he exploited my attempts to escape.

"I'm going to murder you, Brendan Bearon!" I wrenched my knee up toward his groin, but he slid a leg between mine. Heat pooled in my core and I inhaled sharply.

A whistle came from shore. Catcalls. We broke apart and I almost tumbled back into the water.

"Well, you two look cozy," Lars said loudly. "Don't stop on our account. We were enjoying the show." At least a dozen trainees hooted and snickered at his words.

I wanted to drown myself; my face was on fire. "Grow up, Lars. You're just jealous because no one wants to cuddle with you. Try taking a shower once in a while and see what happens." I made a beeline for shore, faking calm while my insides shook. Bren didn't follow, and I cast a quick glance at him. He hadn't moved an inch. Was he as mortified as I was, or did he think this was funny? Probably the latter. My nails dug into my palms.

Pulling myself onto dry land, I took stock of the shadowed faces. The moon didn't want to give up their features tonight. Lars was front and center, and what appeared to be his closest allies clustered around him. A tall, feminine figure caught my eye next. Catanna. Her hands weren't on her hips like usual. They were . . .

I blanched at the sight. She had Iris in front of her, and the poor girl was trembling. Without hesitation, I pushed past Lars on my way over to her. His hand streaked toward my wrist, but I was ready this time. I slapped my arm to my side and spun, capturing his wrist with my other hand. Then I squeezed. Hard. Harder. Until my fingers whimpered a protest. But I didn't dare let go.

Shoving up against him, I deliberately carved into his skin with my chipped fingernails. "Don't touch me," I snarled, practically spitting in his ear. "Or I will invent a special kind of pain just for you."

He chuckled. "You're getting me all hot and bothered, Mute. We can cuddle, if that's what you're pining for." I stepped back and released his limb as if it was covered in maggots. His grin was disgusting.

I faced Catanna. "What are you doing with Iris?"

She shrugged delicately. "It's initiation night. The little weakling doesn't know how to swim. We're going to teach her."

My blood boiled. "You'll have to get through me first." Several guffaws. I was so dead. They could see straight through my bravado to the squirming mess within. And I didn't have anyone to protect my back.

Lars sauntered up behind me. "That's the plan, Mute." He must have signaled Catanna because she dragged a sniffling Iris toward the water. I lurched forward but Lars clamped onto my arms and bent them together until my elbows were almost touching. I cried out as my shoulder muscles stretched too thin.

Bren roared. "Let her go, you piece of—"

The smack of bone hitting flesh drowned out his next words. Lars's hands fell away and I stumbled to the ground.

In a flash, I raced for the lagoon where Catanna already had Iris submerged chest high. Just as I reached the water's edge, Catanna shoved the girl's head under the surface.

"No!" I jumped in. Five seconds. Ten. *Hold on, hold on.* Fifteen seconds. I tangled my fingers in Catanna's hair and yanked. She screeched, shrill and long, but didn't let go of Iris. I kept pulling until a chunk of hair ripped free of Catanna's scalp.

Her blazing eyes whipped my way. "You're dead!" She released the girl and fixed her claws into my shirt. With a shove, she dunked me in the water. This I could deal with. I could hold my breath a lot longer than Iris could.

I hooked a leg around Catanna's and rolled; I felt the moment she lost her balance. My fingers groped for the hidden pants pocket as I planted my boots on the lagoon's floor and shot to the surface, dragging Catanna up with me by her hair. With a flick, my blade was at her graceful throat. "Enough." I dragged in a breath of victory.

Iris was sputtering not far from us, but she was alive. Thank the stars. And then she pointed toward shore. "Bren."

That's when I heard it. *Thump.* Grunt. *Thwack.* Groan. "You shouldn't have chosen her, outsider." Cackling laughter.

I scanned the area where Lars had grabbed me, and my heart plummeted. Four trainees held Bren in place while Lars railed at his face, ribs, and stomach. After a roundhouse kick to the gut, Bren thudded to his knees. And then a flash of silver. Lars had a weapon. I couldn't breathe. All it took was a flick of the wrist and Bren's cheek split open.

"Lars, don't!" Panic crashed into me and I almost loosed Catanna. But my brain functioned just enough to cement me in place.

Iris. I had to protect Iris.

A great weight pressed on my chest as I watched, helpless. Lars pointed his knife at Bren's heart. No, no, no. Tears fell in droves down my face. This couldn't be happening. It couldn't end like this, with Bren thinking I hated him. Thinking I didn't . . .

I felt sick. Bile laced the roof of my mouth. An image popped into existence, blinding me from my surroundings. And yet, I was seeing the same setting—just not the same events. The image whirred to life, in it a scene of Lars jamming his knife into Bren's chest.

The scene faded and I was left gaping, blinking away the afterimage. *That* had never happened before.

My body shuddered as it righted itself, as the here and now sharpened into focus. And there was Lars, his knife still hovering over Bren. But the knife wasn't in his chest. It was poised, ready to strike. It was descending . . . I sucked in air and let it burst forth in a blood-curdling scream.

The knife paused.

Everyone gaped.

"What's going on here?"

Dead silence, except for the vestiges of my scream echoing across the water. At first, I feared that a trainer or guard had heard the commotion. But out from behind a tree stepped Ryker. I frowned. Ryker? His boots were sound-less as he made his way to Lars. The two men assessed each other, and whatever Lars saw made his feet shift nervously.

"Just a little fun," Lars tossed out casually. "These two tried to interfere with our initiation night, and things got a bit heated. It's all under control, though. No harm, no foul." He slowly slinked backward, knife nowhere in sight.

Ryker just stared, his black tattoo stark against his pale neck. "Break it up or you'll all be reported."

That was all the trainees needed to hear. They bled into the night. Catanna squirmed in my grasp and I let her go. "This isn't over, Princess," she hissed, and disappeared from sight. My shoulders sagged. I looked to Ryker—he was staring at me intently. No, intensely. All words froze on my tongue. Somehow, I didn't think he'd appreciate a thank you. A second later, he faded from view, leaving me and Iris and Bren.

"Bren," I breathed, treading water. When I made it to shore, he was slumped over, hair covering his face. My fin-gers itched to brush the strands aside. I kneeled in front of him and reached a hand out despite myself. "Are you . . . are you okay?"

Slowly, his head lifted, and I caught sight of his eyes. They weren't sad. They weren't angry. They weren't even laughing. They were . . . "I knew you still cared." He smiled softly.

IT WAS ME

"I'm guessing you have first aid supplies stashed away in here somewhere?"

I had sent Iris to my dorm room and told her to lock the door. Now I was in Bren's room, a complete ball of nerves. The gray box looked the same as mine, only it smelled of him. I refused to breathe any more than necessary. I'd never been in a man's room before. It was awkward. And forbidden. But after what we'd just endured, I couldn't care less. A growing part of me felt out-of-control reckless at the moment, adrenaline still simmering in my blood.

"Yeah, in there." From a slightly slouched position on his bed, Bren gestured at a dresser. His eyes tracked me as I walked to it and pulled open the top drawer. I withdrew a kit and involuntarily jerked at what lay underneath.

A book.

A real, leather-bound book.

I slammed the drawer closed as if it contained a venomous serpent, upsetting a cup on the dresser's surface. My free hand snatched it midair and I returned it with a bit too much force.

"Nice catch."

I didn't respond, my brain too busy calculating. Books weren't allowed in the city because of their power—I hadn't seen a book in *years*. According to Renold, societies fell when the citizens filled their minds with knowledge. The influx of ideas made them discontent and prone to riots. The penalty for possessing a book was imprisonment. I didn't know what happened to the prisoner after that. They were never seen again.

What if . . .

I hated myself for even thinking it, but thoughts of revenge flooded my mind. All the pain Bren had caused me. If I reported the book, would Renold finally trust me? Would he relieve me of Bren duty? Would he stop the abuse?

My greatest competition in the Trials would be eliminated.

A battle waged in my head. What kind of person would I be if I betrayed for vengeance, to increase my chances of survival? But doing nothing, after all I'd suffered, left a sour taste on my tongue. Grimacing, I turned to find Bren staring at me. He scanned every inch of my face and I squirmed like a worm on a hook. It was as if he could sense my inner turmoil and gauged which course of action I would take.

I pulled up a chair in front of him and opened the kit. My hands kept busy, distracting me from my thoughts. Nervous energy assaulted me as I prepared to clean the cut on his cheek. But I pushed through the mire of discomfort and wiped at the blood. Bren winced, and I pursed my lips, lightening my touch.

His gaze was pinned on my face; my skin heated. I shifted on the chair, aching to dispel the charged silence. "The cut," I blurted. "It's not that bad. I think I can just glue it shut. Good thing I don't need to give you stitches because you would probably lose an eye."

He laughed softly. "I would risk it just to have you near."

A tremor began in my fingers, and I stopped cleaning the wound. I stared as a thin trail of blood trickled down to his jaw. My brain was a riot of tangled knots. After all I'd put him through this month. After all the harsh words. He still wanted to be near me? Against my better judgment, I peered into his eyes. They were as serious as they could be while still allowing a faint lopsided smile.

He inched a hand toward my face and, before I could move, his fingers gently glided over my cheek. Inwardly I screamed at myself for not pulling away, but outwardly I didn't flinch. As he picked up a lock of hair and smoothed it behind my ear, inward and outward held no meaning—only the tender touch mattered. Until that moment, I hadn't realized how desperately I missed being near him like this. It wasn't like our training sessions, which were brutal and savage. No, this was . . .

I should hate it.

It was against the rules.

I wanted *more*.

Oh no.

I shot up from the chair and Bren followed suit. No. I shook my head and retreated a step. I couldn't do this. Not again.

Ever so carefully, he reached between us. I froze, eyes wide. Warmth enveloped my fingers and palms as he laced our hands together. I didn't pull away. I could feel myself weakening, caving.

Stars above, save me.

He softly tugged on my hands and drew me closer. Bending his head, he captured me with his pleading gaze. "I miss you so much. Come back to me, little bird."

Right then, something in me cracked. The many weeks of silence and anger between us hadn't stopped my feelings for him—time had only forced them into a state of hibernation. Now the feelings were thawing and I was scared out of my mind. How could I still care for him after all he had done to me?

His expression changed then. Oh stars, I was staring at determination as he said, "How about a compromise?" I raised a brow at the question, the same one I had asked him a month ago. He charged ahead. "A secret for a secret. Trust is a scary thing, but you can't move forward if you don't take that first step. I already revealed a secret to you: I have a book. I'm entrusting you with that knowledge even though you could report me."

So, he knew, yet he had still allowed me to see the illegal book. What game was he playing at now? I fought with myself. I should keep things as they were. If all went according to plan, I would be far from this city in a little over a month and would never see Bren again.

And then another scenario pushed its way to the forefront of my mind. What if one of us died in the Trials? All this pain and betrayal and bitterness would be pointless if one of us died. I could feel myself considering the compromise he'd offered. The very real concept of death in my near future hung like angry dark clouds over my head.

Spine straightening, I gripped his hands as if they were the only thing holding me in place. Actually, they were. My heart hammered in my chest so hard it hurt. I drew in a shaky breath. Reckless. Here went nothing. "At the lagoon earlier, if my scream hadn't alerted Ryker, Lars would have plunged that knife into your chest." Stars, what was I doing? This was insane. *He's going to think I'm insane!*

I hardened my jaw and locked eyes with his, daring him to laugh at me. My body quaked at the thought, yet my brain wildly buzzed at having revealed a secret to my possible enemy. The familiar rush of adrenaline pumped through my veins and I fought the urge to cackle like a maniac. I really *was* insane.

Bren looked thunderstruck. "How do you know that? Are you sure you didn't just imagine him doing such a thing?"

"No, I didn't imagine it, you big giant idiot. I *saw* it! And if you *dare* report this to Renold, I will hunt you down and stick a knife in your chest myself." This was it. Right here, right now. I was finally unhinged. Truth came at a terrible price, and I would kill him if he betrayed me this time. Because if I didn't kill him, I would ultimately die of a pierced heart.

He gaped at me, his face turning a sickly shade of yellow. "It's not possible," he breathed.

"What's not possible? That I saw you get stabbed or that you reported me? Because *both* are true." My hands squeezed his so fiercely, I could barely feel them.

"I would *never* report you to Renold. Get that through your head, Lune Tatum!" he growled.

With a snarl, I dropped his hands and latched onto his shirtfront, jerking my body against his. "Don't call me that! And you're lying. A month ago—the day you went to see Renold—you sold me out. You—you *betrayed* me all over again!"

"What?" Bren's voice was weak with astonishment. My breath expelled from me in harsh pants and I dug my fingers more securely into his shirt. Memories of the torture I went through, the physical and emotional pain of that day—the constant agony every day since knowing Bren had duped me again—was a slap to my face. I couldn't do this. It hurt too much, like someone was ripping my chest open.

I released his shirt and dashed for the exit.

"Oh no you don't." He wrapped an arm around my waist and swept me off my feet, spinning my body around to face him once more.

"Let go of me, you insufferable liar," I ground out through bared teeth, the sting of tears threatening.

His lips thinned and his hand tightened on the back of my shirt. "Not until you hear me out. At least now, after an entire month of being left in the dark, I have something to work with. Let me make one thing perfectly clear: I would *never* betray you. I swear it's not possible. No way could I hurt you like that."

"Oh, really?" I cried. My heart was breaking into a million pieces. How could he keep lying? Didn't he see what it was doing to me? Tears burned down my cheeks and I raged at them. But they wouldn't stop, and so I didn't stop. I opened my big mouth and spewed words I wasn't ready to say. "You know that little girl you couldn't save, the one I remind you of? Why did you make her trust you and then let her get kidnapped? Why did you betray her?"

In the next moment, his expression mirrored my own. Complete horror.

Everything stopped. Time, thought, breathing. It all stopped.

Then he sucked in air. "Lune." His eyes widened as they raced over my face. "How did you know that she had been kidnapped?"

My lips parted. I'd revealed too much. No, no, this couldn't be happening. I hadn't meant to—

I wrenched away from his grip only for his hands to clamp down on my shoulders, pinning me in place. "Lune." I dug my teeth into my lip. He shook me, his expression bald panic. "Lune, tell me!"

I was done. I couldn't hold the hurt in any longer, even though I should. I knew someone would probably hear and report me for being in this room, but I couldn't . . . I couldn't . . . Eleven years of suppressed emotion sprang free. I exploded, screamed my pain right at his face. "Because it was *me!*"

A choked sob burst from my throat, the sound of infinite heartache. My soul was bared as I finally unearthed the thing between us. "I'm the girl who haunts you, Bren. The girl you tricked and betrayed. You sold me out to the Recruiter Clan and I never saw my mother again. I've been stuck in this place for eleven years because of you!"

His hands began to shake and he snatched them back as if I were fire. No, as if I were a ghost made solid. His skin was gray ash, eyes dim ember. He placed a hand on his chest, directly over his heart, and his fingers curled into his shirt like claws. "No." He stumbled back a foot, then two. "No, no, no . . ." He repeated the word several more times as if it would erase my admission. Oh, how I wished it could.

"Please," he croaked. He raised a trembling hand toward me. "It—it can't be you. Not you. Please tell me it's not you."

My chin wobbled at the gut-wrenching despair in his voice. Nothing about this moment was fake. It was all too heartbreakingly real. Another scalding tear trailed down my face as I fumbled for the cord at my neck. I should have destroyed the thing a long time ago, but for reasons beyond my understanding, here it was. And here I was. And here he was. We had come full circle in this game of lies and bitterness, betrayal and revenge.

This moment might forever break us apart and I internally wailed. I didn't want it to end like this. I didn't want it to end at all.

But, inch by inch, I exposed the only evidence I possessed of our entwined pasts. Inch by inch, I watched Bren's crestfallen face grow more and more bleak, until his chest heaved and his eyes filled with unshed tears. When the bear tooth dangled between us, a shudder racked his large frame. "You . . . you knew? This whole time?"

I couldn't respond—my throat was closed. So, I simply nodded.

The choking noise he made was awful. Raw. An open wound. He fisted his hair, wrenching his head back. "Oh, God, why? Why *her?*" Abruptly, he whirled and punched the wall. I flinched at the sound of bone smacking cement. Then, with a guttural cry, he did it again. When he drew back, flecks of crimson spotted the wall. He dropped, knees slapping the hard floor; a haunted groan tore from him. He buried his face in his hands as his shoulders shook.

In that moment, I knew we felt the same thing. Shame. Guilt. Self-loathing. I couldn't stop myself from feeling responsible for his current agony. I had wanted to inflict pain on him for so many years, but now . . . now I just wanted the pain to stop.

There had been enough pain. I wanted us to heal.

His words were muffled, spoken behind bleeding

knuckles. "How can you—how can you even stand the sight of me?" He didn't lie, didn't offer excuses or platitudes. There was only misery. So, I found myself opening up in return. His anguish called to mine and I rose to meet it, wishing to wrap our pain in a balm of peace. The suffering had to end before it buried us alive.

"I couldn't, at first." My voice cracked, but that didn't stop me. "I only saw the past you and what you had done to me. I was hurt and angry. So, so angry." I hiccupped, dispelling a piece of the pain. "But the you I see before me isn't the past you. You came in here and helped me, and you helped others when no one else would. You show me day after day that you care despite the way I've treated you in return. I thought you betrayed me again, and I was so . . . so . . . But no matter how hard I *try*, I can't stay mad at you, because you're so . . ."

My eyes burned anew and I scrunched my nose to ward off an onslaught of fresh tears. "Stars, this is hard." I dug my fingers into my hair, then knelt in front of him. The cement was splotched next to his knees. Tears. "I just . . . I want you to be real. I've been lied to my whole miserable life, and—" A breath heaved out of me. I sounded like a wounded animal. "You didn't report me to Renold?"

"I swear, I didn't," he rasped. "I would never." His head hung low, defeated. He didn't offer further explanation, but I didn't need it. Not right now, anyway. I needed . . .

I placed a trembling finger under his chin, and he slowly, almost painfully, met my gaze. My lips quivered at the dullness in his eyes, normally so vibrant. I still haunted him. What I planned to ask him next was another reckless gamble. But he was right. Trust was about taking that first scary step and hoping you didn't fall.

And so, I said, with a touch of steel in my voice, "Please tell me you're real and not a lie, Brendan Bearon."

Twin tears glistened in his red swollen eyes. And fell. In the next beat, he was moving. He locked my knees between his and crushed me to him. His whole body trembled against mine. Desperately, I twined my arms around him in return, fusing us together. He pressed his face into the crook of my neck and inhaled.

Every molecule inside of me became hyper-aware of him. And this time, they reached for him and begged not to be separated.

I filled my nose with his scent, memorizing it. In this moment, my mind decided on a truth: I was safe with him, here in his arms. Despite everything. It didn't make sense and yet it made all the sense in the world.

"I'm real," he murmured against my skin. "I'm right here."

CLOSE CALL

Something.

I needed to ask Bren something, but I couldn't remember what.

It was important, I knew that much. Otherwise I wouldn't have gotten out of bed.

Bed.

I should be in bed.

But I was floating. My arms and legs couldn't move, though. They were frozen. A chill sunk deep inside my bones and I became aware of a repetitive clacking noise. I focused on the sound. It was my teeth.

"Hurry, I think she's waking up!"

Scuffing, cursing, jostling. My body dipped, then resumed floating. The strange motion and noises snapped me back to reality. I cracked my eyes open and saw a large shape bob in sync with my body. Squinting, I tried making out the face, but it was too far away—or too dark.

I flexed my arms and legs, wishing to be free of the odd constraints.

The shadow-face jerked my way. It cursed. "She's awake. Get her in the water *now!*"

My brain sluggishly clicked to life. Water?

Splashing surrounded me, then my limbs were set free.

I fell. Being fully submerged into freezing liquid was not what I had been expecting, so when my lungs seized from the icy impact, I sucked inward. Water speared down my throat like icicles. It was so cold, it burned. The sensation kick-started my survival instincts and I clawed toward the surface.

But something held me down.

Stark fear flooded me; I thrashed like a rabid beast. My hands struck something solid and I latched onto it, tearing at what felt like sinewy human muscle. It wouldn't budge. My lungs were now on fire and they cried for air, convulsing once, twice. Eyes wide open, I aimed my legs for the undulating shadow and clamped them around what felt like a torso.

My waterlogged body dragged the shadow under the water with me and I quickly twisted free, shooting toward the surface. Frigid air blasted my face and I gulped it down, immediately racked with hacking coughs as my lungs dispelled river water.

I knew where I was now and what was happening. The how and why, though, would have to wait. An arm snaked around my neck from behind. My sharp elbow found a home in an unsuspecting ribcage. The would-be murderer grunted and loosened his hold. I could hear that he was male and feel that he was physically stronger than me.

But apparently, he wasn't smarter.

My head whipped back, striking true. A gratifying crunch and muffled yell was all I needed to hear. I shimmied out of the slackened hold and scrambled for the riverbank, slower than I should be. My body was already shutting down, preserving what precious little heat it had left.

And so, I couldn't outrun what happened next. My gut didn't even warn me. One second I was reacting and the next, a frozen statue. Then pain registered. First a spark, then a blaze, so fierce that every nerve locked in place, unable to compute the level of agony.

My pain threshold had been reached and I was tipping over to the other side, literally. Down, down, down I went until water embraced me yet again.

My grave.

I was floating, this time just my legs.

At least, I thought they were floating. I couldn't feel them.

I couldn't feel anything, really. If I was dying or dead, it wasn't so bad. It was sort of . . . peaceful.

My eyes rubbed against their lids and I worked on prying them open. They were gritty, heavy. It was like lifting a seventy-pound sack of grain. Everything was blurry when they finally opened. And gray—a dreary, colorless shade. I blinked lethargically, trying to sharpen my vision. After a moment, I realized the sky was misting, hence the hazy view.

I was shrouded in a deep fog, completely confused as to how I ended up in it. Was I really dead? Was this . . . Heaven?

With a monumental effort, I raised my head to get a better look. The small movement sent spikes of pain into my left shoulder blade, and a pathetic whimper puffed past my lips. The peace was gone now, in its place worry. I wasn't in

Heaven. More like hell on Earth.

Memories crashed into me and I fought for calm. Someone, or several someones, tried to murder me. They had
almost succeeded too. I *should* be dead. But here I was and,
with growing panic, I realized where *here* was: the riverbank. Half of my body still lay in the water, which explained
why I couldn't feel my legs.

Stay calm, I commanded myself. *Slow, shallow breaths.
In, out, in, out. That's it.*

I studied my murky surroundings, not recognizing this
part of the city. How far had I drifted downriver? I strained
to hear—held my breath as I listened for signs of civilization. Only the river's gurgle reached my ears. Wait . . . I
picked up another sound. There! It was like a zap, or a zing,
or a—

"No," I whispered, crestfallen. It was an electric buzz.

I was at Tatum City's outer wall.

A weak groan rolled up my throat. This part of the city
lay untouched, miles away from help. I was alone. No one
would find me out here. I knew my body wanted to cry in
frustration, so I lifted my head higher, creating the perfect
distraction. A terrible ache pulsed in my back and, before
I could chicken out, I inched shaking fingers toward the
source.

I hissed as my half-numb arm continued its slow journey. I was so weak, like a newborn. Eventually, the pads of
my fingers bumped up against cold steel and I gasped, more
from shock than pain.

I'd been stabbed.

The blade was still embedded in tissue and muscle. Bile
raced up my throat. Acid covered the roof of my mouth. I

clamped down on my tongue and rode the waves of nausea, refusing to vomit. The violent action would render me unconscious.

I diverted my attention by focusing on my predicament. First things first. I needed to get out of this water. The cold temperature was slowly killing me. My mind drifted, thinking about how far I'd have to travel if I wanted to see another sunrise. My chest constricted. Panic overcame common sense as realization hit me. I was doomed. I could barely pick up my head let alone tell my body where to go.

Mortality was a noose around my neck. It squeezed, tighter and tighter, waiting for me to surrender my sorry excuse of a life. And for a heart-stopping minute, I contemplated just that.

"No," I whispered again, fiercely this time. I would not give up so easily. I faced death every day and conquered it. A little stab wound wasn't going to take me down.

I redirected my thoughts to getting out of the water. My fingers curled into hardened clay and crafted an anchor. Arms trembling like a day-old foal, I pulled myself forward. The knife shifted and a guttural groan left me. But I didn't stop. One hand over the other, I crawl-dragged my body fully onto dry land.

And then I collapsed, stiff grass stalks poking into my face. I rested, one beat, then two. But I couldn't remain still. My body desperately needed warmth. Without permission, my brain conjured an image of Bren holding me close and I almost broke down in hysterics. I needed Bren. That's what I needed. He would help me. He would warm me. He would fix me.

He became my motivation.

Bend your knee. Good. You're one step closer to Bren.
Bend the other. Good. You're two feet closer to Bren.

But getting to my feet was one of the hardest things I'd ever done. A strangled sob left me, then another as my legs shook so hard I almost fell back to the ground. I widened my stance and waited for the tremors to lessen. Slowly but surely, my legs warmed, and with the warmth came the sensation of a thousand needles. They stabbed my skin and muscles, even my bones.

Tears dripped off my chin. But I was standing. And my legs were beginning to function. Finally, I allowed myself to hope. Maybe I would make it after all.

As I took that first stumbling step, I knew three things for certain: I would bleed out if I removed the knife, I needed to follow the river, and I was in trouble. I couldn't walk a straight line and worried that I'd fall in the river again. If I did, it was game over. I didn't have the strength to pull my-self out a second time. And so, against my better judgement, I veered right, away from the water's edge.

Several agonizing minutes passed—each one feeling more like an hour. Either the fog was growing thicker or the night was becoming darker because it was getting harder and harder to see. But no, that couldn't be right. It should be closer to day than night by now. In fact, I heard the far-away chirp of a bird. Sunrise was approaching at last.

Yet black dots wouldn't stop following me. They winked and danced until I felt dizzy. I swayed farther to the right and barely caught myself on a tree. The incessant throb-bing in my shoulder wasn't my main focus anymore. Now the real possibility of fainting had my heart fluttering with nerves. I could be lost out here for days, succumbing to hypothermia or blood loss. No one would find me this deep in the woods.

I dug my fingernails into the rough tree bark. I was such an idiot. I'd lost sight of the river.

My weary eyes drifted shut.

"No!" I grunted, forcing them open. Falling asleep could be just as deadly as fainting. I had to stay awake at all costs.

Bend your knee. Good. One step closer to Bren. Now, find the river or you'll never see him again.

That got me going. As I trudged along at a snail's pace, my thoughts strayed to others I would miss—Asher, Iris, Freedom. I had to see them again. I just had to. Eventually, the sound of softly rushing water led me back to the river and I released a sigh.

But, as I stood at the bank on unsteady feet, a sickening truth arose.

My journey had just begun.

My soiled sock-clad feet tripped and stumbled over another root, and I stubbed my toes. I didn't feel the pain. Everything was numb, except for the burgeoning fire in my shoulder. With each step, the torment intensified until I wheezed in every breath.

Clumps of limp hair swayed around my face as my head hung low, so I didn't see the felled tree. I plowed into it and almost pitched over the other side. My body lurched awake in blinding agony, but I could only manage a slight grunt, then collapsed on top of the tree trunk. I sat, hunched, with forearms braced on knees.

I just needed a minute.

Then I would continue.

A shrill scream echoed in my ears.

I jerked my eyes open and frantically searched for the source. The world was on its side and I frowned, baffled. A full minute passed before my brain sluggishly registered the cry as my own, my throat raw from the force of it. I was now on my side, next to the tree. I must have fallen off and agitated my wound. Carefully, I reached back and felt for the knife. Still there.

My arm fell and I rested my cheek against dying leaves, their pungent, decaying aroma thick in my nose. I realized I was like a leaf. First a fledgling bud, blossoming into a vibrant, healthy shoot. With maturity, I had survived battering winds, rains, and hail. Through it all, my spine held true. Finally reaching my apex, I, like a tired leaf, broke free of my mooring and tumbled to the ground. There I wilted, until the earth embraced me with open arms.

Reduced to dirt.

I was fading fast, disintegrating like a leaf. It was as if the earth held its breath, waiting, waiting . . .

The leaves around me rustled, accepting me as one of them, and I smiled faintly. My eyes slipped closed for the final time and I reached invisible fingers toward the comforting threads of peace.

"Lune!"

My throat constricted; the peace evaporated. A tear squeezed past my lid and trailed the bridge of my nose before landing with a soft plink onto a leaf. My mind wouldn't cooperate. It clung to thoughts of Bren. I could hear his voice as if he were here with me.

"Lune!" The leaves sighed and scattered, giving me up as an apparition with Bren's voice dropped next to me. "Oh, God, don't let her be dead," the apparition croaked. The ghost had warm fingers; they pressed into my neck. A gusty sigh burst across my cheek, the heat of it mildly surprising. "Thank the heavens. Hold on, little bird, hold on."

As solid arms slid under my body, I became unhinged, not knowing dreams from reality. It was too much. The world and apparition disappeared.

"...it has to come out."

I awoke to fire licking my bones.

A scream burned its way past my windpipe. I thrashed around, desperately seeking escape from the white-hot pain, but my body was tightly bound. I writhed and shook with ice cold fear. Heavy pressure was applied to the stab wound site and I groaned loudly. Someone was finishing the job. I was being murdered.

"I'm so sorry, little bird. It couldn't wait any longer. The wound needs to be cleaned and stitched before you lose any more blood."

I stopped thrashing.

The familiar voice was a balm, easing the weight of my fear, though my body still trembled with cold and fatigue. I cracked open swollen eyes and drank in his strong features. He looked like an angel. Maybe I was dead after all and Bren had carried me to Heaven.

He thrust a cup into my line of sight. "Try to drink it all. You'll need it."

It took several tries to dislodge an arm from the blanket wrapped around me, but I managed, lifting the cup to my nose with weak fingers. The aroma of dirt and bark wafted up my nostrils and I cringed. I changed my mind—Bren wasn't an angel. No angel would force their charge to drink stinky tree bark tea. My lips puckered as I choked down the repulsive liquid.

When I finished, he took the cup from me and I rested my cheek on the bed again, bone weary. He renewed pressure on the wound and I bit off a whimper. "What happened?" he asked.

"Went looking for you," I mumbled. His hand twitched on my back and I rephrased. "Sleepwalked. Got stabbed."

A low growl rumbled through the room and I stiffened. Abruptly, the growl cut off and Bren shifted on the bed, his thigh brushing against my hip bone. My muscles unwound as warmth seeped through the blanket and into my chilled skin. He was warmer than any blanket.

"I'll find whoever did this to you, Lune. I'll find them and make them pay—"

"No," I interrupted weakly. "Don't." He didn't understand how things worked in this city. Whoever had tried to kill me no doubt had allies. We were highly outnumbered, and I knew Renold wouldn't step in. He had taught me to stand on my own, to never show weakness. The more Bren helped me, the harder it would be to face the Trials. "Just . . . don't."

I expected him to argue, to press the issue, but he didn't. He remained quiet for several long moments, the heat from his body thawing mine.

"When you didn't show up at the stables this morning,

Asher knew something was wrong. He said only sickness would keep you away. And when I didn't find you in your room, I went out looking." He paused. His swallow was loud in the silence. "I thought . . . When I found you face down with a blade sticking out of your back, I—" His heavy sigh stirred something within my chest.

It was my turn to swallow. "Thank you. For finding me."

The tightness around his eyes softened. "Always."

A corner of my mouth curled, then I was drifting on a cloud of sleepiness.

"Hold on there, sleepyhead," he said. Surprised, I popped my eyes open. His gaze held an apology. "The wound needs cleaning and stitches, so I'll need to . . ."

Oh.

My eyes gradually widened in horror. My back. My . . . scars.

I was frozen with indecision, almost demanding he take me to the infirmary for further treatment, but he would suspect. Ask questions. I was trapped. My heart rate jackknifed as my body vibrated with the need to flee. Bren's expression morphed to bewilderment, a line bisecting his brows. He opened his mouth and I quickly cleared my throat, cutting him off. "Yeah. Just give me a second."

My arm wobbled crazily as I propped myself on an elbow, then loosened the front laces of my filthy nightshirt. I felt a moment of relief at the sight. At least Bren hadn't tried to dress me in clean clothing. The task of lowering the material over my shoulder proved to be too much. My arms shook so hard, the action agitated my wound and I hissed through clenched teeth.

Bren's gentle fingers stilled my attempts. He helped

lower me to the mattress once more, then ever-so-carefully peeled the bloody shirt from my skin. I didn't blink, move, or breathe. I waited in agony for the inevitable moment. I'd rather endure another stabbing than this acute torture. As cool air touched ravaged skin, I heard his sharp inhale and wanted to die a thousand cruel deaths.

A nasty little voice jeered in my ear. *You are ugly. You are damaged. You are weak. You aren't good enough. You're a failure.*

Shame dug its unforgiving talons into my chest and twisted maliciously. Without mercy, I sank my teeth into my lip and concentrated on the biting pain. It was better than crying. I would *not* cry.

And then, with the softest touch imaginable, he trailed his fingers down my shoulder and feathered them along my spine, exposing more and more flaws as he went. The infinite care was overwhelming, and my eyes ached hotly. No amount of lip-biting could keep the burn at bay.

"What has been done to you? *Victus est cor meum.*"

It was the hushed, broken tones that did me in. I buried my face in the mattress and released a flood of tears. Drowning in them seemed like a kindness after this humiliation. It wasn't just my back he exposed but my very soul, my deepest insecurities laid bare. I quivered at how completely vulnerable I felt.

He brushed aside clumps of stringy hair, revealing the side of my face, and I peered past the cleared gap before I could think better of it. That's when I saw Bren's face, so near my own that I hiccupped in surprise. His expression held so much sadness, my eyes welled with more tears. He closed his, as if my pain was too much for him, then leaned

203

forward, pressing his forehead to mine.

Lyrical words like soft music spilled from his lips, and though I didn't recognize them, their meaning was clear. He cared. Well and truly cared. It wasn't pity he now showed me, but more like . . . understanding, as if my abuse were his. He radiated mournful sorrow.

An incessant urge to comfort him stole over me and I reached out, needing more contact. I touched his cheek, which was both soft and hard, half-covered in prickly stubble. I almost pulled away, shocked at my boldness, but the rough texture beneath my fingertips fascinated me. I explored his jaw, which was smoother than it looked. I expected the muscles to be as rigid as rock after all the jaw-flexing he did.

My eyes had drifted shut and I slowly opened them to find Bren watching me. My throat closed. A bare inch separated our faces. His free hand slid across the mattress and captured mine, encasing it in warmth. Normally I'd feel out-of-my-mind uncomfortable at the intimate position I found myself in, but the way he was looking at me, the way his thumb swept across my knuckles . . .

I was hypnotized.

"I want you to remember something very important, Lune. Your scars are beautiful. *You* are beautiful, and not just on the outside. Your scars have made you strong—so strong. And that's what I see. Strength."

Somehow, I still possessed tears in my body. They re-newed their trek down my face, further dampening the mattress. But I didn't have words, not after what he had just said. They filled me, uplifted me, consumed me completely. And I knew like I knew my deepest secret that he had meant every word.

His eyes further intensified, as if by doing so I would believe the sentiments the same way he did. That I was beautiful and strong.

But right now, I just felt weak, weaker than I'd ever felt before. My lids pulled shut again.

Bren chuckled and moved his face away from mine, taking the heat with him. I frowned. "Now, let's put that strength to the test one more time today, shall we? It's time to stitch you up."

"Don't poke me in the eye with the needle and I'll do just fine, Doc," I mumbled. A question niggled at the edge of my mind and I spoke it before I forgot. "How did you even find me? It should have taken you days, not hours. There's miles and miles of forest to get lost in."

I couldn't see his face anymore, so when he answered, "Just lucky, I guess," I had more questions than ever.

18

WHATEVER HAPPENS

Somewhere behind me, Bren's voice rumbled, "You opened it again." No, more like grumped.

"So?" I tossed back, knowing it would rile him up.

"There's blood soaking through your shirt. Come here, I'll tape it closed."

"I don't have time." I performed another lunge, ignoring the dull throb in my shoulder. "It'll stop bleeding on its own."

All was silent and I grinned. The calm before the storm. We had been dancing to this tune for the last three weeks as my injury healed. He was like a big mother hen.

I straightened and made to step into another lunge, but a tree sprouted right in front of me and I smacked into it. Oh, my mistake, the tree was actually a cranky Bren. My hands flashed to my hips and I stared him down. Well, more like stared him up. Did he grow another inch overnight? My brows lowered. "Get out of my way, Doc. I'll bite you if I have to."

His eyes glittered. "Try it. See what happens."

With that dare, my body temperature spiked. I ignored the heat as best I could, fingers digging into my hip bones. "Maybe I will," I taunted.

Warning, warning: playing with fire!

But I couldn't seem to stop. It was too much fun.

And then he lunged for me and a tiny shriek escaped my mouth, echoing in the near empty gym. He latched onto my arms and spun me around, marching me toward a deserted corner. A gaping trainee stopped lifting weights and I glared at him. He resumed his task. Bren plopped me into a metal chair, then went to retrieve a first aid kit.

My butt left the chair and he jabbed a finger at me. "Sit."

I hissed and he snickered.

As he got to work patching me up—again—a random thought popped out of my mouth. "So, what is your book about?"

Laughter startled me and I peered up at him.

"Sorry," he said, still chuckling. "You'll probably think I'm strange but it's a book of poetry. I guess you could say reading poems is a hobby of mine. But I'm sure you didn't catch the title because it's in Latin."

Poetry? Hobby? Latin? What gibberish is he speaking now?

I hoped my next question was safe enough. At the moment, I felt incredibly stupid. "So, the foreign words you sometimes say . . . they're Latin?"

"Mmmhmm. How about you? What do you do in your free time?"

My mind blanked. "Uh. I don't know." I decided not to tell him about the dangerous game I played with water. He'd probably think I was insane if he knew I tried to drown myself for fun.

"Huh." He readjusted my shirt and snapped the kit shut. "What if I helped you find a hobby once the Trials are over? You're bound to have some free time then."

The question rattled me—it was like submerging into ice water. The Trials were only two weeks away. That meant I had two weeks left before my life would change forever. Up until a couple months ago, all I could think about was leaving this place. But now . . .

My heart twisted violently, then I shot up from the chair.

"What's wrong?" Bren was instantly in front of me, searching my panic-stricken face. He reached for me but I shook my head, backing up a step. His brows knitted and I relented. He'd saved my life. The least I could do was give him an explanation of what was to come, even if it was vague at best.

"The Trials." I took a fortifying breath. "When the Trials are over, everything will change. I . . . I might not see you anymore." My heart gave another painful lurch.

He frowned and ran a hand along his neck, scratching it. "What do you mean? Do you think you'll fail and get assigned a menial job? That won't happen, Lune. You'll win, I know you will."

I groaned. "No, that's not what I meant. Don't you realize that we're supposed to be competing against each other? If we're assigned to contend in the same segment—and odds are we will—we can't *both* win."

"Actually, we can."

I stilled, a flare of warning tickling my spine. "How? That's not possible. There's only ever one winner per segment. The only possible way we could *both* win Title of Choice is if . . ."

Stars, he knows something.

He watched me carefully, jaw lightly flexing. Whatever he was about to say could drive a permanent wedge between us and he knew it. I prepared myself, fisting my hands and shifting my feet. His voice lowered, even though we had the corner to ourselves.

"I spoke with your father." Immediately, I stiffened and he jerked up a hand. "Hear me out. This was almost two months ago, the day before you decided you couldn't trust me anymore. I told him I couldn't compete against you, so I made a deal with him. We came to an agreement, and now you and I are assigned to different segments in all three Trials."

My breathing was too fast. I clenched and unclenched my fingers. Droplets of sweat peppered my forehead and upper lip. *Brendan Bearon, what have you done? And why didn't you tell me sooner?* I wanted to throttle him. Instead, I asked, "What was the deal?"

He looked away and sighed. "I can't tell you that. It's . . . confidential."

"Oh?" My heart thudded, and then a question I'd been meaning to ask him struck me like a lightning bolt. It was the question that had urged me out of bed and almost gotten me killed three weeks ago. My face simultaneously surged with blood and drained of it. I felt sick with dread. "Bren, why Tatum City? Why do all of this—signing contracts, the Trials, giving up the outside world. What does this city have to offer that the rest of the world doesn't?"

Who's pulling your strings?

This time he scrubbed both hands down his face and blew out a long breath. The conversation had formed a wall of tension between us and I feared it could never be breached. After several agonizing seconds, his eyes met mine. They were clear yet held a myriad of secrets.

Still, he answered me with deep sincerity. I just didn't know what to make of it. "Signing a Trial contract was the only way into this city. Not just one Trial, but all three. If I don't prove my worth in the Trials, I'll be sent to the outside again. But I'm not allowed to tell you why I'm here—like, I *physically* can't. I will tell you this, though: nothing is as it seems. It's not about what the city can offer. Renold has been planning something for decades and I'm—" He choked and rubbed at his throat, like it hurt him.

I could tell by the spark in his eyes that he wanted to say more, but wouldn't. Or . . . couldn't?

After a careful inhale, he continued. "The purpose of the Elite Trials isn't just to prove who is worthy of a new job title. They're so much more than that. But whatever happens, know that I am on your side. Whatever happens, please remember that."

Whatever happens. That was asking a lot, especially now that he had made a secret deal with the devil.

TALL, DARK, & PRETTY

The Elite Trials Winter Gala was a mockery.

This event was held in honor of the Trials contenders, the lesser. In actuality, the Gala was for the elites, a way to lord their social standing over those inferior to them—which was everyone. They flaunted their status and twittered behind devious hands, betting on the Trials. Several of them, as patrons, had a personal investment or two, and openly disputed amongst each other as to whose contender would win.

The Supreme Elite's daughters were required to attend the annual three-day-long Gala every year, to show their support of the Trials, of course. Every year I went, and every year I hid in a corner, making myself scarce. But I feared this year would be different.

Kara—my hairdresser—and Arlyn—my seamstress—fluttered about me with agitated hands as I stiffly stood before Rose's floor-length mirror. I was still in her old room, but I didn't care anymore. Soon, I told myself, I would leave behind all my city-accumulated possessions and begin anew.

Soon.

My stomach clenched with nerves.

Now that the Trials were finally here, my body had gone haywire. I picked at my food, too nauseated to eat. I was easily distracted, making poor decisions during training.

And I barely slept. For the past two nights, I had woken in the middle of my room with a knife in the air, poised to strike.

I shook my head as I envisioned how insane I must have looked.

"Hold still, Miss Lune."

"Sorry," I mumbled to Kara as her hands expertly weaved blue ribbon into my hair, forming a crown of braids atop my head. She looped the midnight satin into place and tied the ends off. A large golden comb was carefully positioned in front of the braid, just in case the crown effect wasn't conspicuous enough.

"Okay, you are ready. What do you think?" I glanced at my hairdresser in the mirror's reflection, noting the slight tremor in her voice. Odd. She was usually so calm and collected. What had her spooked?

My eyes dipped to the new dress I wore, by far the grandest ever made for me. It was blue, a deep pool of twinkling stars. The satin top fit like a second skin, restricting my breaths. The bodice pushed my breasts upward, exposing their curved tops. I not-so-subtly tugged at the material, but it wouldn't budge. Ugh. Capped sleeves covered my shoulders and, thankfully, the seamstress had formed a higher back on the dress, hiding my scars.

The two staff members had seen my scars, but they were both sworn to secrecy several years ago. I didn't know what Renold had said to them, but it must have been effective. There had never been rumors of the elite daughter's scars.

I peeked at my face, not used to seeing so much makeup on it. With dark kohl-rimmed eyes and full red lips, I appeared older. And I looked like an elite.

Invisible fingers gripped my throat.

I needed air.

"It's perfect," I somehow managed to say. "Thank you, Kara. And Arlyn, the dress is beautiful."

They both beamed at my reflection, as if up until this moment they had doubted their handiwork. The strange behavior only intensified my angst. The room shrunk and oxygen grew scarcer with each forced breath. As they gathered their supplies, I made my escape. The relief I felt was immediate.

One last time, I snuck to the fourth-floor observatory and climbed to my secret balcony. After tonight, I might never see this view again. Gone were the vibrant reds, oranges, and golds. The branches were barren spidery limbs reaching for a midnight sky. It had snowed recently, and the light powder covered every square inch of ground from here to the mountains.

A stiff breeze froze in my lungs and rustled the filmy layers of tulle on my skirt. Still, I breathed deeply, clearing my foggy brain. The air was crisp and deathly silent. I felt like an intruder.

My eyes closed, and I imagined my feet leaving the balcony as I rose above this prison where I didn't belong. Up and up my body ascended, until I shot like a star toward the distant mountain peaks. I aimed for the tallest one, feeling wild and free. My chest ached, not with cold, but with longing.

"Soon. Soon you will climb those mountains, and no wall will stop you."

———◯———

I followed the haunting strains of violin as if in a dream. The sound was trancelike; I floated on clouds. Music was a gift so rarely heard and I soaked in every note until my soul's ache was soothed.

"Announcing Miss Lune Tatum, contender in the Elite Trials." The head butler's firm monotone voice broke the spell, and I erased all traces of whimsy from my face.

"Thanks, Dobson," I murmured for his ears alone. "You finally remembered me. This pleases me so greatly, I might remember to name my first child after you. Wait, what's your name again?" His lip twitched, the most he ever reacted to my sarcasm. I supposed I would miss him a little when I left.

No, not really.

I swept into the long, rectangular room that was neglected but once a year. Pine garlands hung over the two roaring fireplaces and tall, warmly lit candelabras chased away the corner's shadows. Bodies were everywhere, bedecked in their family's or patron's colors—greens, reds, yellows and, of course, blues.

A cluster of blue mingled near one of the fireplaces, the fire's blaze reflecting off their golden accessories. As usual, several lesser elites mingled close by, eager for the Supreme Elite's notice. Sickening.

I hugged the outer wall where a row of French doors led to an impressive balcony overlooking the river and mountain range beyond. I wrapped a hand around one of the door's handles, nudging it open, where I planned to flee the stifling room and mingle with the outdoor chill. At least the full moon would keep me company.

But Dobson's dreary voice announced a newcomer and,

as he entered, the room and everyone in it became inconsequential. My hand slid to my side. His midnight blue, perfectly-tailored suit made him appear ten feet tall. He dwarfed those around him, who cast openly curious glances his way. Even from this distance, I could see the gold in his eyes as they scanned the length of the room, clearly on a mission, oblivious to everything else.

An elite's daughter attempted to snag his attention and he ignored her completely. Her bottom lip protruded as she flounced off. I snorted.

It was as though he could hear the soft sound I made over the music and chatter of a hundred voices, for his gaze found mine, and there it stayed. His eyes twinkled as if to say, *"Mission accomplished."* My breath caught. And then he was navigating the crowd without breaking eye contact and my stomach was doing strange things. He had always been handsome, but tonight? He was *beautiful.*

As he neared, his gaze finally left mine and I swallowed, relieved. But a second later, my skin flamed, wholly unprepared for the way he drank in every last inch of me. Bren stopped near enough that I could smell cedar soap and pine and the faint scent of leather on his clean-shaven skin. I wondered what his jaw would feel like now that it was free of stubble.

His throat bobbed, and I realized that I'd been staring like an idiot. But he was staring, too. Finally, slowly, he released a breath. *"Si iam mortuus est, ut et mori beatus vir."* When my brows ticked upward, his grin widened.

"Care to translate?" I asked.

He chuckled. "Nope. Although, I will say that it hurts to look on such deadly beauty, but the pain is worth it."

I flushed even hotter. How could I want to punch him and kiss him at the same time? Wait. My mind caught and analyzed the random thought. *Kiss? What do I know of kissing?* I had never wanted to kiss anyone before. But now . . . My face was probably the color of a raw beet. If I didn't stop imagining my lips pressed to his, I would melt into a puddle of wanton stupidity right here, right now.

Not going to happen.

A coy smile transformed my mouth and his eyes drifted to it. Stars above, he wasn't helping matters. "Forgive me for causing you such great pain. Perhaps I shall ease your suffering and leave." And I did just that. I managed one full step before his hand wrapped around my bicep and whirled me into his arms.

My breath hitched as every nerve-ending sprang awake.

His head lowered, those distracting lips near my ear. "Dance with me?"

I felt eyes on my back—they scrutinized, judged—but I was beginning to care less and less. What could they do to me, really? *They could take away your chance at freedom,* logic snapped. *They could take away everything!*

No. They couldn't take away everything. They couldn't take away this moment I so desperately wanted to know. And so, I replied, "Do I have a choice?"

"You always have a choice," he whispered. "You just have to be willing to fight for it."

Tiny pinpricks of shock skittered up my spine. I pulled back enough to see his smirking face. He knew he'd surprised me by quoting one of my sayings. Apparently, his hearing was as good as his night vision. I returned his smile with one of my own.

"Then yes, Mr. Bearon, I will dance with you."

I'd never been one for shyness but, when he took hold of my wrist and rested my hand on his shoulder, I tensed with the need to disappear. Not to avoid confrontation—more to escape the hailstorm of emotions pelting my sensitive skin. I broke eye contact, his gaze like an unfathomable abyss. It sought to devour me, body and soul, and I couldn't bear the onslaught.

He held my other hand in his. When his palm pressed into my lower back, nudging us closer, fluttering wings beat within my stomach. I'd never have imagined someone touching my scarred back could make me feel so wanted. So safe. My feet almost left the floor as we swayed into motion, easily finding our rhythm.

Even as we softly twirled, I inwardly reeled. How could this boy, this man, who was so wrong for me, feel so right? It seemed like yesterday that he had stolen my free will, but today he was stealing piece after piece of my heart. I was afraid he would take it all. Take everything until I couldn't picture life without him.

My poor heart beat triple-time. "You're ruining every-thing, Brendan Bearon," I blurted, not caring that my voice cracked under the pressure.

"I know." His response was so unexpected, I blinked up at him. Deep conflict waged war in his eyes but, under-neath it all, a longing glimmered dangerously bright. His hand squeezed mine. "I want to change things for good. But sometimes, for things to get better, they first have to get worse."

I couldn't decide if his statement was foreboding or hopeful. Maybe both. *Perhaps you can't have one without the other.*

Before I could think of a reply, a lilting voice spoke quite loudly behind Bren. "Lune, darling, you must stop hogging the new boy all to yourself. I mean, what would father say? I think it's time our newest citizen gets to socialize with the Supreme Elite's favorite daughter." She twittered as if making a joke. But she didn't make jokes—jokes were beneath her. She was the queen of thinly-veiled insults.

If it were anyone else, I would have ignored them, but Rose wasn't to be trifled with. Not now. Not when the first Trial was three days away. I couldn't afford a beating at this time. So, I stopped and faced her.

The triumphant smile she always wore reminded me now of an evil sea witch my mum had once told me about. In the story, the witch put a spell on a prince and lured him away, in the process breaking the heart of a red-haired mermaid girl. The poor girl watched helplessly as he walked out of her life without a single look back.

Rose continued smiling, waiting for me to make the introduction. Her shimmery blue gown rippled like the sea. My stomach tied itself into painful knots and I pressed a hand to my midsection. *Stars above, she really is the sea witch and plans to steal Bren away.* I wanted to laugh at the melodramatic thoughts, but they felt too real.

I relaxed my shoulders and pretended to be bored out of my mind, a favorite tactic of mine. She hated it. "Rose, I'm sure you remember meeting my student, Mr. Brendan Bearon, a few months back. Bren, this is my *younger* sister." She hated that, too. I smiled sweetly when her eyes narrowed.

But she quickly recovered and began her simpering act

on Bren. "It's a pleasure to be properly introduced, Brendan. Father has told me so much about you." She held out a hand as if giving him permission to kiss it. A lump welled in my throat and a faint snarl tickled my windpipe. I had a deep, dark desire to rip the perfectly curled hair from her scalp.

Bren's eyes widened. They ticked my way before refocusing on Rose. He took her hand and gave it a firm shake, smoothly releasing it as he said, "Interesting. He hasn't once mentioned you."

I hunched over in a fit of laughter that I unconvincingly turned into coughs. I covered my mouth in a vain attempt to silence the strange sounds. All the while, Rose seethed. But the fury was solely in her eyes; she was like her father in that way. Those swirling irises—the same umber color as her mother's—sliced into me like the sharpest of blades, flaying skin and muscle.

Snapping her gaze back to Bren, she tossed her hair and batted long lashes. "What a pity," Rose practically purred. "He's been so busy preparing for the Trials that it must have slipped his mind. Why don't I tell you all about myself while we dance?"

I almost lunged at her as adrenaline flooded my veins. My heart galloped in my chest as my body trembled with the effort to remain in control. She all but morphed into a hideous, cackling witch with grasping tentacles. I couldn't stop her from wrapping them around Bren and squeezing.

In this moment, I hated her with a fiery passion. The emotion boiled me alive and oozed out of my steaming pores. I reached for the monster, intent on strangling it, and smacked into a wall instead.

Confused, I blinked at the solid blue wall. I made to move around the obstacle and pursue the witch once more when it spoke. "Of course. Shall we?" But the wall wasn't speaking to me, and it was moving away, transforming into . . .

I couldn't breathe past the terrible ache in my chest. Bren held Rose's hand, leading her to the middle of the room. There, he took her in his arms and they danced. I was bleeding. I couldn't see it but, oh my stars, I could feel it. Blood leaked out of me and formed a puddle on that wretched dance floor. My eyes lowered to the carnage at my feet, but only found glistening wood.

I bolted.

And tripped. Stupid dress!

I grabbed fistfuls of the sparkly material, not caring if I wrinkled it. Colors dipped and whirled in a chaotic mess as I whipped by party-goers. My stomach clenched, threatening to hurl. I moved faster, desperate for the feel of winter air on my overheated skin.

An unforgiving force rammed into my shoulder, spinning me around, and I came face to face with the worst possible person. He wore a suit the color of pine needles, but it did nothing for his appearance—he would always be hideous to me. Those onyx eyes of his slunk downward until they brazenly slid over the tops of my breasts.

Now I *really* wanted to vomit, right onto his shiny shoes. I hardened my voice. "What do you want, Lars? I'm not in the mood."

His oily smile was full of hidden intent. "I would ask for a dance, but I don't think it would end well. Too bad, really." He shrugged, his attention again pulled downward. "Where were you off to in such a hurry? Where is your trusty lap-dog?" His gaze slipped over my shoulder and a second later, lit up in understanding. "Aaah." He drew out the word, finally focusing on my face. "Did he find a new lap?"

My fists shook with their need to punch him in all the areas it hurt most. "Shut your face. And get a life while you're at it. Or better yet, don't. Stay out of my business unless you're looking to lose a limb."

That dumb mouth of his fell open. I brushed past him, but he clamped onto my wrist. I hissed, cursing myself for not expecting it. His fingers squeezed and squeezed but I didn't react. I wouldn't give him the sadistic pleasure. "You small-minded, ignorant girl. You *are* my business. Soon you'll understand the extent of our connection. I can't wait to see the look on your face when that day comes." He let go and melted into the crowd.

My brain perked up at his mysterious and incredibly creepy words, but I slammed walls in place, blocking all thought. This moment was about feelings—foreign, scary, out-of-control feelings—sensations I had no idea what to do with.

Soon, my shoes sunk into wet snow and I was free of the toxic building. Already my heart beat a steadier rhythm as the cold infused my throbbing lungs. I wished the evening chill would infiltrate my heart and freeze it as well. The stupid thing wouldn't stop moping. At least, that's what I thought it was doing. It felt terrible, whatever this feeling was.

Why was I reacting this way? When did I care who Rose set her sights on? She was always flirting with boys and making a fool of herself. She'd done it for years. So, what about tonight had been different?

And then I pictured *his* hand holding hers and felt sick all over again. It was like my heart was ill. *Heartsick,* my mind whispered. But why? *Because he means something to you.* What? My mind remained silent, not having the answer. *I* didn't have the answer.

I was halfway down the stable's main aisle before realizing where I was. Instinctually, my body knew I could find a fragment of solace here. No equine heads greeted me. Most of the chargers were fast asleep. The air was quiet in here, warmer too. I filled my nose with thick hay and animal hide. My shoulders relaxed a notch.

With stiff hands, I collected a meat offering and unlatched the stall's half door, then I was crooning in Freedom's ear as she nibbled the treat. "Hi, sweet girl. Sorry I woke you. I just—" A small sigh escaped me. "I need someone to talk to and you're all I have. I feel so . . . so confused. And lost. My time here is coming to an end and—" This time a strangled choking noise cut off my words. Admitting feelings out loud was horrible. "There's this part of me now that doesn't want to go. But I must. I *have* to!"

Mum. I ached to see her smiling face again. Ached to feel her arms around me. Would she understand the strange feelings I was having? These feelings that clutched at my heartstrings and begged me to stay?

Panic beat against my chest. Why was this happening? Why *now*, with only days left before I either earned my freedom or died in the attempt? I didn't want this burden!

"What's wrong?"

I squeaked like a trapped rabbit, and Freedom yanked her head away from me. My heart settled back behind my sternum when I saw the intruder was only Asher. "You really need to stop sneaking up on me, Asher Donovan." I sniffled and wiped a sleeve under my runny nose. Gross.

He ignored the comment, carefully studying my face. "You breezed right by me. Didn't even hear when I called your name. Want to talk about what's troubling you?" He rested his forearms on the stall's half door.

"No. Yes. Ugh. I don't know how to talk about it. I'd be too embarrassed, anyway. It's stupid."

"Let me guess. *It* is tall, dark, and what girls probably consider pretty?"

I snorted. "Handsome."

"Ah, so you know who I'm referring to, then? Because your face is cherry red."

"Asher, stop. This is weird. Really, really weird. I'm not discussing boys with you."

He shrugged, smile dimming. "You know you can talk to me about anything, though, right? You're my best friend. And even if you spend all your time with 'tall, dark, and pretty,' that won't change."

I stared at him, my eyes round and unblinking. Then I burst into tears. Once I started, I couldn't stop. It was like my body had taken control of the off-switch. Life was cruel. How was I going to leave Asher behind? The unfairness of the situation had finally snuck up on me, and all I could do was weep uncontrollably. I'd never let anyone see me like this. I felt so lost.

"May I?"

Through bleary eyes, I saw that he had entered the stall. He held his arms out—an invitation. I'd never let him hold me in all these years. Not only would people get the wrong idea if we were caught, but I couldn't be weak like that. I was supposed to be strong, every moment of every day. He was never supposed to see this side of me.

But these were my last days with him.

I walked into his embrace, pressed my cheek to his shoulder, and he gently wrapped his arms around me. His thumb softly rubbed my back, and I didn't flinch away, even when I wanted to. But I needed this. I should have allowed him to comfort me years ago, when he was the only one who would talk to me without malice. Without judgement. With no expectations beyond friendship. I didn't deserve him. My tears soaked the fabric of his frayed shirt.

A sound, like a sharp inhale, snapped me back to reality. I jerked out of Asher's arms, swiftly wiping at my wet cheeks, and met Bren's shocked gaze. My mind blanked.

"Lune." His voice was reed thin. He cleared his throat, blinking rapidly, and looked everywhere but at me. "I should . . . I should go. Sorry to interrupt." He pivoted, his shoes clipping briskly on the cement.

He was gone before I could utter a word.

CHANGE OF PLANS

Blaming lack of verbal control on a bruised heart wasn't going to work.

I was in trouble. Like I-might-not-survive-the-night kind of trouble.

It was the second evening of the Winter Gala and I had just exited Rose's old room. My mind had been in a deep fog all day, consumed with thoughts of Asher and Bren. The look on Bren's face when he'd caught me in Asher's arms, like I'd betrayed him in some way . . . Had I? He wouldn't stoop so low as to report me, would he? Instead of mentally preparing for the Trials, my stupid brain wanted to focus on boys. So, my distracted self didn't notice the trap until it had already sprung.

The door to my childhood room whipped open and there she stood: Rose Tatum, killer of hopes and dreams.

"Oh, how beautiful!" she gushed. I blinked. She waved a hand at me. "The dress, of course."

Indeed. It wasn't the first time she had pulled that insult.

But the dress *was* beautiful, despite the color. I let my eyes travel down the royal blue confection. Gold-stitched leaves scrolled up my ribs and wrapped once around the long, pointed sleeves. The skirt was a large shiny bell that swayed when I moved. The scooped neckline was low but not low enough to display my assets like last night's dress, thank the stars. And tonight, my hair hung in loose curls, a single gold comb sweeping the tresses away from the left side of my face.

Her own dress flounced prettily as she hopped toward me and looped an arm through mine. I gawked. "This is perfect. Let's walk to the Gala together!" She practically dragged me down the hall. I felt her assessing eyes but kept a bland expression on the upcoming stairs. "So, Brendan is quite handsome, don't you think?"

Goosebumps pricked my arms and legs. I feigned a disinterested shrug. "Sure, I guess. If you don't mind neck cramps while looking up at him."

Rose ignored the last comment. "And so strong! My feet barely touched the floor as we danced last night." She sighed dramatically. "I think he likes me. We would make a beautiful couple. If he wins his Trials, he will be free to pursue a relationship with an elite." A pause, then, "You wouldn't mind if I showed an interest, right, Lune?"

My pulse thumped in my ears; my head grew heavy and full. I knew my calm facade was splintering under the pounding force. "Of course not. Why would I mind?" I inwardly cursed as my voice projected too much emotion.

She pulled on my arm until I stopped and faced her wicked smile. "Because I'm not stupid and I know you like him." Her cloying perfume further deadened my brain cells as she stepped so close our dresses crinkled against each other. "I may not be the Princess of the Trials like you are, wielding weapons of steel, but I will always be Princess of the Elites—perhaps someday Queen—and I have weapons of my own. You know I do. And right now, I want Brendan,

226

and you will *not* stand in my way."

At the threat, adrenaline shot through my veins. I bared my teeth. "He's not a toy, Rose. You can't steal something that's not yours to take. You think he *wants* a relationship with you?"

Her big eyes flashed at the bald insult. "Yes, he will, as long as you don't mess it up. I'll have Daddy talk to him. Make him understand what a perfect match we are."

I blanched. Before I could stop them, my fingers dug into her bicep. "You'd be a *terrible* match for him. Leave Renold out of your boy-toy fantasies. Bren doesn't deserve to be manipulated and embarrassed by the two of you."

Her drawn-out gasp was like a splash of ice water to my overheated veins. What had I just done? I'd lost all sense and allowed the conniving witch to wriggle past my defenses. With a twist of her lips, she broke free of my hold. "I'm surprised at you, Lune. You've said some treacherous things in the past, but this one is by far the worst. My only regret in all this is that I won't be there to witness your punishment."

As she whirled and descended the stairs in layers of undulating blue, I grasped the bannister with trembling hands.

What would my disloyal words cost me this time?

Staring at the crackling flames in the fireplace didn't ease the tension in the air. The orange flickering glow only reminded me of the people behind me, swaying and twirling to the music. Of Bren dancing with Rose. My nose scrunched up and I focused on Bren standing beside me instead. I opened my mouth to speak with him about last night, but I didn't know what to tell him. What could I say? Somehow, I had hurt him, but I wasn't sure why.

So, I ended up asking the dumbest thing possible. "Everything good?"

He scratched at his neck before answering, "Sure. Yeah, everything's fine." After a few more tense-filled moments, I let the matter drop. My mind was currently too full for such complex issues.

"You're awfully distracted tonight."

"Huh?" I snapped my gaze to his.

He cracked a faint grin. "You've been staring at the fireplace for the last three minutes, and," He brushed a thumb over my cheek, "you have whipped cream on your face." Then he licked his thumb.

My jaw slackened. Suddenly, the air was too hot. "Stop eating my food." The whisper was breathy. Ugh.

"But I'm hungry. And now I don't have to hunt down something to eat." He licked his thumb once more. And the old Bren was back.

I might have drooled a little in response. Pathetic. My body craved to be near his, and I didn't know what to do with myself. Everything felt awkward, my movements, my words. Everything. Something was happening to me and I knew that it was dangerous. Maybe more dangerous than the entirety of the Trials.

I was doomed.

"Miss Tatum, the Supreme Elite requires your presence. He said you'd know where to meet him." Dobson's inflectionless words beat holes into my sensitive skin and I cringed. Noting my nodded reply, he returned to his post.

Too soon. I wasn't ready. I would *never* be ready. Sweat

beaded on my forehead and slid down my rigid spine.

"What's wrong?"

I blinked sluggishly. "Huh?"

"Something's bothering you. What's going on?"

"Uh . . ." I set my sights on his suit coat, not willing to meet his eyes. Gold buttons shone in the fire's rippling light. "I have to go. I just . . . I have to—"

As I turned away, Bren wrapped a hand around mine and tugged. I followed blindly as he wove through the crowd and out of the stifling room. I hid behind his broad back, knowing my mask was cracking. Pieces of it pinged off the hardwood floor with each step. A shiver rocked my body and Bren's warm hand squeezed mine. My chin wobbled.

We descended into a shallow green pit. No, a garden. The Winter Garden. Lush, exotic plants swallowed us whole. I wanted to get lost in the labyrinth of flowering plants and trees, and never be found.

Bren tucked us underneath a weeping frond, hidden from prying eyes. "Look at me," he urged. I did, and I knew my mask was completely gone as his eyes widened. He reached for me, callused fingers sliding into the hair at the base of my neck. He bent down, our foreheads almost touching, and I didn't pull away. I needed his nearness like I needed fresh air. "What has you so afraid? Please let me help you."

My mouth opened and a squeak emerged. I was in so much trouble already. What was a little more? This could be a test, I was painfully aware of that, but what if Bren truly wanted to help? The weight of my darkest secret was a burden I no longer wanted to carry alone. Its ugliness shouldn't see the light, yet my lips shaped words never before shared with another.

"He's going to punish me. I said something I shouldn't have and—" I exhaled shakily. "It's going to be bad."

His expression changed. First concern, next confusion, then seething anger. I felt the loss of his hand as he jerked back a step. "That monster." A chill slid up and down my arms at the barely restrained rage. I'd never heard him speak with such utter contempt, and I quaked at the thought of that wrath directed at me. "This has gone on long enough. It ends *now*. Let's go, I'm coming with you."

He took my hand again and tugged me out of the green maze. "Bren, stop!" I ripped my hand free. "There's too much at stake. He can't know that I told you. Think of the Trials—think of our contracts!" I was pleading now. My head shook as my feet shuffled past him, my hands gesturing for him to step away. "I have to do this alone. Maybe this will be the last time and—"

"Haven't you been listening?" His eyes holding mine captive rivaled the sun for intensity. "When will you see that you're not *alone* anymore! I'm right here and I'm not going anywhere."

"How can I trust you? I don't even know why you're in this city or what Renold wants with you. I don't even know what you want with *me!*"

His fierce gaze softened, as did his voice. "I just want to *be* with you. It might be safer to go it alone, but I don't think you want that, little bird. And you don't have to. I'm here, even if I can't give you all the reasons why." He held out a hand. Waiting. Asking.

Hoping.

Doubts crawled to the recesses of my mind. My next act could cost me everything, but my hand betrayed all logic and reason and accepted his.

His teeth ground together. The grating noise wound my nerves tighter and tighter until I knew we couldn't enter the room of horrors in our current agitated state.

Nudging his arm, I directed him through a side door and into a dusty, shadow-filled room far enough away from *the* room to give me a sense of safety. Renold couldn't hear through walls, could he? It was deathly still, like a graveyard. Bren's teeth clacked together and I reached up, touching his flexing jaw. "It'll be okay," I breathed, allowing myself to explore. His face was smooth for once and the rough pads of my fingers slid toward his mouth.

His lips looked full, hard yet soft, like the rest of him. The longer I looked at his lips, the more I longed to feel them. What must it be like . . . ?

He caught my fingers with his. Exposing my palm, he bent down and pressed a kiss there, lingering. My stomach clenched; the rest of my muscles went limp. The tender gesture stirred awake a slumbering beast, one that sent pinpricks of awareness up my arm, spreading outward until my entire body tingled pleasantly.

"When we're in there, follow my lead. I won't let him harm you. Can you trust me with this?"

Trust.

Was he really asking me to trust him?

It was impossible to blindly trust a person shrouded in secrets. Right?

Trust him, my instincts implored—begged, even.

I nodded, my pulse spurring into a sickening spiral. "You'd better be real, Brendan Bearon."

"I am. I promise you, I am."

So, with his body shadowing my back, I opened the door at the end of the hallway.

Fingers laced behind him, Renold cut a solitary figure in the room's cold center. He turned as the door's hinges slightly creaked, and his cool gaze absorbed the length of me. His lips parted, then clamped shut as his attention snapped to the surprise guest. "Mr. Bearon, I wasn't expecting you. I only have need of my daughter. You may return to the Gala."

The big fool didn't heed Renold's subtle warning. Instead, he nudged me aside so my dress didn't obstruct the entrance, then closed the door behind us.

"With all due respect, sir, I can't do that. It would seem your daughter is in danger, her life threatened more than once these last couple of months. I believe someone wants her eliminated before she can contend in the Trials, so I have given her my protection."

A flush spread from my scalp to my toes. No. No, this was all wrong! Bren was screwing me over by painting me as a weak girl in need of a strong protector. Shame tore at my insides.

Renold sliced his eyes toward me, dicing me to pieces before speaking. "Is that so? The student is protecting the trainer? I raised you to be capable, to take your punches. Now you're letting someone do it for you?"

My fingers curled into twin balls; my chin jutted defiantly. "No, sir. I would never allow that. But . . . I'm not on my own anymore. I have someone in my corner."

The silence was a rod of writhing electricity. It pierced my skin.

And then Renold laughed, low and deep, each sound controlled, precise. "I'm beginning to understand now. With the amount of time you two have spent together, it's only natural that you'd form a bond, of sorts." He let the statement dangle in the air. My stomach dipped uncomfortably.

He stirred into motion and paced in front of us. "My eyes and ears informed me that you've been hiding something, Lune. A *big* something."

I swallowed and forced myself to look him in the eye.

"I didn't believe it at first. It seemed so . . . trivial. But my source is, shall we say, motivated. I'm afraid it's all too true that my daughter has an extreme fear of mutant beasts."

A cold sweat doused my body. I felt exposed. Betrayed. But by whom, I couldn't be sure. Bren shifted slightly, as if worried of where my mind was taking me.

"I'm assuming by your silence that this information isn't news to either of you. Perhaps you've bonded more than the contract rules allow?" He stopped pacing and cocked his head. "I've heard rumors . . ." I held my breath, waiting. Something very bad was about to happen. A smile crept onto his face, and it was the scariest thing I'd ever seen. "I believe the deal I made with Mr. Bearon needs to be amended. It's only fair. You break one of my rules and I change your contracts."

The blood in my face drained away.

"The deal still stands: you will not contend in the same Rasa Rowe or Faust Night segments. But you will now contend in the same Arcus Point segment. If you don't want to fight against my daughter, then you will fight *for* her, Mr. Bearon. It would seem she needs your protection against the beasts. Unless . . ." He rolled his gaze to mine, "she wants the win more than she wants the protection, in which case you are free to pursue the win for yourself. I wonder if my daughter will play the victim or become the victor. We shall see."

With a wave, he brought the meeting to an end. "Choose wisely. Your futures depend on it."

Dismissed, we shuffled out the door, the only sound a faint squeak of rusty hinges. I knew my feet were still attached because I moved down the hall and up the stairs, but I couldn't feel them. I couldn't feel much of anything.

Nothing.

I wanted to be nothing.

As I twisted the door handle toward temporary freedom and away from this oppressive house, Bren gently wound a hand around my left bicep. I stared at his fingers. So strong. So willing to protect. Or was that just a front? Had he been a part of this scheme all along, to control the outcome of the Trials?

"I won't be a victim, Bren." The words held no anger or bitterness, not even sadness. They were flat. Emotionless.

"I know," he said, drawing me to him. I stiffened and he froze. "Talk to me, Lune. Please."

"There's nothing to talk about. Only one of us can win Title of Choice now. Renold made sure of that. I . . . I need some fresh air."

"You really want to be alone? Let me come with you."

"If I had remained alone, none of this would have happened. But now that I *care,* the world is a million shades of gray. I—" A breath that sounded too much like a sob burst out of me. "I have to go. You have to let me go."

A swell of panic crashed into my chest. Emotions flooded back in a flash and I was drowning. My eyes whipped to his and I knew I'd made a mistake in looking. His expression was pure hurt. Agony. I couldn't breathe. With a weak yank, I slid the door open and stepped through.

I waited for the hand on my arm to pull me back, but those careful fingers released their hold, leaving a ring of cold in their wake.

I melted into the night.

LAST HOPE

He didn't come after me.

I should have felt relieved. But I didn't.

I saddled Freedom and led my charger from her stall. The stables were empty of human life. Good. I didn't want to see another face for the rest of the night, not even Asher's. I needed solace in the only friend who understood exactly how I felt right now.

I patted her bristly hide before swiftly mounting, the rich blue fabric of my dress like a cloud over her back. She took off at an even canter, eager for a late-night run. I let her instincts and the moonlight guide our way. The dress's thin sleeves did little to ward off the winter chill and, unfortunately, the cold seeping into my body ripped the last of the emotional numbness away.

I now felt the full extent of the night's treachery, and a sob knotted in my throat.

My prison master didn't deserve my tears. I bit the inside of my cheek until I drew blood, staving off the flood that threatened to gush from my eyes. How had it come to this? How had I let this place so thoroughly burrow beneath my skin and poison my veins? For a decade, I had been careful not to form strong attachments so that I could eventually leave this city with no regrets.

But now . . . now I regretted everything.

Bonding with Freedom.

Befriending Asher.

Protecting Iris.

Caring for . . . Bren.

The price of letting others in was pain. Because caring hurt. And I couldn't seem to stop. I cared more and more each day, giving away pieces of myself until my heart was scattered throughout this black city. Even if I did make it out, I wouldn't be leaving whole.

Freedom.

What was it, really?

The heady idea of it had kept me going, kept me fighting, when all I wanted to do was quit. But could I ever have total freedom when my heart wished for one thing and my body another? Freedom was almost within reach, but I'd never felt more trapped.

The splash of hooves against water and the river's rush colliding with Freedom's underbelly distracted me. But only for a moment. We were heading west toward the Arcus Point Trial site, where some of my greatest fears resided. I didn't change our course.

Anger, hot as acid, coursed through my veins. Anger at myself for fearing the beasts. Anger at the beasts for existing. Anger at the dangerous Trials. Anger at Renold for creating them.

Anger at Bren.

I wanted to scream into the night, too much of a coward to scream in Bren's face. *Who are you, Brendan Bearon, and what are you scheming? Why won't you tell me?* Because I wasn't a complete fool. I knew he was up to something—something bigger than the Trials. Whatever his end goal was, it wasn't the same as mine.

Seemingly out of nowhere, Arcus Point's glinting metal cage blocked our path and I yanked on the reins. Freedom skidded on the slick forest floor as I slipped from the saddle, less than gracefully. There was a loud rip, followed by a snap. A section of my gown fluttered to the snow-dusted ground. I felt a moment of guilt for being so careless with Arlyn's flawless masterpiece, but the dogged pressure in my chest smothered the feeling.

I approached the cage that would imprison me with several mutant monsters. A stupid idea formed. It promised a delusional sense of gratification and I grabbed ahold of the flickering hope with fisted hands. I loosened my fingers, surprised to find rocks resting on my palms. When had I gathered rocks?

Didn't matter.

A spark of adrenaline was all it took, then I was hurling rocks at my cage of death. The echoing clang of metal rang in my ears and, instead of backing away, I surged forward, searching for another rock. "I wish you didn't exist!" The words hurtled from my gut toward the structure, bouncing off harmlessly. I picked up another ice-encrusted rock and threw it. "I hate you!"

I threw rock after rock, sometimes sticks. Whatever I could get my hands on. The anger was a firebrand beneath my skin. Slowly the cage morphed and, in my mind's eye, Bren stood before me. I paused, wavering and unsure. Friend or foe? Protector or betrayer? The doubts crept in again, now that I would have to compete against him in a Trial. I knew he cared for me, but did he care enough to let me win?

Renewed anger snapped through me and I growled through clenched teeth as I pelted the cage all over again. Throwing and throwing until I mentally defeated Bren and a new image appeared.

Me.

My chest heaved for breath. I hiccupped on a sob. Bren, I could defeat. I couldn't trust him to protect me during the Arcus Point Trial. But me? I couldn't trust her most of all. And I needed to. I needed to trust my instincts, the very ones that betrayed me, if I was to ever escape this caged city and all the contending beasts prowling around my waning strength. My walls had lowered too much. Was it already too late to reinstate my defenses?

My arm lifted to throw another rock when another sound rose above my rage. I froze. My senses pricked. The sound . . . It was a scream.

Human.

The noise was followed by a savage roar. It flipped my anger to fear. The rock tumbled from my fingers. In a flash, I scrambled toward Freedom, plowing into her side before launching into the saddle. We plunged into the woods as I frantically groped for the dangling reins. A second roar spiked my adrenaline and I glanced back, convinced we were being chased by a demon.

I gasped as the shadows shifted, taking the shape of a tall form. Either my eyes were playing tricks on me or we were being pursued. With a tug on the reins, we veered right, away from civilization and safety. I told myself I was leading the beast to a secluded place where I could take it down and protect the village, but if I had indeed heard a human cry of pain, I was a hypocrite. A fake. I was running away again. In this moment, I hated myself and my crippling fear of beasts.

The panic grew as I realized I was weaponless.

Idiot!

No way could high-heeled shoes take on a beast.

We galloped and galloped.

"Stop running away," Bren's voice whispered to my mind. "Face your fears." Instead of gritting back anger at his reminder, I pressed my heels into Freedom's flanks even harder. And we ran. We ran and ran until we ran out of land.

Freedom huffed when I eventually yanked on her reins. She shook her head and nickered as her sides heaved. I could feel the power of her annoyance ripple through my body. I rubbed soothing patterns along her sweat-soaked shoulder while gathering my bearings.

The outer wall now loomed before us.

We changed course again and, this time, galloped alongside the thick slab of never-ending steel, giving the wall a wide berth. The power was always active and charged with so much electricity that it could stop a grown man's heart.

I'd seen this happen once. Five years ago, I had hid behind a bush as a man chopped down a tree. It crashed against the wall, branches draped over the very top. As soon as his boot touched the wood, he stiffened and fell, the high voltage traveling through the trunk's sap and into his body like lightning. He was dead before he hit the ground.

There was no escape.

Dimming hope demanded I try, anyway.

I searched for a hole, a flaw, anything. Like I always did. I was stupid to think I'd win all three Trials and make it out alive.

It felt like Freedom and I had traveled the city's perimeter for hours, scouring for a way outside the wall. I'd ceased caring if a beast was following our trail. Seeing those shadows transform into my nightmares must have been a trick of the moonlight. Or my grieving mind.

My fingers were fused to the reins, frozen stiff. My bones creaked with every jarring step—brittle, breakable. But I wouldn't stop. Couldn't. This was my last hope.

I was going to die in here, my heart and body ripped in two.

I had always known that death might claim me before I could attain freedom, but now it felt *real*. I had spent so many years training for the eventuality and, now that it was finally here, the weight was too much. Too heavy and suffocating. Too final. I couldn't breathe.

Something in me broke then and I finally stopped my heaving mount. My legs were two icicles and I fell as I dismounted, a layer of snow softening the impact. But it still sent dull stabs of pain throughout my shivering bones. My hands sunk into the glistening white fluff, oblivious to the wet cold, and I crawled toward the wall.

As I neared, closer than I'd ever dared before, slits in the wall's structure allowed teasing glimpses of the outside world. A keening, primal wail rolled from my mouth and shaped into vapor.

"Help!" I screamed. Desperate, I hunted for a sign of life beyond my prison. There must be *someone* out there. Someone brave enough to rescue a trapped soul. "Please, help!"

The broken pleas tore a sob from my throat. Then another. I was an insignificant blue speck against an endless field of white. My throat was raw, my chest was raw, but my heart . . . it bled.

"Mum," I whimpered. "Mum, I need you. I don't know how to—" The words hurt too much to speak. Tears dripped unnoticed into the snow.

But no one was going to rescue me. If I ever wanted to see home again and, more importantly, my mum, I would have to save myself.

THE REAL ME

In the fairytales, Mum always said a knight in shining armor would rescue the princess, and they'd live happily ever after. But I'd long ago given up hope of being saved. I had allowed myself a weak moment where, in my mind, Bren protected me from the beasts and let me claim the win. When that moment vanished, thoughts of death had consumed me. But I still had a chance. I could still earn Title of Choice and shock the entire city with what I truly wanted.

And so, after I'd picked myself up last night, I decided I was done running. Bren's words rung true. The Trials were my fate and I would face them. Life wasn't a fairytale. The princess needed to save herself, not cower in fear.

My newfound courage—or maybe it was just plain stupidity—urged me to do something daring. Reckless. Something I'd never done before. If I was going to fight in the Trials, I'd do so as the real me, Lune Avery—not Lune Tatum, adopted daughter of the Supreme Elite.

"Do you have access to gold fabric, Arlyn?"

The seamstress straightened from her bent position near my bed and nodded. She had just begun gathering supplies for my final Gala dress. The strain of threading together so many elaborate gowns while still attending her regular duties had aged her delicate face this week. Guilt niggled at me again, but I squashed it. This had to be done.

"Tonight, I need to stand out. Make a statement. Will you help me with this?"

The whites of her eyes grew and her fingers slightly trembled. Elites didn't ask the lesser for help. Ever. They demanded, but never asked. And maybe that was why she nodded her assent even as fear pinched her lips.

A single pair of eyes slid the length of me as I descended the spiral staircase, no doubt shocked at my appearance. My dress was a golden waterfall, refracting every light source that touched it. The material hugged my upper body and arms, flaring like a spray of foam when it reached my thighs. A complex knot of braids swept my hair atop my head, thin gold ribbon woven into the strands.

But those intent eyes lingered the longest on the leather cord. My hand crept toward it until the bear tooth was hidden by my fingers. I froze, six stairs from the bottom, my decision a scraping noose around my neck. Perhaps I'd been *too* daring.

Then he held out his hand, a hand I was growing accustomed to, a hand I still ached to depend upon. I knew I shouldn't. I teetered on the edge of something. Bren was asking me to make a stand with him. I just had to reach out and grab hold. And, stars above, I did.

Strong fingers engulfed mine, guiding me toward the floor, until inches separated us and I was looking up into eyes the color of my gown. A sense of rightness wrapped its arms around me and filled me with calming quiet. The

Trials were a battle I needed to face on my own but, right now, knowing that he cared for me despite everything, this was exactly where I should be. With him.

"I'm sorry," Bren said. I could still see lingering pain in his sorrowful expression.

"I'm sorry, too."

We didn't have to explain. Our secrets were many, our futures uncertain, but tonight—maybe just for tonight—we could lock it all up and be a girl and boy dancing the night away.

One step. I took one small step away from him, making for the Gala, when I knew he'd caught sight of the most scandalous part of the dress. "Lune Tatum." He gasped, then I was being propelled around the staircase to its underbelly where a private nook shielded us from view.

He whirled me around for a better look at my back, a small window illuminating the length of me. The dress was completely backless and exposed every scar that marred my skin. "It's Lune Avery, actually. I'm done with pretenses and expectations. Tonight, I'm just me. The real me."

His reaction wasn't what I'd presumed. I thought he'd order me to cover the scars or, at the very least, question my brash behavior. But he was silent. Except for his ragged breathing, like he'd just run a mile uphill. I peeked at him over my shoulder, curious. He looked like a man on the brink of losing control of something. A thrill zipped through me at the thought.

Bren noticed me watching him. His eyes held mine as he said, "Lune Avery, it is a pleasure to meet the real you." Hesitantly, he touched the back of my neck and, when I didn't pull away, his fingers lightly skimmed down the length of my spine. My eyelids drifted shut, the feeling over-whelming my ability to think. It was warm lightning under my skin. The currents exploded when his hand slid over my stomach and drew me to him. As my back met his chest, I melted, completely and utterly lost to the sensations.

This.

Maybe dying here would be worth it, if I could have this.

Tinkling laughter from above broke the spell and I quickly pulled away, my legs like a newborn foal's. A pair of elites descended the stairs and proceeded to the Gala. Bren sighed through his nose, frustrated, not hiding the fact that the interruption was unwanted.

I had the urge to laugh. We were precariously close to breaking all sorts of rules and, instead of panicking, I struggled to contain laughter. What had gotten into me? "We should go," I whispered, biting back an idiot grin. "We can't miss the last night of the Gala."

Air puffed from his cheeks. "Yeah. Let's go before I do something I'm not supposed to do." I arched a brow but he just smirked, then threw me a wink. Holy stars, we needed to leave. Now.

We entered the overflowing room together, arm in arm, my usual trepidation muted. Tonight, this city's taint couldn't touch me. Tonight, I was free to be me. Tomorrow held no promises and so I would live in this moment, con-sequences an afterthought in comparison to the challenges that awaited me.

A day from now, I could be dead.

Or Bren could be.

My arm brushed his as I leaned into him, seeking com-fort. He looked down at me, his smile a balm to my aching chest. Gasps, murmurs, and hissed whispers followed us across the room. My spine straightened as someone blurted, "Look at those scars!" The words whipped my back and I steeled myself against a cringe of shame.

"Dance with me?" Bren asked. All it took was three little words and shame lifted like fog giving way to sunlight. The soft whisper became the loudest sound in the room, absorbing my attention. "And this time I won't let anyone come between us."

The teasing note in his voice drew a shaky grin from me. "They couldn't even if they tried."

He drew me close and twirled us. I laughed, unable to help myself. I let the room disappear. The music ebbed and flowed like a meandering brook. Wrapped in his arms, I decided right then that I'd never felt safer. Maybe I was delusional to think so, but my heart didn't agree, as if it had found a home, at long last. The thought made my conflicted heart pump harder, and my fingers dug into his shoulder. The room spun; I felt dizzy.

Bren must have noticed my shift in mood. He leaned in close, his breath stirring wisps of my hair. "I think we should sneak away."

"Oh?" My pulse jumped. His nearness wasn't helping my equilibrium.

"Yeah. You up for it?"

A challenge. Of course he would extend a challenge.

I snorted. "Do you know me at all?"

Even though I couldn't see them, I knew his eyes were twinkling. "Follow me." He let go and faded from view. With a smirk, I lifted my skirt and followed.

He led me on a wild chase: through a side door, into the

bookless library, up a ladder to a secret passageway—wait, how did he know about this passage? I shrugged and continued. Would I ever learn the secrets of this mysterious boy? I trailed him down a little-used stairwell and out into the night. The brisk air slapped my face, stealing my breath. I stopped and silence greeted me.

"Bren?"

Arms grabbed me from behind and I squeaked, ramming my elbow into rock-hard abs. I whipped around, prepared to fight, only to find Bren doubled over with laughter.

I rolled my eyes. "Serves you right." I swept up a clod of snow and chucked it at his face. He ducked.

His mouth widened into a wolfish grin. "Careful now. Don't dish it if you can't take it."

We stared each other down, neither moving a muscle. Then in a flurry of motion, snow was spraying, a large chunk sliding down my neck, and I was laughing so hard I couldn't breathe. I backed up a step and his eyes narrowed wickedly. With a squeal, I hightailed it for the stables, as fast as heels would allow me. When I arrived, he was already there, leaning on a post just inside the double doors.

"What in the—" I wheezed, rubbing at a stitch in my side. "How did you—? You know what? Never mind."

He chuckled and pushed off the post, grabbing a bridle and saddle blanket on his way toward Stalin.

"Where are you going?" I followed, cautiously curious.

"You mean *we?*" He opened the stall and offered the mammoth beast a morsel of meat. "You'll see. Come here."

I rubbed at the goosebumps prickling my arms. "Um, I don't think that's such a good idea . . ."

He threw the blanket over Stalin's back then led him into

the aisle, halting next to me. Without a word, he removed his suit coat and draped it over my shoulders. Still gripping the lapels, he tugged me close and dipped his head until our faces were inches apart. I was now fully awake and quickly warming as his woodsy scent surrounded me.

I inhaled it greedily, barely restraining a groan that pushed against my lips.

"Better?" he asked.

"Huh?" I blinked dumbly.

He cracked an amused smile. "You looked cold," he said, untying his bowtie and tossing it aside.

The gesture made my mouth twitch. "Not anymore. I mean, yeah . . . thanks."

His smile grew at whatever had spewed out of my mouth. "You ready?"

I glanced at Stalin, then back at him. "Uh, no, not really. Do you see what I'm wearing? I can barely walk in it let alone straddle a charger."

He laughed loudly at that, probably envisioning the image I just gave him. "Come here." He crooked a finger and I backpedaled, leery of his intentions. But my dress-clad legs were no match for his. He ate up the distance in one stride and placed both hands on my waist. I was in the air and sitting astride the monstrous animal before I could utter a protest.

Not used to riding sidesaddle—especially without the saddle—I wriggled, seeking a somewhat secure position. "Next time warn me or I might accidentally throw a punch . . . or kick."

He looked up in mock terror. "Yes, ma'am."

I felt for the reins and grabbed hold. "Is there a reason

you left off the saddle or—" He swung onto Stalin's back before I could finish, shifting until I could feel the length of him along my side. Words fled my brain as he reached around me and plucked the reins from my limp fingers.

"So I could do this," he murmured into my hair.

I suppressed a shiver. Barely.

Bren clipped something large and bulky to his belt, a bag I hadn't noticed because I was too busy noticing him. "What's that?"

"You'll see." His lips quirked, and I rolled my eyes. The boy of too many secrets.

We left the stables and I squirmed, not knowing what to do with my body. His arm halted my movements as it wound around my waist, fitting me snuggly to his chest. I sighed, content to be near him and traveling away from the root of my troubles.

One night.

One night to be me.

I'd make it count.

Before I knew it, Antler Hill Village came into view, a soft yellow glow outlining its edges. Usually the village was pitch black this time of night from curfew. Finally, Bren explained, "I spoke with Asher earlier today. He mentioned the curfew was lifted one night a year in celebration of the Elite Trials. Thought we could make the celebration a bit more . . . enjoyable." He jiggled the bag, which I now guessed was packed with food stolen from the Tatum House kitchens.

I pressed my lips together, overwhelmed. He really was ruining everything.

Bren led Stalin to a small open stable, and somehow

250

supplied the beast with a sliver of meat. Did he stash it away in his pocket? I almost fell headfirst into the hay when my gown tangled up my graceless dismount, but Bren grasped my shoulders and set me upright. "Stupid dress," I muttered.

"I'm rather fond of that stupid dress," he practically purred in my ear.

A typical blush stained my cheeks. "You can have it then." Wait. But it was too late. Bren choked on a cough. "When I'm not wearing it, that is." He barked a laugh this time. "You know what? Never mind. I'm going to cut it into pieces."

I left him behind as he cackled like a lunatic. Was it hot out here?

The revelry was in full swing and, with the help of a violin and clapping hands, the entire Village Square was transformed into an undulating sea of dancing faces—most of them smiling. They had so little to celebrate but, for a few, this night could be the last of their misfortune. Tomorrow, a child or mother or father could win a Trial segment and change their family's future. And so, they celebrated, even if that loved one could very well fail or die instead.

Hope. They celebrated because of a sliver of hope.

"Whoa," Bren breathed next to me. I looked up in time to catch the awe in his expression. "I expected weeping and sad tales around the campfire. Not . . . this."

In that moment, I felt a touch of pride for these people. *My* people. Despite my efforts not to get close, not to get attached, *these* were my people—the hard workers who made up this village. "Those with less find joy in little things, Mr. Bearon."

He directed that awed expression my way and I plucked the heavy bag out of his hands, needing space from all that intensity. I went in search of Asher—he would never miss a chance to socialize. But I'd never been to this annual event before. Had never dared. And when several dozen heads finally turned my way, I doubted my recklessness. My heart sank as my eyes darted around. The murmurs and whispers grew in volume until the dancing and music slowed to a halt.

I stopped, my pulse pounding out of control as hundreds of faces gaped at me. Not in awe. No. In fear. I was, after all, the Supreme Elite's daughter. A threat to their way of life. An intruder. My throat closed.

The moment lasted an eternity. Then came the sound of scuffing feet. "Excuse me. Pardon me. Lune!" The familiar sight of blond messy hair, twinkling blue eyes, and deep dimples greeted me, and I started to breathe again. "I can't believe you came!" He laughed, completely oblivious to the tension surrounding us.

I thrust the bag at him, my tongue a useless lump. He took it with raised brows and quickly peered inside. Whistled. "You're an angel," he said, a little too loudly. "Let's share this with others. They should know who you really are, Lune." My lips parted. Tears pricked my eyes. I was going to miss him so much.

"It was Bren's idea, actually," I rasped, and cleared my throat. "He came too." I pointed to where I'd left him. Sure enough, he was still there, watching our exchange. Holy stars, his eyes were even *more* intense, if that were possible.

Asher snickered. Baffled, I met his gaze. "I think now would be a good time to dance."

"If you didn't notice, I kind of crashed the party. I don't think—"

But he wasn't listening. With a few whispered words, he passed the bag off to another villager. Then he yelled, "Hey, where's the music?"

Several people chuckled as they threw looks of adoration his way. Someone clapped their hands to an invisible beat, and soon more joined in. It was as if they were accepting me as one of them. A tear slipped down my cheek.

"This isn't a night for crying, Lune. This is a night for celebrating." Asher offered me his hand, eyes alight with merriment. I held back a laugh as I shrugged off Bren's coat and tossed it onto a nearby table. When I placed my hand in Asher's, he all but jerked me off my feet. The dance moves were fast and frenzied as we kept pace with the tempo, twisting and twirling. My skirt flared like a child's spinning top.

Finally, a laugh burst out of me and I let myself go. Soon we were but two bodies in a tangle of dancers, weaving, stomping, and clapping to the music. The pins in my hair popped loose and I shook my tresses free, letting them float down my back. It hit me then: I hadn't heard a single judgmental whisper about my scars.

Iris joined us and I squealed. Literally squealed like a little girl. She beamed up at me and I decided my odd behavior was worth it if I could put such a large smile on her face. "You look like a princess," she said, her hazel eyes round with wonder. And for once, I didn't flinch at the word.

I DARE YOU

I didn't know how long we danced.

Long enough for my feet to hurt. If this was to be my last night on earth, at least I had spent it as me, not the closed-off human being I had been for several long years. Maybe this was a taste of what freedom should be.

My eyes searched the shifting crowd for Bren, wondering if a village girl had pulled him in for a dance. The thought dampened my mood and I slowed. I came to an abrupt stop when I finally found him. He was still standing where I had left him, and . . . his eyes were on me. Air stalled in my lungs.

"I did the best I could. Now it's up to you, Lune," Asher said, slightly winded. He and Iris watched me watching Bren, and from my peripheral, I could see they wore matching grins. What was going on? Asher nudged my shoulder with his own. "Go. You'll never find that peace you're always searching for if you don't give this a chance."

My eyes flew to his.

He smiled softly, dimples winking. "I see you, remember? Now go. He already left."

I jerked my gaze back to where Bren had been standing and, sure enough, the spot was empty. Swiftly, I dodged twirling limbs and fancy footwork as I snatched up Bren's coat, then slung it over my shoulders. My heels slowed me down once I hit snow, but I pressed on.

He was almost to Stalin by the time I caught up with him. "Bren!" He froze. I was completely out of breath at this point. I heaved in mouthfuls of the cold, still air. "Were you going to leave me stranded here? If you say yes, these shoes are going to magically sprout wings and smack into your face."

I was teasing, still hyped up on adrenaline, but when he turned around, his expression was pained. He tried to smile and failed. "No, I would never leave you in such dire straits. What kind of gentleman would do such a thing?" He meant to be funny, but the words came out flat, strained. "I just thought it would be best if I waited for you here, that's all."

"Oh." I blinked. My adrenaline nose-dived.

His jaw muscles bunched, and he looked away. "So, you and Asher?"

I blinked again, not comprehending. "Huh? Asher and I, what?"

He sighed, like he was agitated, and met my confused stare. His lips thinned, and then he blurted, "You like him?"

My brows pulled together. "He's my best friend. Of course I do. What's going on, Bren?"

"Best friend," he repeated under his breath, yanking a hand through his hair. Dark strands fell over his forehead. "And what about me?"

My stomach flipped at the bold question. "I . . . I . . ." I was tongue-tied. And apparently struck stupid.

I was still reeling when he reached for me. I squeaked when he lifted me onto Stalin's back. My foot itched to give him a swift kick for startling me yet again. "Come on, we have one more stop for the night," he said, swinging up behind me and nudging Stalin into a trot before I was fully seated. Bren secured an arm around me, but this time my back was stiff against his chest. Where were we going? Why was he acting this way?

After several minutes of meandering southwest in complete silence, we found ourselves at the river, the full moon glinting off its surface in never-ceasing ripples. Bren flicked the reins and Stalin's hooves dove into the frigid depths. I lurched forward with a gasp. Bren's arm tightened, keeping me from tumbling head first from the charger. "Don't worry, I've got you. I won't let you fall."

I raised my feet and watched as the tips of my shoes skimmed the water's surface. "It's not the fall I'm worried about. I'm wondering if I head-butted you one too many times because the Bren I know wouldn't willingly cross a freezing river. You do realize we passed a bridge a few minutes ago?"

His chest rumbled against my back as he laughed softly. I relaxed a little. "I'll explain when we get to the other side."

"You mean *if?*" I had an evil desire to grab the reins and create a storm of chaos, just for the fun of it. Maybe it would shake him out of this strange mood he was in.

He growled, low and menacing. "Don't you dare."

I held in laughter, but the need was strong. "If I recall," I drew out the last word, "you failed to heed my warning when I told you not to dare, so it's only fair that I return the favor."

Bren nudged Stalin into a faster clip. I snickered as we climbed the opposite bank and onto solid ground. We stopped in a small clearing near the river's edge and Bren slid down, shoes crunching in the snow. And then he peered up at me, hands lifted as if to break my fall.

I went still.

His mouth tipped sardonically and he waited, a clear challenge on his face, daring me to trust him. What game was he playing at now? I almost jumped down on my own. Almost.

But I found myself accepting his help. My hands left the blanket and rested on his shoulders and, when I leaned forward, he grasped my waist and eased me toward him until my body brushed down his. I swallowed loudly as heat pooled in my veins. When my shoes sunk into powdery snow, neither of us made a move to separate.

Bren's expression changed then. The lost look from earlier was gone, and in its place . . . My stomach fluttered at that look of want.

His lips parted and my eyes gravitated to them. "You have a cruel sense of humor, little bird."

I didn't know what he was talking about. Was there something funny about this moment? I swallowed again, with difficulty. "You're the one being cruel right now."

Did I just say that out loud?

He smiled, slowly. *I think I just died.*

"My apologies, ma'am."

He dropped his hands and put space between us. I wanted to pout. Pout? Inwardly, I rolled my eyes at myself. To appear natural, I busied my hands with pulling Bren's coat around me, and then resisted the urge to sniff it.

Thank the moon and stars, thoughts can't be heard.

"This is where it all started, you know," he said, sweeping an arm out. I glanced around the clearing, once more confused at the topic change. "This is where you first made me face my fear of water. This is where I first heard you laugh—a *real* laugh—deep and unchecked and . . . perfect. That moment, I knew I'd do just about anything to hear that *perfect* sound again."

As he spoke, I noticed the rock where I had sat to empty my boots of water after our fall into the river, the stone now buried in crusted snow. That day seemed so long ago, when my heart had been full of anger and bitterness.

And now . . .

He approached me again, this time from behind. I didn't flinch, didn't stiffen in fright like I normally would. With a shock, I realized that somewhere along the way, I had stopped reacting negatively to his presence at my back. My heart lurched. I knew he was close, warmth radiating from him like a furnace, and I leaned backward, my head connecting with his shoulder. His arm slid around me, securing me to him.

Home, my heart purred. I couldn't breathe.

"You've changed me." His voice rippled pleasantly against my skin. "I'm not the same person I was when I first entered this city. Your strength makes me want to be stronger—and not just for myself. For *you*. And so, crossing this river tonight was no big deal because I have you here with me. You give me the courage to face obstacles I would normally run from."

My chin quivered. I could tell he believed each and every one of those words, and I felt . . . humbled, yet empowered. I twisted in his arms, his face inches from mine. I didn't know if I was capable of speech in this moment, but I tried anyway. For him.

"I'm not the same either. I used to hate you, and now . . . I—I don't know if I can do this without you. Maybe that makes me weak, but—"

He interrupted, shaking his head. "It doesn't. You've faced your fears again and again. Lune Avery, you are the bravest soul I've ever met. You don't need me. If you wanted, you could tame this river or make it boil."

I laughed, heart swelling. But a second later, my smile faltered. "You're wrong about one thing. I *do* need you. And the thought of you dying in the Trials—" My breath hitched, pulse beating frantically in my chest. What if this was our last night together? What if he never held me in his arms again? What if he—What if, after everything we'd been through, I lost him?

With death lingering in the shadows, greedy for our blood, I pushed upward and held his head in my hands before I could talk myself out of it. "You can't die, Brendan Bearon," I whispered fiercely. "You just can't."

His eyes swirled, reflecting the moonlight. "I won't. I swear I won't. Just as long as you don't. Because if you died, I . . . I'll never—" His voice quavered to a halt, and my heart hurt at the heaviness in his words. His nostrils flared as his gaze ran over my face, memorizing, searching. It stopped on my mouth and stayed there. "Dare me."

I blinked. "What?"

His throat bobbed as he repeated, "I need you to dare me."

"Um. Okay. I . . . dare you?"

"Thanks," he breathed.

Then his lips ever so softly touched mine.

I froze, eyes wide. My brain short-circuited, not

knowing what to do. I hadn't even seen him bend down. The soft pressure lingered, begging me to accept, to respond. I trembled but held still, afraid that if I wrenched away then I would disappear for good. And as the warmth of his skin seeped into mine, I felt only one thing: a bone-deep ache for more.

I let my lips move against his, kissing him back, and my eyes finally drifted shut. A breathy groan left his mouth and my insides reacted, fluttering, flipping. My fingers scraped along his jaw and entwined behind his neck. His skin was smooth, softer than silk.

I pressed my body closer to his.

A chill hit my back as Bren's coat fell from my shoulders. A moment later, his palm set my lower spine ablaze, drawing me closer still. It was hard to tell where I ended and he began as he curled his body to mold against mine, and I marveled at the feeling. His other hand fisted my hair, tilting my head. Our kiss deepened.

Fire lit every nerve ending.

I might have whimpered as his full lips devoured mine, like a man starving. I might have attacked his lips with equal fervor, desperate to be close, closer. I might have gotten a little carried away and sucked his bottom lip into my mouth. And bit it.

He jerked, then stilled. My heart thundered harder than it ever had before.

Loosing a growl, he shuffled me backward until rough bark pricked my shoulder blades. The needling pain only enhanced my ache for him. I whispered his name and his body pinned me against the tree as my knees gave way. He was the only thing keeping me upright.

I thought I couldn't feel any more than I did now, but that was before he bit me back.

The noise I gasped into his mouth should have embarrassed me. Should have, but didn't. I was lighter than air, yet I knew I was drowning. And I never wanted to break the surface. When his tongue ran along the bite mark on my lower lip, soothing the slight ache, my blood ignited with a roar.

I needed to taste him, *consume* him. I was burning up.

But his lips left mine. He leaned back slightly, sucking in air.

I felt robbed and almost whined, like a puppy denied a treat.

His chest rose and fell sharply, working as hard as mine. I must have forgotten to breathe the last couple of minutes. I could have lasted longer . . .

"I guess that answers my earlier question," he panted. His forehead thunked against the tree.

All was silent except for our loud breaths. Then I started to laugh—or maybe I was crying. So unaccustomed to these feelings, my body reacted all at once. Emotions flowed out of me in the form of tears, trickling faster and faster when I realized that, for once, they weren't tears of pain or rage or sadness.

Here in this prison, with a boy who should be my enemy but wasn't, I had found real happiness.

THE ELITE TRIALS

I expected to feel regret about last night.

But I didn't. I felt liberated, like I had made a decision for me, come what may. Burn the consequences. Reckless thoughts, but I couldn't stop myself from thinking them. Maybe I had truly snapped this time.

I had slept remarkably well, all things considered. Maybe the fact that I'd used Bren's pilfered coat as a pillow had something to do with it. His scent had wrapped me in a cocoon, staving off the usual nightmares. He would never see that coat again.

Today was the beginning of the end. The start of something I had waited eleven torturous years for.

The Elite Trials.

Blood would spill this day. Lives would be lost.

Maybe my own. I was finally ready to face that all-too-real possibility, but my mouth still went dry at the thought.

The Trials were split up into four days—Rasa Rowe on the first, Faust Night on the second and third because of its many contenders, and Arcus Point on the fourth. There were only two segments, each consisting of seven contenders, on this bitter cold day. I could barely feel my toes or my nose; my fists were jammed into my armpits for warmth. A lock of hair tickled my cheek but I left it there, too cold to care.

Many years ago, I had dared to ask Renold why he'd created the Elite Trials to take place in the winter. Thinking the question impertinent, he had whipped me. But while doing so, he explained that the contender's and even the audience's comfort was irrelevant. One of the Trial goals was strength, and overcoming the elements was the ultimate test of a person's endurance.

The path to greatness required pain.

Fourteen lives were about to change today, for better or worse. Mostly for worse. My Trial wasn't until later this afternoon, but my nerves were currently firing on all cylinders as I waited for Bren's Trial to start. It was then I felt rather than saw a presence materialize a little behind and to the right of me. I should be safe here, surrounded by thousands of onlookers, but a well-placed knife stab to the ribs in the middle of a crowd would cause just as much damage as one delivered in an isolated stretch of woods.

I searched for the source of my unease and locked my sights on steely blue trapped in rings of shifting black. Ryker. I inwardly shuddered. His watchful eyes never failed to unnerve me.

My brows lifted, and I peeked at his striking tattoo before I could stop myself. Finally, his neck was at the right angle for me to clearly see the design: a black crescent moon with three slashes through it, like claw marks. Ominous, but strangely beautiful. My tone was flat as I said, "Am I in your way?"

He settled his frame at the railing next to me and I locked my knees, refusing to broaden the gap between us despite my instincts screaming at me to do so. With a grunt, he replied, "Not at the moment. But when we're on that track, keep your distance."

"*We?*" My brows became soaring eagles above my head.

He huffed softly, but it was loud with annoyance. "Your shortsightedness will get you killed someday. First rule of survival: always know who your enemy is. Second rule: know where they eat, breathe, and sleep. You'd know that I'm contending in this Trial if you paid attention to detail."

My jaw hit the concrete slab beneath my boots. Was he for real? I could feel the snark sliding out, thick and decadent, reserved for the extra dim-witted. "And what's the third rule? Know what your enemy's favorite dessert is and stick a razor blade in it? Wait, that might not be subtle enough. Maybe glass? Poison?"

Ryker was facing me fully now, looking for all the world like I had given him the gravest of insults, worse than a spit to the face. I stared back, waiting for a response in mock expectancy. He snorted and a muscle in his jaw feathered. "I don't know how you survived this long with a forked tongue like that."

I laughed, but there was nothing funny about this moment. "I compensate for it in other ways. And I *do* pay attention to detail. A fork would make a great weapon."

He stopped talking to me after that, exactly what I had been hoping for. Holding a conversation with him was worse than facing off against the Smart Bot while a gaggle of trainees jeered and cat-called. A staccato beat, fast and sharp, drowned out the chattering voices in the high-rise stands. With each passing second, it tripped faster and faster, like a runaway heartbeat. Thousands of bodies stilled as elites of all classes, dressed to impress, slapped their left shoulders with their right hands, and then thrust their right arms straight, palms facing outward.

The sign of loyalty to the Supreme Elite.

All of them, except for the elite-born, had stood down here in the lower stands at one point in their lives, fighting for the position they now clutched with viselike fingers. But having risen above, quite literally, they now regarded everyone beneath them with disdain. We were but entertainment, something to mock and wager against. Some cast curious glances my direction, but quickly looked away.

I smirked. To me *they* were the entertainment. Too self-important to realize how shallow and desperate they were.

The drums trilled now, announcing the creator of the Trials. Above the stands, Renold appeared at the open window of his special glass viewing box, Rose and his wife Blanca a little behind and to either side of him. Clasped to his shoulders was a knee-length midnight blue cape he wore but once a year for the Trials, a gold lion's head stitched between his shoulder blades.

He raised his hands. The drums ceased. The only noise was the snapping of white Rasa Rowe flags, a black charger head insignia on each one. Sapphire and gold glinted on Renold's fingers, the rings catching the morning light. Then, with the aid of a voice amplifier, he began his speech, the speech he gave every year. "Citizens of Tatum City, it is my honor to bestow the annual Elite Trials upon you all! Every year, many of our brave citizens train for the Trials, knowing that only through them can they earn a better life. These contenders before you today fight for an esteemed title, one worth dying for. Depending on their personal skills and Trial wins this week, they could become our next guards, trainers, doctors, or advisers."

He spread his arms wide. "And let's not forget: two Trial wins earns you the coveted title of Elite!"

All around me, a chorus of cheers swelled. I remained tight-lipped, hands squeezing the rail.

"But this year," Renold cut off the noise, "is unlike any we've had before. We have not one, but *two* contenders competing in all three Trials for the ultimate prize!" There was a collective gasp as many had not caught wind of the news before this moment. "Since the start of the Trials thirty-one years ago, no one has won all three Trials. Sadly, no one has earned the right to choose their own destiny."

He paused—for effect, no doubt. Shifting feet and low murmurs followed his last statement. The fact that no one had beaten the Trials in their entirety was a sore point for this city. But no one spoke above a whisper, waiting in obedience for Renold's final words like well-trained dogs. His voice thundered as he asked no one in particular, "Do you think one or both of these contenders will earn Title of Choice this year?"

The explosion of noise rocked my body. But it was his question that weakened my knees. *Both?* Why did he word it that way? Was it to fuel the flames of hope? It was false and it was cruel. Renold's gaze flicked to mine, just long enough to send a message. One that sent liquid ice spurting through my veins. He was aware that I knew his words were a setup. And he commanded me to keep my mouth shut.

His eyes released mine and my shoulders uncoiled their rigid hold. He crossed an arm over his chest, then thrust it out, spurring the Trials into motion. Automatically, the citizens mimicked the action, including myself. Loyalty. He demanded it. "Speed. Strength. Precision," he shouted. The crowd loudly echoed the Trials motto. "First contender to cross the finish line wins!"

The roar of the masses was a dull thrum in my ears, as if they were underneath water—or I was.

From my perch, I watched Bren and Stalin enter the Rasa Rowe Trial track. They were formidable, a dark wall of muscle and tightly-reined energy. Yet out of the three Trials, this one had me most worried—not for myself, but for him. They were fast, and suitably paired, but could they keep up with the others?

I realized I was rooting for him, an oxymoron if there ever was one. He alone posed the greatest threat to my winning all three Trials. If Renold hadn't pitted us against each other for the Arcus Point Trial, we might have both been able to win Title of Choice. But that was impossible now. Bren should be my number one enemy, and yet . . . he wasn't. Far from it.

A gusty sigh puffed from my mouth, sending plumes of pale white before me. I was in so much trouble.

With a final clang, all seven chargers were locked into their starting gates. A hush settled over the crowd. I could hear the charger's impatient snorts. An echoing crack rent the air, and the seven beasts sprung free. Two of them immediately tangled. The unfortunate animals and their riders screeched and yelled, tumbling to the packed dirt in a heap of flailing limbs.

Instead of gasping, the mob roared excitedly—because when it came to the Trials, most of this city became bloodthirsty and merciless. The Trials brought out the worst in people. I was relieved that Bren hadn't fallen, then felt pinpricks of shame. Those riders deserved concern; one of them was still a crumpled ball on the track. I didn't know the extent of his injuries and probably never would.

But my eyes couldn't linger on the still form any longer. They swept toward the five remaining contenders just in time to witness a three-foot solid metal wall shoot out of the ground with a grating clang. The lead charger was too close to the obstacle and its body slamming into metal sounded like a thunder clap.

The other four chargers cleared the jump, and then it was raining. All around me people raised their chosen projectiles and lobbed them onto the track—apples, sticks, rocks. I even caught the flash of steel. A rock struck Stalin's neck and I leaned forward, squeezing the frozen rail that blocked me from rushing onto the track. But the gigantic beast plowed on as if a mere pebble had pinged off his tough hide.

Just as the deluge of objects ebbed, a series of spikes dotted the track like needles haphazardly stuck into a pincushion. The chargers threaded their way through the dangerous maze, and I noted with relief that Bren had Stalin tightly reined. One rider recklessly wove his charger into the obstacle course; the brown beast brayed as its shoulder struck a sharp spike. They made it out, but a bright red gouge was the price. Despite the animal's pain, its rider laid on the whip, spurring the poor beast onward.

My lips pulled back and I bared clenched teeth. I promised myself then and there that when I was free of this prison, I was going to steal all the whips and burn them to ashes.

The other three contenders were neck-and-neck on the track. The charger next to Stalin lunged sideways, its teeth narrowly missing Bren's leg. I hissed as those around me chattered gleefully. After a few more swipes, Stalin whipped his head around and latched those scary big teeth onto a soft muzzle, the most vulnerable spot on a charger's body. He shook his head and his captive shrieked, kicking out its hind legs, nearly unseating the hapless rider.

Bren leaned into Stalin's neck and I saw his lips move. A second later, Stalin released his prey, charging ahead of the insipid beast who'd dared challenge him. A grin tugged at my mouth. Why had I been afraid they wouldn't be able to keep up with the others? They were formidable.

And then a black pit opened and swallowed them whole. My heart skipped a beat; my eyes strained to see into the gloom. I heard a scream from the stands, then another, until dozens of screams burst against my eardrums.

Finally, I caught a glimpse of Bren's face, pale surrounded by so much darkness. The hole writhed, as if alive, and with a shock I realized that it *was* alive. Coils of undulating rope slithered over Stalin and Bren. They could barely keep their heads above the constantly moving mass. "Snakes," I whispered, a chill shooting down my spine. If they were venomous . . .

Two more chargers plunged into the pit and the snakes became an angry obsidian sea. The animals neighed their fear; the riders weren't doing much better—a female contender clung to her mount, her face leached of all color. Bren swung off Stalin's back and waded through the snakes, the reins firmly in his grasp. With a few words directed at the charger, he led them to the other side where they clambered up a ramp obscured by snakes.

A shudder shook my shoulders as phantom scales slid

over my neck. Ugh. Snakes.

Pounding down the final stretch, they were now in the lead, followed closely by the charger Stalin had bitten. The other two contenders were still stuck in the snake pit. I felt lightheaded. I was holding my breath, teeth chewing the insides of my cheeks as I fought the urge to cheer Bren on. I couldn't. But my throat ached with the desire to roar, "Go, Bren! Faster!"

The other rider whipped his mount with a vengeance and they crept forward, nearly nose-to-nose with Bren and Stalin. The crowd was a wild thing, whistling, yelling, jeering. But the noise was drowned out by a new one, one that I feared most: water. I feared the great whooshing sound because Bren did, and now he was heading straight toward it. Water erupted from a trench, forming a geyser that spanned the width of the track. There was no way around this obstacle. They had to go through it.

"Come on, come on, come on," I breathed, unable to keep silent. My fingers wrung the metal rail, chipping off flakes of rust.

Bren slackened the reins, giving Stalin control, and I stifled a gasp. It was reckless, beyond dangerous. But as they moved faster and faster, I couldn't help but think it was glorious. I braced my body for impact, as if by doing so, I could lend Bren courage. With a final burst of speed, they hit the roaring wall. Time slowed, and I waited for something awful to happen. Waited for Bren to lose his grip and tumble to the packed earth.

The knot in my chest expanded. Then a dark streak, drenched and beautiful, sprang from that raging white inferno as if fear were a trickling fountain. "Yes!" I was jumping in the air now, oblivious to everything but the sight of Bren still clinging to Stalin's back.

They hightailed it to the finish line, spraying dirt and water in their wake, a shadow close on their heels. The shadow inched forward, sneaking up on their rear flank, beast and rider heaving, but it was too late. Stalin's black hooves touched down on the finish line.

CRUEL

Metal jangled; leather creaked. A charger pawed; another snorted. Comforting sounds. Familiar. Out of the countless hours spent training for the Trials, racing on Freedom's back was the one thing I had fallen in love with. Wind snatching at my clothes, raw power beneath me, pure adrenaline pumping through my veins—the knowledge that one misstep could send my fragile human body sailing through the air at break-neck speed.

I craved it all. And maybe my fixation with danger made me reckless, but it was better than feeling helpless.

Freedom and I were ushered into the number six starting gate, the thin metal door latching with a clang behind us. This was it. Our last race together. Unless . . . unless I could bargain for her freedom as well. She tossed her head and I shoved the worry aside. I had to think of the here and now, and nothing else. I soothed her agitated state by running a palm down her neck, and she settled.

"You again?"

I glanced to my left and there was Ryker. I almost laughed at the irony. Pretty soon he'd think I was running into him on purpose. "What's his name?" I asked, jerking my chin toward his dark bay charger sporting white socks.

"Napoleon," he said, which surprised me. His response

almost sounded human. "And don't get too close to him. He bites."

I rolled my eyes. That was more like him. "Oh, that's okay. I bite back." I could have sworn his lips twitched into what appeared to be a grin.

A final gate clicked shut and I forgot about the strange man beside me. I forgot about the high-rise stands holding my many enemies and very few friends. My muscles tightened, and I felt Freedom's tighten in response, her weight shifting to her slightly bent haunches. She was ready. She craved this just as much as I did. My senses swirled around her, fusing us together, until we were one and the same.

I inhaled; she inhaled.

Crack.

Bang!

Freedom exploded out of the gate. She quickly found her stride and I nudged her left, closer to the inner rail. A wall of deep brown blocked our progress and I hissed as Ryker slammed his charger into mine. My leg took the brunt of the impact. Before I could retaliate, a spiked fence blasted out of the ground and my focus zeroed in on the obstacle. I tightened the reins and Freedom bunched her muscles for the jump. My stomach bottomed out as we took to the air.

With a thud, we landed on the other side, and a grin tore at my face, the thrill of racing a staccato beat in my chest. I gave Freedom her head, long enough to cut in front of Ryker and Napoleon. Vengeance had never tasted so sweet. Something whizzed toward me and I flattened against Freedom's neck. But I was still pelted by flying debris. A fist-sized projectile—probably a rock—struck my lower spine. I bit back a curse. Stupid, bloodthirsty crowd.

Another burst of pain slashed my outer thigh. I tore my eyes from the track to peer down at a three-inch slice in my leather pants, now leaking blood. I didn't have time to growl at the idiots in the stands because a terrible screech announced the next hurdle. Several steel planks shot across the track from one wall to the other, level with a charger's head. Oh stars. My brain calculated the odds and came up short.

I almost whimpered as realization dawned. There was only one way past this horizontal ladder: I had to dismount.

As much as I dared, I asked Freedom to decrease her speed. The soles of my boots balanced on her saddle while I rose to an unsteady crouch. Hesitation would get me killed. I blanketed my thoughts and let my instincts roar to the surface. I dropped the reins and leaped. This time the rush of falling didn't bring a smile to my face. I was scared out of my mind—my aching bladder told me so.

Thick steel rang beneath my leather boots. Then my feet sprouted wings as I flew along the remaining rungs, eyes doggedly tracking Freedom's progress below. The speed was swifter than I could normally sprint, an out-of-control dash for an unknown ending. The last plank came up fast. With a grunt, I pushed off its tip and blindly pinwheeled through the air, hoping that Freedom was somewhere down below. Her saddle greeted me sooner than expected. The impact jolted up my bones and knocked the breath from my lungs.

I wheezed in, grateful to still be alive, right as a heavy force barreled into Freedom's left side and threw me off balance. My leg was once again pinned between several tons of charger muscle. A pained cry tore from my throat. Teeth bared, I threw a glare at Ryker, only it wasn't him. A man

I didn't recognize glared back with equal fervor, his eyes morphing into twin pools of hate. Without knowing why, I understood that he had a personal vendetta against me, and he was going to show me just how deep that feeling went.

It must have been shock that kept me glued in place. Shock that a stranger could direct so much rage my way without a moment's hesitation. His whip snapped my head back, the strike to my cheek burning like hellfire. My balance tipped sideways and then I was falling, falling, falling . . .

I choked on a gasp, fighting my gag reflex. Eyes wild with fright, I blinked at the angry man still racing beside me. How . . . how was I still in the saddle? I'd fallen.

Air left my lungs as I came to the only conclusion. A vision had happened again. A warning.

Movement in the man's hand caught my attention and I noticed his knuckles whiten on the leather whip. I didn't further question my luck, only reacted. I punched his nose. Blood spurted from his nostrils, the droplets whisked away by the wind. After a split second of utter shock, he roared in fury, bringing his whip up. But I knew what would happen next.

I ducked.

The leather tail brushed against escaped strands of my hair. He let loose a string of curses as I spurred Freedom into the lead. On impulse, I jerked the reins sharp to the left and moved into his path. His charger bumped Freedom's rear. There was only one thing that could flip my sweet charger into epic witch mode and that was being pushed from behind. Her ears flattened as she snorted, and then she did what she always did in situations like this.

She bucked.

Freedom's hooves punched into her pursuer's chest, but I didn't anticipate the damage it would do. I heard the animal stumble, then a clap as it nose-dived into the dirt. And gravity wasn't finished yet. I craned my neck around in time to witness two more chargers go down as their riders vaulted over their heads. The contenders looked so graceful while effortlessly soaring through the air right before they slammed to the ground. My stomach churned miserably at the mess of limbs and screams.

Stars.

I faced forward again, but the track was watery. No, my eyes were drowning in tears. The price of freedom was steep. Maybe too steep. I hadn't realized how it would feel until this very moment. Furiously, I blinked away the tears—they wouldn't help the poor souls I had doomed. But, no matter how many times I blinked, the track wouldn't sharpen.

When I finally realized why, it was too late.

Without me to guide her, Freedom attempted to leap over the abyss. Not even halfway across, we were sucked downward. Down, down, down, until deep brown sludge reached out and enveloped us in a slimy embrace. I first felt relieved, glad that we weren't surrounded by snakes, but then my body began to itch. Everywhere, in and out of every crevice, tiny pricks moved. My skin begged me to scratch and my fingers burned with the need to oblige.

But I pushed past the discomfort and slid from Freedom's back. I sunk and lifted a foot, the thick ooze bubbling up to my chest. It was like wading through mashed potatoes. By now, the other contenders—at least two of them—were also in the dank, smelly pit astride their floundering chargers. There was much shouting and cursing, but I blocked out the noise, too busy trying not to lose my boots. I loved these boots.

A slow, excruciating minute ticked by.

My legs shook; my shoulders ached from keeping my arms aloft. Ryker and Napoleon fought through the sludge barely a yard to our right and a ball of panic stuck in my throat. Faster. We needed to go faster. I leaned forward and picked up the pace, my thighs on fire as they churned. Even as I panted, I spoke calmly to Freedom, so she wouldn't thrash and waste energy. Another step, then two. The mud receded a few inches, then a few more. We were on a ramp, the upper half of my body free of the grasping stench.

With scrabbling fingers and slick boots, I mounted Freedom, the action nearly impossible as mud weighed me down. But I was in the saddle once again, nudging her to solid ground. And then I kicked and she sprang, flecks of mud from her mane pelting my face. I could see the finish line just beyond this final stretch of track.

So close, so close . . .

Hoof beats echoed in my ears. A dark bay nose bobbed in my peripheral. Someone else had made it out of the pit. I peeked at our competition. Determined, electric blue eyes met mine. The unnerving gaze practically shouted that I was in the way.

I hunched over Freedom's neck and slackened the reins. "Fly!" I urged her. Ears flat against her scalp, she charged down the track. There was a reason I had trained her to recognize that word. For, in moments like this—when she put everything she had into the here and now, when she gave herself up to speed—she did indeed fly.

We were unstoppable. I knew we would win. I could feel it in the way she moved, as if every muscle had loosened and wind now propelled them.

I was weightless, a bird winging for freedom.

Ahead, a sharp sizzling buzz broke my euphoria. My heart stuttered, then climbed up my throat. No. Not that. Anything but that. White zigzags of tiny lightning bolts flexed across the track. One last obstacle—an electrical field—stood between us and the win. Ryker was still a pace behind; he wouldn't outrun us. No charger could best Freedom's speed.

But . . .

I hesitated.

Once I'd experienced the paralyzing stab of electricity jolting through my veins, the feeling never really went away. My muscles locked in instinctive terror. I could do this. I could force myself through and endure this torture like I'd done many times before. But to make Freedom bear it? The act would be like inflicting a scar upon her, intentionally. Even as I mourned how this would forever impact her trust in me, I was whispering encouragement to her.

Asher was wrong. I *was* cruel.

I braced as invisible bands snaked around my limbs and squeezed. The field held us in its snare for what felt like an eternity. I shook uncontrollably as aftershocks crashed through my system. I desperately clutched at the reins as Freedom went wild, braying in pain and fright. She lunged and bucked, and she wouldn't listen to my commands, and I had to . . . I had to . . .

I tore the whip from my belt and screamed, in shame and

agony, as I brought the wretched thing down on Freedom's hide. It was the first time. The first time I had ever struck her. She squealed in shock, and the sound ripped a hole through my heart. *I'm so sorry, I'm so sorry, I'm so sorry.* But no apology could ever fix the rift I had just caused. My sweet, faithful charger obeyed, lurching over the finish line a second before Napoleon and Ryker, but elation over the win never came.

Not when I realized the price of freedom was betrayal.

THE PRICE

Knock, knock, knock. "You're up, number three!"

I stood from the bench in the single person changing room and double-checked my pure white suit for holes. The only other color was on the back, a number three stitched in blue. Faust Night's white suits were specially designed for this Trial, lightweight and flexible, yet able to withstand shallow nicks and slashes. Just the face and hands were left unprotected, a fact that many contenders used to their advantage.

It only took one cut from a steel weapon to lose this Trial. The internal wiring of the suits detected even the barest hint of blood, programmed to release a shrill chime when the wearer's skin broke from the sting of steel. And somehow it knew the difference between another's blood and blood spilled from a punch or finger gouge. How Renold had accumulated this superior technology was a mystery. He never divulged the Trial's secrets.

If your suit chimed, you lost. If you didn't stop fighting, the suit transformed into an electric hug, zapping your body until you lost consciousness. It was like Renold was obsessed with electricity, shocking his subjects at every opportunity.

My Faust Night segment was the first of two taking place

this evening. The other two would take place tomorrow.

"Who's tough?" My voice shook as I whispered in the quiet space. "That's right. You are." My mouth was drier than a concrete slab.

The room's metal door groaned inward, and Drake's frame filled the doorway. "Don't disappoint me, Instructor Lune," he said, holding out my twin golden daggers. The title was meant to rattle me. I was heading to battle, and no title would stop a contender from sticking a blade into my chest.

I grasped the dagger's cool handles, a sense of relief rushing through me at their familiar weight. "Maybe disappointment is all you will ever know in life, Drake Stonewood," I countered. I had never spoken to him that way before, and doing so now liberated another piece of myself. As his jaw dropped, I breezed out of the room. I wasn't free of this city, but from here on out, I would be free of him.

My footsteps echoed down the long concrete corridor lit by dangling bare bulbs. This was it. This was really happening. My legs trembled.

I was at a disadvantage in this Trial. Fear aside, not many women attempted this Trial because of its brutality. Most of Faust Night's contenders were like Elite Instructor Drake: completely and utterly merciless, driven by physical strength and testosterone. My only edge was my size. I was quick. That and I wasn't drowning in male pheromones.

Nearing the end of the tunnel, I heard Renold's amplified voice shout, "Speed. Strength. Precision." The crowd parroted the motto. "Last contender uncut by steel wins!" I couldn't clearly hear what he said next, only the sound of my name. The frenzied crowd roared. I flinched.

Whatever he was saying wouldn't help me win this fight. In fact, it would only drive my competition further into a state of bloodlust in their desire to gain the crowd's—and Renold's—favor.

My stomach lurched. Maybe I could still back out.

No! I had to get free. I had to find my mother!

The tunnel spat me out into Faust Night's amphitheater and my thoughts cut off. The crowd appeared as rippling water and bobbed with color. The other four contenders were like blurry bleached pillars, barring the way. And then the glass door silently yawned and swallowed us whole. I was inside—trapped in a cage with four others who craved spilled blood.

Stars above, what am I doing?

The door sealed shut, but it didn't cut off the feverish screams and *beat, beat, beat* of the heavy drums. From my position along the left wall of The Pit, I glanced up in hopes of finding Bren's or Iris's friendly faces, only for white lights to burn my retinas instead. I was under a spotlight. Except my audience didn't want to watch *me*. They wanted to see my flesh pummeled into the ground.

The ground.

It was then I noticed how the cement floor was blanketed in sand, obscuring the vents. I knew there were vents on rotating poles high above my head as well, even though the blinding lights made them impossible to see. The cage almost looked harmless—if it weren't for the four other people in it watching my every move. Good thing I had just used the bathroom or I would have peed myself right about now.

I rotated my neck and shoulders, and warmed up my wrists, pretending for all the world like this was a simple training session—not what could very well be the last day of my life. Like I wasn't afraid of a blow to the head that could mean lights out for me—permanently. Like the steel objects inside this cage were dull and incapable of penetrating my suit—or my skin.

Chink. Chink. Chink.

My eyes gravitated toward the strange noise and widened as they fell on a medieval spiked flail in the hands of a bald, dark behemoth-sized man. He shook the ball and chain, then swung it in a circle, leering at the other contenders. Intimidation tactics. It was working. I swiftly catalogued the rest of my competition. A boy my age of average height and build slipped knuckle knives through his fingers. A man in his late twenties thumbed the blade of a tomahawk, his raven hair tied back in a low ponytail. And the last . . .

Soft brown skin. Sable irises.

My stomach dropped.

Catanna.

I shouldn't have been surprised, and yet my brain struggled to accept her presence. When our gazes collided, she flashed perfect white teeth, her eyes shining with hunger. Hunger for my blood. Her curved sword caught the overhead fluorescent lighting and glinted. It was a katana, to be precise, the blade she had trained with for eight years. Her obsession with her chosen weapon was legendary. She had even changed her name from Catarina to Catanna many years ago.

I knew she would carve me to pieces, if given the chance.

Blood thumped in my skull, so loud I almost missed the sharp bell chime announcing the segment's start.

The tinny shriek unlocked my muscles and, with a jolt,

I lunged for Catanna. My gold daggers were a blur in my hands. My gut gave a sickened twist, warning me, and I rolled, barely avoiding a tomahawk in the back. It sliced toward Catanna and she jerked away before engaging with the dark behemoth and his ball of horror. I sprung up and lashed a kick at the man with the ponytail. Blood spurted from his mouth, but his suit remained inactive. I needed to cut him with steel.

His weapon chopped at my arm and I danced back a step, forcing his follow through to swing wide. My left dagger sliced at the wooden handle. His whole right side was undefended. I quickly tore through his suit with my other dagger, careful to keep the cut shallow. His suit dinged, startling me out of my cold focus.

The punch of adrenaline warped my concentration and I almost missed the knife sneaking toward my left side. I whirled and blocked its trajectory, steel clanging on steel. The boy's other knife zipped for my throat. The thrust would have impaled me if I hadn't swiveled my shoulders. The knife shot past me, so close I could hear a hiss. But I didn't avoid the strike completely. Steel knuckles bludgeoned my jaw.

I stumbled back, blinking away spots, both my daggers raised in hopes of warding him off until I could see clearly. No such luck. The kick to my stomach sent me flying into the solid glass wall. My skull cracked against it, once again plunging my world into flashes of white liberally splotched with black. This was the end. The boy's wavering shadow inched closer, knife poised to skewer me against the wall like an insect.

Then the vents turned on.

Sand burst into the air, and everything became white noise. The storm swallowed me whole; high winds made the sand a weapon. Instinctively, I squeezed my eyes shut. Tiny stinging granules pelted every exposed inch of skin. Particles sought entrance into any crevice, clogging my ear canals, my nostrils—even managed to slip past my tight-lipped grimace.

My body curled on the floor, not knowing up from down. The sting intensified and, before I could stop myself, I gasped. Sand raced down my throat and lodged in my lungs. Hacking coughs racked my chest. I inhaled even more sand. Something bumped my back and I squeaked, lashing out with a foot. Surprisingly, the kick met with resistance—something hard, like a skull. Over the wind's wail, I heard a dull thump, as if someone had toppled.

And then the unnatural elements switched off. Franti-cally, I scrubbed grit from my watering eyes. I pried my lids open despite the burn behind them and cast my gaze around the cage. Knuckle Boy was climbing to his feet—a three-inch gash on his forehead dripped blood. His arm cocked back. My body was slow, still recovering from the sand that had blasted down my windpipe. I wouldn't be able to block him in time. I braced for pain.

His shadow grew, not because he was closing in, but because of the hulking figure behind him. *Smack!* Warm liquid spurted onto my face and I flinched. I threw myself into a roll to avoid the body pitching forward. Knuckle Boy thumped against the glass; his lifeless form slid to the floor.

Staggering, I forced my body upright and glanced at him, a second later wishing I hadn't. His skull was caved in where a spiked flail had crushed it. I didn't even hear his

285

suit chime as blood rushed into my ears and bile surged up my throat. But if I got sick now, I was done for. My head would soon look like his. I swallowed the bitter tang and faced the Behemoth, his face contorted in a sadistic grin.

"You're next, little girl," he said, swinging the ball and chain that now glistened red.

I crouched, my daggers at the ready. He took a giant step and whipped his weapon toward my face. Air whooshed over my head as I ducked. More blood spattered my exposed skin. It snuck into my mouth and I spit it out, shuddering at the awful taste. The taste of a dead man.

The grinning Behemoth let loose a belly laugh, as if the sight of me choking on another's blood was his idea of entertainment. It probably was, considering the raised scars on his hands, neck, and even his face. He looked like a man who fought for sport—for the pure pleasure of it. Suddenly, his laughter cut off, mouth wide open.

And then I saw what had shut him up. The end of a blade stuck out of his chest. He looked down and touched the sharp tip, pricking his finger. He stared, transfixed, as a bright drop of blood welled to the surface of his skin. Then his eyes rolled upward. He dropped to his knees and fell face first into the sand.

Behind him stood Catanna, a purpling bruise on her cheekbone. "That's for messing up my face," she purred, wiping her bloodied blade on the dead man's back. His suit dinged.

She maneuvered around him until nothing but ten feet of floor separated us. This time her flashing teeth were red. "I've waited eight years for this moment, you know. Fitting that it should be you and me, Princess. But do you have what it takes to win? Can you kill? Because that's what it's going to take to defeat me." She spat out a mouthful of blood.

"Why me, Catanna?" I made sure the ten feet remained as we slowly circled. "Why do you want my blood so badly? Because you always have—ever since that day we were ten years old and I asked you to be my friend."

She laughed, but the sound trembled. "You're so *blind,* Lune. Look around!" She swept her blade in an arc, pointing at the crowd, at the elites high above. "This is the only way to a better life for us *lesser.* But then there's you, living the perfect life up in that big house, surrounded by wealth and luxury."

Catanna laughed again, this time edged hatred. "But it wasn't enough for you, was it? You climbed down into *my* world and entered the Trials. And for what, recognition? To be the best? Is Daddy not paying enough attention to you?"

Each accusation was a shock to my system; they were blows to my sternum. All this time and that's what she thought of me? Years and years of whispered taunts and threats, because she thought I wanted *attention?* My throat throbbed. The price for my silence was a city that believed I was an elitist, the very thing I hated most.

My eyes burned, and I squeezed the dagger's hilts. Wrong. This was all wrong. I couldn't do this. "Listen to me, Catanna. The last thing I want is attention. I've kept my head down for *years,* trying to blend in, trying to survive. If there was another way, I wouldn't be anywhere near the Trials. I hate them, do you hear me? Hate how they divide us and pit us against each other. But . . . I'm desperate for a better life, too. Just not the one you think I want."

She stilled. I stopped moving. Her mouth spasmed, as if she were trying to hold back the words, but she blurted, "What could you possibly want that you don't already have?"

My heart was a drum in my chest. If I told her, she could ruin everything. She could spread a rumor of my plan and the whole city would take up arms against me before I could finish the Trials. But . . . but what if she didn't? The look in her eyes—it spoke of uncertainty, and maybe a sliver of hope, that I wasn't who she thought I was. That maybe we weren't so different after all. "Freedom." I released my breath in a rush. "I want to earn my freedom and leave this city."

Those calculating eyes widened; her full lips parted. And she laughed. Threw her head back and cackled. Scorching heat blistered my face. She waved her blade at me. "I never took you for a liar. You had me going there for a moment. This is what's going to happen, Princess. We're going to put on a good show, you're going to die on the edge of my blade, and I'm going to earn a title that secures a better future for me and my family."

We were circling again, this time with weapons at the ready. "Neither of us has to die today. We can become allies in this!"

But with a sinking feeling, I knew I'd lost her. It was written like permanent ink in her eyes. "You're wrong," she said, her body tightly coiling. "You can never trust an elite."

She sprang.

Sparks danced as steel collided. Thoughts were nothing, reaction everything. I crossed my daggers and shoved her katana sideways, then ducked in with a swift kick to her thigh. She snarled; her blade sang as it sliced for me. Our feet leapt and spun to the musical tune of ringing metal. The seconds we fought felt like hours. She kicked my left wrist and my dagger skittered out of sight. My hand went numb.

I twirled around her and dropped into a slide, reaching for the lost dagger. My tingling fingers closed around the hilt a second before the sharp whine of Catanna's blade rang over me, aimed for my neck. Rolling onto my back, I jabbed my legs up, the soles of my boots punching into her gut. She went airborne and smacked into the glass wall. I wasted no time scrambling to my feet. As she took a moment to recover, I was already in motion, swinging with all my might at her blade. Her precious katana soared out of her deadened fingers.

She cried out, equal parts shocked and furious, as I pressed my other dagger to her throat. "It's over, Catanna," I panted. "But I won't kill you."

"Do it," she snarled through bared teeth. "You'd be doing me a favor."

I gasped. How could she say that? Did the Trial win mean this much to her, that she'd rather die than lose? But then it struck me that I was doing the same thing and I felt sick to my stomach. I removed my dagger from her skin. "No. You should live, Catanna. Find something worth living for." I neatly sliced the material covering her bicep and watched as a thin line of blood welled up.

The crowd's roar crashed over my heightened senses. The thunderous sound drowned out the impending chime of her suit. My limbs vibrated with adrenaline as I focused outside of the cage, and I immediately became overwhelmed by a sea of animated faces. The sight of Bren, pressed close to the glass, settled my world somewhat. I took a shaky step toward him, then another, my eyes seeking out his. The comforting gold of his irises warmed my insides, that wicked grin of his stirring my heart to tripping over itself.

And then it all changed. Horror. There was horror on that face and he was pushing toward me, his body slamming into the wall as if he could force his way through by sheer will alone.

I felt a wrinkle form between my brows. What was he—? *Crack!* My skull screamed in agony as something rammed into my temple, driving me to the ground. I smacked the sand with enough force to make me bounce, and I lost a dagger. My spine bowed as a solid weight pushed me farther into the sand. Air left me in a rush. Fingers pried at my remaining dagger and I clenched my fist, refusing to give up my only chance at survival.

Something, maybe the hilt of a katana, bludgeoned my temple once more. Stars burst across my vision. I was jerked onto my back, the dagger ripped from my fingers. Strong thighs pinned my arms to my sides, all before I could blink away the floating black and white lights. Catanna's exultant grin swam into view. I frowned in confusion. She should be writhing on the floor right now, bolts of electricity snaking through her veins.

But as she leaned over me, my dagger now clutched in her hand, confusion was replaced with acceptance. It was me or her. There was no way around it now. If I didn't kill her, she would kill me. I felt her place the tip of my blade to the delicate skin of my left temple and I stilled, stiller than death itself. A muffled whump-whump sound—as if a body repetitively threw itself against an obstacle—pricked at my ears, but I quickly shut the noise out.

Catanna giggled, sounding like a girl unhinged. "It must be my lucky day. A malfunctioning suit. Or is it?" My lips tightened at her words. She babbled on, all the while twisting the blade tip against my skin. "What if someone wanted me to win and sabotaged the suit? I mean, I could just pretend ignorance, that I didn't know I'd been cut."

Her breathing escalated then, and she look scared. Her eyes darted around the room, searching. She must have found something, because her gaze jerked back to mine, victorious. "This win is mine. I won't let you take away what I've worked so hard for. But before I end your life, I'll put my initials on your face, so that the city knows who the *real* Princess of the Trials is."

And with that, she began to carve. Steel dug into my skin in a slow, torturous half circle. The searing heat was too much and I screamed, hot tears obscuring my view of the sad, twisted girl trying to kill her past. Warm blood trickled into my hairline, mingling with the flow of tears as I realized what I had to do. I didn't hesitate. My stomach muscles clenched, and I jerked my knees upward. Catanna flipped over my head. I followed her in a backward somersault; my fingers clawed at the dagger still clutched in her hand.

We rolled several times, each trying to gain leverage as we fought over the weapon. Four hands struggled for the dagger's slick hilt as our bodies slammed up against the glass barrier, as Catanna landed on top, as she raised herself up and shifted her weight forward, driving the blade's tip down, down, down, until it broke through my suit and pierced the skin of my chest. I screamed, the pressure a shrieking firestorm.

The elements joined the fray. Winds and sand blasted my beaten body, tore at my shredded throat.

No.

I wasn't beat.

I wasn't *beat!*

Everything froze. We were cocooned in a cyclone of sand and heat and wind. I couldn't see, hear, or think. All I had left were my instincts. They were the only thing the elements couldn't snatch away.

I pushed, with every last drop of rage and fear and helplessness. Helpless to stop what was going to happen next. Fear because I knew. I knew what was going to happen. I felt it before it even came to pass. I felt the weapon slip from her grasp, now firmly in my control. I felt my body roll with my victim's. I felt the blade slip through material and skin, tissue and muscle, until it found a home in a desperate heart.

The wind stopped. The sand settled.

In the silence, my mind denied what had just happened, even as crimson bloomed and spread over material white as snow. A wet cough. Another. Catanna was choking on her own blood. It spilled from her lips. "You . . . you took e-everything from me. You s-selfish elite . . ."

I looked into her eyes. Oh stars. Oh, how I wished I hadn't. They were murky brown pools of emptiness.

A chill deeper than I'd ever felt before seeped into my bones.

I had . . .

I had killed her.

A fierce wave of nausea surged up my throat and I twisted, splattering the contents of my stomach. The ground was

292

a wasteland. I deserved to wallow in it. My body sank toward the concrete slab and shifting sand as it yawned, gladly accepting the offering. But a strong pair of hands slipped under my arms and lifted me away from the carnage.

STAY

Halfway to the barracks, my legs completely gave out. Bren scooped me into his arms and carried my limp body close to his chest. I couldn't feel it. I couldn't feel anything.

A mechanical hissing sound made me flinch. I looked up and a dingy shower stall took shape. How had we gotten here? Bren lowered me to my feet, keeping a solid arm around my waist. I felt like I would float away into nothing without that arm holding me to the earth.

"Lune."

Slow blink.

"Lune, can you hear me?"

"Mmm."

"Can you wash yourself? Quick in and out, just to get the blood off. I don't want the cold water putting you into further shock."

Shock . . . Is that what this was? I wanted to bathe in its numbness—wash all thought away and drown the pain.

Without replying, I shuffled into the small square stall, clothes and all, and slid the curtain closed.

A sigh. Then soft retreating footsteps.

Silence, except for the spitting shower-head.

I was alone, at last.

The chill dug deeper into my bones, to my very soul. My

whole body chattered; my jaw ached with each clack of my teeth. As the water penetrated my suit, I dropped my chin and watched, detached, as rivers of red and pink swirled down the drain. My blood mixed with several others'.

My knees liquified and my back smacked against the shower wall. I slid until my butt hit the floor. And there, in a cold empty corner, I pulled my knees close to keep from falling apart. But it was happening. The numb nothingness was lifting, and I saw her dead eyes. I jammed my eyelids closed and threw out a hand, trying to push away the image. My knuckles cracked against tile.

The image was replaced with another, of Catanna's blood-flecked mouth. "Killer," the lips accused.

I whimpered, the noise high and frail. "I'm sorry. I'm so sorry. I didn't mean to."

The red lips sneered. "Liar."

"No." I shook my head, clumps of hair sticking to my wet cheeks. "That's not—"

"Elitist."

"No!" The scream tore at my throat, ripping away the last of the numbness. The press of emotions was like being held under water, my lungs starved for air. My mouth opened but no sound came out. So, I did the only thing I could think of. I punched the wall. The agony of bone colliding with tile sharpened my focus. I could breathe again. I imagined my pain was a ball and squeezed it tightly in my fist, then drove it into the wall, again and again.

Red rivulets ran down the tiles.

And then my body bucked, head wobbling to and fro. I was being shaken. Vices clamped onto my wrists, stopping my assault on the tiles. I wrestled against the constraints, but no amount of fighting could set me free. I was a prisoner—forever a prisoner. A faraway noise, muted and garbled, distracted me and I tilted my head, wondering at the notes of panic.

"Stop. Stop, Lune. You're hurting yourself! This won't help."

I desperately wanted to shatter into droplets of water and slide down the shower drain. My nerves were deadening again, and I shook uncontrollably. The water shut off and a towel wrapped around me, then I was airborne.

I had enough sense left to recognize my own room as my sopping boots touched down on concrete. Gold eyes, lit with life—so much life—filled my world and a fierce ache squeezed my heart. Bren's hands left my shoulders; the warmth of his gaze and touch disappeared. He was back a second later, my nightclothes in his grasp, but the bone-deep chill had already returned. I drifted, focus blurring at the edges.

"Stay with me, little bird. I need you to get out of that suit. Can you manage it?"

I nodded—at least I thought I'd nodded—then reached for the zipper at my neck. Bren glanced away, even went so far as to show me his back, and my heart squeezed again. My chin quivered and not from the cold. The dull hiss of a zipper and my awkward attempts at peeling the material from my slick skin were the only sounds in the room. With a thump, I kicked off my boots and stepped out of the suit. And that's when I noticed, as I shivered in nothing but my underwear, that the suit was covered in pink stains—stains that would probably never wash out.

I crushed the suit into a ball and hurled the miserable

thing across the room. With a splat, it settled into a corner, like a venomous snake waiting for its next victim. Bren stayed silent, didn't even flinch. I donned my gray nightshirt and pants, then cleared my throat. The sound was weak, raw.

I expected to see pity in his eyes when he turned and approached me once more. The last thing I deserved was pity. I was a killer. He shouldn't even be here, helping me. But his emotions were tucked away as he slowly lifted his hand and looped the stubborn lock of hair behind my left ear. His fingers trailed along my jawline, gently tipping my chin up so he could inspect the crescent moon shape carved into my temple. The cut still leaked blood.

His expression didn't change, but his fingers shook ever so slightly. "You'll need stitches," he said softly, as if afraid the news would destroy me. But what was another scar? They were just reminders of what I'd endured. They were my shame. My burden.

"Fine." My voice was hollow.

And then his expression *did* change, to one of worry. But that wasn't all. There was this fierce gleam, so blindingly bright I almost looked away. It shot straight into my heart. His palm cupped my cheek and I tried not to lean into his warmth. "I can see that you blame yourself," he said, sliding his thumb across my cheekbone. "But she gave you no choice. If you hadn't done what you did, you wouldn't be standing here right now."

"Maybe . . . maybe I don't deserve to be standing here right now," I managed to confess past quivering lips. At his growing look of horror, I launched into my reasoning. "You don't know how hard it is for the lesser of this city. Why do you think so many of them enter the Trials, or send their children instead? The little bit of food I manage to smuggle into the village is *nothing* compared to the people's needs. I—I took everything from her. From her family. If I had just accepted my fate, none of this would have happened." *I wouldn't be a killer,* is what I wanted to say but didn't.

Confusion blanketed his troubled gaze. "What do you mean by that? What is your fate?"

I grimaced. Telling Catanna the truth hadn't made a difference. Would Bren laugh at me too? He was from the outside, after all, and had willingly entered the confines of the city and the dangerous Trials. He was the least likely person to believe me, but . . .

The price of my silence.

I couldn't bear for him to think of me as a shallow glory-seeker like everyone else, even if his reasons for winning the Trials led him down that very path. Maybe the truth would change his mind about what this city had to offer.

"My fate is to be the loyal, humble servant of Supreme Elite Tatum," I began. "I am his conquest, his *slave*—to do with as he pleases. But I am more than just a captive daughter to him, and I'm afraid to find out what that is."

My mouth was so dry, I couldn't force a swallow as I finished. "The truth is, I don't want any of this, Bren. I don't want to be a trophy, an elite's daughter, or even a Trial winner. I desire my *freedom* more than anything, and not just to escape the cruel hand of a madman. I want to be free of this horrid place, this city. I want . . . I want out. I want to *live.*"

As if a hand gripped my neck, my throat closed. The air was static electricity, poised to strike me down for uttering such blasphemy. In all my eleven years trapped in this city, I had never once dared whisper such traitorous words. And now they were in the open, naked and vulnerable, and I feared what Bren would do with them.

His breathing had picked up pace, eyes wild and burning. He looked like an untamed beast ready to explode, and I felt my insides recoil in terror. I had known him for such a short amount of time and had no idea what he was truly capable of. What if he got angry and . . . My pulse hammered erratically. His fingers, now tangled in my hair, formed a stronger grip. I was about to jerk away when he spoke, his voice laced with an emotion I couldn't define.

"You really want to be free of this place?"

"With every last breath in my body."

Those wild eyes burned even brighter, with a passion that fluttered my heart. A strangled exhale slipped from my mouth as he crushed me to him. My palms rested on his chest where his heart thundered out of control.

"Good," he murmured. "You have no idea how relieved I am to hear that." The words warmed the crown of my head. He drew me in tighter, and I fitted my nose to the valley his neck and shoulder made. And breathed. Sparks danced in my stomach, chasing away the numbness, worry, and fear.

"Stars above, you smell good, Brendan Bearon." Muscles jumped in his neck as he chuckled, and I froze. "What?"

"You think I smell good?"

Oh stars, are my thoughts leaking? "I didn't say that." I pulled back, my face a flaming ball of embarrassment, but his hands wouldn't relinquish my waist.

His head dipped as he tried to force eye contact, but I evaded the look, too mortified that I must have spoken the thought out loud. "Yes, you did," he persisted. "Your exact words were—"

"Don't you need to stitch this up?" I blurted, jabbing a finger toward my temple.

His lips curled knowingly, but he dutifully transitioned into doctor mode. "Yes, ma'am. I'll get right on it."

I bit my cheek. "And the other cut?"

"What other cut?"

"Where she—where my own dagger almost pierced my heart." My earlier embarrassment faded at the vivid memory. Hollowness crept in once more.

His expression grew pained, as if the memory hurt him as much as it hurt me. "Show me," he said softly. I loosened the laces on my shirt and exposed the still-weeping wound directly over my heart. The brackets around his mouth deepened, as well as the crease between his brows. "I'm sorry for what you went through."

My hand dropped. "Pain is the price."

"The price of what?"

"Freedom."

I heard keening, the sound of brokenness.

Squinting, I peered into the fog, but couldn't locate the source of the awful noise. No matter where I looked, the fog's thick tendrils blocked my view. I whirled when a soft tsking came from behind my left shoulder, but no one was there. Still, I heard dark laughter.

"You can't see us, Princess. We're dead. How many more will suffer before this is over? How many more will *you* destroy?"

My fingernails bit into my palms. "I'm not trying to hurt anyone, Catanna. I just . . . I just want out. I need to find my mother before it's too late. And this is the only way. I don't have a choice!"

She sighed in disappointment. "Wasn't it you who said that you always have a choice? Oh, Lune, don't you realize what you've become? A liar. You even lied to that precious beast of yours—the one you whispered false promises to for the last decade."

I had no defense against her accusations; they pried open my ribcage and punched my heart. A strangled sob left me and I didn't bother stifling it. Wrapped in fog with no one to see, I let the shame and the guilt squeeze from my eyes. The emotions tasted like acid.

"I'm sorry." The words sounded broken.

"Your tears and apologies cannot undo what you've done," she spat. "You're a monster, and monsters only deserve one thing. Death!"

A black shadow stirred just beyond the gray wisps. The obsidian shape elongated, forming a sharp point, like a dagger. I blinked at it, completely frozen. Then it flew toward me, plunging into my heart. I screamed.

My eyes jerked open. I could still hear the keening. It was in my head, in my chest, in my throat. I released a whimpering breath. My fingers poked and prodded at my heart. Still there, whole and frantically beating. A dream. A horrible, realistic nightmare that waking couldn't erase. My knees buckled, striking the concrete floor.

Panic seized me when I realized I wasn't in my bed, but a quick glance around showed that I was still in my room.

A chill slid down my spine when I noticed the damage I had caused. The blanket dangling over the side of my bed now had a new tear. Fresh slashes crisscrossed the room's far wall. I looked down and saw a thin red slice along my right forearm.

And next to me lay my hidden knife, blood darkening the blade's tip.

It had been awhile since I'd last experienced a waking nightmare, where the dreams were so strong, they became reality. This was different than sleepwalking, like the time I'd searched out Bren, instead landing in the hands of my enemies. No, this was much worse. Under its spell, my body was controlled by the nightmare, unpredictable and danger-ous.

Reactive.

I really was a monster.

A feeling hit me so hard I curled into a ball, arms tightly crossed over my galloping heart. Fear. But it wasn't fear of the monsters lying in wait outside of my locked room. I was afraid to be alone . . . with myself. The fear closed in—mov-ing, reaching, grasping—until a single word pulsed in my head.

Bren.

I pulled myself to a stand and felt my way to the door. This room was a cell and I had only one thought: escape from this tomb-like silence, escape from my reactive body. With a soft snick, the lock sprung open, the door after that. My bare feet carried me into the hallway and I sighed, relieved. My heart rate kicked up again but for a different reason. If someone caught me sneaking up to Bren's room, there was no excuse I could give that would spare me the consequences.

Was I willing to risk my future for this brief moment of escape? My body was a statue, my brain firing conflicting thoughts as I stood in the chilly hallway. And then, farther down the hall, I heard a cough. The creak of bed springs. My legs whisked me in the opposite direction, toward the stairwell, before my brain could make up its mind.

What am I doing, what am I doing, what am I doing?

I slid up the stairs on silent feet, barely breathing. As I slipped past several closed doors, I waited for the inevitable moment when someone would hear my loud heartbeat and jump out with a, "Got you!" I found Bren's door and all but flew toward it, not even pausing to knock. The door should have been locked, putting an end to this idiotic venture, but it wasn't. I'd scold him later for his foolish oversight.

My nerves gave a sickening jolt as I closed the door behind me and swiveled toward his bed. *I shouldn't be here. I'm an idiot. He'll think I'm crazy. But I am crazy.* My feet were stuck. Maybe I was still in a waking dream.

"Are you going to stand there and stare all night?"

I about leapt out of my skin at the sound of his voice. It was amused, I think. Hopefully. "Maybe," I murmured lamely. My arms formed a protective barrier over my chest.

"Come here."

The invitation did funny things to my stomach. I couldn't hold still. But I didn't budge. "This is . . . this is a really bad idea. I should go." Uncrossing my arms, I reached for the doorknob, and he shifted, as if preparing to spring.

"Wait," he said, and I froze. "Is Lune Avery afraid of me? After all that we've been through?"

"I'm not afraid *of* you. I'm afraid of what this"—I

303

gestured between us—"will do to me."

In the dim moonlight, I could see him lean closer, resting his forearms on his thighs. "I'm afraid of what it will do to me, too. But I just want—" He cut himself off, as if realizing he'd said something he hadn't meant to say.

"What?" I dared ask, the question barely audible over the thumping of my heart. "You just want what?"

But the moment stretched into silence, and I felt a piece of me shrivel up and die. Instead of answering, he asked, "Why are you here?"

I laughed weakly. "Because my nightmares are eating me alive, and I-I can't—Being alone is just . . ." I shrugged, feeling a burning behind my eyes. My fingers blindly reached for the door.

"Stay?"

I paused, breath sticking in my throat. No. Yes. I shouldn't. I should. How could such a simple word fill me with so much terror? And yet, it gave me the courage to take a step, then another, until I was looking down at his up-turned face brimming with hopes and doubts and possibilities. He shifted backward and laid down, pressing his spine against the wall, leaving me plenty of room to . . .

Stars above, I was really doing this.

With my lower lip trapped between my teeth, I sank onto the mattress. And after a slight hesitation, I flipped so my back was to him. Every muscle was tightly wound as I anticipated and dreaded what he would do next. *Would* he do anything? Did I want him to? But the minutes ticked by and Bren lay unmoving, so quiet I wondered if he had somehow snuck out the window.

It took a while, but my muscles eventually relaxed and I

drifted to sleep, comforted knowing that, even in my night-mares, he watched over me.

HIS WEAKNESS

"Don't touch the prickly coat. Or the mane. Or the . . ." I chuckled and slid my hand underneath Iris's much smaller one. "Let's just practice feeding her, okay?"

She shivered when I placed the raw meat in her palm. "Ew. Disgusting."

"I like the taste of pig, actually. So much flavor." I lifted both of our hands toward my wide-open mouth. Iris squealed and I barked a laugh, offering the meat instead to Freedom.

As the charger's large teeth gingerly nibbled at the food, Iris giggled, and my heart melted. They liked each other.

"What's her name?" Iris asked, reaching upward to touch the beast's nose.

"Cleo—" I paused, glancing around the stables, then whispered, "Can you keep a secret?"

The girl's eyes rounded and she bobbed her head.

"All of the chargers are given a name at birth by the Supreme Elite. But I wanted my charger to have a special name, and I've never told anyone else what that name is. Until now. I want you to know that I named her Freedom, because I think you are like us. I think you want the same thing we do."

My breath hitched as I watched her process the information. I was almost certain that I was right, but I didn't know how she would react.

Finally, she spoke, her lips quivering. "I want to see my mother again."

My throat all but choked me as I exhaled shakily. I wiped a tear from her cheek. "Me too, Iris. Me too."

Questions hovered in her hazel eyes, and I knew I'd answer every single one of them. She and I, we were the same. Without even asking her, I knew that Iris was from the outside, just like me. I knew that she had been kidnapped—compelled to contend in the Trials. But unlike me, she didn't have the heart for it. Our little knife-throwing lessons wouldn't be enough to save her.

"It's not easy tracking you down, Mute."

The sound of Lars's mocking voice was salt in an open wound. My back snapped straight as I faced him. He prowled closer, peering down at Iris. I shifted in front of her. Lars grinned. "Aw, was I interrupting a touchy-feely moment?"

My gaze flicked over his shoulder, noting that he had two of his cronies with him. I searched for Catanna and my brain froze.

"Did you forget?" Lars whispered in my ear. I flinched back and he snickered. My pulse hammered. He had caught me at a weak moment. I had no comeback or ready sarcasm. My scars were on full display, and he leered. "I honestly didn't think you had the guts to kill Catanna. Maybe I've underestimated you, Mute. And yet here you are, playing with your two pets. Revealing all your weaknesses."

At that, the world quieted. I casually crossed my arms, cocking a hip. But hidden from view, my fingers curled inward, forming tight fists. "Everything makes perfect sense now, Lars. The dirt. The smell. You have a fetish for charger dung. Cleopatra here is due for a crap if you want a fresh batch."

The two men behind him chortled, but Lars only smiled, as if my insult was endearing. He slid into my personal space and roughly grabbed my chin. Iris gasped. He brought his face close to mine and I stopped breathing. His stale breath shriveled my nose hairs.

"That wicked, wicked mouth," he crooned.

His other hand shot around me and gripped my butt, then jerked me against him.

Even as my blood roared, my voice remained calm. "If you think my mouth is wicked, wait until I introduce you to my knee." I thrust my arms out and knocked his hands off my body, then pegged him in the groin. I danced back and prepared to punch his ugly nose. At the last second, I changed my mind and slapped him. Hard. The cracking noise was glorious.

"Iris, run," I said, preparing myself for the inevitable fight.

"Grab the kid," Lars ordered his cohorts.

Time stopped.

Iris whirled, but not toward the stable's exit. She ripped open Freedom's stall door and slammed it shut behind her. *No!* Freedom wasn't used to strangers. Iris would be trampled, or bitten, or . . .

Oh stars.

"Get her!" Lars shouted this time, and the two men launched toward the stall. I didn't move. I couldn't turn my back on Lars.

One of the men reached for the door's latch and Freedom's chestnut head streaked toward him. He pulled back, but not fast enough. Her sharp teeth clamped down on his hand with a crunch. The man's scream raised the hair on my arms. The other man pushed at Freedom's neck, then her cheekbone, trying in vain to break her hold on the now gushing hand. Blood rained on the light gray floor.

I smirked. *Good girl, Freedom.*

The man gave up his attempts at freeing his wailing accomplice and dashed away. I wanted to crow in victory, but he swiftly returned, this time with a whip in his white-knuckled grip. He raised his arm and struck my charger across the face, a mere inch from her right eye. She shrieked and wrenched her head back, jaw loosening. The wounded man stumbled out of biting range.

As the other man lifted the whip a second time, I broke. With a battle cry, I launched onto his back, winding my legs around his waist. I wrapped his neck in a chokehold and squeezed and squeezed. The whip clacked to the cement as he clamped onto my forearms and dug his blunt fingernails into my flesh. I only squeezed harder, my muscles shaking.

Just as he wavered on the edge of consciousness, something bludgeoned my skull. My limbs slackened and I fell. I smacked the ground, air whooshing out of my lungs. Lars's smiling face loomed over me.

"Secure her."

My growl was a pathetic wheeze as the man I'd almost successfully choked dragged me upright and locked my arms behind me. Before I could drive my heel into his kneecap, Lars drove a fist into my ribcage. Bright stars shot across my vision as fire ignited my ribs. I grunted, still unable to breathe. My eyes darted around the stable's interior. I needed help, but the main aisle was empty.

Most of the city was headed for Faust Night's second evening of Trial segments. Lars should be there, not here. His Trial was today. Why was he here and why was he doing this? Was it because of Catanna?

"You know," Lars began, and punched my cheekbone. Blood filled my mouth. "I was only going to have a little fun with you. Remind you of who's in control."

My boot inched backward, and Lars barked, "Help us out here." The injured man grabbed one of my arms with his good hand and wrenched it up my spine, higher and higher until I whimpered and stopped all movement. Lars swaggered in close. "I admire all that fire in you, but I like you best this way. At my mercy." He touched my outer thigh and my teeth clenched as I fought to hold still.

His hand moved, sliding over my hip bone, up my stomach, where it paused at my sore ribs. "What are the outsider's weaknesses?"

The question caught me off guard and I gasped. "What?"

Lars jabbed two fingers between my ribs, right where he had punched. I cried out, curling forward as pain consumed me. "Tell me!" He dug the fingers in deeper and I screamed.

My whole body trembled and blood dribbled down my chin. I started laughing. It sounded more like crying, but either way, the noise ended the torture. Lars stepped back, eyes narrowed, as I said, "I know what *your* weakness is, you sniveling pig. You don't have any balls. Not anymore."

And with that, I whipped a leg up and pegged him in his unprotected groin, this time with my boot.

He doubled over, groaning, and I cackled like a crazy

person.

"Someday," he wheezed, "I'm going to crack that head of yours wide open and spill *all* your secrets." The rage in his eyes. Stars. I was done for. He slowly straightened. "But in the meantime, this'll have to do."

I saw the fist coming but didn't have time to brace. Ready or not, I was going to lose consciousness. Or worse. The blow struck my left temple, right where Catanna had carved her mark. I lost my vision, but I felt warm blood trickle into my ear and down my jaw as the stitches ripped open. I heard familiar shouts and the pounding of feet as my knees gave out.

Asher.

Bren.

Lars chuckled, close to my ear once again. "Well, I think I know what Bren's *biggest* weakness is."

As I lost touch with reality, I heard him whisper one final word.

"You."

FIGHT

Beep, beep, beep.

The annoying chirp wouldn't stop. It was relentless, beating in time with the pulse in my left temple.

I batted at the noise, but something tugged my hand back down. My eyes popped open, and I cringed at the sterile fluorescent lighting. Slowly blinking, I took in white sheets and curtains.

Did I die? Death was annoying.

The beeping wouldn't stop. It was then that I noticed the multitude of tubes and wires attached to my body. The beeping intensified.

Ugh.

With a swipe of my hand, I detached the intrusive objects. The beep became a solid blare. I couldn't stand the obnoxiousness a moment longer. I rolled off the bed and hit the floor. Literally hit the floor as my legs gave out. "Stars, I feel like a pile of crap." I groaned, muscles shaking as I stood upright, or as close to upright as I could force my body.

Bruised ribs? *Check.* Splitting headache? *Check.* Possible mild concussion? I assumed that's what the beeping was for: to monitor my vitals. Well, I had somewhere to be. *Sorry, doctors, ready or not, the patient is checking out.*

They hadn't removed my clothes or shoes, which made me think I hadn't been unconscious for long. I gently probed at my left temple. My torn stitches had been repaired.

Through a slit in the curtains, I waited until the hall emptied of traffic. There was some rushing around, chatter about removing an eye, then silence. I sucked in air. Had I missed Bren's Trial segment? I didn't know if his was first or last. Was he injured, or . . . ? I lurched into the hall, pulling my hair down around my face. No one noticed me until it was too late.

"Miss Tatum? Lune Tatum? Wait, we haven't—Wait!"

But I pushed through the exit door and scurried down the short hallway that connected the medical wing to Faust Night's main amphitheater. A small part of me was ashamed at causing them worry. They might even be disciplined for losing me. And then they were the last thing on my mind as I heard the crowd chanting a name.

"Bren! Bren! Bren!"

For a moment, I felt relief that they weren't focused on me anymore, but that meant Bren must be in the cage. And I was missing his Trial.

I sped up the ramp toward the crushing mob, my headache keeping time with Bren's shouted name. No one saw me slip into the throng, awkwardly trying to protect my ribs from getting bumped by enthusiastic body parts. That is, until a hand squeezed my shoulder. My elbow slammed into someone's gut before I could stop myself.

The unfortunate person coughed, wheezing out, "Lune, it's me. By the way, your elbow is super pointy."

I twisted around and drank in the sight of Asher's friendly face, and almost wrapped my arms around him. But, my ribcage whimpered at the thought. I had to raise my voice over the ruckus. "Do you know how I got here?"

Even as I asked, I turned toward The Pit's occupants. There, in the middle of the glass cage with a su-yari clutched in his hands, was Bren. He was dressed neck down in pure white, except for a blue number seventeen that was stitched onto his back. I couldn't help but note he looked good in white. Well, better than good. His tanned face and hands practically glowed bronze, his hair like a crow's wing.

"Bren carried you here after we chased off those guys." Asher started laughing. "You should have seen Bren. He was like this raging beast when he confronted them, and then he went ballistic when the guards wouldn't let him into the medical wing. Kept babbling about being your doctor or something. I said I'd look after you when you came out and that seemed to settle him down some. I knew you'd find your way out sooner than later."

Two men, one dark as night, the other with spiked blond hair, had Bren backed into a corner. They seemed to be teaming up. I'd never seen teamwork in the Trials before, not even when a past contender had attempted to win Title of Choice. But these Trials felt different, and I couldn't figure out why.

The three engaged in a flurry of strikes, blocks, and kicks. I could hardly tell who was who. My eyes flew wide as the su-yari whipped in an arc, the wood shaft cracking against Spike's skull. I knew Bren was dangerous with that stick, but stars above.

I was distracted watching his body move with deadly grace, so I didn't notice the other contender until his heavy ax was practically an accessory in Bren's back. Ice shot down my spine. I couldn't help him. But he pivoted at the last second and the ax sailed past him, along with the man attached to it. The su-yari kept twisting and swept the man off his feet.

I sucked in a gasp and whipped my gaze to Asher. "Iris. Where's Iris? Is that how you found me?"

"Oh, she's fine. Went to stand with the other tier one contenders. And no, it wasn't her. This serious guy with creepy blue-black eyes told us you were in trouble, actually."

I blinked. Ryker? No way, it couldn't be. "Did he have a dark tattoo on his neck?"

Silence. Asher's mouth popped open as he stared, riveted, at something in The Pit. Those around us wore matching expressions. Dread ate a hole in my gut as I focused on the cage once more.

Bren was looking down at his stomach. There was a tear in his suit.

Everyone held their breath, waiting for the suit to chime. I stared at the punctured material but couldn't see blood. Did a weapon open his skin? Still, no chime. Apparently Night, the dark-skinned ax wielder, wasn't going to take any chances because he swiped for Bren's neck. With a flick, the su-yari glanced off the man's wrist and sent the ax clanging across the floor. Then Bren drove his fist into the man's mouth.

The crowd gasped when Night spit out a bloody tooth, then roared when he flashed his new snaggle-toothed grin. Insane. They were all insane. The blond man, Spike, must have thought Bren's attention was still on Night because he lunged forward with his heavy sword, only to be met with a fist between the eyes. I didn't even see Bren move. For a full five seconds, the blond man teetered, then tipped backward, until his skull bounced off bare cement. I winced. He would have a wicked headache when he came to.

Bren's su-yari bit into Spike's bicep. His suit chimed.

There was no sand on the cage's floor, I now realized. Nothing to cushion a fall, but also nothing to blind you. What elements would Bren face? No sooner had I thought of them than they exploded from the vents, quite literally. A pillar of fire shot up between Bren and his remaining opponent, the blast knocking them off their feet. Thank the stars, it wasn't water. But as I watched Bren climb to his feet, clearly in pain, I wished it had been. There were burn holes in his suit; the skin on his arms looked angry.

People jumped and cheered, as if watching someone get burned was the most exciting thing they'd ever seen. I bit my tongue, so I wouldn't rail against the sea of idiots I was swimming with. If only I could stick *them* in the cage and get my hands on those elemental levers.

Night and Bren were back at it, and Night got a lucky shot in: a kick to the back of Bren's knee which drove him to the cement. *Get up, get up, get up!* The wicked-looking ax swung for Bren's neck again, but he launched himself into a forward roll.

The dark man roared and chased after him, striking out with blind ferocity. *Crack!* His ax chopped downward, splintering the su-yari in two. Bren paused, for a moment looking put out that his precious stick had broken, then reverse-gripped the two short spears with a wolfish smile.

I snickered.

He exploded, undulating like a snake, his moves a hypnotizing dance I had no desire to contend against. A tiny part of me felt sorry for the ax-wielder, but only for a millisecond. His clunky weapon thunked and clanged against wood and steel; sweat rolled down the man's face. The pace was unrelenting and . . .

I rolled my eyes. *Stop playing with him, Bren!*

It was over ten seconds later, Bren's prey bent at the waist heaving great gulps of air, a shallow cut on his right bicep.

I let out a loud whoop, then shoved a fist against my lips, hiding a smile. Surrounded as I was by a bloodthirsty mob, cheering for my enemy probably wasn't a bright idea. My attention strayed to the other two contenders fighting in the far corner. Particularly to the brown-haired man ramming a boot into his opponent's gut. I practically jammed my fist into my mouth to control the rage and fear his appearance unlocked inside of me.

Lars. My upper lip curled.

Despite the shaggy hair in his face as he hunched over a contender laying lifeless on the floor, I knew it was him. Knew it in the way he gripped his victim's suit while pounding a fist into his unconscious face, over and over again, the poor man's features bloodied and bruised. Lars was sick and he needed to be stopped.

My eyes flitted to Bren again—he was the only one who could end this brutality. I tried to force both fists into my mouth when I saw that he was already on his way to the far corner. Lars dropped his unfortunate victim, then stepped over the body, his red knuckles glistening. He jabbed a finger at Bren, then at the bloody contender at his feet. I couldn't hear what he said, but I could guess.

Bren seemed unfazed, leisurely rotating his neck and

shoulders. Lars's expression changed, the arrogance morphing into fury. Now he gestured at something outside the cage, in the direction of the medical wing. Bren's calm vanished. I'd so rarely ever seen him angry, but I watched as his spine stiffened and knuckles whitened, face etching into deep lines.

What was Lars saying to him?

His movements, usually so precise and carefully controlled, were now unhinged. It was like watching myself, which scared me. He threw his short spears down and lunged at Lars, who was the picture of arrogance once again. Bren barely avoided a kick to the gut in his haste, and his attempt at a leg sweep was sloppy. Lars simply hopped over it. Then he drove a fist into Bren's temple for the trouble.

My hands trembled, in shock and anger and fear—so much fear. What had Lars said to unravel Bren like this? Why wasn't he using his weapons? He was going to lose the Trial if he didn't snap out of it soon. They exchanged a series of vicious blows, each taking hits. Bren regained some sense and managed to plow a foot into Lars's stomach, sending him sprawling, but the wiry cretin popped up on a handspring.

They both froze mid-step when a wall of orange burst from the floor vents. The heat must have been intense based on their cringing expressions. Bren and Lars stared at the wall of waving fire as if expecting it to do something. And then it did. Fireballs shot at them like bullets exploding from a gun. But they were huge.

Impossible to dodge.

A scream climbed up my throat as both men sprinted for the far wall and the fireballs gained on them. They were

318

trapped; they would burn to ashes. They jumped, running up the cage's wall as high as they could while the fireballs smacked into heat-resistant glass. The impact obscured them from view. Time slowed to a crawl, the noises around me muted as I waited . . . and waited.

Two figures burst through the smoke, both mid-backflip. They cleared the fire, just barely, landing on solid cement. The crowd whistled and stomped their feet, but all I could see was Bren's suit on fire. I lurched forward, needing to help him, only to earn a wayward jab to my sore ribs. Even as my body curled around the pain, I was pushing past it, pushing past everyone until the glass wall stopped me.

I splayed my hands on the surprisingly cool surface and watched, stunned, as Bren tore the upper half of his suit off and flung it into a corner. Lars rolled on the ground nearby, extinguishing the flames licking at his legs, but I couldn't part my eyes from Bren's bare skin. His chest and stomach. His back as he twisted. He was flawless, with sculpted muscles only an angel should possess. I could feel the fire's heat after all—it seared my face first, flickering down my neck, where it then burned something fierce in my gut.

"Are you okay?"

I flinched, a squeak slipping past my lips. The skin on my face was all but melting. I peeked up at Asher, almost guiltily. "Yes. It just got . . . intense there for a second. They, um, they seem to be all right, though."

Asher snickered, as if he knew, and I quickly glanced away. *Oh my stars, awkward.*

Lars at last picked himself up, his pants smoking and ruined, though still covering the important bits. His earlier arrogance was gone, and so was Bren's fury. Nothing like a close brush with fire to cool a temper. They launched into more kicks and punches, feints and jabs—both would be heavily bruised after this match. Sweat slid down their faces, dampened their hair. It must be a sauna in there. Bren had a split lip, Lars a nosebleed.

And then they tangled, bodies pulled to the ground where they grappled for top position. Bren excelled at ground fighting, but apparently so did Lars. With his arms and legs pinning Bren to the floor, he leaned so far in, their noses practically touched. The arrogance was back, his mouth twisted in a mocking jeer as he said something, something that made Bren freeze. Lars took advantage of the moment and bashed Bren in the nose. Blood spurted. I growled.

I was going to accidentally break Lars's nose after this.

But he didn't stop at one shot. He pummeled Bren, like he did with the other faceless contender. In the eye, on the cheekbone, on the chin. He kept going and going, and Bren wasn't moving, and I was pounding on the glass wall with my fists, shouting until my throat was raw. I didn't care if my ribs burned or my head exploded or my knuckles split—I just wanted Bren to get up, get up, get up.

"Fight, Bren!"

And maybe he heard me, or maybe he remembered why he was doing this, even if I didn't, because he bucked his hips while Lars's arm was cocked for another blow. Lars tipped forward, hands splayed on either side of Bren. He was wide open for a—

I screamed, this time with satisfaction as Bren head-butted him. He ripped his arms free next, slinging one around Lars and flipping him onto his back. Blood dripped from his nose and onto Lars's face as his lips moved. Oh, how I wished I could read lips. The moment didn't last long. Calm once more, Bren clocked Lars in the head so fast, I almost missed it.

The arrogance vanished. Lars was barely conscious as he watched Bren pick up *his* weapon, a thin silver saber. Bren hovered over the defeated man, as if deciding where to mark him. I held my breath. With careful precision, he dragged the blade's tip across Lars's left cheek. Then did it again, carving a red X.

MY STRENGTH

I waited in the shadows.

The wait wasn't long. I knew he would come.

When the door softly clicked shut behind him, I whisper-yelled the chant.

"Bren! Bren! Bren!"

He spun toward me. The dim light of my bedside lamp just barely illuminated his eyes. I watched as they flicked up and down my body, as if making sure I was still in one piece. Then he was reaching for me and the chanting stopped. A sigh escaped my mouth as he wrapped me in his arms, cradling me to him carefully. Too carefully.

"I won't break," I whispered against his skin. I burrowed my nose into his shoulder and breathed in the scent of clean shirt with just a hint of smoke. He shuddered. Even though it hurt my ribs, I stood on tiptoe and curled my arms around his neck, molding my body to his. A sigh gusted from him, stirring my hair.

Time was a gift and a curse when he held me like this. I wanted the embrace to last forever, but it would end all too soon.

"I thought I was going to lose you," he spoke softly, roughly. "When Ryker said that Lars had you, I—I couldn't breathe."

The confession tightened my throat. When Lars was pounding on Bren's face, I couldn't breathe either. My arms slowly unwound from around his neck and I leaned back. It was so dark in this corner of the room, I couldn't see the damage that had been done. "I need to . . . Can you let me see what Lars did to you?"

"Yes, but don't scream when you see how incredibly frightening I look, okay? It'll hurt my ego, maybe even cause permanent damage."

I rolled my eyes as he shuffled us toward the light, his arms still banded around my lower back.

As we shifted positions, shadows no longer hiding his features, my first impulse was to gasp. I swallowed the sound. He may have been joking, but his eyes had a vulnerability to them I wasn't used to seeing. An ache swelled inside my chest, a desire to make that vulnerable look disappear.

One of my hands slid into the hair at his nape, tugging him closer. And when he bent down, I rose on tiptoe once again. My lips gently touched his jaw, kissing the bruise there. His breath hitched, and my heart skipped in response. I moved on to his left eye where a purple crescent darkened the skin underneath, and swept a kiss there, too. Black lashes fluttered against my sensitive mouth. His nose was in the worst shape, swollen at the bridge, and I ran my lips down to the tip.

I saved the cut on his lip for last, giving him plenty of opportunity to pull away if he wished. But he didn't. In fact, with my mouth a mere inch from his, I could hear and feel his breath quivering, as if he were restraining himself. My pulse thudded in the silence, lips tingling with want, with need, and I finally erased the small distance between us. His mouth, soft and warm, molded to mine, and my insecurity melted away.

My body would have stayed this way forever. But I needed to see his reaction, so I broke the kiss. I met his eyes, their color deepest amber, and cracked a smile at what was written there. That sliver of vulnerability was gone, and in its place . . . Stars help me. I swallowed thickly. "Well, I think you look dashing, like a rogue pirate."

He loosed a strangled laugh. "What's with you and pirates?"

I shrugged. "I don't know. Something to do with water, I guess. Mermaids fascinate me too. Someday, I hope to see the ocean, find out for myself if they're real or myth. I'd invite you to come along, but I don't think all that water would be good for your health." I smirked, but I knew my words were weighted. I was fishing, sharing my dreams in hopes that he would share his.

Bren smiled, but it looked pained. My hope floundered. He cleared his throat; his arms dropped to his sides. "You should rest. You'll need it for the final Trial tomorrow."

He shuffled backward and I panicked. This was the last night we could be together, just him and me, nothing separating us but a contract stating we weren't allowed to have what we had already taken. I just needed one more night of this, whatever this was, before I had to give it all up. Because I would have to, I realized now. If I won tomorrow and chose freedom, he wouldn't follow me.

Not only because he couldn't, I didn't think he wanted to.

"Stay?" I asked, so softly the word was barely a sigh. My heart was naked before him, and if he left tonight, leaving it bare and bleeding, I was certain it would never heal again.

He was quiet, so quiet, and I could feel my heart begin to crumble. I was about to turn away when he moved, pulling off one shoe, then the other. I tracked him with my eyes as he crawled onto my bed, laying down beside the wall as if he knew I wouldn't want to be trapped against it. I continued to stare, not sure what to do now that a man was in my bed.

I blinked. *A man is in my bed.*

Bren waggled his eyebrows and crooked a finger, effectively breaking the tension.

Even as I mock-huffed, my heart felt ten times lighter when I laid down, this time facing him. Okay, now I was a little bit nervous, or maybe a lot. He was studying me and I him, our bodies close but not touching. "If you keep staring at me like that, I can't be held liable for my actions," he purred.

I was going to jump out of my skin any second now. "Bren?"

"Hmm?" His hand inched toward my waist.

"What did Lars say to you earlier that made you so angry?"

His hand stilled. Everything in him froze. I held my breath as I waited for his reply, if he replied at all. But surprisingly, he did. "That night, when you got dragged into the river? Well, that was his idea. Catanna was the one who found you wandering the halls, and the one who stabbed you. But Lars? He wanted to drown you, slowly, without actually killing you. Same with your encounter in the stables. He wants you rattled."

"Wow." I laughed, not because it was funny, but to disperse some of the heat coming off Bren. Maybe I shouldn't have brought up the subject. "Did he say why he has such a personal vendetta against me?"

"No. Just that he wants you incapacitated, but not dead. And if . . . and if—" He blew out a breath and looked up at the ceiling.

"And if what?" I whispered, brow wrinkling.

His jaw clenched. "And if I'm not around when the Elite Trials are finished, he has plans for you. Plans much worse than death."

My brain skimmed over the words but didn't land on any of them. They were all too awful. "Hey." I reached over and touched his flexing jaw muscles. "He can try, but he won't break me. And you're going nowhere. We're both making it out of that Trial tomorrow, and—and . . . Bren, stop looking at me like that. You're not going to die."

"And neither will you. I'll be there, and I won't let anything hurt you. And if that means—"

"No," I interrupted. "Look at me. You can't fight my battles. Otherwise I won't—" I cut myself off with a groan. Flopping onto my back, I flung an arm over my face. I couldn't win the Trial if he fought for me, no matter what Renold had said. The only way to win was to fight alone. "It isn't supposed to be like this."

A hand gently grasped my arm, pulling it aside until all I could see was Bren hovering above me. "You're right. It's not supposed to be like this. But you and me? Now that makes sense. And I'm going to do whatever it takes to keep us from being torn apart, even if that means breaking all the rules and upsetting the Trial gods." I gaped at him. His voice lowered to a growl. "Starting right now."

Oh stars.

As he pressed his warm lips to mine, I melted into nothing. My toes curled at the dizzying rush of heat, at the perfect taste of him on my tongue. I grabbed his shirtfront and yanked, drawing him closer. The hand not holding my wrist splayed on the mattress next to me, his body my shield.

His mouth lifted, and I whimpered a protest, only to sigh a second later when that mouth trailed kisses along my jaw. He softly breathed into my ear, his teeth nipping at my earlobe. My spine arched off the bed, then his lips were on mine again, torturously slow, exploring every curve and dip.

This.

One night of this.

"You are my weakness," he murmured against my lips, kissing gently, reverently. I felt a spike of alarm at that, remembering words from earlier today. But before I could frown, tell him how dangerous that was, he finished with, "But more than anything, you are my strength."

THE LAST TRIAL

The viewing screen dimmed. Arcus Point's arrowhead insignia replaced the horrific images. But I still saw red. The reddest of reds. Thick and dark. Oozing.

Nothing was redder than fresh blood.

Ryker had won the first Arcus Point segment, single-handedly shooting down five out of the ten beasts. But not without casualties. He'd earned a dislocated shoulder and several gashes. Even miles away from the Trial site, watching safely from the middle of Antler Hill Village Square, the large viewing screen couldn't hide the horrors he'd just went through. Despite his tenacity, he'd struggled greatly to survive.

And now my confidence was shot. In fact, I felt down-right lousy.

"Hold this." I thrust my meat pie into Bren's hand and stumbled to a low shrub mashed between two buildings. My body shook, tears forcefully torn from my eyes as I expelled what little food had been churning in my stomach.

If Ryker had barely made it out alive, how could I, with my phobia of mutated beasts, walk out of this last Trial in one piece? I retched into the scraggly leaves again. A large hand smoothed down my back and my stomach unclenched, just a little. I needed more of his comfort. I needed to wrap my body around him and sink into his warmth. But I couldn't. We couldn't. Eyes were everywhere, watching us even now. I straightened, swiping my mouth on a sleeve.

"Just think, this time tomorrow it will all be over," he said, dropping his hand.

I snorted. "Is that line really supposed to work?"

He blinked. "No. I don't know why I said it, really. Knee-jerk reaction, I guess."

"Now you sound like me." I waved away the meat pie when he offered it back. "You can have it. I don't think I can keep it down."

His mouth popped open, eyes glazing over.

"What?" My face heated. "It's not the worst thing in the world to sound like me."

"N-no," he stuttered, pointing aggressively at the meat pie. "You just—you just shared food with me for the very first time. I think that means something. Something huge. I'm not sure what, though. Let me chew on it." And he took a ridiculously large bite of my pie, smearing the guts across one cheek. I had to take a deep breath as my stomach lurched.

I crossed my arms, cocking a hip. "Don't think too hard. This is a one-time deal."

"Your protests are futile. This is the beginning of some-thing epic."

My eyes rolled skyward. Only he could be so relaxed as to joke at a time like this. But I could feel the effects of his calm loosening my muscles even more, and I was grateful for it.

Two hours later, we waited just outside the faintly buzz-ing Arcus Point cage under a roiling, sporadically-spitting sky. My muscles were clenched tighter than a steel trap. This time of year, the weather was unpredictable—one morning a cheery yellow with sleepy insects peeking out of their resting spots, and the next evening, bitterly cold, wet, and dreary. I could tell, as the dull afternoon grew dimmer and dimmer, we were in for the latter.

I counted my arrows again, running my fingers over the fletching. Fourteen of them. All gold. Under normal circumstances, the arrows would be Tatum blue, but Bren had received those. I was sure Renold paired me with gold for a reason. He left nothing to chance. I slung the quiver over my head to rest against my spine and right shoulder blade, putting extra care into buckling the belt snugly across my chest.

Bren was doing the same, and I snuck glances at him repeatedly. Last night, cradled in his arms, I had drifted to sleep feeling warm and safe. Now, I was cold and nervous. Cold from the drizzle and brisk wind, and nervous that I wouldn't be safe with Bren once we entered the cage. He was driven to win, and so was I. We were two unwitting forces about to collide.

But then he looked up, caught my stare, and winked. That's all it took—one little wink—and I was a mess of confusion. I couldn't compete against him. Could I? My freedom and finding my mum were the two most important things in the world to me. I would do anything to make those things reality. *Even if that means hurting Bren?*

My heart gave a slow, miserable thump. The only solution was to separate from him as soon as we entered the cage. Fight our own battles. Because whoever killed the most beasts would win the Trial, and there were five contenders going in. We couldn't team up. I had to ditch him at the gate.

Yes, that's what I needed to do.

But what if he needed me? Suddenly, I could hardly breathe. An image of him laying on dead leaves, throat ripped out, skin and clothes stained red, flickered in my mind's eye. The blood drained from my face.

A shadow fell over me. Warm hands cupped my cheeks. "Lune? Lune, talk to me." I knew it was Bren who spoke, but he sounded so far away. "Breathe. Don't do this right now. Show me the brave girl I know is in there."

Then the noise that I dreaded most, the grind of metal sliding open, snapped me out of my stupor. I gasped in a breath, rapidly blinking, realizing Bren held my face and thousands of people were no doubt watching. I decided I didn't care anymore. My gaze locked on his and I let him see how terrified I was. "I don't think I can do this alone, Bren."

He could have shrugged and said, "Not my problem. You're my enemy now." I half expected him to.

"Segment two, Arcus Point contenders, you're up! You have five minutes to get into position before the ten beasts are released into the cage. In ten, nine, eight . . ."

My eyes widened; my body shook uncontrollably. I couldn't do this, I couldn't do this, I couldn't do this. Bren's forehead touched mine as he leaned in so close, gold was the only thing I could see. "You don't have to be alone," he whispered.

". . . five, four . . ."

And then he said two words. Two words that should be easy, so easy to give into. But they weren't—not with the secrets between us. Not when he had spoken those same two words eleven years ago, and nothing but pain and suffering had come from them. So, when he said, "Follow me?" my heart stopped beating. How could I? It would be all too simple for him to lead me to my death. He, more than anyone, knew of my weaknesses. With a quick thrust, he could push me into the path of a beast and watch as I—

". . . one! Into the cage, contenders, go go go!"

Bren didn't wait for my reply—didn't need to. My answer was written clearly in my expression. As if realizing my feet were two useless stumps, he grabbed my hand and pulled me into the cage. Several yards in, he released me, steps swift and purposeful as he led us away from the electric fence and grassy fields, and toward the dense center. I didn't let myself think, just focused on his broad back and the bow and arrows shifting with each pump of his arms. We hadn't quite covered a mile when Bren headed for a two-story cement building, the top floor partially caved in.

My first instinct was to protest. The front door was missing, the windows dark empty holes. A death trap. But after a glance at my thin wristwatch, I clamped my lips shut. We were out of time. Right on schedule, a siren went off, a low-high whoop warning us that the beasts were now inside the cage. I could almost feel the vibration their paws made against the ground. The pounding jarred my teeth, my skull, the marrow of my bones.

Strong, capable fingers tangled with mine, ushering me into the building's entrance. "You can do this, little bird. I'm not going anywhere."

Inside felt damper than outside, the air heavy with mold and rotting things. We were in a black tomb. I stuttered, my tongue dry and swollen, "How—how do you know where to—to go?"

He didn't say anything for a beat; panic tickled my throat. Then, "Training. My eyes can adjust to darkness faster than the average human. Watch your step, we're coming up on stairs."

Training? That's it? Sure enough, my boot struck raised cement a few seconds later. As we ascended, our surroundings took on grainy shapes. Light from a second story window illuminated the stairs just enough that I avoided a particularly crumbly step. A cat-like scream came from that open window and I practically crushed Bren's hand.

He paused on the stair above mine, head slightly cocked. With a gentle tug, he urged me into motion again. "The animal is a good half mile away. Its cry just happens to carry long-distance."

"Oh, is that it?" I released a shaky laugh. "How do you even—How do you stay so calm and aware under pressure?"

His shoulders lifted in a shrug. "Training. Even though you were young, you've been on the outside and know how dangerous it can be. To survive out there, you must adapt. Learn new skills. In a chaotic world, the calm live long."

"Nice saying," I muttered. "Let me guess, a lesson you were taught?"

"Yeah," was his reply. As much as I cared about him, right now I had an overwhelming urge to shake him until his teeth fell out. The secrecy had to stop, and soon, or I was going to explode.

But for the moment, all I said was, "We were raised in vastly different worlds, you and I."

"You have no idea," he distractedly murmured, rounding the corner of the second-floor landing. As we picked our way down a narrow hall, I wanted to scream, *"Well I would know if you'd just tell me!"* Instead, I savagely chewed on the inside of my cheeks.

There was only one room with a door still attached, directly ahead at the end of the hallway. Bren released my hand and poked his head into each room we passed, but I ignored them all, shooting straight for that closed-off room. In a creepy way, it called to me, like it had been awaiting my arrival. Or maybe I just knew I was destined to go in there.

I reached for the knob, only for a hand to grab my wrist and a giant body to nudge me aside. I gave the hulking idiot my most squinty stink-eyed glare, but all the look did was make him smirk. Arrogant, overprotective meathead.

After thoroughly scanning the room for dangerous dust mites, he waved me inside. "All clear. The window has an unobstructed view of the field and tree line—a perfect shooting spot. You'll just want to keep an eye on that man-sized hole over there, in case, by some miracle, something crawls through it." He gestured at the outer wall on the right where there was indeed a large jagged hole.

"And where will you be?"

"The hallway."

I looked at him sharply. "Bren, no. I know what you're doing and I don't want you to. The hallway is a blind spot and too risky. I won't let you do that. Not for me."

He gave me a stern look of his own. "Too bad, little bird. I'm doing it."

A growl rumbled in my chest. My hands clenched into fists. I was going to knock some sense into him. Stupid, stubborn fool. I wouldn't have his death on my conscience too. And then he was in front of me, fingers sliding through my braid and cradling my head. I placed both fists on his stomach and pushed, to no avail. His ridiculous abs were made of rock.

"Lune." His voice softened and I felt myself weakening. As I met his eyes, my fingers unfurled and clung to the sides of his waist. I couldn't lose him, I couldn't lose him, I—A hot tear slid down my cheek. Bren groaned, as if that tiny speck of salt water hurt him. He leaned down and pressed his lips to it, murmuring against my skin, "I'd make it all go away if I could. But I can't. So, please, let me protect you."

More tears joined the first and I slowly shook my head. "You can't. I'm not a victim. Despite what Renold said, we can't team up. We shouldn't even be here together. We should be enemies."

"Never." His fingers clenched, gripping at my hair. "We will never be enemies, no matter what happens, you hear? Just let me do what I came here to do. Let me . . ." His tone was pleading, almost desperate. His mouth was still on my skin, caressing, teasing . . . distracting.

I managed to pull back. "Let you what? Why are you *here?* Why can't you just tell me?"

He grimaced and shook his head, not meeting my gaze. "I—I *can't.* I want to. You have no idea. But . . . but if I do, I'll—" His mouth snapped shut and he grunted. Pain. He was in pain.

"What's wrong? What's happening?" I searched his body for injury as he hunched over, hands on his knees. His face turned red and his neck tendons strained. Could he not breathe? Oh stars. What was I supposed to do? I'd never done CPR before. "Bren!"

It can't end this way!

That's when I heard it. A scuffling noise from outside.

I froze. In a flash, Bren straightened and made a bee-line for the window. His wide shoulders blocked the view and I stared stupidly, feeling lost and scared and . . . He was dangerous for me. I was distracted, worried about him when I should be focused on the Trial. On *winning*. What was I doing, hiding out in this room with him when I should be fighting? When I should be earning my right to choose freedom?

My stomach wanted to spew all over the floor. Was that why Renold put us in this Trial together? So, Bren would be a distraction? My weakness? So that I would *lose?* Oh stars, I was blind. I was the most idiotic idiot. But what had me doubling over was the real possibility that Bren could be in on it all. Toying with me. He could lock me away in this room while pretending to be my knight in shining armor, then abandon me and take the win for himself.

Lines that had blurred were now sharpening. I clutched at my cramping stomach.

"Lune." He grabbed my shoulders and hauled me upright. His breaths were labored, but he was breathing. That's all that mattered. "Get ready. Another contender is heading this way and a beast is on their tail. You can do this." He pressed his lips to my forehead, then he was gone, sealing the door shut behind him.

Now I was completely alone. Was I a prisoner? But I didn't have time to check the door. The next moment brought the sound of running feet and a high-pitched shriek. I unslung my bow as I spotted a blonde-haired figure dashing for our hideout. She was lithe, young, and scared witless. Bren was right. A beast must be on her scent. She bounded through the front door.

Claws scrabbling on cement was the only warning I got before pale-yellow paws stretched through the wall's jagged hole and pulled a saber cat halfway into the room. Every muscle in my body locked. This wasn't a synthetic machine. This was real, my nightmare in the flesh. Its eyes were twin suns, wholly trained on me. How the animal had found that hole and ultimately me was a thought I quickly shoved away.

I had to move. Run. Hide. Anything! My feet were cement.

Arrows. I needed one. My brain felt stuffy, useless. I was out of time. The cat was fully in the room now. If it weren't for years of training, I never would have moved. I reached for an arrow and nocked it to my bow. My hands shook, and the shot flew wide, sinking into the beast's shoulder. Its maw opened and it screamed, revealing the longest teeth I'd ever seen.

Holy stars above, I was dead meat.

The cat's front legs lowered as it readied to spring and I knew, without a doubt, that I didn't have time to prepare another arrow. I wrenched my body from its frozen state, slinging my bow across my back as I whirled for the far-left corner where I'd seen a chair earlier. It was wood and missing a leg, but it felt like a sword as I grabbed hold and swung.

The legs snapped off as they cracked against the cat's thick skull. Pieces of wood flew in all directions. The impact numbed my hands and the flimsy weapon careened into the wall. While the splintering crash distracted the cat, I slammed my boot into its face. Before I could kick it again,

337

the air practically shook as something thudded against the door, causing the wood to split down the middle.

Bren. My lungs seized. He needed my help. I knew it as I lunged for the door. *Crack!* The door caved inward. I immediately rolled to avoid being flattened to pancake proportions. Another saber cat leapt into the room only to whirl and trounce the lithe blonde girl I'd seen but a moment ago. My brain switched off. I focused on the blue arrow sticking out of the monster's tawny chest, then its glistening fangs as they ripped into the girl's throat.

A throat that should have been Bren's.

In the span of a breath, her terrified screams became wet gurgles, fear-stained eyes a dull gray. I choked, gasping on helpless sobs. Just like that, she was dead. I should have helped her, I should have . . .

The noises I was making drew both cats' attention like moths to a flame. Four bright eyes fixed on me and I knew it was over. No. An arrow was nocked to my bow, ready to shoot. When had I—? *Don't think, just shoot!* The arrow burrowed deep. An eye winked out, leaving only three. One of the giant cats, muzzle slicked red, crumpled on top of the girl, and I winced.

"Lune! Run!"

I hesitated, and that split second of indecision was all it took for the other cat to rip its claws into me. My leather vest tore like paper. The sensation of fire igniting my stomach and bruised ribs was instantaneous, and I screamed, long and agonized. In a flash, Bren was up, yelling at the beast. He loosed an arrow into the cat's side and, with horror, I realized the wound only enraged the animal further. A massive paw swiped for my legs and I leapt backward, scant inches to spare.

"Run!" Bren roared again.

But where? And then I knew. I didn't head for the hallway. No, I dashed for the man-sized hole in the wall, not even pausing when Bren started shouting words I couldn't decipher. And then I jumped into nothing. The leap was a gamble, one that could end with me broken on the ground. But I'd glimpsed the flat, one-story building only yards away and took the chance.

The roof came at me faster than expected and I tucked into a roll too late, landing heavily on my side. I groaned. My ribs—of course the injured ones—took the brunt of the fall. The sky winked out and I looked up in time to see the cat soar over me, alighting on the rooftop with agile paws. Carefully, I stood, trapped with only a flimsy bow and arrows between me and this nightmare. Two broken arrow shafts protruded from its body, but the beast was still very much capable of tearing me to shreds.

My hand rose a notch, inching for an arrow, when the cat shot toward me. I raised my bow like a sword and thrust one end into the cat's face, but with a flick of a paw, the bow clacked across the rooftop. Several hundred pounds reared up and took me down, my back and skull bouncing off cement. The cat's dagger-like claws pierced through leather yet again, this time hooking into the skin right above my chest. The claws flexed and a scream ripped from my throat. Pressure, so much pressure. Pain—sinking, stabbing, consuming.

The world swam, pulling me under, and this time I couldn't escape. I would finally drown.

I failed.

Breath hotter than the pits of hell hit my neck, a drop of acid saliva striking my collar bone. I squeezed my eyes shut. My last thought would be of my cowardice. I wasn't enough. But instead of tearing out my jugular, the cat dropped all its weight on top of me.

The great pressure on my chest pushed the air right out of my lungs, depleting them completely. My whole body seized, eyes and mouth flying wide as I strained for air. Nothing. What was it doing? Taking a nap? I wouldn't die in a pool of blood after all. I would die of suffocation. Dark splotches stole my vision and I knew in a matter of seconds I'd be gone. I had failed . . .

And then all pressure vanished. At least death wasn't heavy.

The dark spots shifted into the shape of Bren's face and I frowned. Was Bren dead, too? I gasped in pain, lungs burning. Tears welled and spilled over. Not Bren. I choked on a sob. "No. Please, no."

"Don't move," he ordered. He didn't sound happy about being dead. He sounded . . . scared. I sucked in air too fast, coughing most of it out. The movement hurt. I hurt all over, actually. Bren wasn't looking at my face anymore. His intense focus was on my stomach. Shaky yet determined, I strained to raise my head. He unbuckled my vest and peeled away the leather to reveal a gray shirt soaked in blood.

I half cried, half laughed. "I'm alive. You—you're alive." I was smiling and frowning, tears falling, but I was alive. Bren had saved me. The pain became manageable as I held onto that thought. Then he lifted my shirt hem and cold air rushed over my torn flesh. I hissed, clenching my jaw.

"Breathe, Lune." He had on his doctor face as he hiked

the shirt higher, baring my bruised ribs. His lips turned bloodless.

"Are . . . are my intestines still in there, Doc?"

He glanced at me sharply, then cracked a wobbly grin. "Was that a joke?"

"Maybe. I do feel lighter though, like something fell out along the way or—or got squished."

That got him chuckling and my muscles slightly uncoiled. But when he rocked back on his heels and unbuckled his vest, removing it along with the gray shirt underneath, my stomach muscles cramped. That chest, those abs, right there in front of me. So much more perfect up close.

"You're going to set me on fire with that stare," he said, tone a bit cocky. My eyes snapped to his, horrified. If I wasn't in such pain, I would no doubt . . . He leaned forward, whispering, "You're adorable when you blush."

I groaned. Maybe death would be a mercy.

The sound of fabric ripping was a welcome distraction. Bren tore off the entire bottom half of his shirt, hands gentle yet efficient as they wound the makeshift bandage around my midsection. I tried not to think about the fact that he was looking at and touching my bare stomach. A stomach covered in blood. Ugh. His eyes briefly flicked to mine. "Since the animals seem to like you so much, all this blood isn't helping matters." He paused. "Something about this seems off."

"You think?" I snickered, then flinched as the action stretched my wounds. I turned serious at his continued frown. "What seems off?"

He tied the bandage and lowered my shirt. "The way they entered the building, as if they could sense you were in there."

"Me?" I squeaked. "But didn't the girl lead the cats to us by accident?" My breath caught. "Is she . . . ?"

His head lowered. "No, she didn't make it. Sadly, she was just in their way. Those animals were after *you*, Lune."

"Well that isn't creepy or anything," I muttered and dug my elbows into the cement as I attempted to sit up. The dead cat was sprawled next to me, a blue arrow protruding from the back of its skull. I shuddered. My adrenaline was wearing off, leaving me with way too much feeling—mostly pain. Even with cold rain pelting my skin, sweat stung my eyes. "Help me up," I panted, hating the weakness. But I needed him. I could only hope he wouldn't be my downfall.

He grunted. "Something tells me you won't listen if I ask you to rest for a few minutes. You were almost gutted, you know." I leveled a stare at him, letting my eyes do the speaking. He stood and buckled on his vest and quiver, grumbling, "Worst patient ever."

I was only sad to see his bare skin covered once more.

Ever so carefully, he scooped me up, and I marveled at the ease of it, as if I weighed nothing at all. *He's carrying me and I'm awake. That's a first.* He slowly released my legs, keeping an arm wrapped around me as I regained my balance. We stayed that way for several seconds, and Bren didn't seem in a hurry to move anytime soon. I sighed. "I have to go. There's still eight more beasts out there and two other contenders hunting for them. I can't let them get ahead. I can't let them win this Trial. You . . . you know what this means to me, Bren."

He tensed. Then his shoulders fell. "Yeah. I know. But I'm scared that you'd rather die than walk away without the win, and that kills me, Lune. Kills me."

The confession punched a hole through my chest. I held my tears in; they trickled down my throat instead. "I'm sorry," I whispered. It was the only comfort I could give. I'd known from the beginning that death might be my only form of freedom from this place.

His eyes narrowed, forearm flexing against my back. "Not good enough. I want you to *live*. I *need* you to."

"But don't you see? Trapped in this city, I die a little every day. How is that living?"

"You have me. And Asher and Iris. You're not alone, little bird, and that's what you continually fail to see."

32

ALONE

The rain's patter and soft rustle of the tall grass I crouched in should have been soothing. No padding of animal paws. No screaming or growling. But all I could hear was a word—just one.

Fail.

He might as well have shouted it. At every turn I was confronted with that word. It was my very own personal wall. Yes, I failed to see the people in front of me. Yes, I failed to detect foe from friend. But after a decade spent in a city of lies, I didn't know what trust meant anymore.

So how then could I not feel alone?

Even now, knowing Bren was hunkered down in another patch of grass across the clearing, I still felt isolated. He had tricked me, had kidnapped me, had stood up for me, had saved me. He had chased my nightmares away. Had cared for me, gently and without judgment. In my heart, I knew I'd forgiven him for lying to me all those years ago, for being the cause of my imprisonment. Whatever his reasons, he wasn't the same person he once was. People could change.

At least, I hoped so. With all my soul, I hoped so.

Because I was trusting him right now, to have my back and fight fair, and to not steal the win. And to not steal my heart and then break it. *Please don't break my heart,*

Brendan Bearon. He had been so certain the beasts would find me, not the other way around. Had all but begged me to stay in that dark cement building. But I couldn't. I needed wide open spaces where I could run or climb or hide, if I so chose. And I couldn't stand to be trapped under the same roof as a dead girl.

So I left, and he had followed me.

I had found a spot in the heart of Arcus Point, heavily wooded with a small clearing of pale gold grass at its center. Several trees were nearby—climbable trees. I was itching to climb one right now.

Before I had the chance to so much as twitch, the sound of snapping twigs echoed in the clearing. For what felt like an eternity, I couldn't tell if the noise was animal or human, but the harsh panting that came a few seconds later eased my fears. Human. A very loud human. In fact, they were being *too* loud, going *too* fast. My pulse sped up and I gripped my bow tighter.

I was about to find out what else lurked in this cage.

A wild-eyed man crashed into the clearing, and my flight instinct kicked in. My legs shook with their need to flee, but I inhaled a breath and released it slowly, inhaled another, refusing to budge. Halfway into the expanse of near waist-high grass, the man dropped out of sight as if he'd fallen into a pit. I strained to glimpse him through the pale stalks, finally catching the glint of a lacquered bow as he prepared to shoot. But shoot what?

He was aiming at a bush. A bush that was morphing into charcoal gray fur and bright yellow, intelligent eyes. My breath stalled. A magnawolf. It was huge. Probably weighed more than Bren. The man shot and the beast exploded into the air, sailing above the arrow which thudded harmlessly into a tree. Bravery points went to the man. He held his ground as the magnawolf landed and began pacing in front of him, looking for a weak spot.

I contemplated remaining still. It didn't feel right interfering, possibly killing the beast under the man's nose. But this was a competition, after all. I crept forward, just a few inches, and that's when I saw them: two black magnawolves to the left of the clearing. And they weren't looking at the man. They were looking at me.

Oh. Stars.

"Lune, get out of there!" Bren bellowed as he sprang from his hiding spot.

The urgency in his voice set my legs into motion. I whirled, plunging through the grass toward the trees. As I ran, I spared a second to sling my bow across my back. It would be of no use to me. Not right now. Not when every hair on my body stood on end, warning me to run, run, run, and not look back. *Don't look back. Don't look back!* One of the beasts yelped, as if in pain, letting me know just how close they were on my heels.

All my attention was on a large oak tree, namely the low-hanging branch within arm's reach. I barreled toward it, planted a foot on the trunk, and launched myself at the branch. I only had one shot at this. My fingernails gouged into bark as I scrambled upward, pulling, grunting, shaking. My stomach and ribs were hot and aching, my head a swarm of bees, but I was soon standing on the branch, bow in one hand, arrow in the other.

Two black streaks raced toward me, only yards away. Quick breath in, sight down the arrow, and release. The beast on the right crashed to the ground—instant death with an arrow protruding from its eye socket. My heart leapt, elated, only to stop when the other magnawolf kept coming. It was going too fast. It would hit the tree, or . . .

Crap.

It sprang off the trunk into the air, wide open mouth aimed for my legs. The moment came slowly. I watched, stupefied, as two-inch-long canines sunk into my left calf, as the sensation of being tugged had my boots slipping, as my body floated to the ground. The impact of landing on top of the animal woke me up. In a flash, I rolled, but its fangs were still in my skin. The beast jerked me backward and shook its head. The pain of tearing flesh was debilitating.

I cried out, flopping onto my back, and made a vain attempt at kicking it. The teeth unclenched. Stunned, I didn't react, and in the next moment, a black muzzle filled with razor-sharp fangs lunged for my face. On instinct, I squeezed my eyelids shut, not wanting to see the moment of my death. But it didn't happen. My arms quaked under a terrible writhing weight, holding aloft a thing that sunk closer and closer toward my face—whining, growling, panting. It stunk like old bloody meat.

My eyes flew wide.

I was gripping my bow. A stick of wood was all that separated me from an animal consumed with a need to sink its maw into skin and bone, all to feast on flesh and blood. I pushed against the weight with every last ounce of strength, determination, and terror left in my worn-out body. I was not going to end up as dog food. My arms dipped, weary from the strain, and I was forced to turn my head as teeth grazed my cheek.

I snarled, furious at the world for its cruelty. The beast was going to eat me alive and I wouldn't have the strength to stop it.

Strange sounds left its throat—hacking, coughing, gagging—but I couldn't see what was happening. My head was still twisted to the side. Its long tongue lolled and brushed against my cheek. I whimpered, tears leaking past my closed lids. I didn't want to die. Not as a rare steak. Then came a series of moans and dry heaves, popping and cracking. And one loud crunch.

The noise was so awful, bile rushed up my throat and I sputtered, sucking in short gasps. The weight lifted after that, but I couldn't move my arms. They were numb, welded to the bow. Hands ran up and down my body. They tried to take away my bow, but my fingers were vices.

"It's okay. You're okay." The cadence of Bren's voice was less than reassuring, but his presence made up for it, even if his eyes looked wild with fright. "Where are you injured?"

"Everywhere." I chortled, which became a cough, which became a groan.

He saw the blood soaking through my pant leg, and despite how carefully he rolled up the stiff material, I couldn't hold back a small cry. The bite burned something fierce.

"I'm sorry," he breathed, face stricken.

"It's not your fault."

His tortured gaze met mine. "Isn't it? You wouldn't be in here, if it weren't for me. If I hadn't—" He cut himself off. It was becoming a bad habit.

My mouth worked silently. I didn't know what to say, anyway. He was right. When I didn't reply, he got to work on my leg, pulling out the torn gray shirt he'd tucked into his vest. Smart. Patching me up was becoming a full-time job. Always a good idea to carry extra bandages around. Finally, I spoke, unable to stand that guilt-ridden expression a moment longer. "You know, we really need to stop meeting like this."

He blinked at me. "Like what?"

"With me lying on the ground while you try putting me back together. It's getting cliché."

A choked laugh left him, and I breathed easier. Then his mouth turned white around the edges. "It hurts me seeing you in pain and helpless."

My heart melted at the honest words. But he was getting too serious again. Him hurting over my pain was making the pain even worse. So, I fixated on one word. "You think I'm helpless?"

His lips twitched. "Okay, maybe not helpless."

I relaxed. "Good. I thought I'd need to remind you what I'm capable of, and that wouldn't be very fun for you."

"Oh, I don't know about that," his voice deepened, and my pulse jumped. Stars above, how did he do that?

I needed a distraction before we both did something incredibly stupid, like make out in the middle of beast-infested woods while time raced on without us. My gaze outlined his lips as I contemplated the possibility. No, that wouldn't be a good idea. "I've got two kills. How many do you have?" There. That was a safe topic. Sort of.

Those sinful lips stretched into a smirk. "Wouldn't you like to know."

My eyes narrowed. "Brendan Bearon, don't you dare hold out on me." Too late, I realized I'd used the wrong word. He *always* dared. If I wasn't so busy skewering him with a death glare, I would have rolled my eyes.

But he surprised me by actually answering. "Don't worry, I have the same as you. That guy in the clearing killed the gray magnawolf."

At the news, several emotions flooded my body: relief that another contender didn't die because of my hesitation, satisfaction that Bren didn't have more kills than me, and a wedge of guilt that I could only think of them as competition—not people.

I forced myself into a sitting position and reached for Bren's hands, stilling their ministrations. He watched me, a line bisecting his brows as I finished securing the bandage before wiggling my pant leg down. I painfully got to my feet. By the way his hands were fisted, I could tell my unexpected actions troubled him. Hurt him even. And I hated myself for causing him pain. But I had to finish this.

Alone.

"I have to go, Bren."

He stood, slowly, carefully. "And I'm going with you."

"No, you're not." My head pounded. This was harder than I thought it would be. "You need to let me go."

His face contorted as if I'd just sucker-punched him. "I can't. Not this time."

I was the worst person in the world for what I had to do next. The only thing I *could* do. This was the only way. I stepped into his personal space, fingers fisting his vest, and stood on tiptoe, placing my lips near his ear. "You will. If you care about me at all, you will." A warning. Maybe even a threat. I was sick. I took a step back, fully intent on leaving without another word or glance, but my traitorous heart couldn't bear to walk away without one last glimpse of his face.

A part of me died, shriveled to dust when I saw the gutted look he was giving me, like I'd fatally wounded him. I held it together until I was out of sight, then the tears came, fast and blinding. My chest was a hollow pit. I was poison. It was better this way. He said I was beautiful and strong, that even my scars were something to be proud of, but I knew the truth of the matter. I was swimming in fear every second of every day, and I would do anything to break free of this prison.

Even if it meant hurting him.

I would probably die in here tonight, but at least my conscience wouldn't hold the burden of taking Bren down with me.

My chest tightened and I gasped, fingers kneading the ache. I never should have let him get so close to my heart. The organ bleated pathetically as I widened the gap separating us, until all I could hear was sizzling rain and slogging footfalls. Think. I needed to think. Without a plan of action, I would no doubt stumble into one or more of the remaining beasts and get my head ripped off. Or maybe they would toy with me and prolong my death.

I shoved the morbid thoughts away. To distract my brain from thinking of death, or Bren, I pondered over the strange visions I'd had recently. They were sporadic and unexpected; they brought a whole new dimension to the gut warnings I'd had for years. In them, I could see *exactly* what would happen next if I didn't react quickly. How did they happen? How did they work?

I stopped walking and leaned against a tree to rest my throbbing leg and head and stomach. I throbbed all over.

After a quick perimeter check, I let my eyes slide shut. Concentrated. Focused. On seeing what was impossible to see.

The future.

My mouth twitched. I wanted to laugh at my foolishness. There was a good chance I was being tracked, and not just by mutant beasts. Cameras were positioned all over the inside of the Arcus Point cage, and soundless camouflaged drones too tiny to see, unless you knew where to look. Was the city watching me even now, wondering what I was doing? Perhaps they thought I'd given up.

I fine-tuned my senses to that of the remaining beasts. Where were they? How many were left? Focus, focus, focus. And then, in the span of a blink, my stomach bottomed out and I was staring into the face of a monster. I'd never seen anything so huge or hideous. Its eye sockets appeared empty, the pupils large and opaque. The muzzle was bent as if caving under the weight of countless teeth. Then the vision threw me backward. I helplessly flew past trees and buildings and rusted objects. But no, my body was going *through* them, as if I were a ghost.

Stars above, what was happening?

My body jerked upright where it was propped against the base of a tree. All movement stopped. Lashes fluttering, I scanned my surroundings and promptly bent over, dry-heaving. When the nausea eased, I straightened again, blinking stupidly at the sight before me. I hadn't moved an inch. My back was still pressed to the tree I'd chosen to rest against not moments before. I checked my watch. No time had passed. I hadn't been sucked into the future after all.

Then what had just happened? I began walking again, subconsciously correcting my course to a northerly route.

My senses quivered with the knowledge that the monster I'd glimpsed was in that direction. Still, I plowed forward without hesitation. One thing I'd learned over the years: always listen to your gut. And right now, my gut was chattering like a crazed squirrel.

Five minutes later, my hair stood on end. The monster was close. Every last inch of me knew it. *Come out, come out wherever you are, you big ugly thing.* And then a roar shook the world. Trees swayed, rain gusted, the very ground trembled at the horrific sound. My confidence shrunk to pea-sized proportions. *Help.* But I was on my own. I'd abandoned the only person brave enough to stand by my side. *Stupid, stupid, stupid.*

I realized I hadn't moved, cementing myself in place. There was a second of utter silence, when not even the wind dared breathe, and then . . .

Pandemonium.

TOGETHER

There was shouting that sounded too much like Bren. Another roar that was far too close. Twigs snapped, leaves crunched, trees cracked as something big, something *huge* barreled through the woods, heading straight for me. I hated being right. One thing was for certain: this rampaging beast was more terrifying than anything I'd ever faced before. And the best place to face it was from above.

I picked the nearest tree with low branches, knowing the monster would find me on its own. Bren was right. The animals seemed to sense when I was near and, for some reason, it drove them mad. Lucky me. I was a good fifteen feet off the ground when a bright red streak dashed for my tree. Pausing in my climb, I gaped as the fifth contender launched himself at a low-hanging branch and scrambled up after me.

My hand frantically waved at him. "No, get away!" I whisper-yelled.

But he wasn't listening. This was bad. This was bad for both of us. The monster was almost here, tearing through the woods with a ferocity that stole my breath. It wanted me, and this redhead was going to complicate matters, either dying or getting me killed because of his idiotic choice in trees. He reached my perch and stopped, inches away.

Winded, he raised a finger in a "give me a second" gesture.

And in that second, the monster exploded into view, its roar booming like thunder. My eardrums rang and I stared, slack-jawed, as the animal—half bear, half enormous freak of nature—rose onto its hind legs. Up, up, up, ten feet . . . fifteen. Those soulless eyes leveled with mine.

Holy mother of—

"I have a message for you," the redhead said. What was he talking about? We should be climbing, not socializing!

"From who?" My lips barely moved. A whisper of wind.

"Wrong question."

My gaze finally flicked to him, just as his fist crashed into my jaw. White bursts of light robbed my sight, so when he wrenched on my arm, I wasn't prepared. The sensation of falling—something I normally craved—was the most horrific feeling I'd ever felt. My nails clawed at porous tree bark, bending and breaking in their attempt to keep me aloft. I slid, one foot, then two, my arms and legs clamping around the trunk until I sputtered to a halt.

Before I could catch my breath, my assailant was beside me once more, arm reared back for another blow. Instinctively, my muscles locked, but my gut told me I would fall this time. Fall and hit the ground where the monster would disembowel me. With nothing left to lose, I sucked in air and loosed a shrill scream. The redhead paused. The monster paused.

The world paused as I finished emptying my lungs.

Then the tree shook as the freak of nature charged toward us. The redhead ditched me in favor of saving his life, shimmying up the tree. I was too low, easily within paw-swiping range. The chances of reaching safety in time were slim, but I moved my body faster than it ever had before, grasping, pulling, swinging. Higher, I needed to get higher!

A shockwave struck the tree. It vibrated the trunk and rattled my very bones. I gasped and clung to a wobbling branch, stomach lurching. *Don't look down, don't look down.* I looked. The monster-bear was peering up at me so intensely, I felt my bladder loosen. *No, no, no, do not pee right now. Animals are attracted to pee!*

A paw swiped at my feet and I tucked my knees to my chest, hoping the branch was sturdy enough to hold my weight. The monster lowered to all fours, retreated a step, then another, until it quietly stood a few yards away. My feet found purchase again, fingers fumbling for my bow. Now was the perfect time to—

Several tons of ultimate predator rushed the tree. The impact was ear-splitting. No, the tree was splintering under the assault. Holy crap, it was going to knock the tree down. The freak bear backed up for another pass and a green arrow whizzed past my head, sinking into the monster's shoulder. I glared up at the redhead. Had that arrow been intended for me? The bellow from below was ravenous. Chills prickled my flesh, but I almost leapt out of my skin when that monstrous beast decided it could defy gravity.

Claws longer than fingers gouged the tree's bark, and the scariest thing I had ever seen began climbing. My eyes didn't want to believe what they were witnessing. Nothing this big should be able to scale a vertical obstacle. It wasn't possible. But it was happening. The tree shook and I nearly lost my grip as I inched upward, closer to the homicidal contender. Was I safer with the idiot or the bear?

The animal chuffed, like it was inhaling my irresistible

scent. I took my chances with the idiot. He had stopped, the thin branches at the top unable to support his weight. When I neared his position, he swung a boot for my face. Really? I was so done with this. At the next kick, I captured his ankle and gave a sharp tug. I'd only meant for the action to warn him, so he'd cease his ridiculous antics. But he lost his grip—or maybe the branch snapped. I would never know. It all happened so fast.

With a sharp cry, he plummeted. His body smacked into countless tree limbs as he inevitably lost to gravity. I was a good twenty-five feet off the ground, so when he landed, the noise was muffled. I could almost pretend he had made it down with just a few bruises instead of instant death.

Bile raced up my throat. I shouldn't have looked. His leg was on backwards. Oh stars, what had I done? I'd just, I'd just . . .

My horror amplified at the sound of crackling. Were the woods on fire? Deep groans joined the cacophony and my world tipped ever so slightly to the left. My head spun as I stared at the forest floor a million miles away. The tree was breaking. Literally breaking in half as the bear continued to inch toward me. Unable to hold the weight, the trunk snapped like a twig, my haven now a death trap. If I jumped, the fall would kill me; if I climbed down, the monster would kill me. The world was tilting, tilting, tilting.

The sound of tearing wood was a continuous peal of thunder as the tree picked up speed in its descent. Then I spotted a third option and made a split-second decision. I ground my teeth together, holding my position.

Wait.

Not yet.

Now!

Bending my knees, I sprang into dead air. But my aim wasn't downward—it was across. The broken tree housing the bear hurtled past without me as my own destination came up fast. Way too fast. Oh stars. My midsection collided with a neighboring tree branch. I wheezed as all oxygen escaped my body. It felt like someone had cut me in half. In that moment, I could sympathize with the felled tree.

A jarring thud rocked the forest floor, and I peered through leaves and limbs, hoping against all hope that the monster had been crushed by the tree. I didn't even care if that meant one less kill for me, because right then, all I wanted was to stay alive. Maybe I wasn't quite willing to give up everything for freedom after all. Maybe some things were more important. Maybe I wanted to live out the day.

But the mutant creature shook its mangy brown coat, as if falling out of trees were a normal occurrence. My hope of surviving this day dissolved. I was off the ground, yes, but for how long? My ribs and stomach were a mess of blood and bruises, fiery pain my constant companion. Breathing hurt. Blinking hurt. Thinking hurt. *Give up now. You're a failure, Lune Avery. A waste of time. A waste of breath.*

I hung from the branch, defeat crushing my lungs.

"Hey, Ugly, over here!"

The words, though shouted, were music to my ears. The sight of Bren emerging from the woods, though covered head-to-toe in blood, was the most beautiful thing I'd ever seen. "Give me a break, I'm having a bad hair day," I shouted back, albeit weakly.

He glanced at me, eyes scanning my body for injury. "You all right?"

"Nothing I haven't dealt with before. Well, except for the freaky bear. That's a new one."

The animal in question had almost recovered. It watched Bren now, not me. I didn't know whether to feel relief or panic, so my body decided on a heavy dose of both. "Listen carefully, Lune." Bren pulled out two arrows, affixing them to his bowstring. "You'll need to climb down as fast as you can, then run. Run like demons from hell are on your tail. Got it?"

"Roger that," I said, earning a grim smile from him. "But Bren? Try not to kill the teddy bear. He's mine."

"I make no promises. I'll kill him if it means saving your life. I know how you feel about this, but I'm not going to lose you. Not when I finally found you."

I didn't say anything. I couldn't. My throat was too tight. Yes, he was stubborn, but he was trying to save me, yet again. Maybe I did still have hope as long as I had him. So, when he told me to get ready, when he released the arrows and barked for me to go, I obeyed. Adrenaline surged, boosting my speed, but I was shaky, clumsy. The monster thrashed and released a long bellow. Bren's arrows must have penetrated its thick hide.

My concentration broke and I all but fell the last eight feet—my bent knees absorbed most of the impact, but agony still shot through my entire body. My muscles tightened as I prepared to bolt, but I hesitated. Just for a second. I threw a look over my shoulder, needing to know where the freak bear was, and that one little look ruined everything.

On the ground, this close to the animal, I finally realized how big it was. Fear, wave after wave of it, gushed through my veins, and the monster paused. Inhaled. And whirled, onyx eyes rooting me to the spot. Every hair on my body stood on end, but I couldn't move. Stark terror had me in its clutches.

"Lune! Run!"

I'd never heard him sound so afraid. That fear reanimated my limbs—gave me purpose, gave me strength—when it should have had the opposite effect. But Bren made me feel things and do things I never would have done on my own. And so, I ran like fear had given me wings. Like a desperate girl wanting a few more seconds of life, even if those seconds were inside a cage.

I weaved through trees and jumped over bushes, blazing a confusing path. How smart was this beast? How fast? My chest was scorching fire as air sawed in and out of my lungs, the stitch in my side like a hand twisting my intestines. I started to limp, but I couldn't stop or spare a second. Deep in my gut, I knew that if I dared to peek over my shoulder or slow down in the slightest, I was dead.

Something bright caught my eye. It winked at me, beckoning. Metal sounded safe right about now. If I could only get there. The monster's presence was all around me, its grunts and heavy tread faster than my own breaths and unsteady footfalls. I was out of time. So, when the rusted car came into view, it was my salvation. I raced toward it, scared senseless that the doors would be locked.

If they were . . .

My body slammed into metal, then bounced off. I lurched for the front door handle, wrenching the door open so hard, it hit me on the rebound. But I didn't feel the hit, too busy scrambling into the front seat. Until an outside force rammed the door and pinned my ankle not yet tucked inside. My bones ground together and I couldn't breathe.

A shrill scream shook my frame, nausea a roiling sea in my stomach. With all the desperation I possessed, I kicked, opening the door just enough to free my ankle. The door shut with a crunch. Back and forth, the car rocked, creaking, squealing. Saliva and blood invaded my mouth and I spit onto the floor, the need to vomit overwhelming. I must have bitten my tongue. But my ankle was what worried me. Was it broken?

And then glass rained down on me, the front windshield now a jagged hole. Through the hole, a paw the size of my head entered. My whole body flattened against the seat as claws scraped along my scalp. Oh stars, oh stars, oh stars, it was going to gouge out my brain. The paw suddenly jerked back, taking several strands of my hair with it.

I made a dash for the back of the car, shimmying between the front seats, when the monster reached in again, this time snagging my boot. I tried to free myself, kicking and pulling like snared prey, but I was an idiot. Perhaps this had been Renold's plan all along—the best way to rid himself of a daughter who only brought him disappointment. My body was yanked backward, dragged over glass and then the dashboard. The whole time, my fingers clawed for a handhold, finding and losing them again and again.

They latched onto the steering wheel with a vengeance; I could feel my body stretched thin. As I held on to my last moments of life, fingers slowly unraveling, I screamed one word. I could have cried anything in that moment, but only one could save me now. *Bren.* I poured all of me into that word.

He came like an avenging angel. He swooped in and

clobbered the monster's skull. I felt the vibration, and then I didn't. Claws unhooked from my boot as the animal wheeled around to face its attacker. Eyes glued to the fight, I slid off the car's hood and pressed my back to the metal exterior. I couldn't tear my gaze from Bren as he single-handedly took on a beast twice the size of a charger.

His bow and arrows hugged his spine, untouched, and my heart skipped a few beats. Was he risking life and limb because of me? Because I had selfishly asked him not to kill the bear? There he was, swinging a stick—more like a small tree, actually—at what could arguably be the top predator on the planet. And here I was, watching. *You idiot, do something!*

I stood, unstrapping my bow and three arrows. It wasn't often I'd practiced shooting with multiple arrows at once, and now I wished I had. There was no way one arrow would take down this leviathan. Maybe not even three arrows. But I shoved doubt aside as I trained my weapon on a patch of muddy fur directly behind its front leg joint, the most vulnerable spot on its body. The heart. That front leg lifted, revealing its weakness, and I would have hesitated, hating to exploit another's weakness—even an animal's. But that paw with impossibly long claws was aimed for Bren, ready to deliver a death blow.

I shot.

Three gold arrows buried into the heart, and the monster bellowed in surprise and pain. And fury. Its wounds leaked blood but the freak bear was still very much alive. And now swerving toward me. Crap. Two bounding steps and it was practically on top of me. One swat and I was airborne. My back struck the ground several yards away, knocking the wind out of me. I laid there, stunned, not really seeing the angry ash clouds above as I struggled for air.

I couldn't move, couldn't even panic at the thought of paralysis. I was just . . . existing. But I could hear every horrible sound: scraping claws, panting, shuffling, a sharp snap of metal . . . Wait. What? I could see the monster now, lumbering my way, and I could do nothing but stare as its head lowered, nose nudging my boot. *Ah crap, don't eat my feet first.*

And then a long silver object wrenched that monstrous head sideways and all I could see was Bren, his tall frame a shield. Legs planted on either side of me, his bare arms rippled as he gripped what looked like a piece of metal torn from the car. "Look at me. Look at *me!* Not her, you over-grown hamster."

I would have laughed at his description if I had any breath. He swung at the bear again, landing a hit to the shoulder, and the animal swatted back, raking claws across Bren's chest. Air leaked into my lungs as a strangled gasp left me. I fought with my numb body. *Get up, get up, get up!* He needed my help, and here I was, a useless lump yet again.

"Stay down, Lune," Bren ordered, taking another swing. I strained even harder. The monster retreated a step and Bren darted behind it, then lunged onto its back. Using the metal object as an arm extension, he wrapped up the animal in a chokehold.

Now I *really* wanted to laugh. As the odd pair brawled, I painfully scooted out of trampling range. My body was failing; this needed to end soon. I grasped for my bow but only caught air. Where was it? Now I felt panic. Lots of it. I was nothing without that bow. How would I kill the beast? How would I . . .

I was going to lose. *No, no, no.*

How a mere human could strangle a several ton beast was beyond my comprehension, but sure enough, the animal keened, shaking the ground as it dropped unconscious. Seconds later, Bren skid to a stop at my side. "Where are you hurt? Where—"

"Bren, my bow. Where is my bow?" I tried to rise and he helped me into a sitting position.

"It's broken. I'm sorry," he said. My heart plummeted. He unslung his compound bow. "Don't give up hope, little bird. This animal is still yours. Give me two of your arrows."

"What? Where—where's yours?"

"Gone. I used them all up on the other bear." He plucked two arrows from my quiver when I failed to do so.

But I couldn't move. I was too busy gaping at him. The blood. That would explain why he'd been covered in blood. "There was *another?*"

"Yeah, but I killed it. No, don't look at me that way. They would have both gone after you and I couldn't let that happen." His expression was firm, determined, not a single line of remorse. But how could I blame him?

This was a competition.

"So . . . so you won then." I nodded, swallowing roughly. "Go ahead. Take the shot. They'll know it was you despite the arrow color."

"No."

My brow furrowed.

"You're going to take the shot." He said it with such finality that I sputtered nonsensically. He leaned in, lips brushing the shell of my ear. "Just trust me."

Just trust me. Trust me. Trust. Trust. Trust.

"A secret for a secret?" Now was not the time for truth-telling, but I had to know something. This could be my last opportunity to ask. "Secret: I'm afraid. Every day, all the time. Especially right now. Your turn. What *are* you?" Because he wasn't a normal human. He *couldn't* be. Not when he did the things he could do.

His breathing intensified. He sounded afraid, too. But this wouldn't work if we couldn't trust each other. Finally, he whispered so low, I strained to catch the words, "I am many things. A Sensor, for one. It's how I . . . it's how I found you all those years ago. Why the Recruiter Clan used me. The world is changing, Lune, and we are changing with it. Whether we want to or not."

My brain scrambled to make sense of what he had just revealed. I could tell that it was just a tiny corner of the puzzle but, in this moment, it was enough. Even though I didn't know how to trust, I did it anyway. I grasped the offered bow and arrows. "You better be real."

"I'm real. I'm right here."

The monster huffed, and my pulse roared. It was stirring awake. In a flurry of movement, I kneeled, Bren directly behind me. My arms trembled as they pulled back the string. Quaked when the draw-weight was too much. I hissed in fear and frustration. The beast was rising. I wasn't strong enough. Bren wrapped his fingers around mine and lent me the strength I lacked.

I let him.

"Stronger together," he whispered, the words warming my scalp. When the bowstring was sufficiently drawn, he slowly released my fingers.

I would never forget this moment, when two supposed enemies became strong allies. When my kidnapper did everything in his power to set me free. So, when the raging bear charged, I didn't waver. I didn't run. I didn't hesitate.

I faced my fear and destroyed it.

THE WINNER'S CEREMONY

My fate would be decided today.

I hadn't won the Arcus Point Trial, but I hadn't lost either. And the not knowing—the teetering on the edge of a precipice, helpless to stop the inevitable tip one way or the other—was excruciating.

But one thing was for certain. I was now an elite, regardless of my wants. I had risked becoming what I hated most for the chance to earn what I desired most. They gave me my old room back, not a single trinket of Rose's to be found in the airy, circular space. I'd always loved this room, despite what it represented. The walls and furniture were palest peach and yellow—not blue, like the dress I now wore. More than anything, I hoped this day would be the last I'd ever have to wear royal blue again.

The material was heavy, as I was expected to stand outside for the Winner's Ceremony. I was going there next, as soon as my new hairdresser finished securing the elaborate braid she had pinned to the crown of my head. "Were Kara and Arlyn not feeling well today?" I asked her reflection in the mirror.

Her eyes flicked to mine, widening like a doe trapped in a hunter's crosshairs. "I—I don't know, my lady."

I frowned. Usually the staff kept close tabs on each

other—it was necessary for their survival. One must never keep an elite waiting. Something was wrong. But, as I studied the woman's trembling hands and downcast expression, I decided not to push. I'd been the cause of enough pain this week; I wouldn't cause further harm.

It took me twice as long to navigate the hallways and winding stairs, a pronounced limp slowing my progress, courtesy of the monster. The very much *dead* monster. My finest hour. I hadn't frozen. I'd done it. My lips twitched into a faint smile.

Dobson opened the front door for me, and maybe it was just my imagination, but his face seemed less grouchy when I thanked him. Huh. I guess winning a few Trials was the way to earn respect around here. Yesterday's rain made for a wet, bitterly cold morning. Upon exiting the heated house, a plume of fog curled from my mouth. I placed a fur wrap on my shoulders, and a shudder went through my body as the fur tickled my neck. I'd had enough animal fur brushing my skin to last me a lifetime. By sheer willpower, I managed to not chuck the thing down the steps.

I knew hundreds, if not thousands, of eyes were now focused on me as I gingerly descended the handful of limestone stairs. I hobbled toward a tall podium erected in the center of the massive front lawn where the majority of Tatum City's population now congregated. I locked my gaze onto the structure. The fixed object was now my lifeline as I navigated an ocean of sharks. I'd never seen an actual shark before, but the stories my mum had told me of the high seas were vivid. Even now, I could imagine the smooth, undulating bodies circling closer, closer. Scenting me, sampling me.

Yes. The city's populace were sharks. Maybe not all, but

jealousy and desperation changed and dehumanized people. They would strike at the first sign of weakness, tearing others down so they could rise instead.

My gait evened, and I bit the inside of my cheek as my ankle and calf throbbed. *You're not out of the water yet. Push past the pain. Show no weakness.* I slipped into the first row of bodies, then another. And that's when the whispers started.

"Attention whore."

"She doesn't deserve Title of Choice."

"She's weak."

"Killer."

That last one punched a hole through my chest. Maybe all the whisperings were true, but that one . . . that one would haunt me for eternity. My eyes betrayed me then. They let go of the lifeline and plunged into the fray, searching for that last voice. And they found its owner. The woman was an older version of Catanna. Her mother? And clinging to her threadbare clothes was a little boy and girl. Her siblings.

Instantly, my throat closed. My eyes burned hotly and my chin wobbled. "I'm . . . I'm so sorry." The woman's expression didn't change. But I didn't blame her. My apology wouldn't bring her daughter back, or better her way of life. I had condemned this mother and her two young children to a life of wanting but never getting. Unless she forced her remaining offspring to sign Trial contracts. And even then . . .

It was too much. I was floundering under the weight of so much hate and envy. The sharks were swarming, taking bites out of me, hungry for more.

A warm presence brushed my back, and then banded an

arm around me, just under my collarbone. I knew without looking who it was, by the way he moved, in the way he felt, and by how he held me.

"Looks like you need saving again," his deep voice rumbled in my ear, and I sighed.

For once, I didn't have a snarky reply on the tip of my tongue. Because he was absolutely right: I needed saving. And right now, here amid so many unfriendly faces, I needed *him* more than ever. I leaned into his touch, soaking up his offered strength and protection. And I didn't feel weak. I felt like I could face the sharks and come out the other side, whole and alive.

Together, we made it to the foot of the podium where the other Trial winners anxiously awaited their fates. They didn't get to choose their new titles—Renold and his pack of advisers did. Bren and I were the only anomalies. Who would get Title of Choice? What title would Bren choose, if given the honor? A swarm of bees found their way into my stomach. The not knowing. It was eating me up inside.

Renold finally joined the throng. Rather, he strolled down a red carpet that magically appeared, then took to the stage during riotous applause. I didn't clap, and neither did Bren. The strike of a loud gong quieted the noise. Renold raised his hands.

"Citizens of Tatum City, welcome to the Winner's Ceremony! Those who strive for excellence will be rewarded. So, without further ado, let us present the winners with their new titles!"

My world narrowed to him, the decider of my future. His mouth moved and, one by one, winners were allotted their new titles. But I didn't hear a word he said. Not even when he announced Ryker's title. Then Renold looked down at me, his lips forming my adopted name, and the blood rushing in my ears drained from my face. Maybe even my entire body. If not for Bren's support, I might have fainted, proving to everyone just how weak the Princess of the the Trials really was.

Renold called another name, Bren's, and his fingers curled over mine, urging me onward. I could do this. Whatever the outcome, I could do this. *I am not weak.* We climbed the platform steps together. The people below were a rainbow sea, eyes winking, bodies rippling. I fixated on my guardian's mouth, and watched with mounting horror as the corners tipped up. He had an ace up his sleeve and was about to play it.

"Ladies and gentlemen, let me tell you a story about the two fine young people standing up here. Brendan Bearon, our newest resident, and my adopted daughter, Lune Tatum, both wanted the same thing: to win all three Trials and earn Title of Choice. But here's the tragedy. They tied. And a tie does not equal a win." Several gasps sounded from the crowd, and Renold lifted a hand. "Hear me out. There can only be one winner per Trial segment, as stated in the contracts, so I've come up with a solution."

My heartbeat was out of control. I might very well die of a stroke before knowing who won.

"Here's another piece of the story," Renold was saying. "Mr. Bearon couldn't bear to fight against my daughter in the Trials, so I amended his contract. That is, until I discovered they were breaking the contract rules." Like a light being switch on, the crowd became a mob, hissing and booing. The evil man before me allowed their anger, encouraging it with his silence. Bren's fingers tightened around mine. They were shaking. A flare of worry ignited in my gut.

Eventually, the jeers quieted enough for Renold to continue his public persecution. "I understand your anger, citizens. The rules must never be broken. They are what unite us; they keep the peace. As punishment—and dare I say it was lenient—they fought in the Arcus Point Trial together. But they once again broke the rules, not fighting against each other, but fighting *together*. You all saw it on camera. And so, you will all bear witness as I announce my solution to this problem. There will be a winner, but only one; and since they both killed three beasts, the one who shot the most arrows wins. And that would be Brendan, who buried all fourteen of his arrows into those beasts."

I died.

My soul left my body, too broken to hold me together a moment longer. The stage buzzed with the energy of the people, but I couldn't see faces—I saw black holes yawning wide, eager to swallow me whole. Renold was talking again. I didn't want to hear it. He would twist the tragic tale into a victory by knighting the outsider and ushering his daughter back into the elite fold. My life was over. And yet, his words slowly filtered into my mind and took root there.

"But here is where our story takes an unexpected turn. When I initially amended Mr. Bearon's contract out of the kindness of my heart, he willingly forfeited his right to our most coveted title. So, my people, once again we must conclude another year of Elite Trials without anyone having earned Title of Choice." Several more gasps. A vein ticked under my right eye. "But before you go back to your lives, sad for these two star-crossed lovers, I've decided to bestow upon them both a title I came up with myself. They are the best of us—strong, brave, loyal—and so they will protect us with their lives. I present to you Tatum City's very first Elite Guardians!"

The world was an undulating wave. I didn't wave back. I felt my blood freeze. If it weren't for Bren's fingers twined with mine, my stiff body would have stayed on that platform where it would eventually collapse, or perhaps float away into nothing. I didn't care. I couldn't feel. I was done being hurt.

A block of ice took the place of my heart.

THE MISSION

Two weeks later, Bren disappeared.

I'd pushed him away after the Winner's Ceremony, not able to cope with the final loss of my freedom. I knew he just wanted to comfort me, but I also knew a part of me blamed him for everything. "Trust me," he had said. This was what came of trust: a lifetime of servitude to a city that hated me. And so, a great wall formed between us, taller than any previous ones.

"It's going to be okay, little bird," he had said after the ceremony and wrapped his arms around me, even as several elites and villagers looked on. "Just wait and see."

For a moment, I had leaned into the embrace, unable to stop myself. But I made myself pull away and say, "If you think I'm okay with this, then you don't know me at all."

That was the first time I had rebuffed him. It would become one of many.

What an idiot I was for allowing someone to distract me from what mattered most. Stupid for letting Bren wrap himself around my heart. And now I was paying the price for that mistake. The image of my mum was but a faint flicker while the image of Bren was larger than ever, now that I worried. Worried that Renold had done something to him.

I was given a chance to recover from my many injuries

before starting my new job as an Elite Guardian. I didn't even know what the position entailed. For two weeks, I had filled my days with Iris and Asher and Freedom, trying my best to ignore Bren, and now I had a gut-wrenching feeling that my new duties were going to be harder than anything I'd done before.

Renold would make sure of it.

So, when a knock sounded on my bedroom door two days after Bren's disappearance, I was prepared for the worst. What I didn't expect was Ryker. I leaned on the door jamb, arms crossed. "Are you here to clean my room? I don't think the title of maid suits you. I can put in a good word with Renold if you'd like, see if he'll reassign you out of the kindness of his heart."

He stared down at me with those two-toned irises and didn't bat an eyelash. Ugh. He was no fun. "Supreme Elite Tatum sent me to escort you. Said you'd know where to find him."

And with those words the numbness ripped away. The emotions, the feelings . . . I hurt all over. "Then let's get this hide-and-seek game over with so you can get back to your cleaning duties." I had meant for my voice to sound flippant, but it was reed thin. Panic set in with a vengeance.

As I made my way into the bowels of the house, with my enemy before me and an unknown at my back, I couldn't help but compare my present with my past. The past me would have been scared to be called down here, no doubt for punishment. The meetings had only affected *me* though. I could handle what he did to me, mentally and physically. But the present me was more than scared. I was petrified. Not for myself, but for the people Renold wanted me to protect. Deep down, I believed Renold was grooming me to become something horrendous. To become what I feared most.

A monster.

Like him.

My fingers pushed open the door before I was ready. And there he was, the greatest monster of them all. I would have rather faced the raging mutant bear in that moment than the soft-spoken, meticulously dressed man standing in the middle of the room. He looked straight through me. "As always, thank you for your service, Mr. Jones. Your loyalty will be rewarded. Wait at the end of the hallway, if you please. You know what your duties are after that. Oh, and say hello to your father for me."

"Yes, sir." Ryker shut the door, sealing me inside with my fate.

The keeper of my destiny finally slid his eyes to mine. He stared hard, unwavering, unblinking. My eyes burned under the scrutiny, but I didn't dare show weakness by breaking contact. Then his face broke into a huge smile. I wanted to run. I wanted to run so badly.

His mouth opened. "Do you know why I value loyalty more than anything else?"

I stiffened. Renold hardly ever offered up information. *You don't give up your secrets for free.* I slowly shook my head. "No, sir."

"Because this city was built on it. Without loyalty, everything I've planned—everything my father and his father had planned—would be destroyed. This city is special and, from the beginning, I knew you'd be an asset. You're different; the Trials proved that. After thirty-four years of waiting, the Trials finally did what I created them for. They revealed what a person is *truly* capable of. You don't think like the rest. You think *more*. You feel more. You do more. You're pure reaction, Lune. It's incredible."

He stirred, hands behind his back, circling me like he always did. I stared straight ahead, willing my muscles to stop trembling. "But you are impulsive and lack control. You're like a wild animal that can't be tamed. I see that now. No amount of beating will make you submit." He stopped directly behind me, like he always did. His breath was hot on my neck as he said, "But I discovered another weakness of yours—a greater one. You *care* more. And that is why I made you an Elite Guardian. That is why you will do as I say with unfailing loyalty. I have a gift for you."

A velvet blue box was nestled in his palm. It looked like a jewelry box one would give a loved one. But I knew better. Whatever was in that box would rock my world, and not in a good way. My hands noticeably shook as they accepted the box. As they slowly opened it. At the sight of what lay inside, my fingers spasmed, and the box slipped from my grasp. I watched, shocked senseless, as the contents bounced and rolled along the floor.

I couldn't tear my eyes from the grisly objects. They looked like . . . human thumbs. A massive wave of nausea overtook my body; I couldn't hold it back. Stumbling, I heaved up my breakfast into a corner, the wet splat almost undoing me yet again. My breathing was ragged as I straightened, wiping my mouth with as much dignity as I could muster.

"Whose . . . whose are they?"

"Your old seamstress and hairdresser, Kara and Arlyn.

377

It's all that remains of them. They betrayed me when they agreed to help you publicly flaunt your scars, your *failures*, at the Gala. You see, Lune, this is what happens when you double-cross me. I know now that beating you isn't the way to your loyalty. But punishing the ones you care about? Judging by your reaction just now, I believe I've finally found a way to control the wild beast."

And he had. Oh stars, he had.

But he wasn't done. I didn't know if I could survive this.

"Truth of the matter is, I need you, Lune. You are the future. Things are changing, and we need to change with it. Those who don't adapt will get left behind, and I'm like you: I won't sit on my hands and let life pass me by. But I'm needed here while you aren't. You can better serve this city from the outside." His icicle eyes penetrated mine, forcing his words into my brain. From the outside. The outside. *Outside.* His soft grin was of the devil. "That's right. You're leaving. I need you on a secret mission. In doing so, you will protect the ones you love. And if you don't . . ."

He let the sentence hang, his expression commanding me to respond. I dragged in air. "And if I don't?"

His thumb stroked his chin as he watched me closely. "I heard about your little friend. Iris, is it?" My heart beat out of my chest, breath hitching despite my best efforts to control the sound. The corners of his eyes crinkled. "Ah, I've struck a nerve. Well, rumor has it her guardians plan to disown her should she fail her Trials training. They say she's weak and not worth the expense. But I also hear she looks like you, and that intrigues me. Makes me consider adopting her."

My breaths were coming too fast. I was giving myself

away. I was giving *her* away. The thought of her under his sadistic hands . . .

Black spotted my vision.

"Tell you what," he went on as if he hadn't just torn up my insides. "Complete this mission and I'll make sure Iris finds a nice new home. If not . . ."

There was no "if not." My spine snapped straight as an arrow. "What's the mission, sir?"

His smile was cunning, victorious. "Two days ago, I let someone out of the city gates. They have a mission of their own, but I'm beginning to question their loyalty. I need you to hunt him down, spy on him, and make sure he completes his mission. If he deviates from it, I want you to kill him. Understood?"

Why did it feel like someone was digging a knee into my chest? Maybe because I knew, without a trace of doubt, who I would be hunting. But I had to ask, to be absolutely certain. "Who—who am I hunting, sir?"

He destroyed my heart with two words.

"Brendan Bearon."

After that, the conversation was a fog. I had my mission and my ultimatum. Iris or Bren? I didn't know if I could save both. I was a puppet, tangled up in knotted strings. I was a pawn, controlled by those more powerful. The game was only beginning; a game I still didn't know the rules to.

Ryker led me to my room with instructions that I wasn't allowed to speak with anyone. Renold's orders.

I donned my heaviest gear, fur-lined coat and boots, and packed personal items I would need—gloves, thick wool socks, hygiene kit. And as I reached for one more pair of heavy socks at the back of my drawer, my fingers bumped into something hard and smooth. It was leather, rectangle-shaped. It fit in the palm of my hand. Bren's book. I gaped, disbelieving.

How? Why?

My fingers trembled as I cracked open the book's cover, something I hadn't been allowed to do in over a decade. The book was a message, that much was clear. With a faint rustle, I flipped through the pages, searching. There had to be a clue. Something. And then I found it.

I stared, horrified.

"No," I whispered brokenly. It couldn't be. I should have seen it. I was blind. *How?*

Maybe I was interpreting the words wrong. It had been so long since I'd last read. But no. The words were short. Simple. Shocking.

She is your sister.

Iris.

He had to mean Iris.

Oh stars. And now I was leaving her all alone and she wouldn't have a clue. There was no one to protect her from Renold. From Lars. A giant sob heaved out of my very soul. I curled forward until my forehead touched the cement floor. I shoved a palm over my mouth to muffle the noises coming from it, certain Ryker could still hear.

Too much. Too much. This was all too much.

I couldn't leave.

Someone impatiently cleared their throat beyond my bedroom door, making me jump. "Two minutes," Ryker said. I hesitated for another few seconds, quickly scrubbing my face free of tears, then shoved the smuggled contraband deep into the bag I was packing.

After a quick look-around, I left the room, intending to make my way to the supply room and kitchens next. Who knew how long this mission would last. But Ryker held up a large hiking pack. I paused before taking it, rifling through the contents to make sure everything I'd need was in there, namely a first-aid kit. How much did he know about this mission, anyway?

He hefted another hiking pack that had been hidden behind him, and shoved his arms through the straps, snapping a buckle across his chest. I observed his movements, noting too late that he was dressed similarly to me. When had he changed? Alarms rang in my head.

"What are you doing?"

"What's it look like? I'm going with you." He bent, then straightened with several weapons in hand. *My* weapons. He thrust them at me and my hands mechanically took them. He slung a belt laden with knives around his hips. "Arm yourself. You're going to need them."

A strangled squeak left my mouth. "No. Absolutely not. There's no way I'm going on this mission with you."

His eyes slowly raised to mine. Ah crap. He stalked toward me, and with so many weapons in my hands, I didn't know which one to ward him off with. I still hadn't moved when he reached me, grabbed my arrow quiver and shoved the leather strap over my head. His words were a quiet growl as he said, "Are you brave enough to question Elite Tatum's orders?"

My eyes widened a fraction.

He grunted, collecting his bow and remaining supplies. "I didn't think so. Let's go."

With long strides, he was down the hall, taking the stairs

two at a time, and out of sight before I could protest. But what could I say? Renold had me firmly pinned beneath his thumb. If he wanted this rude and wildly unpredictable man on the mission, then I had no choice but to go along with it. Could things get any worse?

But as I exited the house, I realized I'd spoken too soon.

A wet fluffy ball splattered on my nose. Another on my cheek. Tilting my face to the sky, dread weighed me down. It was snowing. A soft white blanket already stretched across the empty front lawn. I followed Ryker's fresh boot prints to the eastern gate, the only gate leading in and out of this prison camouflaged as a city. When I'd entered through those gates eleven years ago, my hands had been bound. I'd been kicking and screaming, terrified.

Today, I did none of those things. My hands were unbound. My head was clear. But as the guards gave the command to open the gates, as the outside world came into sharp focus, I was more a prisoner now than I had been going in. Freedom pulled at me, urging me to take what was rightfully mine. And yet . . .

My chin quivered.

I have a sister.

Renold was right. I cared too much. And that weakness was now iron shackles around my wrists and ankles.

But maybe that weakness would get me through this mission. Keep me focused. Keep me from running away. And Bren. Stars above. How had he known?

Determination spread through my limbs as the gates opened wide. In this moment, it was his image I saw clearly. He watched me, eyebrows raised, daring me to trust him. To take that first scary step into the unknown.

He held out his hand.

A challenge.

I readjusted the pack on my shoulders and snorted. *Game on, pretty boy. Game on.*

When the guards waved us through, I didn't hesitate. My boots crunched in the untouched snow—one step, then two. And, just like that, I was on the outside for the first time in eleven long years.

I held my breath.

Took another step.

And didn't look back.

ACKNOWLEDGMENTS

Without God's strength, this book never would have been published, so I thank Him for His unfailing grace!

When I started this adventure, I had no idea how complex and tiring and thrilling the journey would be. How it takes a team to write a book. So I want to thank every single person who ever answered one of my countless writerly questions, who convinced me to follow my dreams, who encouraged me to keep going, to not give up. Because of you, this book transformed into a story I could be proud of, one that I hope will have an impact on others as it does on me.

I promised myself that I would keep this short, so I'll end by personally thanking those who read Reactive in its earlier, rough stages and lent me priceless feedback! All of the hearts go to: Melissa, Tyffany, Jesikah, Daphne, Grace, Virginia, Hannah, Danielle, Shiza, Sarah, Marissa, Belle, Adelaide, Allisa, Baj, Chloe, Emily, Lyn, Stephanie, and Russell. You each had a hand in shaping this story and I can't thank you enough!

Oh my stars, did you think I forgot *you?* I could never! To all of my readers, fight for the future that you want. The choice is yours.

Thank you for reading!

ABOUT THE AUTHOR

Becky Moynihan is the author of *The Elite Trials* trilogy as well as the coauthor of the *Genesis Crystal Saga* with Tyffany Hackett. She lives in central North Carolina with her family

For more on Becky and her work, visit her website at www.beckymoynihan.com

If you enjoyed this book, please leave a review on Amazon! Thank you!

Printed in Poland
by Amazon Fulfillment
Poland Sp. z o.o., Wrocław

53424919R00233